PANDEMIC-19

JASON MCDONALD

GOOD TWIN
PUBLISHING ™

www.jason-mcdonald.com
Twitter: @JasonMcD_Writer

Good Twin Publishing
333 University Avenue
Suite 200
Sacramento, CA 95825

Good Twin Publishing and the Good Twin Publishing logo are trademarks of Good Twin Publishing LLC.

www.goodtwinpublishing.com
Twitter: @goodtwinpub

Paperback ISBN: 978-1-7378299-0-4
Hardcover ISBN: 978-1-7378299-1-1
eBook ISBN 978-1-7378299-2-8

First edition: December, 2021

Library of Congress Control Number: 2021951193

DEDICATION

For my wife and precious children. You are my rocks, my support, my everything. I love you.

ACKNOWLEDGMENTS

I first must thank my wife for her take on my book and the support she gave to see it materialize. I love you.

Second, my heartfelt appreciation to my children for putting up with me frantically writing and editing as I multitasked. Love them both.

Third, to my select group of editors, readers, and also dear and trusted friends these many long years. Sebya Sinona for taking time from a busy schedule to read and offer insight. My father Jay McDonald for valiantly trying to read and provide encouragement before he passed away. Their contributions were valuable.

For the amazing feedback on the cover design and all its iterations, a huge thank you to Wynter Mahal. Your creative suggestions were greatly appreciated. I was able to take so many ideas and realize a vision that really brings this book to life.

Last, to my wonderful fans and followers. Without all of you and your support, I would be writing this all for myself.

This book would not be possible without the unfortunate events that transpired at the beginning of 2020 when the Coronavirus-19 emerged. At the time, I was working for Emory University School of Medicine in Atlanta, Georgia. With the Center for Disease Control, or CDC, located close by campus and hearing the latest information, I witnessed what would become one of the worst pandemics to affect the planet. Having a front seat to what was happening and the information that played out across campus and in the media, the story for this book developed through the events of 2020 and into 2021.

A novel was born.

This is a work of fiction that takes information from everywhere and twists it to write a suspenseful and psychological thriller using intricate details that spin a tale for the sake of entertainment. The truth is never what it seems and the lies shades of gray. The unabridged version goes into much more description and information. This version is the result of wonderful feedback and discussions with trusted people whose opinions and ideas matter to me.

I hope you enjoy it.

Jason McDonald

PANDEMIC-19

CHAPTER ONE

The tremors came slowly at first.

Short waves rolling and undulating one after another until they manifested into full-blown shakes and rattles. Cold sweat soaking his body to the bone. The excruciating pain of muscles contracting, freezing in place, contorting his body. Nausea building up ready to spew forth frothy vomit chunks and dissipating, only to return.

Throw in blurry vision that created a migraine, reminiscent of a nose freeze from drinking a cold beverage or eating ice cream.

It was a nightmare with no end.

The day puking really sucked if it hit with the shakes. Getting vomit all over yourself was crushing to the soul, even without an audience around. Any one ailment could leave you extremely vulnerable during the day if they decided to manifest, and since praying them away didn't work, God wasn't really on the friends list anymore, you simply hoped for the best and struggled to stay one step ahead and alive.

Dammit. I hate this. This shit sucks.

He could think of more descriptive words that really conveyed how it felt. Sometimes, using words like *shit* and *suck* seemed to be more grounded in being part of civilization, a grasp at the past that was gone.

The convulsions always seemed to come in the dead of the night, once the calm set in and R.E.M. had taken hold, right as he slipped into a deep slumber. It was a roller coaster ride he didn't ask to go on and one that threw his body this way and that with no safety bar to protect him from the G-Forces.

That wasn't to say that they never hit during the day or any other time.

They did.

For some reason the nights were the worst. If percentages and statistics mattered anymore, which those days were long gone to care, once all the

1

adrenaline and fear subsided and the body could ease itself out of fight or flight, the tremors found a small window to screw up the only time he had to regain his strength and sanity.

Safety and security, *the calm*, that seemed to be the catalyst.

He only wished for one night of peaceful sleep to actually have a chance to get some decent rest before the light brought the horror back to reality.

Is this going to be the new normal? Will they ever go away or is this life from this moment on?

Ryan Carmichael lay motionless in his bunk, eyes fixated on a faded brown stain on the ceiling, concentrating on a thought from long ago to ride this one out. Julia, her long brown hair blowing in the wind as they sat at the beach, watching the waves patter in. A perfect hue of vibrant reds and oranges across the clouds and skies above as the sun began to set.

The wonderful smell of lavender lotion from her skin.

A sly smile, the left corner of her mouth slightly upturned, looking out over the ocean as the wind and water performed a concert of sound. The roar of the waves crashing on the breaker rocks along the length of the jetty that left them both relaxed and in love as they sat at the end of it, enjoying a rare moment of me time.

It was as if he was right there with his wife again and he swore, he could see and smell everything. It was his last good memory before the end came.

The long-ago recollection of happier times, still vividly painting a picture inside his head, unlike many others that had faded to dust, helped ease the muscles in his body from rigor and trembling to slowly regain his senses and take in his surroundings.

Coming back to reality, Ryan took a deep breath, sighed, and closed his eyes.

Focus on relaxing Buddy. Let it all out.

At least until the next one came tomorrow night, he could go back to sleep and get some much-needed rest. The day had been a grueling disaster and pushing that out of his mind was the next task to conquer.

Food supplies dwindled and searching every single day meant the difference between life and death. He had goods stored away, cans of every imaginable thing, powdered this and that, rice and pasta, and even the sacred fresh fruits and vegetables he managed to find in abandoned gardens that wild animals hadn't wiped out. Most of the canned beans and meats had expired and taking a chance past the expiration date was a gamble.

Botulism or some other gastrointestinal issue was not the kind of thing you wanted to deal with, especially during the end of times.

The world was an unknown, events transpired without warning, and preparedness kept you alive for another day. Broken bone or need surgery to fix something?

Best of luck.

Infection?

You were hosed if you didn't stay on top of it.

He had ventured out like every other time, intent on adding to his horde. Some days he found huge bonanzas, others simply a few scraps. Yesterday was one of those where he hit the mother lode only to have life piss right in his face. A cardboard box of pinto beans turned out to be putrid, the cans pierced and a slow rot eating away at the precious commodity inside.

Even medical supplies like alcohol and peroxide were necessities to prevent infections, and his stock needed replenishment.

A tiny gash could turn into a life-or-death hazard. Start as a small scratch and go all red and MRSA or really screw you and wind up with gangrene.

He had found a crate of hospital grade bottles of alcohol and peroxide that someone must have pilfered before leaving it, all neatly packed and secure, though the glass containers made him uneasy.

Taking what he could, he called it a day and ventured back to where he called home.

Halfway there a wild pack of dogs, desperate for food, decided he might be on the menu. He felt for them, once someone's beloved companion now left alone without love or any kind of affection and their own lives hanging by a thread between living and dying, being a larger predator's next meal.

Instinct to survive cemented its hold over being man's best friend again.

He took his cue to get the hell out and ran like an Olympic sprinter trying to go from last to first, hopping fences, over cars, the pack in hot pursuit. Right when he thought he was safe, climbing on top of a dumpster to scurry over a retaining wall, he hit a greasy patch, slipped, fell on his back.

The crunch of broken glass and leaking liquid drained the life from him.

If crying was an option anymore, he might let a minutia of a split-second think the thought before burning it with a flame thrower. His scent was all around the supplies and path back, and given past experience, the hungry dogs would likely guard the remaining bottles for some time. He hoped he didn't need more until well past his aroma died out and the pack moved to better digs.

That was the thing.

With the world as it was, smell and the senses were on overdrive. There weren't all the competing odors like fast food or restaurant kitchen exhausts that sent plumes of awesome aromas into the atmosphere.

Cars and their exhaust were long gone.

You had the decay and rot mostly and once you either blocked it out or focused your nose to catch whiffs of what was around the corner, that opened up a new dimension on what you could sense. Kept your ass one foot ahead if you could manage to hide your own stench among the filth that remained.

As consciousness crept back, his mind wandered. The past was becoming a distant memory and trying to grasp a hold of any tidbit he could muster kept his world going. Even the bad ones, the last in particular, countered the positive feelings and ate at his soul.

Still after three long and desolate years, alone with much more to worry about in staying above ground and beyond the grave, losing his family haunted his dreams.

The good times soothed the tremors until they subsided, a gift at least as the nausea crept back to the recesses of his gut. The nightmares only added to his grief. If only he had been a step quicker, a second faster to act, they might still be alive. No guarantee of that for sure, though the maybe persisted.

They didn't deserve it.

Thick as cobwebs, Ryan tried hard to remember how it began.

Three years was a long time to pass and keep events straight in his head. The details were a bit hazy, the line between reality and what were now his own faded memories twisted in the wind.

All he knew for sure was what had happened to him.

The virus came upon the world slowly at first, a few cases here and there. China, the reported epicenter, by all initial reports was the first to be hit hard. Then, it spread like fire from country to country, across mountains and borders and even traveling over every ocean until nowhere was safe. The United States had been infected earlier than originally thought, a full three months before anyone realized it.

Colds, the flu, that's what the medical professionals thought since it was winter and the season for the yearly fevers, coughs, and runny noses to spread.

When they realized the gravity, stay in place orders, masks, social distancing.

Government officials tried to implement safety measures and safeguards. Businesses closed and the economy faltered. Contradictory messages from the White House, CDC, FDA, and the virus task force kept changing protocols. States didn't know what to believe or who to trust and began to open back up.

Some people felt the virus wasn't serious enough and went right back to life.

Social media posts and news feeds coming from all sides didn't help. The proliferation of false information mixed with what was portrayed as the truth added to the confusion and mistrust of what were lies and what was real.

That was what occurred during the first wave.

The truth was more complicated than what played out on television or in public. Ryan had a peek into it. When the second wave hit because of all the chaos and unrest that percolated, the virus brought a tsunami of death and destruction that bore down with a vengeance.

All the money and resources put toward vaccines proved catastrophic.

Approvals for trials had lackluster results and vaccines were put to production that during any other time in modern history, would never have seen the light of day.

Many people desperate for a cure consumed cocktails of medicines and snake oils that didn't work.

When promising vaccines came and people flocked for a shot, and all seemed on the road to recovery, hell rose from below and stoked the ashes of destruction.

New York City fell first in the U.S. and turned to ash.

Having plateaued from the first round and seemingly on the glorious path to recovery, the virus antibodies the experts thought would stay, faded away to leave people vulnerable again. The mutations multiplied until nothing stood in the way of the virus.

Seattle succumbed, ceased to exist.

Already hard hit from the first wave and fires and smoke that raged across the West from drought conditions, the second coming flooded communities lean on resources to protect and preserve life. Like dominos it went from city to city, town to town until every corner of the country suffered the same fate and the bodies outnumbered the living.

The rest of the world fared no better as the virus spread when countries lifted restrictions before a vetted and reliable cure was found and violence gripped the planet in response to the chaos and uncertainty of life beyond the next day clouded sensible thought. As television and radio covered events as they unfolded and began to drop off the air one by one before signals completely died, the glimpses of information before it all went dark were devastating and distressful.

Technology, once the binder of modern civilization to keep connections and information at the fingertips, simply went away and never returned.

The Stone Age would be a pretty good description, if anything positive could describe the world reverting back to a non-tech time and survival relied on what you could produce with your hands and any tools you could find.

Australia vanished.

As goods dried up and ships stopped sailing to deliver essentials, and a lifeline to the outside world blew up, it was only a matter of time. Still trying to recover from the devasting fires earlier in the year that killed a billion animals, the flames came back with even more vengeance as there were no people left to fight them.

Russia, fell soon after.

The virus passed along to shop keepers and their families and soon brought down the Kremlin, even with all of its precautions and protections. People died en masse, with sporadic groups finding refuge here and there isolated and alone.

China swelled again and an infection from a new strain simply depleted the population in one swift pass. With planes grounded and absolute travel restrictions in place, the virus withered away with the few fortunate left stranded among the billions of bodies and their stench.

Europe and Africa devolved at the same time.

Nationalism among countries and tribal warfare saw power grabs from groups that previously had little influence. Taking fear and what they saw as weakened governments lacking power, they threw chaos into society and the response from militaries and police to quell discord only brought more death and destruction until no leadership, positive or dictatorial, stood.

The Middle East fared better for a few months longer, desert lands offering some refuge.

They soon crashed and withered away to the sands of time.

The rest of Asia shriveled as the N95 mask supply that had been supplied by close neighbor China disappearing like puffs of smoke. With no protection, death washed over villages and towns that had been spared the first round. Like migrating birds, it went from continent to continent until nothing of substance was left standing above ground.

South America and Latin America were reduced to rubble.

The poor rebelled against the rich and entitled who had the resources to prolong their existence. Soon, Brazilian favelas and ghettos fought for food and medical supplies horded away. Fires were set to drive the oppressors out who had corralled every resource for themselves, and in the process burned down all in their wakes. With all essential lifesaving goods exhausted or burned to dust, starvation and death drove madness and people of all levels of society simply died out.

Canada vanished as well, though it took around the same time as the United States to wither and decay to oblivion.

For those who were left, the virus still lived inside, the last promising vaccine holding firm. There was no cure for the aftereffects and the debilitating way it ravaged the body. And worse yet, there was no telling when or if the antibodies would die, leaving you susceptible all over again to either manage to barely eke by or succumb to a horrible and agonizing demise.

Life forward was a roll of the dice.

As Ryan lay motionless, sleep felt like it was not in the cards. His mind kept playing over and over the events that led up to the end. It should have been the United States leading the charge and showing the planet what to do to fight the spread.

Wasn't the U.S. supposed to be an example for the free world? The leader to show the rest of the planet the way to salvation?

Not like salvation was any better. That was more a religious sentiment, and Ryan wasn't a church guy.

Government simply failed at every level regardless of political party or left or right-wing ideology to stop the madness until anarchy and catastrophic decimation of the free world was all that was left.

Nothing tangible remained. Everything came with a price.

No laws or people to lead. The world absent any sense of order or structure, even if people didn't like authority. PTAs, book clubs, hanging out at the gym. The ordinary concepts of people getting together for a purpose. Religions to comfort the masses who followed along with the ideologies. It all vanished with a flash. Foreign concepts when you looked around.

When all of that was gone, what remained was even worse.

CHAPTER TWO

Morning decided to make another visit, and with it the light of dawn brought a new day.

Splinters of rays wriggled through cracks in the old wooden pallet planks boarding up the windows. They danced off every miniscule and remaining shiny surface they could find, until the room illuminated with enough brilliance to catch Ryan's eyelids and raise him from a deep slumber.

The white paint, peeling and stained from years of neglect, left shadows as the light moved around the room.

An old overhead fluorescent, long ago ceasing to work, swayed as a breeze crept through the broken glass and past the boards. Its soft creak like a wave rolling in and washing back out to sea.

The cold air felt good against his skin.

He sighed, opened his eyes, and stared up into the abyss. Hoped it all had been a really bad dream and he was back at home, tucked under the covers and rested, the sea foam green paint of his bedroom ceiling a familiar greeting to put a smile on his face. Julia snuggled next to him and soon the kids barging in, loud and boisterous, urging everyone to get up for Saturday morning cartoons. Logan and Luka standing next to his sleepy face, their Boxer tail nubs swishing back and forth, urgent to go outside to pee. Chloe and Ceamus insistently meowing for breakfast before anyone else.

Seeing the cracks in the sheetrock overhead, no such luck.

The night aches left an impression in his muscles while at rest. The pain would subside, fluidity of movement returning to normal once he got out of bed and stretched. It was the initial period of horizontal awareness and awakening that his body had to overcome. He rolled to the side, tucked an elbow underneath, grunted, and threw himself to a sit.

Leaning slightly forward, head bowed, eyes closed, Ryan took in deep breaths, slow and methodical, an old cleansing and relaxation technique Julia had taught him. After a minute, he stepped into his boots, laced them up, and stood. Five minutes of stretching to warm the muscles and ease the pain left him feeling refreshed and ready for what lie ahead. He made his bunk, a reflexive action, smoothed out the wrinkles, tucked in the corners, and folded the old gray blanket. Grabbing his holster off the chair, he belted up and stopped by the mirror.

You look like crap Carmichael, he thought to himself.

His bright green eyes were contrasted by the dark circles staring back at him from all the restless nights of sleep. The flecks of gray in his tousled curly brown hair that was in need of a haircut. The salt nearly taking over his beard.

Some beard dye would take some years off for sure. I'm not that old, he sighed with a shrug.

Personal upkeep was a bit low on the list. Toothpaste and other essentials for health took priority. Besides, Julia had always liked his gray and complimented him on it.

She was a trooper.

A stray gray strand for her?

Immediate coloring ritual. That made him chuckle and feel some warmth of spirit.

Maybe today was a good day.

Peering out, he glanced from left to right down the dimly lit hallway. Morning light from the other rooms offered some visibility. He could see well enough, though it was never a sure thing.

He took precautions.

Trip wires hooked to bottles acted as sentries so he could hear any intruders who breached the stairwell and managed to remove the welded door. It would take a blow torch or a well-placed C4 brick to remove it and by that time he'd be long gone. Broken glass strewn haphazardly about would crunch under unsuspecting feet, giving him enough warning to act. Chuck some grenades down the hall or light them up with his rifle.

Pull the fire alarm as a last resort to unleash some water spray and let it soak pretty good, throw the battery cable out his door, and electrocute them.

He had options.

Ryan knew the path to zigzag to the kitchen. Mornings meant usually grabbing a bite and something to drink. Start the day off right like a champ. He worked his way right and past empty stretchers, beds left in the hall during the final chaos, and through the open door. Sitting atop the counter was Pete, staring intently at him, a scowl protruding from his lips.

"Hi Pete," Ryan winked affectionally as he walked over. "I missed you last night."

Pete stretched out as Ryan petted the cat's head and scratched his chin. The gray short-haired feline enjoyed the attention, moving his body rhythmically to capture the affection. Soft rumblings erupted that turned into purrs until he rolled on his back to offer up his belly.

"Too easy Pete. You need to play a bit harder to get."

Grabbing a can of powdered milk from the shelf, Ryan popped off the top, scooped out some contents, added water from a jug. Stirring quickly, the ingredients melted together and formed a nice frothy drink for his little friend.

"Here you go Buddy. Drink up."

For himself, he decided on a cup of coffee. He had a stockpile of food, some canned, some fresh, there were a few choices. He really wasn't in the mood for anything. Trying to push the blahs away, Ryan poured some water into the percolator, added some coffee grounds to it, and placed it atop the camp stove. Grabbing a match from the box, he turned the dial to high, rubbed the stick against the striker, and lit the propane gas. Fire erupted beneath the pot and a steady stream of flame flowed, bright orange tendrils dancing below his impending hot cup of Joe.

From his third-floor lookout, Ryan had a perfect view of the world below and as far as he could see in the distance.

Tall buildings dotted the skyline.

Some, having been ravaged by fires and explosions from the riots, were shells of their former existence. Others seemingly left intact and alone, stood like beacons of hope from a long-forgotten time.

That was a false sense of a picture that no longer existed.

They may still stand, the madness lurking inside hidden from view, a danger to the unsuspecting scavenger or group that sought refuge from the outside world.

He learned the hard way and almost lost his life.

Any expeditions for supplies or fun artifacts to keep some sanity followed a precarious routine of preparations and observation. Vigilance ensured a more positive outcome than shoddy prep work that nine times out of ten, brought death. The city had been his newest residence since rolling into town a little over a year ago. Given him time to roam around, learn where he could go freely without any issues and the hot spots to avoid like the plague.

Coffee brewed and now short sips to relish in its heat, the liquid went down as best as it could since the dry beans lacked the enriching oils that made it a drink worthy of contentment. He was always on the lookout for a tin or bag to bring back from a walkabout.

Sometimes he hit a goldmine and came across a café that roasted its own beans and the bags were still there to offer a bit of home brew for later.

Other times he came up empty or got a punctured tin from a grocery store that long ago had dried out. He could still drain some taste from the old grinds if he mixed the old with new collections.

It wasn't the same as a good sit at a real café for a fresh beverage or at home on the patio, reading the newspaper, enjoying it fresh and hot from his

French coffee press.

Pressed coffee, his mouth watered at the thought.

Ryan watched as Pete scampered about the staff kitchen, chasing a ray of light that glinted off the side of the soda machine. He would draw himself flat against the ground, ears back, watching intently ahead. Suddenly, he would pounce, paws frantically patting at the light in a vain attempt to attack and subdue. Fifteen minutes of back and forth trying to kill his prey finally sent him to the chair next to Ryan where he curled into a ball and soon fell asleep.

That cat was his last friend in the world.

Staring at the almost empty mug, Ryan relished in the last few drops of his first cup. He had another two waiting. Those would go inside the thermos he stuffed into his rucksack and keep him warm as he wandered outside searching and scavenging for goods.

Finishing his cup, he wiped it out, and put it back with the others.

The wall map had kept him busy as he drank, tracing and retracing routes around the city he had walked. Searching for places that might have food, survival gear, camping supplies, whatever he could bring back and use to keep on living. Push pins dotted its landscape, colored coded to show the good areas and the bad to avoid. Great finds with more in store or depleted and leave alone. It was in constant flux as he updated the current living conditions.

Most stores had been ransacked at the beginning.

It was the diamonds in the rough, places people forgot about or fell off their radar, that he tried to target. Some more visible locations still had the occasional find that was overlooked in the melee. He only ventured in if he felt it was worth the risk.

You never knew who, or what, might be inside.

He put some dry cat food in Pete's bowl, scratched his head, and grabbed his ruck off the floor. Pete would stay put and safe. He learned long ago when Ryan had found him as a small kitten to be weary of the outside world. With an inside window ledge where he would lay absorbing sunshine and from his perch could watch Ryan come and go, the cat would wait until his human's return. As he left, Ryan looked back at the cat munching on his food and gave a wave.

"Be back soon Buddy."

Stopping by his room, Ryan grabbed the rest of the things he needed for a day out. His tac vest was already loaded with clips and extra ammunition for his Sig Sauer pistol and the built-in camel pack filled with purified water. He was in need of another round of purification batches to keep his water supply fresh and had at least another few days' worth of the life-giving liquid to tide him over.

He threw a few more items in his rucksack he might need, climbing rope and D-rings, extra batteries for his flashlight, a bottle of bleach to clean or remove his scent, and threw it on his back. Sunglasses and field cover for his head from the nightstand, handkerchief wrapped around his face to keep putrid smells at bay, gloves to keep his hands warm and safe from scrapes.

His M4 rifle leaned against the wall next to the door, ever ready.

He picked it up, ejected the clip, popped it back in, chambered a round. With the safety engaged he shouldered it and left his room, longing to be back to its safe and secure surroundings later. Tomorrow was never guaranteed, and neither was today. His wits and gut more often kept Ryan in check.

If, he survived a day out in the wild.

CHAPTER THREE

Leaving the security and comfort of the abandoned hospital from the third floor was not easy, but a necessary ritual followed to stay alive.

He had to contend first with silently watching and listening from the window he used to crawl out onto the roof to make sure no one hid behind any of the air conditioning units that lined the way to his exit point. As the tallest building in the neighborhood and none in close proximity to spy on him, he had the advantage of being able to come and go without much issue.

It did not leave him complacent though.

Ryan knew firsthand what happened when you let your guard down and making that mistake again was not a road he wanted to travel.

Feeling confident the path was clear, he quietly slid the window open, climbed out, and grabbed onto the gutter drain. Reaching over he slid the window closed and shimmied down the pipe until reaching the landing below.

From there, it was a short hop down to the rooftop.

Shade from the building hid his movements, every motion could reveal his location, silence and slow movements critical until he reached his destination.

As he passed each AC unit he paused, listening and scanning ahead.

With each successful pass he felt better, more at ease, though never fully confident. Crouched low and continuing along Ryan reached the end.

A retaining wall offered cover and a last secure view of the landscape.

He glanced around, searching, squinting, focusing on every detail for a misplaced item or sign of intrusion into his surroundings. The parking lot was nearly empty except for the occasional car that had been left or forgotten. Beyond it a fence encircled the lot, still chained shut to prevent access.

Ryan had his secret way out.

It meant traversing the pavement in the open. He preferred to use it on his way back when the dark offered shadows to conceal. Today though, it was the way he needed to go to begin this morning's hunt. To the right pine trees and oleander bushes lined the fence and gave him a way to weave his way through until his exit location. It meant an hour of time to do quietly and unseen. Leaving any other way meant hours to get around the hospital massive grounds.

It did mean thirty yards of exposed blacktop.

He hopped over the ledge and holding the top, used his boots as leverage against the wall to shimmy down the drainpipe to the ground below. Moving quickly, Ryan rushed across the parking lot and under the low branches of an oleander.

Waited.

Time was not like before. A minute felt like an hour, an hour like a day. A day like an entire week. Sometimes it went by in a flash as adrenaline coursed through the body. Mostly, it felt *different*, a new way of life that wasn't close to normal.

Just the way things were.

Everything depended on what the current situation was and the heightened awareness or chaos that ensued. He wondered if there would ever be a return to the mundane, or at least a sense of routine where the world did not have 24/7 to worry about a safe place to hide and ride it out or the constant thought of impending death hanging over your head.

Maybe, one day.

He checked his watch, scanned the clearing, listened. Not a sound beyond a slight gust of wind rattling the leaves.

Fifteen minutes of nothing.

Hunched down, rifle ready to drop anything that moved, Ryan worked his way gently through the bushes and trees, stopping every ten feet and dropping low to the ground to watch and wait. It was a labored excursion, time consuming, and frankly boring as hell.

The precautions kept him alive.

Keeping a level head kept you upright and breathing. Panic usually found you disoriented making stupid decisions and winding up dead.

He preferred to avoid being dead, since "dead" was really not quite descriptive enough and had multiple levels of examples like a kid's picture book. If the dictionary revised the definition to attribute it to the current state of the world it would be more confusing and head scratching than anything. Upright and breathing the stench of decaying garbage and bodies was better than the alternative.

Make the right choice and keep trudging along.

Forty minutes later he arrived at the heavy maintenance hole cover. Hidden from view by an embankment to the right and concealed by overgrown bushes and tall grass, it was his way out into the drab world.

The storm drains beneath it led to a run-off basin for winter rains.

This time of year, he didn't have to worry about any excessive water blocking his way. Carefully raising the cover up, Ryan dropped his ruck, climbed down the ladder, careful to pull the lid back into place.

Natural light from the storm grates in the streets above bathed the passage with enough brilliance to paint a guiding path. It was roughly a half mile to get to where he needed. Every hundred yards the tunnel branched off to the left and right and led to other destinations he used to move around the city. Approaching each juncture with caution, he listened for any sound, the click of metal, the slosh of water, a voice or groan, anything that betrayed the security of his transport system beneath the streets above. He had spent nine months securing the end points to prevent discovery and breaches.

Nothing was for sure or even permanent.

He could only hope his precautions held tight and kept anyone or anything out.

Standing close to the wall and bent down at the last four-way juncture, he focused on the sounds that caught his ear. First tilting his head to the left, slowly to the right.

Nothing seemed out of place.

Slowly straightening up, he walked the remaining distance to the end of the tunnel. He could see out across the basin, overgrown with weeds and trees, but nothing that prevented him from seeing clearly if danger lurked. The grate door on this end was hidden from view unless you happened to be right on top of it. Set back in the embankment, it had long ago been overgrown.

Not to the point of preventing seeing out.

It was more camouflage than anything, and a couple of old cans of olive-green spray paint on the bars and surrounding concrete added to the illusion.

Ryan took out a key and unlocked the rusty chain. Carefully moving it, he pulled the grate door open. Normally, it would creak and make a loud noise from being unused.

A can of motor oil kept the hinges lubricated.

It whooshed silently inward, enough to let him quietly pass. He pulled it closed, locked it, and turned, staring out.

Five minutes of pause and he would be gone.

The city, or what was left of it, was a dark, depressing, and increasingly colorless place. Paint fading and peeling from being left unkept, dirt and dust a grimy film left on every surface. Even the snow and rains didn't completely wash them away.

With no traffic or people to disrupt it, it simply stayed.

Litter and garbage decayed everywhere along the streets and sidewalks as occasional gusts of wind whipped things around. Grass fed by winter water was one of the few colors emerging that offered vibrant shades of green as a contrast against the bleakness. It would only last as long as the rains came only to die off, drabs of mottled brown until fall came and offered a palette of leaf colors to add hues to the miserable and drab reality.

Ryan called it modern life.

He walked the desolate streets, keeping close to the sides of buildings as he maneuvered around obstacles. Walls offered shade and some concealment versus being fully exposed in the open. He could easily dive into a recessed doorway or go prone, flat against the sidewalk, if he felt threatened. Mostly, it was taking his time observing ahead, looking, searching for movement, peering into windows and doors for any sign of life.

Keeping his guard up to keep vigilant and painstakingly aware of his surroundings.

Ryan had walked this street many times. Every nook and cranny, every object left behind, every seemingly misplaced and lone article of clothing familiar. Locked inside his mind were the photos he took and meticulously categorized away.

It was the subtle nuances that his trained eyes focused on.

A bottle rolled a few inches and its previous indentation noticeable. A car door slightly ajar. A path through the dirt that appeared swept of footprints.

Every detail important to capture.

Each could have any number of explanations. The wind could have moved an empty bottle.

Car doors and sweeping?

Those meant something else.

He knew which doors were closed and which open as he had checked every single one for supplies and pilfered what he could. An open door meant someone had been here. Swept paths to hide trespassers meant a conscious effort to hide one's presence.

Friend or foe, that was the question.

The answer usually behind a bullet.

His morning walk was uneventful as nothing was out of place. He kept going until he reached his first stop. The old neighborhood hardware store, tucked between a bicycle shop and delicatessen, kept him supplied with required materials and thankfully was still well-stocked. Today he only required a few items, more necessities really, key finds that kept life a bit more acceptable for its current state and comfortable for the long nights until summer came.

The front window was intact, the old mailbox still jammed up against the front door. Feeling secure he went in through the back of the store near the loading dock.

The rear door had been unlocked the first time he found it.

After scavenging the store, he decided to check the office for a set of keys and found them. Added them to his collection and kept the store locked to ensure if he ever found it unlocked or a door open, he better leave, in case whoever was still inside. He always locked it behind to keep him safe.

If he had to run, the push bar would swing it outward to escape.

Standing a minute to let his eyes adjust, Ryan listened. Silence was all he heard. Through the stacked boxes and past the counter to find what he needed. Then, onto the next stop.

Propane camping bottles were on Aisle 3 and charcoal on Aisle 10. Why they were not in the same location left him puzzled. It didn't make much sense. The only reason he could think of was keeping camping and summer cooking and related activities separate as the shelves and inventory in the store themed each activity. He had a few other things to grab and depending on how the supplies looked he might be in and out quickly and onto the next adventure for more treasures.

Grabbing four propane bottles and wrapping each in a thin dish towel to keep from clanking together and making any noise, Ryan placed them in the bottom of his rucksack.

He learned that one the hard way when he first encountered the new world.

Metal tent spikes caught his eye, and as they had many uses, he grabbed two bags, wrapped them tightly with string, and threw them in. He went to get some charcoal, not for a great BBQ to invite people over for some burgers and hot dogs and not even to cook with on a grill.

Smoke and smell floated through the air, catching the wrong kind of attention.

He wished he could sit outside with an ice-cold beer, flipping the meat, having a conversation with someone, really anyone at this point, and bite into a juicy mess he had not tasted in years.

That dream was not a reality anymore, at least around here.

No, charcoal was a part of his water purification system. He grabbed a small five-pound bag and shoved it down. Last stop was for some mesh screening material to help with his water system, the fine mesh that caught all the tiny bits of yuck. He grabbed a roll, wrapped it with string, and slid it down the side of his ruck.

That should do, Ryan thought.

Traveling light and not being burdened down was the way of the future. If he happened upon anyone or anything that required a quick exit to safety, the lighter the better. You never knew when you would be running, diving, and climbing to avoid a hungry pack of dogs or whatever had gotten loose from the zoo.

Being eaten alive was not how he wanted to go out.

Thankfully, he didn't have to worry about any flying sharks taking off an arm or a leg, and when he thought about those old movies, he couldn't help chuckle. There were some lighter moments left, even with as crappy as things got when you were a one man show.

Humor was the best medicine.

Satisfied, he left the same way he came. Locked the door, snuck down the alleyway until he reached where it intersected the street. He took cover behind a large bush, scanning his surroundings for the small things out of place. Cars lined the street in either direction, long ago left abandoned, parked at the curb or in traffic with the engines running, batteries now dead. Trash piles of everything imaginable, clothing, appliances, decayed boxes of food, cans, bottles, even pictures and paintings, lay strewn about and rotting from exposure.

With no movement in sight, Ryan ran across to the other side and down the alley. It dead ended thirty feet in at the back of a building with a roll up door partially open and a dumpster against it.

Climbing on top of the dumpster Ryan jumped up to grab the roof of the building, pulling himself up and over the small wall. He knelt, crouched low, surveyed ahead. He could go left or right and run the length of the block to either cross street. The grocery store was long pilfered of any food supplies so it wasn't on his list.

It still provided coverage and vantage points to spy on the city, and Ryan liked to use it.

Today was a going right day, deeper into the city. He crept along, listening, looking, until he reached the end. Stretched between the grocery store and the next building was a cable attached to two cell towers on opposite sides.

Competing providers looking to expand their networks.

It was a sturdy line some long gone resourceful person had put up to cross the street below and avoid encountering anyone. A smart and resourceful idea for sure. He used it all the time and today was no different. Grab the pully, swing over, tie it for the return trip, and continue on his way.

As he grabbed the line and began to swing across Ryan stopped cold, fear gripping his body. A bead of sweat, not from heat, from panic, slowly drawing across his forehead.

The sound was unmistakable.

Low voices mumbled.

He couldn't quite hear the words, yet the sound was recognizable. He quietly and deliberately with slow precision inched his way back and off the small retaining wall. Looping the cable back to secure it, he bent down to his stomach and crawled over.

"I don't know," the first voice almost whispered.

There was barely enough volume to catch Ryan's focused ear.

He couldn't make out man or woman, or see anything from his current location. Careful to remain hidden he crawled to a small break in the wall used for water runoff. Peering out the gap, his eyes darted back and forth to find the source.

A loud thud echoed between the buildings accompanied by a groan. Looking left and immediately right to focus, he found it in the image of a window across the street. Fifty feet to his left, near the sidewalk, he saw them. Half a dozen armed men, dressed in mis-matched military fatigues, encircled someone on the ground.

He could tell they were not real military by their dress.

A unit would be wearing the same or similar clothing. This group looked like they had raided an army surplus store. Desert camo, olive drab jungle, and urban city gray battle dress uniforms, or BDUs, stared back in the reflection. Professionals, if they still acted as a unit, would all wear the same uniform at least and not have on a bunch of flashy athletic shoes.

This group, by the dress and weapons they held, were much worse.

"Tell us where it is," a man from the group hissed. "My patience is thin, and I want information."

The response must not have been the right one. Another loud thud filled the space between the walls and the group parted enough for Ryan to see.

A small figure hunched over on knees, clothes tattered from years of abuse or maybe the current interrogation, coughed from the blows of the baseball bat.

Cries of pain whimpered out as each came down and connected with the back.

The assailant, a large husky man with a long brown beard that flapped with each strike, took pleasure in inflicting the right amount of pain without breaking bones. A grin pursed his lips from ear to ear and he jumped up after each one, doing a circle dance with a hop at the end.

Appalachian moonshine brewer came to mind.

Ryan could picture the guy deep in the woods, copper still and a fire burning beneath it, a makeshift hut with animal skins on the walls of his home. The occasional ladle below a spigot to grab a taste to check the potency as he cooked up batches of illegal booze to sell to the locals.

The person who had to be the leader, a small skinny man with a shaggy dirty-blond mullet, walked around the figure, leaning in talking, not loud enough for Ryan to hear. He shouted lifted old truck with a gunrack full of rifles. American flag one side and some wanting to be funny bumper sticker the other side of the rear window. Probably too many DUIs to count and nights sleeping them off.

Not the cream of the crop citizens.

It went on for what seemed like an hour, in reality maybe only five minutes. Mumbled voices, blows, and cheers from the rest, egging the two torturers on. They all seemed to enjoy it, a big beatdown party in the middle of the street with plenty of pain to go around if skinny man had let each take their turn with the human piñata.

From somewhere off in the distance he heard it.

Low and steady, building up as it got closer. He closed his eyes and listened. It was a sound lost in his memories. Sweet and beautiful, like a classical concerto playing the lost masterpiece of Beethoven or Mozart. Happiness and joy, dark and brooding, violins and cellos deep and resonating without any words.

A smile washed over him.

V8, dual exhaust, pedal to the floor as it raced nearer. It was only a momentary feeling as he had no clue who or what was coming. More of the group below, rescuers, or the others.

From the direction of the engine pistons firing and screech of tires, he would find out soon enough.

CHAPTER FOUR

The smell of burning rubber hit his nostrils.

Carried along by a swift breeze it filled the air with the sounds of crashing objects and the roar of a high-powered engine.

A battered old Ford Bronco, its green paint pockmarked with dents and scratches down to the metal, came barreling around the corner, oversized tires trying to grip the street as it leaned into the turn, sliding to the right before the rubber made contact and caught the road.

The relic shot forward like a bolt of lightning, the blare of rapid bursts of gunfire erupting from it.

Ryan, unable to see what was going on as the crowd took cover, moved to a different vantage point. Taking safety behind a break in the crumbling retaining wall, he lay prone, his right eye peering far enough around to see unobstructed down the block.

The gunfire came from a makeshift steel-welded mount in the rear cargo area of the Bronco. A .50 caliber gun shot bursts down the block, whizzing past Ryan's location. He figured the shooter was aiming at the mob beating the small figure in a rescue attempt to break up the violence.

To his surprise, shots echoed from behind.

He rolled on his back and nudged up against the wall. Coming down the block towards the Bronco, a group of thirty more armed men, dressed similarly to the group below, worked its way along, taking cover behind abandoned cars, in doorways, and some simply walking straight ahead firing one shot after another. The bullets flew back and forth, the noise deafening, as glass shattered, bullets ricocheted off the buildings and concrete, and people cried out as lead penetrated bodies and blew out muscle tissue and blood through exit holes.

The scene playing out below was surreal.

Ryan rolled back and tried to gauge the carnage erupting below. The

Bronco had come to an angled stop to protect the driver's retreat from the vehicle. A woman, he could tell by the long hair pulled into a tight blond ponytail with a pink scrunchie, fired from behind the safety of an old Subaru SUV that was wedged against a wall.

The shooter, an older man whose wild gray hair whipped around as he panned the machine gun back and forth as it fired in rapid succession past Ryan, was yelling directions to a third person firing at the mob from behind a mailbox.

He couldn't hear anything above the mayhem.

Could easily guess the old man and woman were providing cover fire while the third person attempted a rescue.

Shocked, he watched the assailants fall one by one, being outmatched by the heavy caliber death dealing of the machine gun.

Except the skinny man and his enforcer.

They had managed to run off and find a recessed doorway hidden by shadows and crawl through a broken window. The small figure was still on the ground, even as bullets whizzed all around. Finally, as the shots subsided and the mob lay bleeding in the streets, the person raised up slightly, a face grimaced in pain revealing a hint of features. In an instant the mailbox rescuer darted out and grabbed the figure in a man's bear hug, lifting what Ryan now recognized was a small boy off the ground and away.

Within twenty seconds the rescuers were gone.

Ryan lay staring, what had played out reverberating in his mind. An Old West style gun battle with a modern twist.

Good guys and bad guys in this future world were vast shades of gray areas.

He had seen good turn bad in the days leading up to and right after the fall of humanity. Defining people into categories of right and wrong was misleading at best and subjective, depending on the party or person on the opposite side of the situation. Life tottered on making it to another day.

A balance beam with one wrong step and you fell.

The instinct to survive caused many to do things they normally wouldn't, and you couldn't really blame them. It was you or them in this festering armpit and he'd seen what happened when food ran out. Family and friends turning on one another.

For this one though, he sensed which party was which and could make some calculated deductions.

Beating a small child, bad.

Rescuing small child, good.

It might be a stretch to make such a determination. Given the joy and pleasure the husky bearded man seemed to take in violently cracking a bat over a little kid, his intuition was likely right on this one.

What threw Ryan completely off his game was the momentary glimpse of the small boy's face. It caught him off guard and by surprise. The long wavy and curly brown hair wisping in the wind, covering his eyes, revealing just enough *familiarity*?

Was that what sent shudders down his spine?

It was a split second, not enough time to peer and dissect his face to know. A tiny fraction of a passing glance to plant something in his brain that sowed dissention to what he thought he knew.

He closed his eyes and rattled his head back and forth to clear out the cobwebs forming inside. Gaining his senses was a priority over being lost in thought or the past.

As he prepared for what to do since moving on with his day to retrieve supplies had been blown up, the shrieks jarred Ryan awake. The high-pitched screams of the *dead*, though dead was not necessarily a permanent state and had multiple layers to what constituted being a corpse that stayed that way.

No, in this new world you could be really dead and at peace or "dead" and tormenting anything that lived.

His world had suddenly been thrown into complete chaos. The last year had been a life void of people. It had been filled with the actual dead that littered the streets, buildings, and parks leaving decay and smells as they rotted away from the sun, rain, and cold. He called these the *Perma-Dead*, since they were not going anywhere except to dust.

A step up were the *Un-Dead* or to make it short, *Dead*, and these were a spectrum and various degrees of death waiting to happen. Some were slow, sluggish heaps of flesh that wandered aimlessly and posed little trouble beyond being an annoyance.

They weren't zombies or anything like that.

Humans now morphed into completely brain-dead survivors was more like it where the virus had eaten all the portions that assisted in normal functions. Their eyes looked beyond you with nothing left inside that remotely hinted they were alive, and they were more scavengers wandering until death finally took hold.

There were the slightly more energetic who fancied human flesh as their next meal. You could classify them as living zombies, though they were better described as messed up people affected by the virus and who had left sanity behind. These were the *Lurkers*, opportunistic shadow dwellers who seemed to come out of nowhere, as if they spied on you hiding in the dark and then attacked with vengeance. Sprinters that could be outrun if you got them past fifty yards where they fell to the ground exhausted. Fast and furious, they lost it all past the maximum distance and were easy targets to extinguish after.

The nightmares of your dreams were the vigorously rampaging hordes, the track stars of death dealing he called the *Bolts,* because of their speed and keeping it light with an Olympic reference. They seemed to be amped up on steroids, meth, and caffeine. If they got you in a run, since they could cover

23

more ground than the average person, you likely wound up as a corpse. Ripped apart while alive and eating their victims, they relished in the slaughter.

You really wanted to avoid them.

The last bunch were the B*rain Dead*, an old description of people that had taken on a whole new meaning in the new world. He called them *Brainers* for short. They were not technically dead just like the rest. They had brain function and were not walking corpses eating brains or people.

They simply had their moral compass and all human traits gone.

Reasoning, empathy, sympathy, right versus wrong. You name it, something that made someone human and not evil, well, they were evil times a thousand. It was like a part of their brain shriveled up or the neurons stopped transmitting signals. No matter what, if you encountered them, you died.

It might take a day, a week, or a year.

Eventually they tired of the torture and fun desecrating a living, breathing, and innocent soul, and would dispatch them without even a blink.

Ryan thought the Brainers were the absolute worst. They were still alive after all. Carrying on conversations, cooking meals, driving vehicles. The others were dead in the sense they could never be human again. They had no choice in the matter and were doing whatever it was that they were infected to do. The Brainers might be or might not be infected.

He really didn't know.

Maybe the loss of the world, life as it used to be, maybe that turned something inside off like the humanity switch. Or maybe they were pre-disposed to it and the catalyst, the sociopathic killer button, got turned on and smashed and the rest was nature. Whatever the reason or answer, they were back in his city and life was now a hell where a bloodbath worse than the one that played out minutes ago would soon be the next phase of death coming to them all.

As Ryan sat and absorbed the mess strewn across the street the screams grew louder. The hail of bullets must have drawn them out of hiding and towards the mayhem. He knew these were the Bolts the minute he heard the pounding on the pavement grow closer. He could see the mob below, the dead, the dying. Even with their brain function short-circuited, they still felt fear when death approached.

There was no way they didn't know what was coming. If you made it this far in life and survived the hell dropped upon the planet, at some point you encountered the screams, heard the footsteps approach, and saw the outcome. Knew what it meant and ran if you could or hid and held your breath. Though hiding never seemed to pan out.

Hearing the pathetic crying and begging voices asking for help, there was no savior who would suddenly appear.

It seemed odd to Ryan that every other human aspect was gone except that one. Maybe fear was an innate human attribute that no matter what happened, would never cease. Death came for everyone at some point.

Never like this.

Not as it came in this world. Not like a sea of carnage ripping flesh from the bones and leaving a trail of intestines in its wake, all while the living still breathed. At least until they succumbed to a real death or transformed into a shade of death that kept on hunting and killing its prey.

He'd soon find out.

CHAPTER FIVE

Ryan stayed motionless, his breathing regulated.

He needed to ride out the storm as if he never existed. The last thing he needed was to be trapped on this roof, no food supplies, no way of getting back to safety.

The Bolts traveled in packs with the upper count no more than thirty.

Normally, they were a small bunch of five and outlier groups ten at most. You could pick them off if you had the high ground or the advantage of a secure spot to take them out.

You had to make it quick though.

Their speed presented problems if you were not a crack shot and if they homed in on your location, you better prepare to die as they were ruthless in breeching any blockade or door to make a kill. He had seen them wear their arms to stumps scratching and clawing at doors to try and get past. Beyond persistent, their drive to find and kill whatever caught their attention was boundless. They were also runners and not adept at climbing obstacles.

Simple north/south fullbacks if you threw in a football analogy.

If you could manage to outrun them and get to a position high enough to start shooting them one by one, you had a chance. If you spent too long, you risked drawing more of them to you. Ammo better be plentiful or else you better hope salvation struck, or a rescue plucked you out.

They'd wait you out forever.

He lay for hours until the sun began to fall, and the sky grew dark. The sounds were almost unbearable to listen to so close to him. The shrieks, the screams of terror, the sound of flesh being ripped and eaten. The overpowering smell of iron from all the blood being spilt a few feet below wafted through his nostrils, bringing back hard repressed memories locked deep away.

He had seen the slaughter before from afar, that experience subdued

26

compared to being right on top of it.

It had been years ago, during the fall of civilization when the virus peaked and recovering from it a lost cause.

How did we get to this? Ryan thought, the simple statement etched in his conscious mind and a question asked countless times. He'd been a participant and bit player, although not in a capacity to realize until it was too late.

He thought he knew.

The response to the virus outbreak and ensuing miscalculations, or outright dropping the ball, did nothing to help matters.

Politicians from both sides of the aisle, ever the world class showmen and Teflon figures who could not walk a straight line of truth, took no responsibility for the chaos.

As they failed to lead and engage solutions, blaming each other for the pandemic, some on the fringes promoted medications and off the wall science as cures. Hydroxychloroquine, a malaria drug, was the first fringe treatment, much to the perplexed minds of actual doctors and researchers as there was no real science validating it. People began trying to make a connection with tonic water and quinine, a medicine distantly related to Hydroxychloroquine, as a substitute medication to prevent and fight of the virus. Alternative research sought to get a leg up and get the FDA to approve, which they reluctantly did because of threats and intimidation by politicians and government officials who had investment stakes, or constituents who did.

Respected institutions soon followed to prove or disprove the remedies.

When trials and real data began to suggest and show Hydroxychloroquine was ineffective and, in some cases, extremely harmful, the promoters acted as if they never mentioned it as a treatment. They then promoted the use of UV light outside and inside the body and in the same breath brought up household products used to sterilize surfaces like bleach and disinfectants. Manufacturers immediately put out press releases warning the public in direct language to not attempt to use their products for any medicinal treatments as not only common sense, but as protection against severe consequences.

Doctors, researchers, and experts in medicine all blasted the outright lies and in promoting procedures that had no scientific basis, data, or research to back up any assertions.

Competing press conferences by the left and right to answer the people's concerns had politicians failing to answer even the simplest questions and went on to tout different solutions to combat the virus. When the officials were called out by legitimate medical professionals and respected press organizations, many claimed it was all sarcasm. The FDA finally took a stand and released a statement ending any and all trials for hydroxychloroquine as ineffectual and dangerous with no conclusive positive results.

The profiteers shuddered at the news and loss of stock prices.

It was yet another example of poor leadership and yes men and women who sought their own fame and fortune in the spotlight over responsible medicine finally succumbing to the harsh reality and science published against their wishes.

The facts could no longer be twisted to support the lies.

The medical experts and virus team leaders working for each party faction all failed to protect the public by immediately stepping up and putting the health and safety of the people first by calling out the rogues lying at press briefings.

They instead played politics over life.

Not a single person stood up with integrity and called bullshit. The White House brought up further testing and trials that were full of misinformation. Officials pushed off to states unequipped for large scale disasters and withheld critical resources from them when they disagreed with their representatives in the House or Senate. Governors who banded together to coordinate action and pool supplies faced strict reprisals in going against administration policies that were inconsistent, false, and all failed to provide a national plan and framework for the entire country to follow.

Complete disorganization at the federal level and from the Administration caused chaos. Each political party did little to step up and provide leadership or guidance.

Words were big and forceful, with no bite behind them.

No cohesive response to the virus, no plan for the future, no holding the Administration accountable with legal or congressional action. There was a critical window to step forward and wrestle the incompetence of the current leadership away and chose to put personal ambitions and political aspirations as a party over their constituents.

Even when evidence showed many Administration and elected officials were profiteering and making decisions to benefit themselves while people died, politics versus conscience and oath to protect made the swamp even murkier until it was a festering cesspool. Taking a hard stand and putting integrity first got lost in the shuffle. When reality finally caught, even the most hardened skeptic convinced, there was no way to stop it.

The virus won.

Filtering back to the present Ryan took a chance in the growing darkness and peered over the break in the wall. It had been quiet for some time. Enough light from sunset still offered visibility, so he panned the street to assess.

Nothing moved.

There was zero left of the mob that resembled human. Body parts and pieces littered the street. Internal organs were haphazardly strewn about after the feasting and trails of intestines left gray-white bloody lines. The Bolts had performed well and left while Ryan was lost in thought.

Damn, he grimaced, pissed at himself. *I haven't seen a group like this in forever and I have no idea where they are.*

Trying to track them down without a solid plan was a sure ticket to dead. Plus, it was getting dark and he was far from a secure hideout where he could manage a retreat and last them out if things went to shit. His ruck wasn't packed for a prolonged excursion and food and water would be necessary if he got into it with anyone or anything out here.

Taking more time to survey his surroundings, Ryan could see the Bolts had left going in the direction of the old Bronco. The parts and pieces of flesh and dark drag marks that were likely blood went off and around the corner in that direction.

Taking it as his cue to get back to Pete, he left quietly, intent on returning the next day to investigate and find out who and what, the people in the old Bronco had to do with the Brainers.

CHAPTER SIX

The hot water felt good against his skin.

It was a luxury, one he felt a necessity to make him feel a small bit normal while surrounded by devastation and death. The old hospital, as one of its last efforts before the virus took, had retrofitted the entire campus with solar panels. The parking structures and lots all had tall pillars affixed with solar, a future investment to reduce costs and provide an ample energy supply to negate what was purchased and sell back to the energy company.

All of the hospital electrical grid worked, he had checked it out when he took over residence.

To keep a low profile, he turned off all non-essential circuits, lights, heating, AC, anything that would draw unwanted attention or power resources. He left the electric water heaters for the third floor working, far enough up and internal to be quiet and functional. He also left the electrical plugs for the floor working, though he disconnected everything from the outlets except what he needed. It left life a bit better, far from comfortable and way off the grid rustic, livable and with some amenities that made it bearable.

As the dirt and grime fell and the water cleansed his body, Ryan's old memories flooded his head. Thoughts of his last good memory of Julia. The last time he had a beer with Mike and John before hell boiled over. Placing his children on the medivac helicopter to fly out to the hospital ship, the last remaining safe haven miles around. Julia's hand ripped from his grasp as he was pushed out of the last rescue chopper and fell into the ocean. Seeing the aftermath of the explosion.

Being left with nothing, his family gone.

Their old house flashed into his mind. The beautiful old rancher with wrap around porch. The porch swing they used to sit in, holding the kids tight and telling them their favorite stories. Coffee or tea on those cold or cool mornings, iced sweet tea or lemonade on warm evenings. Hot chocolate with marshmallows for those special occasions.

Even the stereotypical white picket fence Julia had to have that he hated having to paint.

It was the picturesque dream home for them, checking off all of the boxes for each. Large backyard for him with plenty of space for the kids, his workshop for all the mechanical toys and projects, and the garden and fruit trees to feed their bellies with fresh produce.

Open floor plan for her with great natural light and space to unwind.

Gourmet kitchen with top-of-the-line stove for his amateur chef creations that fed the soul with wonderful tastes and delights. Oversized island and bar top seating for her to sit and drink her wine as he dazzled the family with meals.

He missed their home, their sanctuary, the culmination of their hard work and sacrifices as he built his business and turned a profit and Julia managed their crazy and chaotic lives. The house had required a huge makeover to update it from the old couple who owned it before, and hustling to get things done before babies crashed the party was an expensive, yet worthwhile adventure. He longed for it again, to wake in his bed, to sit on his couch. Catch a soccer match on the weekend or enjoying their Friday family movie nights on the big screen.

What did he have for comfort?

A bunk and broken windows, peeling paint, and barely sufficient necessities to get by. If he had his family here it might feel better, even huddled up on the really cold nights for warmth.

Those days of familial interactions were long gone.

Leaning with his left hand on the shower wall, head down and eyes closed, feeling the hot liquid on his neck, Ryan took a deep breath. He knew what he saw that night. It was clear, as if he were right back in it.

I saw it. I saw the ship blow.

The images were vivid, the smells returned. The taste of saltwater spewing from his mouth as he surfaced and the plumes of orange fire shooting high into the air as diesel fuel erupted somewhere inside the ship. Watching helicopter pieces shoot into the air.

The feeling of abject helplessness watching the ship slip below the waves and the moonless night casting complete blackness as far as he could see out. The long cold swim to shore as his body ached, trying to stay above water and not slip below the waves.

He had lost everything that night. His wife, his children, his friends. All gone to leave him alone in a world not worth living in, though not one he would volunteer to leave on his own.

He was stronger than that.

Taking the coward way out would be spitting on the memory of his family and not something Julia would want. She would want him to keep living, to try and find a life, to honor their sacrifices for the kids.

Seared in his mind was the one image that played over and over.

Seeing the evil in Mark's eyes as he pushed him out of the helicopter, the venom in his words, still rang in his ears.

You are not part of the plan.

Ryan up until that point was only doing his job, security for the researchers and scientists working on a cure, to protect them from the conspiracy nutjobs and lunatics who wanted the virus to continue to protect their own delusional interests. He ran it all, in the loop enough to be around and hear everything, though not deep enough to know the real intentions. It ate at him for a long time as he picked up the pieces and tried to navigate what was left of society.

Going back, searching through the records and files, he found some of the answers.

Given the way the end played itself out, it shouldn't have surprised him, and as he read each file page and mouse clicked screen after screen while power still prevailed on the grid, it no longer did. It all began to make sense and as he rummaged through crates for what he needed for his life ahead, the rage seethed inside, wishing for a last chance to stop it.

Too little and too late to the parade.

Rinsed clean and feeling better, Ryan dried off and put on a fresh set of clothes. Always prepared in case you had to leave in a hurry. You didn't want to have to scramble for pants and a shirt in the middle of the night.

Every second counted.

Pulling on legs and arms through holes could mean getting out in one piece or getting caught literally with your pants down.

He sat in the kitchen eating a can of stew heated on the camp stove, the point of his going out earlier to get a fresh canister and backups for the next few weeks. Pete had already eaten his food. He lay in Ryan's lap, purring away, happy his friend had returned. Dinner was a bit of a lonely time since he had no conversation partner to talk back.

He ended up talking to Pete and provided responses to his own questions. Sometimes he worried he had slipped off to crazy town by having the dialog. Then, he remembered it was something he had always done with his other cats and even the dogs. Made them more human to him and in a way, he knew what he was inserting for their part was probably what they'd say if they could actually talk.

Sanity had not left quite yet.

"I don't know what I saw today, Pete. Bullets flying, chaos, just a mess. A split-second glimpse and with a poof, was gone. That kid, the one getting the beat down, there's no way..." Ryan thought, his voice trailing off.

He took another bite of stew, the pepper hitting his taste buds. Not as good as his homemade, although as good as it was going to get in the apocalypse. It wasn't like he could go to the grocery store and get fresh meat cubes to brown. Peel some potatoes and carrots. Dice an onion and celery stalks. Throw it all in a big pot and slow cook for hours.

Ryan longed for those days.

He stroked Pete under the chin, the action calming and putting his uneasiness of thought a few degrees lower. Even the purrs helped his erratic mind. He searched his memories, compared them to today. The similarities, though fleeting, pecked away at his consciousness.

"My mind must be playing tricks on me. Maybe my eyes are in need of glasses finally as the 20/20 vision flies away. Lack of sleep. Probably all of it."

Pete looked up as if to confirm.

"Quiet peanut gallery."

The boy had to be what, eight and some change?

It had been three years since he had seen a real kid. Most that survived got evacuated. The rest were fragile shells, nothing inside left as human. The last one of those had been over a year ago. Saw him wandering with a pack of scavengers, ragged and dirty, his bones barely keeping his skin on. Poor kid was lucky to have lasted that long and seeing him in such bad shape, Ryan knew at the time his clock was almost out.

He teared up thinking if the boy was anything like his own son David, the kid loved to play ball and ride his bike. Probably fixated on video games and the latest cartoon. Smiled with a big toothy grin minus a few teeth the Tooth Fairy had paid for. Seeing an adolescent who no longer really looked like a child but more like a corpse on feet left his mental references pretty slim for comparison. No pictures left, no cell phone images.

Nothing.

All he had was what was inside his head and that wasn't much of an authoritative source. Still, it was the best he had to go on.

The curly brown hair. The split-second look, green eyes piercing back.

The words played over and over in his head.

The medivac. Putting young David next to his sister Emma. The fear in both of their faces.

Emma holding Boo Boo close, her favorite doll offering a small amount of comfort. Touching her cheek to wipe away a tear, tell her everything was going to be okay. Waving goodbye as the pilot lifted up and banked left out over the ocean.

Ryan had seen terror before. The young boy was scared, the fear for his life visible in the stature of his body as it slumped under the blows of the baseball bat. His eyes wide as basketballs as the man scooped him up and off to safety.

Relief? Was that what caught my eye? Relief at being rescued from a certain death or because his tormenters were being hacked down?

The deductions were based on slim evidence, and he was pulling for an explanation. Grasping for a thread that he knew wasn't there. He had seen the explosions, the ship going down. Waited on the shore for days to see what washed ashore. Left when nothing came.

Fast forward to the present. Three years of being alone. It was reasonable his mind played tricks on him. Anyone who had experienced the trauma he had would be in the same boat. Seeing things that weren't real. Memories that you thought you had lived only in a dream.

He knew in his mind that his precious kids were gone. Facts were facts. Especially seeing it with your own eyes. Being there as a witness. Hard to argue any of that.

Logic and reasoning went a long way. Even for a guy all alone who talked to himself. He could flip it any which way, upside down and right side up. The result still the same.

But, what if?

CHAPTER SEVEN

His body tossed and contorted.

The spasms gripped his muscles and rolled from his feet to his head and back down. The pain was excruciating, the worst he had ever felt. On and off for over an hour they came and went.

Ryan could do little except wait.

Getting up would find him thrown to the ground during an episode. Trying to clear his mind and relax was all he could do to wait it out.

The virus had infected everyone. The effects simply degrees of susceptibility and reactions to it. It had morphed as well, the third incarnation as it evolved becoming the most concerning to medical professionals. There were medications that staved off many of the reactions, though the side effects could be worse than the disease.

Crazies had promoted the charlatan cures, and the desperate flocked to acquire the medications, or in many cases, the peripheral cousins like quinine that came in tonic water. At each supposed cure and procedure, they ingested remedies or rubbed some weird salve on the skin.

Many took vaccine after vaccine.

It became a cumulative effect on the human body. The mixed cocktails of ingredients counteracted one another, until they mutated the virus beyond any chance at real treatment.

Some died outright.

Most turned after "death" into crazies. Had their brains fried and became the evil left walking the Earth.

Ryan and what remained were the fortunate ones.

If you could call it that. They didn't buy into the bullshit the nut jobs tried to sell to the public. Ignored the ravings of the internet trolls who professed to know the golden solution to fix it or go and try every suggested home remedy some do-it-yourself doctor prescribed. They followed the science, the medical leaders who had stellar reputations unclouded by bribes or dollar signs from backroom investments in pharmaceutical companies.

The real heroes who put people ahead of greed and narcissism.

For Ryan and those that fell into the level-headed group, waiting for the vaccine that passed every test and research trial with supposed remarkable and positive results helped them to win the fight, albeit at a huge cost. What the research missed, and he had come to find out after the world was gone, was that the "cure" could be worse than the virus.

The side effects disabling in a future where having your faculties present all the time kept you alive.

Maybe it was the shock to the system seeing the world go to hell that let it loose or a mutation of the virus spawned from an incubation period that the vaccine missed.

There was no way of knowing.

All he knew was that whatever the hell happened, the virus put a plague on the planet that had never been seen before and left those trying to survive up against odds that Las Vegas would pay by the armored truckful if you managed to beat them.

And Vegas hated losing.

He managed some sleep for a few isolated hours after his body finally found the calm. Left early, using the advantage of sunrise. The psychotic dead seemed to be more day trespassers and night terrorists with the early morning a time you could move about more freely.

A small window, but you take what you can get.

It took less time to reach the scene from last night and even in the growing light, the picture was a horror movie in the making for multiple sequels.

After surveying the aftermath from above Ryan circled around and took a different route to check it out, intersecting the street three blocks to the south and moving along slowly as he searched for some answers. He hoped to find at least where the Bolts had come from and a possible direction of the Brainers.

Two blocks up he found part of what he needed.

Two abandoned delivery trucks, flatbeds with liftgates and homemade armor siding for walls, sat across the street to the east. He had never seen them before. As he searched through the cabs looking for information, he came up empty. The only plus was getting some extra ammo and that he threw in his rucksack.

The flatbed cargo areas were disappointing too with nothing of value left behind. He took one last walk around to doublecheck, was satisfied, and left the trucks alone. Someone would inevitably be looking for the group that left and never came back. The dead bodies and bullet holes, which he knew was from a firefight and the Bolts, would lead whoever to probably think the Bolts came across the group, they tried to fight them off, and lost.

That was if the kid was not part of the original deal.

The shell casings from the rescuers away from the pile of dead Brainers might say something else if any amount of logical thought still existed in them. That all depended on how it all transpired in the first place.

He could only venture how they'd try a guess.

If the trucks were tampered with, there would be added suspicion. If the Brainers put two and two together, he'd have a hard time keeping his presence quiet. They would send search party looking to exact revenge. That scenario wasn't something he wanted invited to the party.

Leave it to nature and the elements.

Keeping on task, no trace of the Bolts origin along the way was evident. He didn't stray too far down the intersecting streets. From what he could tell, nothing seemed out of place, no disturbances of trash piles or foot traffic in the dirt from such a large mass of movement. Taking his leave, he moved on to the corpses, or what was left of them.

The stench of death permeated the crisp morning air leaving it heavy with smells that seemed to leech into your nose and never leave.

Even with his handkerchief covering his face, the aroma was horrid. Scavengers had been and gone during the night, likely rats and other mammals looking for protein to survive.

Probably some of the Un-Dead and Lurkers who were in search of sustenance too.

The last time he saw this much carnage up close was a bomb blast that spewed remains over a city block and left only bits and pieces.

Seeing eyes and faces staring back blankly was much harder to reconcile.

The real dead always provided something, supplies, information, and ammunition was always in short supply. Most scavengers would loot the bodies and take whatever they could. That also drew a lot of attention when people came looking for their lost friends and group members.

He didn't know the details of what brought the two warring parties together and adding to it was not an option.

Ryan inspected the remains carefully, looking for things that could easily be replaced and give him information and clues as to who this group was, maybe even where they came from. The city had been quiet and free of Brainers for a long time, and something drew them in. Was it the kid? The group the boy was part of?

He needed to know.

Ryan finished his search and not wanting to get caught if more Brainers came, headed off in the direction that he last saw the old Bronco. Before that though, he figured to do a clean-up job.

Eliminate any presence of spent ammo casings from the rescuer group.

The less for the Brainers to think, the better off for him in the long run if their presence was a short-lived incursion into his city. If he could make them think they were attacked by only the Bolts, it could afford him some time to figure out what the hell was going on.

Random casings were one thing for them to come across.

A pile of brass with the fresh smell of gun powder might draw unnecessary attention and a canvas of the city if their numbers were huge and desire for revenge absolute.

His anonymity and security were priority over anything else.

Working quickly, he went to work, chucking spent shells at the storm drains on either side of the street until enough disappeared to keep suspicions light and confuse more than anything if questions arose.

Sleight of hand to draw attention away.

The street the Bronco took ran from one side of town to the other, more like a thoroughfare. The group could have taken it anywhere as it intersected a large part of the city. Following it would take hours and eat up most of the day, leaving him far from Pete and what he called home. He had stashes around, safe places to hide and stocked with minimal food rations. MREs mostly that he had pilfered from abandoned posts.

Meals ready to eat was not the best name for them.

They were high caloric foods meant to keep a soldier filled with enough nutrients and fat stores to burn when in the field, stuck in battle, or screwed for food. If you had never eaten them as a civilian, you were lucky as the horrible taste was not something you'd forget.

They kept you alive at least.

For those battle hardened or unfortunate to have caught base duty without a good canteen that could try and hide the gross taste of mess food, you never got used to them. He had four safe places along the route between his current location and the edge of the city. Secured and hidden, he could wait out for a bit and catch some sleep without burning himself out reversing his tracks.

He moved methodically, hugging the sidewalk in case he needed to jump and hide inside one of the many recessed doorways along the street. Eyes purposefully scanning the entire path forward, looking and searching for information.

It was mostly a dead end.

He got little from the Brainers except some bits of intel that made no sense incomplete. It could spell out significantly if he could add to it. The Bolts veered off a few blocks down, taking the tunnel towards the arena. Dark and about a quarter mile long, he passed on following them.

He didn't have the gear with him, and his focus was on finding out more on the boy.

He could come back and travel above ground first across the rooftops, safer and with more visibility further out. If they were holed up inside, he'd prefer a better plan to engage and get out alive.

Plans kept you above ground.

He had to keep moving even if his journey was a lonely one. Three years with no intimate connections to talk to, friends to laugh with, strangers to smile at and wave back when they reciprocated, family to hold.

His mind filtered in and out old memories, good times, and even the bad.

The last fight with Julia over something stupid around leaving his boots next to the front door and not in the shoe cubby. Hide and seek with David and Emma in the house, running around like crazy soccer hooligans only to fall into a tickle game that nearly broke a lamp.

Good times there.

Seeing the world fall apart right in front of him, finally taking some control when those directing efforts failed to act, and saving others' lives only to see those close to him lost.

His failure ate at him every day.

As time passed it took less of a toll, crept at a snail's pace, yet would never totally leave him free of guilt.

Time could never erase the scars.

Three hours into his expedition with it being a bit after nine in the morning, Ryan took a break. He had a hideout on the second floor of an old apartment building that led to the roof and a terrace. It gave him a chance to rest and eat some energy bars along with some coffee to warm up while processing his observations. The group had not left the street yet from what he could tell.

Tire tracks and moved cars pointed to that conclusion.

He also found additional tracks, slightly offset, all going in the same direction. He had come across a grouping about an hour before that seemed to indicate a group of vehicles had traveled together and then separated. Likely done in search of the boy, they converged back and journeyed together towards their eventual destination. It seemed he was looking for not some isolated and small band of people, but a larger set.

He didn't know their numbers.

From the tracks could tell it was at least three larger vehicles, the old Bronco and two trucks, one dually and another full-size. The fact they had working transportation meant a collective decision to travel and venture from their location.

Every piece of information began to paint a picture.

The Brainers used transport to scavenge and find victims. The fact these two groups collided was troublesome. No indications that either had a need to come this far into the city and had not in over a year since the only incursions were the Un-Dead. Something drew them. Lack of supplies? Scouting parties in search of people?

The boy.

Ryan's thoughts kept coming back to the child. The skinny Brainer had mentioned something about information. Was he blindly interrogating, or fishing for specifics? Had the boy been acquired in some raid, or simply found haphazardly during a hunting party gnawed at him. The boy's group going to rescue him didn't offer any clues really to answer his internal question. All it meant was he had a value, or a connection that meant he was loved or under some protection.

None of which Ryan knew.

Key to deciphering the broken shards of his thoughts was what that connection was and the need to find out. There were many more questions he had to understand in order to gauge the relationship of being a friend or mortal enemy.

Any unknown was a foe until proven beyond a doubt.

Ryan knew a friend was a superficial category until the other party decided your bond was breakable.

Once broken, their evil intentions poured forth without a hint of sorrow.

Human interactions had changed. What once were cordial or at least superficiary smiles and handshakes had devolved into a kill or be killed mindset.

Everyone was out for number one, and rightly so.

The oblivious might not know the quirks of a Brainer. Meet one and think you've found another survivor and suddenly wind up on a table being filleted alive for the fun of it.

Survivors believing they had met like-minded people only to end up at odds when food supplies ran out and you had a starving family to feed.

Anyone who had some humanity left, regardless of their current situation, also couldn't fend off a stampeding horde that had you in their sights for food. Banded together gave you a shot. Though it would only be a matter of time before you'd be forced at some point to run for your life, decide to trip the person trailing behind, hoping to give yourself an advantage to keep death at bay.

It was an inevitable conclusion.

Social norms evaporated the moment the world and society got consumed by death and destruction. You did what you had to do to live. Ryan wasn't any different. Maybe had a tiny fraction of his humanity still intact. If only for a few more hours and days.

The future wasn't written in stone.

In reality, the rest of today and tomorrow wasn't guaranteed. The next minute, hour even. Fate was the only defining element that carried any weight in Ryan's mind. When your card was punched, that was it. Fight and run and hide all you want. Whatever was around the corner would get you in the end.

Pray to some god or deity?

Good luck with that one.

The only person to rely on was the one behind your eyeballs. Even that was suspect sometimes with piss poor decisions and taking risks.

If you wanted to live you better be vigilant and keep an eye out for trouble. Wait and observe. Test the waters and see with your own eyes what came your way. And always have a foot ready to bolt out the door at the first sign of danger.

Fight if you had to, but there was nothing wrong with turning tail and running far in the other direction. Not in his blood to do it, but for the regular guy or gal, better to live than wind up dead meat. There was still a light at the end of the tunnel.

Ryan hoped life might find a ray of sunshine once more.

For the next hour, perched atop the roof and hidden from view, Ryan walked through what he knew, didn't know, and questioned. The city had been deserted except him for well over a year, the last real human beside himself caught up in a bad situation that left only Ryan. That encounter brought death back.

I see the shit storm coming. This might be the precursor to something big. Could be nothing and just the wind blowing by.

He hoped this time it passed on through.

CHAPTER EIGHT

Ryan had come across Mitchell a week before the two-year anniversary of losing the world, the lost man scavenging for food.

It was obvious he was barely surviving and a mystery how he managed to still be alive at all. Mitchell was loud, clumsy, and oblivious to his surroundings. It might have been remnants of shock, he had not adjusted still, or a simple lack of caring whether he lived or died.

Whatever the answer, Ryan never found out.

He watched Mitchell for two days to see if he was with others. The Brainers played that game, send a scout to play loner, try and draw survivors out. They could only play the part for so long before their dark side boiled over. The rages, the self-mutilating, the voices that answered back.

Mitchell showed no signs.

Ryan cautiously engaged, leaving a walkie talkie near Mitchell's hideout, and catching his attention with conversation before agreeing to a meet. Mitchell had a lot of information to share that filled in bits and pieces of Ryan's gaps.

The man had been a researcher at a private facility, one of the public-private partnerships that got diverted government dollars. Forced on the public by special interest and government officials, it was a company with no credentials to speak of, no marketed drugs, and little data past a few trials with lackluster results.

They were handed hundreds of millions of taxpayer money and given free reign and support.

Mitchell led virus protocols and potential serums. He was a lower-level guy though someone with enough clearance to have access and see the larger picture. As data came in and got crunched, evaluated and scrutinized, a picture developed that couldn't go public no matter the cost.

Many pushed for the removal of quarantine orders, a go back to normal fallacy. The death rate still climbed with countless weeks of stay-at-home orders, deniers protested and broke protocols, claiming their Constitutional rights for freedom and other bullshit arguments of the individual being more important than the many.

The White House let the orders expire and with no federal support and growing protests, loyal governors and states loosened their reigns and people began to congregate and spread the second wave of the virus, now mutated and stronger with resilience to the vaccines in the works.

Asymptomatic people began to infect others, and the virus spread again. Mitchell's research showed what had been shouted by the real researchers and doctors all along, that quarantine had needed to remain and ride out the wave until validated vaccines were developed and trialed.

It all got buried to prevent the Administration from being blamed and the paper trail leading back.

Mitchell's research findings delved deeper into an abyss that painted an even darker picture and what he told Ryan left even more questions. It probably wasn't a radio conversation to have over the open airwaves if ears listened.

It did assist Ryan in evaluating the man as a friend or foe.

His words were that of a lucid man who had not lost his mind, and as his story unraveled for Ryan to digest, pointed more and more to someone who knew a whole lot and gave credence to the validity of it.

"You talk about these Un-Dead types, shadow dwellers, and these super athletes. If it were the movies, we would call them zombies just because of appearance. Except, they aren't. They are still living, breathing, and very much alive, though not as we know it." Mitchell's words were direct. He sounded like he was fascinated by them, though from what Ryan could gather, was more from a clinical perspective than anything.

Ryan knew that part.

The first level Un-Dead were scavengers, rooting through garbage and abandoned gardens in search of sustenance, not eating people. The Lurkers and Bolts were the odd players in the equation. He didn't quite grasp how they turned to cannibalizing people and not the others.

Mitchell continued. "From what I can gather from the data that I analyzed, the flesh-eating ones, or the ones that prefer some type of meat, the virus caused them to be iron deficient. Like on a maddening and insatiable scale. The desire to eat drives all function. And the best way to alleviate the problem is to eat things high in iron. Like livers. Drink some blood and you quench it until the next urge hits. They are better classified as cannibals, though cannibals if we associate them with native tribes who practiced the ritual, they at least have human left in them. These lot, do not. They're sadistic, ravaging, a real bloodlust with no sense of reason. Crazy beyond insane."

Ryan let Mitchell's words sink in. It made sense to him. He didn't see any of the crazed lunatics until after the fall. "I never saw anyone like it until after the world was gone. The Brainers yes. The people consuming weirdos were months later. Did you know of any of that happening?"

The radio was silent for some time and finally Mitchell spoke. "I only know of anecdotal stories. People being admitted to hospitals that *changed*. When that happened, they were whisked away. My guess to dissect and see what made them tick. The scale of it afterwards, my educated opinion, is evolution of the virus. We know that those that popped or drank every conceivable concoction when they got one of the vaccines, they were affected in different ways. The proliferation of mixed drugs and chemicals interacted with the virus, and we got what we got. A world full of killers hunting and killing survivors."

There was so much to digest and think about. Questions that required answers. The virus stopped the world and created a divide between life and death, with real people on either side of the fence. An impenetrable border wall that if you were caught on the wrong side meant you were lost. The pathetic vaccines didn't work the way they were supposed to and created monsters in their wake.

Still, there was the *what if?*

Could a real antidote fix the mess they were in? He thought about it and with time he was sure he'd know the answer to it.

Ryan played it all out in his head and again the last time he was with Mitchell. The city had been quiet and the scavenger the only person to breach the quiet in a long time. His lack of survival skills and gross inattentiveness must have caught a group of Brainers somewhere in his travels.

Gathering food supplies, split up inside a supermarket after agreeing to meet in person, they came.

Ryan was towards the back, sifting through abandoned shopping carts filled with canned goods. Mitchell had been up front taking first aid supplies. Smashing glass and gunfire erupted out of nowhere. As Ryan took cover behind the meat case, he could hear Mitchell scream out.

It took less than thirty seconds and they were gone.

The Brainers must have tracked Mitchell. Ryan had already been inside for days, holed up in the old security office above the backroom. Mitchell, in their conversations over the radio, had filled Ryan in on more details from his research and the trials that created the Brainers.

Brutal psychopaths, he shuddered.

Void of emotion that contained a deference to humanity. Normal people turned to abhorrent violence that otherwise would not be a part of who they were or ever could be in life. Brain scans showed significant damage to key areas of the brain that the virus simply killed off or eliminated the neurons and pathways between matter.

No vaccine or antidote would ever change them.

Ryan waited until he was sure he was safe and went to find Mitchell, sure of the outcome. He found him, or what was left. Reaching down, he didn't hear the footsteps behind him.

The blow glanced off the right side of his head and sent him rolling to his left.

As he went down, the knife blade came out and struck. Laying in a pool of blood, his head aching, Ryan pushed the body off. It caught the Brainer right under the chin and up through the roof of the mouth.

He was still alive, though death speeding around the track to the finish.

Even as death approached, the eyes glared back at Ryan, filled with rage and hate. All he could do was stare as the life slipped out and thank his luck, he was the one who still breathed.

He thought of Mitchell, the dead Brainer, everything he knew and all he had been dropped into over the last day. His life turned upside down. Brainers had not been around since his near-death experience and were back in full force it seemed. At least, by the number of bodies left scattered and the probable reinforcements who would come if Mitchell's information were correct.

Pack animals was the description Mitchell used.

Once they taste blood, they don't stop until satiated. Ryan had them to worry about and another group now at war with the Brainers. He had no idea who they were or any information to dissect their psyche. Good, bad, or worse?

No idea.

Throw in the Bolts and the others and the Wild West of a shit show was sure to come.

After an hour of rest, Ryan packed his things back in his ruck. Taking a last peek out over the city with his binoculars, he panned the city blocks in search of movement or life.

It was still early in the day and well before noon.

Late morning afforded him some protection from the Un-Dead and the Bolts he tracked. Maybe another hour before everyone came out and plenty of time before the Bolts made rounds to finish what they started.

The Lurkers were another story.

They were a constant threat, though their habits a bit on the predictable side. Dark hideouts, recessed alleyways, areas shrouded by trees and lots of shade, the deep interiors of buildings, open doorways, anyplace that could be utilized as a jumping out point or trap to entice an unsuspecting victim in or attack from behind. There were plenty of Lurker dens around he had identified and a few that were suspect.

He always avoided the hots spots.

Looking up at the clouds he saw it in the distance, faint and perceptible.

The unmistakable shroud of white smoke. It could have been anything really, a fire from some spontaneous combustion, a faulty electrical system with residual juice or wire from some self-sustained power source since the grid was kaput, even an ongoing burn from some pile of garbage that was smoldering and kept alive by the wind.

Ryan knew otherwise.

Short puffs, inconsistent, with enough regular bursts to say it was manmade, a machine being run, or a fire actively stoked. Whatever it was, it meant life and people. Good or bad, he wouldn't know until he investigated. Deciding to take a chance, off he went, with the destination mapped out in his head.

The smoke was on the far side of town in one of the many state parks, tucked inside an old trading post fort. He knew it well, having taken the tours with the kids and as a kid himself.

It offered a refuge, high walls, lookout points, security from exposure and breaching of the walls.

He had not been this way in a long time, there had been nothing living this far out and with mostly residential apartment complexes, supplies he needed he could get elsewhere.

The streets were wide and tree-lined, a grid created long ago from a central point radiating out. Old buildings, Victorian era homes and apartment conversions, businesses, and restaurants, all led the way. The walk offered shade, cover, and too much visibility to be out in the open. Ryan kept off the street and worked his way through bushes and vegetation, snaking along flowerbeds and over fences to keep out of sight.

He wanted to get close.

Not too close to be seen or caught up in a trap. He knew of an old apartment complex a few blocks before his destination with an exterior fire escape he had used before. He shimmied up the drain, jumped over to the ladder, and pulled up a few rungs until he could walk the stairs. Taking care to be vigilant and quiet, he kept a watchful eye for movement or noise as he worked his way to the top and over the retaining wall.

Tired, Ryan had to catch his breath from the hustle to get to safety.

Being exposed made him uneasy and even though the hike to the top was maybe a minute or two, it left him in the open.

He paused and listened.

Focused in on any unusual sounds that meant he had been seen and his safety was about to get compromised. The normal person bent on attacking would immediately try to go after their prey to ensure there was no escape.

The shrewd surveyor would wait and bide their time, watching and looking for the right time to pursue and corner. If a minute passed and nothing sparked his ears, best bet was he either was good to go and must keep his exit different than the entry point to throw off anyone watching and waiting to strike or had slipped any observers and could go about his business in secret.

He took up a defensive position behind an old trellis, the old grape vines long dead and offering some concealment. The rooftop had been an oasis in the city, a place the apartment's residents came to socialize, relax, have cocktails and drinks, all to be part of the vibrant downtown lifestyle.

The set up was original and quite cool he thought.

A tiki bar with stools and a large neon sign as a backdrop. Reclining beach loungers lined up with small round tables separating them. Planters and large colorful pots with small trees to provide shade adorned the area.

Fed only by the rains, their lushness was long gone.

Ryan could imagine the fun parties here, beer or wine in hand, the resident bartender cooking up drinks and laying down shots. Given the age of the building and décor, millennials, Generation X, and Baby Boomers all together as a community having fun and living the life.

All gone, though the neatly left arrangement could host a party in an instant as if time never moved on.

Taking his binoculars out, Ryan panned his surroundings. He looked for broken windows, garbage on a balcony, any sign of inhabitants living in an abandoned building. Nothing as far as he could tell, so he focused in on the old fort.

Shock was an understatement.

Life teemed inside. He had expected a few people, a small band of survivors taking up residence. Instead, he saw a community, young, old, men, women, children playing on a makeshift jungle gym, others kicking a soccer ball in a pickup game.

Scanning the internal grounds, he found the old Bronco parked with other vehicles of varying makes and models. An old yellow school bus, the faded letters of the school district undiscernible, was parked across the old wooden gate, an obvious attempt to prevent ramming it open.

People moved freely about, going into the old structures, coming out, talking and laughing, a scene of what was it, *easiness*, he thought, and not of people afraid or terrified of attack.

As Ryan surveyed the scene, the lookouts positioned in the corner towers, perimeter guards inside and out, he got a sense of what lay inside. Organized, structured, not a group of crazies living within the high white walls. If they were Brainers, it would be evident from the way things were run.

No children playing and people laughing, and not a single smile peering back at him.

Instead, he saw survivors, *people like him*, that had banded together to keep on living and try to make it with what was left.

He sat back, knees pulled up, head titled forward, eyes closed. It had been a long time since he had seen this, people and kids, a group this large as a community. Pre-fall of the world in fact.

It hit him hard.

Ryan breathed deep, letting the emotions subside and the calm of focus to come back. *Just because it looks like it, doesn't mean it is,* he reminded himself. Society was not defined the same anymore. People did not follow old social norms. What looked too good sometimes was a fallacy ready to bite you in the ass.

He had fallen into that trap once before, days after losing Julia and the kids. Alone and nowhere to go, nursing bruised ribs from the high fall into the water, he stumbled upon a group of survivors inland up in the hills. He watched a few days, saw nothing unusual, and took a chance. It was a mistake that cost him. The group was spread across a few houses in a gated community, and it seemed quiet and peaceful.

They came and went, walked the grounds, and gathered in groups.

The lack of children and elderly should have tipped him off. Given the virus and the way it affected people across the board, at the time he didn't think about it.

He approached, straight down the middle of the street, arms visible, hoping to be seen. As he got closer it hit. The stench of death profound. Not something so outside of normal given all the bodies rotting in the streets. What should have grabbed him, pushed the pain receptors away to embolden his senses, were the skulls, lined up along the gate. He had not seen them before as they were hidden from view.

As he grew close, there was no way to miss.

He heard a rifle bolt handle being racked and slammed into place, the metal sound jarred him back to reality. The whizz of a bullet piercing his shoulder cemented it. As he ran away, the pain real, adrenaline taking over, he heard the voices, the guttural sounds of what he could only think were the damned. Human words with strikingly different tones, deep from within and showing no emotion.

What he would come to call the Brainers.

As he slipped over a mound and behind a row of bushes they filtered out, running and firing everywhere. He managed to move fast, bent low along the cinder block wall, hidden from view, his pursuers gaining ground. Approaching the corner of the wall a figure jumped out and swung a bat riddled with nails in his direction.

Ryan went low.

In one rhythmic motion, he pulled his knife from its sheath and slashed horizontally across the stomach, the insides of his aggressor immediately falling out.

He kept running, a mile, two, what ended up being five before stopping for breath.

He found a Walgreen's with the sliding door open, went in and pulled it closed, making sure to click the auto open button off. He rolled some shopping carts across the front as extra measure and worked his way to the rear of the store to the pharmacy.

The pain receptors that had responded for the bruised ribs changed to focus on the hole in his shoulder. Grabbing a chair from the wall and facing the front of the building, he inspected the damage to his body. Lifting his red stained shirt, he found the bullet went through. By the size of the hole a .308 or 7.62mm round from a hunting rifle or former Soviet Bloc surplus that the hunting stores sold cheap.

It missed everything vital at least. Closing it would be difficult.

Finding what he needed, he cleaned and sanitized his wound, stitched up the front and the back as best as he could using a makeup mirror he grabbed from Cosmetics and duct taped to a shelf, and snatched up everything he would need to keep it from creating an infection.

It was the first of many "educational" situations he would encounter over time about the ways of the new world.

CHAPTER NINE

New developments always threw wrenches into even well-constructed plans.

Ryan was on a scouting mission, simply out in search of some intel. He never anticipated coming across a group of people holed up in an old fort in the middle of the city.

He figured he'd find some outliers.

A small band of road travelers that got ambushed and after securing the rescue of the kid, would be long gone to the next town, in search of others or more suitable places to plant roots and make a life.

Ryan never thought he would come across this bunch, men, women, kids, and a picture that sent some shock to his core, people with a variety of disabilities entrenched in this little community.

It drew a warm smile across his face.

He witnessed firsthand what happened to the disabled when the world died as many were left stranded and helpless, and seeing that life was still precious and valuable made Ryan feel society might have a chance to rebuild and unite again.

Someday.

Deciding he'd lay low, he kept a vigilant watch. He spent the better part of the day mapping the fort's complex. He vaguely remembered the interior from when he was a kid visiting his grandparents and they took the train into the city. High up above it gave him added insight to the structures and placement of guards protecting the inhabitants. The added caveat to staying awake up on the rooftop was seeing what transpired over the night.

He had not seen any of the Un-Dead wandering about in any remarkable numbers. No Lurkers he could find in the shadows, and no Bolts making a break to attempt to climb the walls. He also had not seen any trace of Brainers as he took up periodic posts from the four corners of the roof. He knew they had to be looking for their lost comrades, and if they were aware of this place, would be looking for revenge. He found a place to set up his things for the night and simply watched as time drifted and his thoughts centered around what the next hour, day, and week would reveal if shit hit the fan.

The fort dwellers lived as if life simply went on like nothing had every happened.

At least, inside that's how it looked.

People walked and laughed, children played, and he could even catch a bit of music in the air from a group playing instruments around a fire. The nightlife reminded him of camping trips with old friends, everyone sitting around the fire, sharing stories, laughing, and relishing in the good times being together. It even drew a simple nod, reminiscing about his last deployment many years ago. The whole team sitting around a fire, beer flowing, and the camaraderie of people trusted with your life. As many times as your ass got saved in a firefight, you believed in the next man.

The unbroken chain.

Reliance and faith only went so far before disappointment and your life flashed before your eyes when someone you knew tried to kill you. Face that and it threw everything you believed in right out the window.

As night darkened and the camp wandered off to their sleeping quarters, Ryan made a mental list of his observations. The group encamped in the old fort appeared to be survivors from different places and families. The vehicles had different license plates from around the neighboring states and as far as he could tell, not airport rentals as they lacked the windshield decal and bar code usually associated with a fleet rental. The way the people broke up into separate groups suggested relationships of family or friends, especially for meals and when it was lights out for bed. The jovial interactions and children present conveyed a lot.

This was no Brainer band.

If it was, it was an evolution into something else and that didn't fit with all of the research material he had read post-apocalypse and what Mitchell had told him before he died.

These were people that might be just like him.

He had not seen the kid again or even the rescue group. He figured the boy was resting and his injuries mending while the rescue party got debriefed. Guards had not been increased and activity seemed normal with no obvious measures being implemented. He wasn't sure what all of that meant, the lack of heightened security or visible preparations.

Was it a lack of understanding of the current state of the world, not having any previous Brainer encounters, false sense of security and power?

He had seen what Brainers could do and knew the persistence of their drive. You needed Fort Knox level protection to keep them at bay and that only kept them out. Unless you got help from the outside or had a lot of stored food to last them out and the arsenal of a small army, the Brainers would wait. Once your resources depleted, it was soon a slow death from within until deciding to surrender.

Or, it was finally over.

Huddled under his blanket for camouflage and some necessary warmth, an eerie quiet shrouded the night, like an ocean fog that rolled in and you couldn't see your hand in front of you as your mind drifted to pirates making shore to pillage the locales.

The uneasiness of absolutely *nothing* happening didn't feel right to Ryan.

It was too calm, too ordinary, too normal for what he had seen the day before. A child beaten, a guns-blazing rescue. Something either precipitated the event or it was a random grab. Either way the incident should have people on edge and an increase in guards. Something to put the arm hairs on end.

Life just went on.

He thought that maybe whoever led this band of refugees didn't want to alarm them and made every attempt to keep it all quiet to ensure the peace. It was possible there was another motive Ryan was obviously not privy to, but it was for lack of a better description, *weird.*

Maybe Ryan had too high of expectations.

It was possible his bias played a part. Or his history and experience living alone all these years tainted his thoughts. It all crossed his mind. What kept coming back to the front was a simple frame of self-preservation and due diligence.

Throw in plain common sense.

A boy had been brutalized by some group of people and whether there was a pre-existing relationship there or a matter of random occurrence, taking precautions against retribution seemed like the logical approach and answer.

He saw none of that going on.

It was possible the group felt they were being watched, had contingencies in place that he couldn't see, or any number of things that meant they took a threat seriously and were prepared to act. It was also possible they simply had no clue or idea of what the Brainers were capable of.

He shook his head at the next thought and questions formed.

Were they overconfident after the rescue? Did they believe they had the firepower and personnel to fight off an attack?

If they had a history with Brainers, they should know better.

If not, the likelihood of believing in themselves, if any had experience with weapons and real combat, might outweigh the pragmatic approach of preparing for war with an enemy that fought to the death. As he sat and watched through his binoculars, listened for any sounds that betrayed them, Ryan knew the Brainers would come.

It was a matter of when.

Time passed as he kept vigil over the encampment. Being two short blocks away, not those long city blocks but the smaller side street type, allowed for Ryan to keep an eye on his target and be far enough away to catch incoming sounds or movements and give him time to react.

Not like he could really do much except protect himself.

It left him a buffer to act one way or another with enough time to decide. He thought of one thing he could do if he caught wind of the Brainers to let the fort dwellers know to buckle up and get ready for a fight.

Not the best solution, though something he could do.

A well-placed round should spark a security alert while giving him a review of their protection protocols. He kept that thought shelved as a just in case and continued observing while chewing on an old energy bar.

Then, the tremor jolted Ryan awake.

He must have dozed off, the boredom and cold night sending him to dreamland. Pain seared his calves as it turned to spasms and progressed up his body. His left leg jerked out uncontrollably and a minute later subsided. The stomach muscles tensed, his abs on fire. His right arm, which had been at his side, bent up, smacking him in the face. As his head lifted and arched backward, he caught it.

A whisper, faint in the distance.

Competing noise was non-existent. The quietest of sounds traveled in the air. A boot scuff on the sidewalk behind him and down below. There was nothing he could do until his body relinquished control.

The spasms stopped and the adrenaline that had been building up in anticipation of reacting kicked into gear. Ryan shot up, grabbed his rifle and night vision goggles, crept over to the retaining wall.

He listened first, trying to pinpoint more sounds as he put his goggles on.

Heard the shuffle of feet, many of them, as they moved past. Checking his watch, it glowed back 3:00 a.m., and he peered over the edge, careful to remain concealed.

Catch them all asleep and in bed, he nodded to himself.

It was what he would have done, though not for a few days to let things quiet down and complacency set back in.

He lost count after fifty.

Dressed in fatigues and moving systematically, the group worked its way down either side of the street. Hugging the building walls and crouched low, rifles hugged close and progressing forward in unison, the head of each line abruptly stopped near the end of the street and held up a closed fist. Everyone behind immediately paused and took a knee.

The hair on Ryan's arms stood up.

This wasn't an avenging band of Brainers. They were haphazard of movement, worked not in unison, individual over the group, and not capable of this type of coordinated organization. This was military or mercenary, he couldn't say which.

From the looks of it, they were well-trained and focused.

He looked closely, trying to gain more insight. As details emerged, a bad feeling began to grow in the pit of his stomach. A military or mercenary action meant a target of value.

The world was gone and the bottom of the barrel dregs of it left.

Organized security or offensive forces had been decimated and left leaderless when the fall began. Nothing had been seen or heard of since. A group like this meant they were after something and meant to take it by force.

What that was he could only guess.

Ryan scanned the troops, their weapons, any visible insignias, any information he could grasp. Standard tactical gear and setup for a night mission. No markings of any kind and the branch was undistinguishable.

As far as he could tell, they could be anyone from anywhere.

The only thing that stood out, a minor detail that passed him once and caught his eye on the second pass, was one man who seemed out of place. He was armed with only a pistol. Inconspicuously tucked near the rear of one column.

Ryan had missed him in a dark shadow.

When the man bobbed into the light from a reflection of the moon, he stood out. Military training for sure, firepower for this mission not his priority. Command maybe or some VIP tagging along.

As the group waited for the leader to make a call, Ryan couldn't help feel something bad was going to happen.

The columns moved ahead, slow, and methodical. They were two blocks out with a long city block to navigate. They had plenty of cover until they reached the end of it. Taking a right, it was a block down until they reached a cross street and the fort lay opposite to the right. Ryan knew the tree-lined street offered shadows as it blocked out moonlight from above and the buildings hid them from sight. They'd have a street to cross and be exposed until reaching the other side with the only concealment rows of bushes that circled the fort grounds if they could make it.

As he watched them disappear around the corner and towards their destination, Ryan could only think of the bloodbath that was about to go down.

The fort housed women and children, people who were inside trying to move on.

He sensed they were not soldiers, more a ragtag bunch hoping to make it by their weapons assortment, though his intel was still rather sketchy to really make a decisive judgement. A military type of action was not something they probably planned for and certainly ill-equipped to fight. A sneak attack would certainly add to a chaotic response and send everyone into a panic. If they had a chance to put on a defensive, they might stand a chance at surviving the encounter.

He had no idea what or why this was happening.

It didn't feel right, and he knew it.

He could sit it out and see, although a slaughter wasn't something he could live with either.

He did the only thing he could do.

The well-placed shot hit its mark. To the right of the tower where the attack would come was an old bell, probably used to warn the former inhabitants.

The loud ping caught the guard's attention and an immediate reaction from inside.

As Ryan swung the rifle's night scope to the left, he could see it registered on the face of the head soldier who hesitated and stopped mid-step in the street, the column abruptly stalled in place. By the perplexed expression, the soldier wasn't sure if he should keep moving ahead or retreat.

Knowing where to look, Ryan ran across the roof to the other side and focused his scope down the alleyway between buildings and where he could see the last one in line. The face was turned to the right, scanning in his direction. Clear as day, he saw him, and within a few seconds, everything changed.

Mark Simpson.

Shaking his head Ryan refocused, ran the scenario fate was thrown. The trajectory of his shot, up high from the opposite side of the rooftop, meant pinpointing it near impossible as it echoed between the buildings and down through the quiet streets.

There was no way to trace it.

Sending the message meant safety and a chance for the people inside the old fort. Activity was instant as armed responders funneled out of the buildings to specific locations all around the interior.

A large caliber gun by the look of its long and thick barrel, appeared out a small window slit in the tower opposite the soldiers.

Deafening gunfire erupted all around, lighting the area with tracers and billowing smoke from expired gun powder. As he watched from his secure perch and the scene unfolded, he couldn't help wanting to act, to do something more. He knew if he started picking off the soldiers, he'd give up his location and find himself in a bind.

The odds were not in his favor.

From somewhere behind the fort, he heard squealing tires between gunshots and saw an old troop transport head straight down the same street where the troops were firing from at the fort. He could see sporadic bits of fire light up from on top of it and see the tracers go forward toward the soldiers.

At some point, he ducked for cover to keep from being seen and could only listen.

Boots trampled the sidewalk to his left and faded into the night as retreating soldiers left the battle. He could hear the vehicle firing from a stopped position, assumed no pursuit in progress.

As the last of the footsteps died away, he ventured a look to catch the tail end and see where they went. Given the light look of their packs, they didn't seem like they were prepared for a long fight or camped out close by. They dragged their fallen, hustling at a consistent pace during their retreat.

Headlights soon appeared three blocks down, illuminating the way to what must have been their transport back to their base of operations. Ryan watched through his scope, searching for anything that might provide insight.

Nothing panned out.

The troops piled the bodies and wounded into one vehicle and themselves into the others and left. The destination unknown. The whole episode from beginning of engagement to evacuation had only been fifteen minutes at most and swiftly ended.

It was surreal.

Ryan moved to the other side of the building. The old fort was buzzing with activity. Even in the dark he could see the frantic movement of people taking up arms and positions to guard for any incursions that might occur. Soon, there'd be daylight and a new day full of questions and what he hoped would be some needed answers.

If the cards dealt Aces.

People ran from building to building carrying supplies. Children were hustled to other locations from where they slept. Armed men moved what looked like ammunition cans to the four corner towers. Fires were lit too. It seemed an armed battle was not going to stop preparations for breakfast.

He sat for a long time, his thoughts a blanket of confusion. Armed soldiers attacking a survivor settlement. Brainers attacking a young boy and a heated rescue. A successful defense of the old fort.

What the hell is going on? This can't all be coincidence. This group must have something or someone of serious value to get attention like this. The who or what is the question and I need some answers.

As the sun rose and the morning movements played out in front of him, Ryan's plan, or death sentence if it was to happen, developed. There was no way he could live with himself and walk away from this, forget it and move on. In some way, it affected him, though he had no clue how or why. He had to find out and understand.

There was no way he felt he could avoid it.

It would only be a matter of time before his luck ran out and Brainers or the group that attacked last night came across him. Not for lack of hiding or preparation.

He could avoid death for days, months, maybe even years.

At some point though, he knew the inevitable conclusion. As the desperate and psychotic ravaged what was left of the world, a lone survivor was an enigma, a defect in the system. Community offered protection, socialization, a foundation with which to rebuild society.

He was an outlier to it all because of circumstance.

He didn't stand a chance against an army of killers. He could fight them off for a bit and had the skill to really make a go of it, reduce their numbers and pick them off one by one.

Eventually he'd run out of ammo.

As part of a larger consortium, he might live longer and make it to old age. Choices today and in the bigger scheme of it all, were making the right ones that actually had meaning and a purpose.

What the hell, Ryan thought, the quiet laugh coming unexpectedly. *Might as well throw my hat all the way in the game.* He pursed his lips, knowing what he was about to do was insane.

Packing his ruck, he scooped up his rifle and left the way he came.

CHAPTER TEN

Patience was usually a virtue.

Being ready and thinking things through, even if fast-tracked under the extraordinary circumstances dumped in his lap, Ryan had some time to implement his plan and wasn't going to jump right into the fray. He wasn't that type, one to go for it without considering all the details and information.

Life and experience had taught him that.

Not to say that he wasn't a spur of the moment type guy, or someone who could not throw caution to the wind. He could be spontaneous.

Sometimes.

Julia might have told him otherwise if she were still alive. He could do things without a care, throw caution aside to dive in and see what happened. Those were different circumstances and not life or death decisions. Fun times didn't wind up killing you, at least, not usually if you weren't crazy.

Maybe your pride if you failed to do it.

He learned the value of observation, taking information in and dissecting it, constructing a well-laid out plan with contingencies. Back-ups to the back-ups. In this moment, he didn't have the luxury of a whole lot of time to sit and formulate it all out. The troops would be coming back, stronger and with heavier weapons.

He knew that firsthand. Every pissed off enemy reacted the same.

Kuwait seemed like a lifetime ago. He tried to not think. It was hard not to as he thought about what was coming. As he walked the street looking at the boot prints left behind, his right hand ached as the memories flooded back. Two tours there, more over the years in Iraq and Afghanistan.

He knew the mindset, the drive to finish the job.

You can take the soldier from the battlefield, but the soldier is always ready to complete the mission. It was especially true if your work had purpose and your targets high priority.

Been there, done that, he thought to himself as old flashes of his past went by like a slideshow.

Fresh out of sniper school and attached to a scout recon unit, Ryan found his place. The elite of the elite they were, not your fly in mission boys who only operated when the odds were in their favor and taking a single target. He was part of the best of the half-a-percenters.

The last resort you called upon to get it done.

Entrenched, gritty, and living inside enemy lines for days and months, he and his brothers lived in the shadows, gathering intelligence, hitting targets, disrupting supply lines, saving lives. It was for a young man who wanted to make a difference in the world, the time and place to contribute himself to a cause.

When the Iraqi Republican Guard rolled into Kuwait and moved further into the small country and the atrocities piled up, Ryan and his men were HALOed in under cover of darkness. High altitude, low oxygen jumps were an adrenaline rush, but not over a populated city with enemy troops patrolling the streets.

One gust of wind in the wrong direction or failure to hit your landing target and anonymity as a shadow dried up.

The missions kept them busy, protecting life satisfying. Providing critical intel on troop movements as the Republican Guard sought to overrun Kuwait and bully the region, his unit's role was pivotal to the efforts of the international coalition in eradicating their presence.

For a soldier, you either relish the fight or endear to saving life. It's the double-edged sword of battle. You can't be both, not in the real sense. Taking life to save life, that is the dichotomy, the contradiction that sears the soul of the humanist over the realist.

For Ryan, a kill of a bad actor didn't faze him.

Not to say it didn't matter. He respected life. For those who enjoyed killing innocents or torturing them for sport, a well-placed fifty-caliber round to end them was justice. He didn't seek out haphazard death sentences for his enemy.

His were methodical.

The wrongly calculated engagement could reveal his presence if triangulated. He was deliberate with his kill shots or close proximity eradications with a blade, an acrobat of skill, as if a phantom performed the deed. That's how he got his nickname.

Ghost.

He could take a life up close and personal and no one watching through a scope or standing in the same room had any clue he was there.

When his service was up and it was time to move on, private global security provided a level of satisfaction where he could still fulfill a purpose, do some good for the world. With his background and former connections, it wasn't hard to find a job and land at a top-notch and respected global firm.

No one would pass on someone with his credentials.

A highly decorated special operations leader who singlehandedly wiped out an entire enemy intelligence unit after being captured was an asset and resource. A platoon of grunts was no match for a soldier with his background. He wrote his own check and CEOs simply asked how much.

A few years in it was obvious he needed to run his own show. While the work was exciting, the travel and clientele did not necessarily conform to his ethics. He formed his own company, pilfered the best of the best who matched his ideals and had integrity above all else, and created an organization that rivaled any small army. The money was great, the work satisfying, and when the world was on the verge of collapse, he stepped in to help.

In his current state, alone and without everything he loved the most, life was merely surviving without any purpose or meaning behind it.

Stepping back in the real world he spent an hour canvassing for intel and any details left behind. There was little to go on. Standard military issued boots by the imprints left by the soles on the dusty street. NATO 5.56 rounds by the discarded shell casings. Diesel heavy cargo troop transports from the tire tracks and fuel leaks.

Hauling away the dead and wounded. Fear of recognition or adhering to the special operations code of no man left behind.

It could be any branch of government.

Given he saw Mark at the back of the column, a plausible guess was some U.S. branch of service. He could probably dismiss the Air Force and Coast Guard. C.I.A. never did numbers this big. Navy Seals too, since for most of those operators it was small teams and each man had his favorite set of weapons. Being a drone decked out like the others not in the blood. Special detachment of Marines or Army moved the needle. Even ex-military contractors.

Green Berets, Rangers, Delta, special Marine detachment. One of them or an assortment from each. Best of what was left alive and had the psycho mindset. Contractors would only be in it for the money or some tangible asset. With money obsolete they seemed less part of the mix. The precision though painted a mural, spoke volumes of a unit that moved as one.

That meant training and order.

Mark would have called in favors. Utilized resources he could trust or at least followed the strict hierarchy of command. The field began to narrow.

And that realization played into Ryan's hands. A smaller field to choose from meant an understanding of who the players might be, even some of his old friends. He doubted it as his former team and associates were either retired or close to aging out. If Mark pulled together a team, there was a possibility of knowing some of them.

Ryan thought that part more fiction than reality.

The soldiers based on how they reacted likely were a unit even before the world crashed down. Had a history together and cohesion. If Ryan's memory was still any good, he ventured a guess they were the ones responsible for the last evacuation. He could use that if it were true.

He knew enough to draw some conclusions. Bits and pieces falling into place. Not enough to make a definitive decision and a desire to investigate on fire in his gut. It was time to find out more, get the dark questions answered if he could. Figuring what the hell, Ryan set off to the lions.

As a pawn on the chessboard, he prepared to walk straight into the den.

CHAPTER ELEVEN

The lone figure appeared out of nowhere in the middle of the street fifty yards in front of the main gate.

Rifle in both hands raised above his head, Ryan walked slowly towards the old fort. He could hear the commotion inside and voices yelling as the tower guards spotted him and barked directions below. As he slowly moved forward a bullet struck a few yards in front.

He knew what it meant.

Immediately he stopped and kept his eyes forward. When someone yelled from behind the wall, he set his rifle down, put his rucksack next to him, and flopped his tac vest off before carefully turning in a circle. Another order, so he lifted his shirt and twirled again.

Last command to drop his holster.

With one hand he clicked the connector around his thigh and the one at his waist, and it fell to the ground. Naked and exposed, he hoped they bit and didn't shoot him dead.

That would royally suck and defeat the purpose of his visit.

The sound of diesel engines roared to life and the gate crept open enough for four men to exit. Armed with rifles and protective gear that made them look like baseball catchers getting ready to play some ball, the group fanned out in a line and proceeded to walk toward Ryan. He could see the tower guards' rifles trained on him and not wanting to be accidentally shot by some trigger-happy civilian, stood perfectly still. Ten yards away the men stopped. He stared down the barrels of three rifles and waited for what seemed like forever before anyone spoke.

"Who the hell are you?" the unarmed man of the group asked.

He looked in his thirties, tall and muscular, tan and well groomed. He had one of those hipster handlebar mustaches that made him look ridiculous because his outfit of overalls and flannel shirt didn't match the vibe he was trying to portray. He frowned from behind some expensive sunglasses he must have pilfered from a mall and casually propped them on his head.

His gray eyes peered menacingly at Ryan when he failed to answer. "I'll ask you again. Who the hell are you and why are you here?"

Ryan stared back, emotionless. He nodded and smiled, the kind of fake smile that says you are about to be an asshole but have something of some significance to say. "Why is Mark Simpson and his band of merry men trying to kill all of you?"

The statement caught the man by surprise. His head titled to the left as he thought about a response, his lips pursed as one developed, and he nodded.

"Tie him up and grab his gear," the man directed.

A short stocky man about fifty, who had Ryan right in his sights, and a young man, eighteen at most, walked forward while the other armed man kept his rifle aimed at Ryan's head. Circling him, the older man zip-tied his hands together and the teenager grabbed the weapons and rucksack from the ground.

They all started to walk forward until the leader held up his hand. "Did you check his bag for explosives or bother to pat him down?"

Embarrassed looks stared back. The men proceeded to check out Ryan and his bag. Finding nothing that would blow up, they gave a thumbs up.

"Thanks," the muscular man smirked, his annoyance at their indiscretions evident in his voice as he flipped them both off and turned to walk back through the gate.

Ryan passed through the gate and was led straight toward the old office. People lined the way as if he were the first live person they had ever seen. Children wrapped in a protective arm of parents, cowered back as they gawked at him. Cold eyes of hatred burned his skin. Though no one knew him personally, they had recently been attacked and some stranger winds up on their doorstep. Any thought at a warm reception he knew was out of the question.

Not that it even crossed his mind.

Through the office they brought him to a closed door. The leader of the reception committee that greeted him outside, Jeff as he learned from overhearing his name at the gate, knocked twice and opened it. It wasn't a room or even an office as he had expected, but a closet with a staircase leading below ground. A dimly lit small incandescent bulb swayed back and forth at the top and others spaced apart that barely provided any light, led down into the darkness.

A jab in the back prompted Ryan to move.

He followed Jeff and descended the steps one at a time. He wasn't in a rush and needed to observe as much as possible before winding up wherever this led. Ten steps down to a small landing that made a sharp left and more steps. The passage had been carved out of the dirt, propped up with timbers and boards, and opened into a large room.

He thought old root cellar for food storage at first, but the craftsmanship was more recent construction for the expansion effort.

On the far wall hung a large map of the city and outlying areas. Two men, deep in a heated and hushed conversation from the gestures and occasional raised fist, paid him no attention as Jeff grabbed Ryan by the shouldered and pushed him into a chair.

"They will be back John," a man grimaced as he jabbed a finger into the chest of the other. His neatly trimmed salt and pepper beard and short haircut with the sides shaved high screamed ex-military.

The other man sighed and shifted his gaze from the map to Ryan. Older and clean cut, he looked like an authority figure and the man in charge. Gray hair cut super short, tall, yet his stomach a bit pudgy, the man held himself high and calmly, his demeanor curtailed.

"Without a doubt Roger. It's what we choose to do about it that matters."

Jeff walked over and whispered into John's ear. He couldn't hear it. The look on Jeff's face as he led the others out seemed to say Ryan's life expectancy was short.

Two large men entered the room and took up places behind Ryan. He peered over his shoulder, noticed the leather strap in the hands of one of them, and smiled. They stared at him, unflinching, their detachment at this being another job reflected in their eyes. He knew what was supposed to happen.

Allowing it *to* happen was an entirely different situation.

John walked around and leaned against the old wooden desk opposite Ryan. Roger stepped over a few feet from their bound captive. He began to speak and Ryan immediately cut him off. He was working his restraints with a small knife from his back, trying to keep the men off center by taking charge and interrupting to see how they would respond. He hoped it gave him enough time to free his hands, or at least one, to react.

"Who is Mark Simpson after here? That many men means something of value is behind these walls."

A fist punched Ryan in the stomach causing him to cough and bend forward. He sat back up and stared.

"I'll ask again. What do you have to do with Mark Simpson?"

This time, the fist caught his left temple and jolted his head to the right. He straightened up, shook his head, and stared over at the man named John.

"Is this how you treat all of your guests?"

Roger swung again, aimed right at the center of Ryan's face. As the fist came, with Roger's momentum drawing him forward, Ryan leaned left to dodge and his now freed left hand came up to strike Roger square in the jaw, knocking him out cold. His body went limp and momentum carrying him, fell to the ground.

Silence filled the room as the men behind Ryan, shocked at what suddenly transpired, reacted two seconds too late.

His freed right hand had grabbed hold of the metal chair as he came up and it glanced off Roger before he swung around and threw it. The chair caught one of the men in the head sending him sprawling backwards. The other, seeing it, dodged to his left.

Ryan was already in motion.

His left boot caught the man square in the chest and sent him into the wall. His head banged hard against the compacted dirt, and he slid down. The other man, knocked back by the flying chair, couldn't catch his feet. Using the advantage, Ryan sprang forward and planted a left cross. He fell to the ground unconscious. Turning around, Ryan raised his hands above his head.

The message was clear.

John motioned for Ryan to take a seat next to the desk. He nodded towards a small table.

"Drink?"

"I think that would be in order," Ryan agreed.

John poured two small glasses of Scotch, handing Ryan one and air toasting him. Noticing Ryan not taking a drink, John nodded and took a sip. "I'd be a bit hesitant too if I were you."

Ryan reciprocated the toast and sat down. He swirled the glass to check the legs for quality and was impressed. The Scotch hit the spot, its peaty smoke erupting his taste buds in flavors long forgotten. Not your cheap blend either from the smoothness as it went down. Higher end for sure, aged to perfection for twenty or more years by the taste.

"Thank you," Ryan replied appreciatively for the pour.

John saw the way Ryan took his time to taste, savoring the experience. "What's your favorite?"

Ryan looked up. It had been forever since he had talked anything not apocalypse related. "I'm partial to Bruichladdich. Has a special meaning for me."

The men sat for a few minutes enjoying the Scotch without words. Simply nodding in agreement after sips and relishing in an activity that was a luxury.

Finally, John spoke. His eyes were clear and focused, his words cut right to it. "Why are *you* here?"

Ryan sighed and took another drink before settling back in the chair. His choice of words was important, more for conveying a sense of trust with this man, and also to gather his own information to import into the foundation of *his* plan.

"I was out scavenging for supplies when I came across the boy being attacked." Ryan took another sip. "Mark Simpson must really want something you have. Why?"

John looked at Ryan, wondered how to answer. Plain faced with no emotion, he was direct. "So, you tracked us down and thought what?"

The unconscious men stirred, and Ryan knew as soon as they fully awoke there would be hell to pay. Getting to the point was necessary, though playing the coy game and tit for tat discussion suited him to keep drinking a bit longer.

The Scotch was that good.

Ryan leaned forward and stared right into John's eyes. "There hasn't been a sign of life in this city for over a year. All of a sudden, you and Brainers show up and get into a gun fight over some kid. That kind of action sparks some curiosity and a need to find out who the hell is causing trouble in what used to be a really quiet town."

John tapped his chin. "Quiet you say?"

Ryan swirled the glass and stared. "You weren't hard to find if you were trying to keep from being found. The smoke led me here. I scoped you out since I don't know who you are or what your deal is, and come to find out that someone I used to know, thought was dead, and had hoped stayed that way, is after you."

He let the words sink in for a minute. He took another sip, and his glass empty, motioned to John for a refill. John took the bottle of Scotch, obliged Ryan with a healthy two drams, and topped off his own.

Roger and the two large men came to and began to rise up from their slumber and still woozy, attempted to lunge in Ryan's direction.

John held up a hand and yelled, "Stop!"

Not sure what to do, they kept moving until he yelled again.

"Enough. We're just getting to why he is here." Looking back to Ryan, John waved his left hand for Ryan to continue.

Ryan took another taste of the Scotch, let it rest in his mouth, before it slid down his throat. He really needed to spend more time in search of hidden stashes like this. Satisfied he quenched his thirst, he began to speak.

"Mark Simpson kidnapped my family and threw me out of a helicopter. I watched it blow up. Three years later he shows up and I need to know why."

Ryan had been leaning forward, his gaze intent at John. At the mention of his family, he slouched back, the memories of his wife and kids haunting his thoughts.

The older man squinted, deep in thought. "How do you know Mark Simpson?"

Green eyes burned back with fire. "He *was* one of my dearest friends. Now, I'm his worst enemy."

"What's your name?" John asked, his brow furrowed, the look on his face searching for something inside his head and nothing adding up.

"Ryan Carmichael. Why?"

As Ryan's brief story emerged, something in the man opposite from him changed, his hard demeanor softened. John leaned all the way back in his chair, closed his eyes, and sighed. The story was good. Maybe too good to believe.

It wasn't the first time someone tried to lay a load of crap on and see what stuck.

John opened his eyes, no longer dark and brooding but soft and welcoming. His eyes shown back with what could only be described as familiarity with something Ryan had shared.

John raised his hand and gestured to the men behind Ryan.

"Bring him."

CHAPTER TWELVE

Ryan sat for the longest time, silence the only thing in the room.

John didn't speak to him, and Roger fully awake and aware, had moved over to the map on the wall and with eyes locked avoiding Ryan, tried to find something on it.

Still seated, the two men simply drank their Scotch, as if nothing else in the world mattered more than the liquid in their glasses. Ryan had no idea how long it was, fifteen, twenty, thirty minutes maybe, before the door opened behind him. He half expected a bullet to the back of the head and if this was it, finishing his drink instead of looking back seemed like the better way to die.

He heard shuffling behind him, a small cough, and from the sounds of it, a small child.

Great, he thought as he took another mouthful of Scotch, *the kid's going to kill me.*

John stood up and walked over to the front of the desk and leaned back to sit. He looked right at Ryan, no words, searching for the right ones before leaving it alone.

He simply pointed.

Figuring his time had come, and not wanting to eliminate a kid and have that on his conscious, Ryan turned his head to the left, half expecting it to be the last thing he ever did.

Their eyes crossed paths and locked.

Ryan felt it hit, and life immediately drained from his body. Blood pooled, the sweat formed, and consciousness was about to leave the party.

It was instant.

A small boy around eight, tall and thinner than he should be for his age, with curly brown hair that hung over his eyes, stood inside the doorway. Large expressive light brown eyes. The pain welled up from Ryan's gut as it contorted, not sure if the shock would make him vomit or not.

The tense feeling subsided, his muscles relaxed, and a peace washed over him. It had been three long years since he felt like that, at ease, with a sense of longing. He wasn't sure how long it would remain. He hoped the warm feelings never left.

"Dad?"

Tears welled in Ryan's eyes.

He was a battle-worn soldier, a tough exterior to those who didn't know him. He had seen death and destruction, dealt it and suffered from it as a victim. Nothing fazed his emotions when confronted with darkness. To those who knew the real man, he was a soft and compassionate husband and father who loved and lived for his family.

"David?"

The named cracked through dried lips. It came out as barely a whisper.

His son ran to him, and as he did Ryan turned in his chair. David launched into his father's arms, crying hysterically as Ryan wrapped him in strong arms, comforting his son and holding him close.

The father in him wept.

Three long years believing his son was dead and a new truth presented itself. He couldn't fight the grief, the joy that all bubbled together and rose to the surface. His world was upside down, and from all the pain since the last time he saw David, the soldier melted away to relish in the feel of his little boy.

"I guess that answers that one." John motioned for Roger and the men to leave. The need for security was gone.

David finally pulled his head from the chest of his father, tears streaking his reddened cheeks. As Ryan looked at him, taking in how much he had grown, he couldn't miss the red marks across his face. Swollen eyes and bruises stared back at him with a love he hadn't seen in forever.

Ryan looked at John for answers and from the reaction, could see that any response was an adult conversation. He had just been reunited with his presumed dead son, and not wanting to lose him again, was not willing to let go.

He shook his head.

"Ten minutes for some answers to your questions and then you can see the boy. I promise." John picked up a two-way radio from the desk, clicked the button and called for someone named Patty, who came through a hidden partition from beside one of the bookcases to his right.

Ryan stroked David's curly hair, his own tears drying up. "Hey, Son. John and I need to talk for a few minutes on some grown-up stuff. When I'm finished, you and your old man have a lot of catching up to do."

He placed David on the ground and gently patted his back, conscious of the injuries that had been inflicted by the Brainers.

"I'll see you in a bit, I promise. And," stroking David's cheek with a father's love, he smiled, "I love you Son."

David wiped his face on his sleeve, tears and snot streaking it as it passed his nose. Nodding his head, he leaned over to hug his dad and managed, "I love you too," and quickly disappeared through the opening as Patty shut it closed behind her.

Having seen the look on Ryan, John took the moment to start, to ease both men back into conversation. "I know you have a million questions and so do I. The most important ones we need to get out of the way."

Ryan nodded in agreement.

"You're wondering why your son is alive and why he is with us. The group you see here is made up of former soldiers like myself, refugees we've collected, and repatriated patients used for virus testing. Some we rescued outright from the experiments Mark Simpson has been carrying out. David was one of them. We had just rescued him from a patient transport when my group got caught moving the group to a secure location and I lost everyone."

It hung there in the air, thick as smoke.

He wasn't sure what to do or say. He knew of the human testing and what transpired before it turned barbaric. He wasn't sure he wanted to know, felt he had to in order to see where it fit into his plan.

Before he could speak, John asked, "What exactly is your relationship with Mark Simpson?"

Ryan bit his lip, trying to conceal the rage building within. As he tensed up, he could feel his body ache for vengeance, that old feeling locked away for so long that finally found the skeleton key to the door and was welcomed back.

Taking a breath and relaxing his mind, Ryan felt the calm return. "Mark was one of my oldest and dearest friends. Someone you'd take a bullet for and knew he'd do the same. We were special operators for one of those groups you don't know the name of or that even officially exists, a long time ago. The blackest of black ops. We took different paths after we left the service. Came back together when the virus hit."

Another sip before continuing. "My company provided security for all the VIP researchers and scientists working on a cure. His group led the most prominent and promising work. The last night before the fall, during the evacuations when D.C. finally fell, we were being medevac'd to a hospital ship off the coast, a research vessel. He pushed me out the door into the ocean and the last thing I saw when I came up for air was an explosion, the ship slipping below the water, and nothing left except debris."

John leaned and put a hand on Ryan's shoulder. The gesture made him flinch. Soon, realizing it was genuine, he relaxed.

John looked straight at Ryan. "The hospital ship was a cover. The explosion was meant to remove any traces of witnesses and those counter to

Mark's work. A carrier further out to sea was the real destination. My ship. We had no idea about Mark's plans and were caught off guard by what happened. When we realized it, it was too late. He infected my crew and turned them against those of us who looked to stop him. Some of us managed to escape after disabling the ship and the remaining aircraft."

John took a sip and went on. "Locked Mark and the others below deck and sealed off exits. We thought that would be the end of him and began getting people off as we could manage it. Got some out before things went bad and we had no choice but to leave. Your David and family were the ones we couldn't save in time. You can't really just blow up a nuclear aircraft carrier. We've been tracking and rescuing the rest over the last two and a half years."

The revelation didn't faze Ryan.

It bolstered his resolve.

Mark had kidnapped his family, seemed to experiment on his son, though John had not provided details, and was responsible for the deaths of innocent people. Given what Ryan had found out post-world and was hearing, the evil that started as a smudge inside his old friend had grown into a haunting specter replacing his soul.

As Ryan began to speak, John cut him off again. "David was fortunate we got him in time. We tracked a transport here, no idea where they were heading, and managed to hit it hard and free some people. Others, have not been so lucky. Your son is the key to ending all of this and Mark wants to stop it. His antibodies have something that reverses the virus and kills it. Doesn't let it stay half hidden away and keep screwing up your life like it does. He wants him back to prevent that from happening."

Ryan let it sink in for a minute, maybe more.

He had read the research, seen the promise of the trials. Nothing he came across had panned out. Hearing about his son and others, those that were killed to hide whatever was Mark's scheme, brewed up the rage inside that had long simmered and been dormant. Now it burst through the confines of his control. He knew the depths of Mark's madness and for what he did to his son, would pay with his life for it.

Shaking his head, trying to wrap his mind around it, Ryan looked at John. "My wife. My daughter…" he began, his voice trailing off, not wanting to hear more bad news. He had to know for his own sanity.

John grabbed Ryan's shoulder and squeezed it hard. "They're alive Ryan. He has them in some secured location from what we have heard from people. That's why we're here, trying to get them and others."

Tears washed down his cheeks. Julia, Emma, still alive after all this time? His family. His life. Three years grieving, missing them, trying to keep a grasp on their memories. Not a single picture, only small snippets of images in his vision when he closed his eyes. Now, he had one of them back with him. The mission was getting them all safe and secure and having Mark reap what he sowed.

He wiped his cheeks clean and looked up.

"How do you plan on getting them back?" Ryan asked.

John looked, reached behind to grab the nearly empty bottle, and poured the rest into their glasses.

"That's the complicated part. You mentioned something about, Brainers? I'm guessing you are referring to that absolutely nuts group of mercenary types and psychotics running around. Mark has some deal with them, hunting for survivors and coming after us. That's how David got caught up in it. We've been moving people to a more secure and hidden location and one of the buses got attacked. David was the only one to make it and those weirdos took him. This here is a staging area as we get everyone together and move them out."

"You mean there are more people?" Ryan felt he knew the answer. Hearing it would give some comfort knowing there were more survivors out there who could help rebuild the world and take it back.

John nodded. "Many more as we have found out. Most isolated and scared shitless, hiding and barely making it. When we can make contact and prove we're not one of his or the others, Brainers right? When we can prove we aren't the psychopaths wandering about we gather up who we can and move to facilities where we discuss rebuilding communities again."

"Got a plan?"

John's deep sigh spoke volumes. "We've been working on one. However, we can't seem to find the location where the labs and research are being conducted. We've sent out search parties and nothing."

Ryan smiled for the first time in years. "Well, I do. And you're probably not going to like it. It's the best one you'll get if you want to end this."

John, his jaw clenched, loosened it as Ryan spoke. If it could be done, he would listen and see how to move it forward and find the success they needed to stop the madness and move on.

"I'm listening."

Ryan shook his head no.

"First, I need time with my son. I have some catching up. The details I can fill you in on, and quick enough to get the wheels spinning. Let's just say that Mark doesn't know I'm alive yet, and right now, I'm his worst enemy. I know him and well enough to find his compound and destroy it."

The older man stood and motioned for Ryan to do the same.

"Understood. We are under a time crunch as you know he will regroup and try again. Your boy is a high value target, and you know Mark will stop at nothing to get him and kill anyone who gets in the way."

Ryan knew it was true.

His friend was gone, replaced by a monster bent on destruction and eliminating everything and everyone in his path. Mark would keep going until stopped, and Ryan was the only man who could do it. It was worlds away from covert operations, killing low-lifes and the dregs of the world. It was no different though, inserting a former friend into his sights.

Ryan had no issue killing Mark, in fact, he ached even more to deliver death to him.

And not the kind of compassionate end some might want to do for someone who had been a key part of their lives. Mark was going to die, the pain dealt excruciating, and as life crept out of the shell of his former friend, Ryan would take considerable joy watching the eyes glaze over and the evil fade away.

CHAPTER THIRTEEN

David was scared and afraid.

How could an eight-year-old not be who had been through the crap he had for the last three plus years? Even the most hardened adult would find a crack in their exterior if the world they had known suddenly opened up and a ghost from their past showed up and smiled like nothing had happened.

He hadn't seen his dad in over three years.

The last time, he watched from a distance as his father's friend pushed his dad out of a flying helicopter and he fell into the darkness below. Watched as they passed the ship he thought they were going to and it suddenly blew up, a huge orange fireball shooting as high as he could see. He thought maybe it was a bad dream like all the others.

He was asleep and the bad men were coming for him.

Too many nights like that. Being taken and strapped to a hospital bed, needles and pokes that hurt. Mean faces yelling and rough hands, leaving bruises on his body. Hours laying and wanting it all to end. Only to happen again over and over.

He lost count how many times.

David missed his mom and sister, wondered how they were and where they had been taken, and out of nowhere his dad was right in front, smiling like before. He shook and began to cry as emotions took control.

"It's OK, Son. Dad is here. You can let it out."

David sobbed uncontrollably and the tears poured from Ryan's eyes too. For his son he kept it together as much as he could. The boy gripped his dad tight around the neck and wouldn't let go.

He felt if he did, he would never see him again.

Ryan stroked the hair from David's eyes and rubbed his back gently, the things as a father he used to do long ago to comfort his little one. It tore through the tough man like a hot blade, feeling sick to his stomach what his son had been through, having been without a father to protect him. He felt failure at leaving the innocent boy vulnerable, for not being the rock to keep him safe and secure.

David began to calm down and the sobs less vocal. Soft and losing their frequency, his crying turned to sighs until finally he looked up.

"I missed you, Dad."

Ryan smiled from ear to ear, genuine and warm.

"I missed you so much Buddy. There hasn't been a day that I have not thought of you. You're still a stinky little man," Ryan winked, and the tension and sadness that was heavy around them evaporated.

"No, Dad. You're a stinky man."

"Sometimes that's true. I did shower yesterday. But," he sniffed his underarm, "I'm pretty ripe right now. Need some soap for sure."

Father and son laughed. They had not shared anything for so long that it was nice to sit and look at each other. Winks, sticking out their tongues, all the silliness of the past that seemed appropriate and right for the moment. Ryan couldn't help smile, it was hard not to, and keep looking at how much his son had grown.

A few inches taller, a bit more weight, still not quite enough for his frame.

His curly hair longer than normal. Not as long as it was when the stay-at-home orders were in place and they both went forever without haircuts. Julia complained that they were turning into mountain men with long hair and Ryan's growing and shaggy beard. David's hair looked good for the length and suited him, kind of surfer boy meets slacker and reminiscent of when Ryan himself was that age and longer hair was the norm.

The two sat for the longest time, asking each other questions, giving answers as best as they could, simply being with each other to know it was real and not a dream. An hour, two, Ryan lost count. He desperately wanted to take David and enjoy an ice cream or a park, someplace where they could relive life like they used to, no virus around, no crazy assholes trying to kill them, a young boy's freedom to play and live.

He longed for those times to return. A family outing like before, all packed in the car, driving to some destination, and off on some adventure. Bikes hooked to the kids' trailers with picnic blankets and lunch, off on a trail ride to their favorite parks. Even a walk at dusk around the neighborhood, Emma chasing David and stopping every ten feet to pick up sticks.

Ryan wanted all of that back.

"Hey, Buddy. I know it's been a long time since we were together, and I want to sit here forever and talk and see you. But-."

David put a finger up to Ryan's mouth to shush him quiet.

"I know, Dad. Mom and Emma, right?"

Ryan smiled at the boy, his smart little adult.

"Yes, Son. Mom and Emma. Plus, since you've been gone, I have a little cat I take care of who will really love you. He's all alone and I've been gone a while. So, I need to take care of him and get some things if we're going to get Mom and Emma back. You understand Son?"

David nodded.

"I do." His eyes started to tear, but he didn't cry.

"I will be back and it's a lot safer for you right here than with me. John is going to get you somewhere where they can't hurt you and I'll meet back up with you in a day or so, OK?"

David wrapped his arms around his dad. He didn't want to let go. He still remembered enough of his dad and some of the stories that he knew he'd be back. Dad always kept his word, and David knew no matter what he would return.

"Love you, Dad."

"Love you more, Son."

The day was late by the time Ryan left the old fort compound. The sun was low in the sky and clouds moving in from the west. Storm clouds from the looks. Until it rained you never knew since there was no predictability and you couldn't find a reliable weatherperson anywhere in Armageddon.

The last of the children had left with David aboard the old bus, heading to an underground garage that Ryan knew was safe and secure. He had spent his time after leaving David talking to John, getting more information and providing his own as he had spent the last year wandering the city and knew it inside and out.

The old garage beneath the clothing store you'd miss if you didn't know it was there.

It was for deliveries and only accessible from an alley that dead-ended into another building. The entrance to the sub-level beneath was recessed and tall garbage bins lined the wall keeping it well hidden.

He had happened upon it during one of his runs by mistake when evading some Bolts who wandered that section of town in search of their next meal. The door had been partially up and he managed to crawl under and roll it down. He took time to check it out, and it ended up being a useful way point for security and lodging as he scavenged the city and collected goods and supplies.

The elevator with no power meant only a stairwell up to the first floor at street level. It led to a backroom and from the looks when he found it, rarely used. A sliding door kept it hidden and a clothing rack full of prom dresses meant unless you were looking to dance, you'd walk right on by it.

It must have been an old employee parking lot.

As the city moved to discourage cars and encourage its transit and train network, the stairwell for employees found less use and ended up forgotten beyond the occasional need for extra storage.

What made the garage and location a great place for John's people was the old tunnel that led beneath the street and below to the building opposite it. It had to have been used to move goods back and forth long ago from an offsite storage area. Ryan investigated and there was no access to the building above, the only access an old lift lost beneath garbage containers in the alley.

If the group was found, they had a chance to escape and evade, be long gone before the garage was breached.

The old gas generators in the storage room still worked and vented high up through the building's roof. The noise was minimal and provided enough lighting to keep the dark and shadows at bay.

They had expected another attack and watchers around the perimeter radioed all clear throughout the evacuation.

Ryan knew it was coming. John did too.

If there was an agreement with the Brainers, it was likely they would be used first this time to attempt to overrun the fort. Ryan couldn't see Mark trying to sacrifice his own men again this soon and using someone else to die was something in his playbook.

Especially if time was a critical factor.

The smart move was sending in Brainers to take the brunt. Sit back and watch for weaknesses in the defenses. Have them engage and wear the survivors down. Wait in the shadows until coming full force with a vengeance and overrun the place.

When no one showed it surprised Ryan a little. Maybe that had been the plan, wait and watch, follow undetected and pounce. Mark would have had to know the direction John's people were heading and have stationed along the way scouts to report back. With all of the buildings around there was no perfect line of site, so all they had to do was get a few blocks away and they were in the wind.

Throw in a few distractions to keep from being followed and get away free.

Could have been Mark had his tail tucked from getting a beat down by some amateurs. Trying to figure out what to do next. That gap turned to work in the survivors favor to retreat and hide. Get settled in the garage and figure out the next plan to move. Be smart about it.

John's people needed to feel safe. The attack at the old fort, while they were able to fend off the attack, left them vulnerable. Get surrounded with nowhere to run and any heavily armed attackers could look to crash large vehicles to bust down the old walls or blow it to pieces. Siege and wait out the supplies inside, though Mark's timeframe likely meant he needed immediate results.

Hidden in the breeze for a bit gave the group time to buckle up and get ready for what came next.

At least John had people spread out to wait and watch, report for troop movements, and hopefully keep a step ahead. Know what might lurk in the shadows coming for them and have enough warning to react. Nothing was ideal and Ryan knew the only way to be safe was to get far away. That would take time and meant some exposure as enemies closed in. They could wait it out and hope for the best.

Relax and pay the price.

Any amount of complacency would get people killed and worse, David falling into the wrong hands. Ryan had just gotten his son back and nothing was going to ruin the partial family reunion. John had to keep his guard up, his soldiers ready for anything that fell through the cracks.

Stay vigilant, and live another day.

CHAPTER FOURTEEN

Getting back to his own safe haven was bittersweet.

It was dark and the rain had slowly begun by the time Ryan found his way inside. He was exhausted, dirty, and hungry as hell. To prevent exposure and any raiding parties out searching, he had taken a circuitous route back to cover his trail, just in case.

Call it paranoia.

Or, him being diligent and safe as he always tried to be these days. The path home took him through the storm sewers and ruins of old buildings toppled during the mass explosions when the city first crashed under the weight of the rising death toll. As more people succumbed to the virus and turned into the real dead or one of the Un-Dead groups, survivors set fires or blew up gas mains in order to try and kill them.

It had been mayhem since there was no coordinated effort.

The Un-Dead simply went around the destruction. The chaos and smoldering remains left wreckage in its wake. For Ryan, it provided a perfect labyrinth of hidden tunnels and passageways to circumvent the city and remain invisible.

That wasn't to say he went the same way each time he used the alternate travel routes.

Trouble popped up everywhere from time to time.

They liked to use them too. He placed markers, things only he would recognize, along the trails to know if trespassers had been by and sullied his pathways. A bottle or can propped in the way someone or something would inevitably kick out of the way. A branch innocuously blocking an entry point. Anything really to give him an immediate heads-up.

Safety first.

Walking into the kitchen, Pete was in his usual place on the counter, waiting for a fresh bowl of food and water.

On his expeditions Ryan always made sure the gray feline had access to enough food and a water supply in case it took him time to return or never made it home. Pete never gorged himself or self-fed beyond his immediate needs, maybe out of a sense of if he did, Ryan wouldn't return. A superstitious gray cat was a new one, but he'd take it.

They both needed all the luck they could get.

He sat in the recliner and propped it back, feet up and a warm bowl of canned stew in hand. Food first and a much-needed hot shower to ease the thoughts away. The last few days had been brutal as the world he knew exploded into pieces and the wreckage left to sort out meant nothing would ever be the same.

Two days ago, he thought he was alone.

One day ago, he thought his family was still dead.

This morning his mortal enemy resurfaced and later he saw and held his son for the first time in forever. The roller coaster of emotions and thoughts warping through his brain hurt. Trying to process it and compartmentalize into rational and coherent segments seemed irrelevant.

Acknowledge, address, and execute the plan like the old days seemed more in tune with the black hole and vortex he was about to encounter.

It had been ages since he had to put on his soldier mask, eons since he had to kill for a real purpose beyond simply staying alive. He lived his life with honor and integrity, and an old saying rang true.

The battle might be over, but the internal battle rages on for the soldier.

His eyes closed with Pete in his lap, if only for a few minutes while the food settled, Ryan's mind raced. His senses returned the memories of old whiffs of gun powder, the ringing of the shot as it exited his rifle, the fresh smell of blood pooling from a kill. You never lost it, just buried it away in a dark and dank recess of the mind.

For those like him, it never left.

The programming automatic to jump right in and respond. Ryan could feel the knife in hand, plunging it deep into the bowels of an enemy, watching the life fade out. As he opened his eyes, he saw Julia and Emma, laughing and smiling, pointing at him. He knew it was only a memory, but he held it tight, kept it front and center, longing for when the daydream became real and he could see them in the flesh.

Soon. Very soon.

He showered, let the heat penetrate his bones and wash the dirt and grime off and circle the drain. It felt radiant, invigorated him, made him feel young once more. He dried off, decided to shave off the gray stubble adorning his face, and returned to the kitchen for a drink. Pete was curled up asleep in the recliner, head tucked under his tail. The gray cat had been his only companion for an eternity.

No matter what, Pete wouldn't be left behind.

Once a Carmichael, always a Carmichael, was the family motto.

He had to figure out a safe way to transport the beast and keep him quiet, which for anyone who ever had a cat and went to the vet, was not an easy task. He had scrounged a cat carrier long ago, but the journey was rough going to get to David and the survivors. He knew Pete would keep David occupied while he went to handle business with Mark.

Especially as he had no idea when he would be able to return.

At least in that vein if he failed to come back, Pete would be a part of his dad David could hold onto to ease the pain. That was what a good father did. Try to keep your kids happy and ease their boo boos when you could. Ryan had missed a lot of those moments and if Pete could help in any way, not that he envisioned not making it to David, if that was the last thing he did, the good dad award that had been tarnished might see some gleam.

A bit of redemption and better memories moving forward.

He took a clean glass and swallowed some water to wash out the thoughts racing through his brain. Then, a few pets for Pete to say goodnight. He knew in a few hours the gray feline would make his way down the hall and up on the bunk to find a warm spot to curl up.

Pete needed the companionship, just as much as Ryan relished it.

Tired from the day, he headed off for some rest to ease the aches and pains and hope the tremors didn't occupy too much of the night. The morning called and being as whole as practical meant some shut eye.

He barely had closed his eyes before the exhaustion took hold and he was gone.

CHAPTER FIFTEEN

In the dim light of the early morning, the Humvee roared to life.

Ryan had done a few modifications to it. Quick connect battery cables so that it didn't drain down from infrequent use. Simply pop them on, click the locking bolt, and done in seconds. Hood down and ready to roar.

He could have put on a trickle charger. Keep it hooked up and pull the plug out. He'd thought about it. The power drain wasn't much for the solar panels.

Not that he didn't use a charger from time to time.

In the event he had to skip town, the disconnect setup worked better to quickly get on the road and saved the battery from cycling out from too much recharging. A half-drained battery and finding another working plug was wishful thinking and led to certain death if the electrical lost all its juice.

Cables hooked up, Ryan gave the beast a once over and nodded.

Outfitted with a Browning M2 machine gun in the turret, it was an imposing figure during the last days of civilization and must have been frightening to see used on American soil against its citizens. A makeshift aiming and remote firing system meant he could drive and shoot if necessary.

Took a lot of ingenuity for Ryan to design and think that one up.

He kept it all in working order just in case and given the provisions he required and to move Pete safely, there weren't many options on transport vehicles with less visibility.

The streets to get to the garage going the quickest route took him along backroads and into the skirts of the city. He knew there wasn't much out there if he went that way, so it played well for his plan. He could hide the Humvee in one of the old warehouses and walk the few blocks to his destination. Drop off Pete, say goodbye to David, and go back to the work of ending the threat against his boy.

Ryan had picked up the Humvee a long time ago from an abandoned

National Guard outpost that had manned the checkpoints and roadblocks in and out of the city. Weapons and ammunition, along with some really great surprises that were left for anyone to come across, found their way into his stash and arsenal for if and when he needed them.

He also pillaged a Guard armory for the tools of his long-lost trade.

Fifty caliber M82A1s and new MRAD variants that accepted multiple calibers, scopes, night vision, all the things he had expertise in and could come in handy found their way into the vehicle.

Breaking in had been easier than he thought since 24/7 armed guards would normally have secured the location and electrical systems to keep the locks secure and sound alarms if breached. He simply walked in, used a big pry bar he snagged from a big box supply store run, and ripped the storage room door off its hinges. Found a cart in a storage room to transport as much as he could, snipped off the trigger guards locking everything in place, and was gone.

He also had the tactical gear and weapons he acquired from a SWAT locker in the police headquarters downtown.

That one was a bit more of an adventure to loot while avoiding a large group of Lurkers hiding deep inside the complex and picking off the stragglers. Once he managed to get past them and was safe, he used the bolt cutters on the rack locks. It gave him access to a treasure trove of sweets for a kid who fiended for toys.

Besides enough tac vests and armor plates to keep him insulated from most caliber rounds, the modified M-4 rifles, tactical close quarter HK MP5s, and Glock and Sig law enforcement pistols rounded out the flash bangs and tear gas canisters he hoped still worked.

He had thought about pilfering their armored tactical vehicle, which offered robust security against most anything around. Besides overkill and no need when he found it, finding a place to hide and park it and keeping it operational would be a pain. The Humvee would serve its purpose with a bit more agility on the streets and though he wished he had taken the big SWAT BearCat, navigating the roads cluttered with old cars and garbage with the behemoth would undoubtably draw serious attention.

Keeping as low a profile as he could muster was a priority.

With the last of his supplies and Pete in his carrier piled into the Humvee, Ryan set out. He felt odd, being back in a military mindset with a mission to execute. It had been years since his last deployment and assigned to kill a target, and while he knew he was a bit rusty, the security work had kept him vigilant in training and reaction times. Granted, three years living day to day and fighting off the Un-Dead and the crazies kept him on his toes.

He figured that counted for something.

Older and wiser for sure, the feelings were creeping back. Not with any arrogance at succeeding, he was humble. He had confidence in knowing he had an advantage over his enemy. If he could find Mark, he'd take one shot for one kill to eliminate the threat forever this time. Even if he didn't make it out alive and had to sacrifice himself for his family, he knew killing Mark would inevitably change the tide of events and get the world back on track.

If left unchallenged, Ryan knew Mark well enough that the innocent would suffer. The free world survivors longed for soon completely replaced by the insanity and visions of a madman. He'd seen what the world had devolved into, the dregs that rose up and replaced what was once a great country. No more.

A reckoning was coming, and he was the perfect man for the job.

CHAPTER SIXTEEN

Pete took to David immediately, and the boy relished in the newfound affection.

The gray cat yearned for the love, someone to play and scamper around with on a more frequent basis than Ryan could offer being gone large parts of the day. David, having no pets or fur buddies for over three years, soaked up the attention and comradery the feline offered with no strings attached. Ryan gave Pete a scratch under his chin and one last belly rub. He hoped it sufficed until meeting up with them down the road.

Saying goodbye to his son was harder.

Given the circumstances, he was safer with John. Multiple places to hide and sequester off to, if necessary, to stay safe and remain alive. Ryan had to find Julia and Emma and get them back to reunite his family. Ensure they never had to endure the hell of being guinea pigs for a sadistic and twisted old friend of his ever again.

He debriefed with John for any added intel that might have come in since he left to get his gear and Pete.

Unfortunately, John came up empty.

The last refugees from the old fort left unscathed and were able to make it to the underground garage unseen by all accounts. They took a predetermined route full of advanced lookouts and no one followed. Ryan had assumed Mark would strike again, if not him in full force, using his mercenaries to do his bidding.

Nothing transpired which was a bit unnerving and odd.

He didn't want anything to have happened, though it would have provided information, more insight into what the future held and what might unfold.

He could assume a few things, and those thoughts weren't pretty.

As he gave his goodbyes and left for a recon stroll, loaded up with gear and enough provisions to be gone for a while, Ryan dove into his old self. He needed to find his prey and the best way was to find a location, build a sniper nest, and simply observe. He was running blind with no intel, no leads, and haphazardly doing a walkabout with soldiers and Brainers likely on the move which wasn't conducive to his health.

Transforming back into the soldier he once was, the man still inside and locked away, was the only way to prepare and succeed.

Outfitted with gray urban assault gear and BDUs to blend in with the monotone city buildings, he walked, destination in mind, open to other possibilities if circumstances arose.

The bank tower downtown was a great location to pan the city and look for signs of life. It was also the most darkened and dangerous building in town. Full of Un-Dead wandering around and for sure a group of Lurkers called it home.

He knew that from his previous patrols for provisions.

Only a nut would try to go in the building as they'd wind up dead. He knew no one would attempt it. For him though, that made it the perfect spot to set up and find his target.

Twenty-seven floors of glass with a three-hundred and sixty-degree view.

Go high enough and you could find the right office to watch one side of downtown and to the outskirts. Switch it up and find another side if one provided zilch to see.

Make it to the roof and you had one spot, with multiple areas to see everything.

The problem was the ascent.

The elevators had no working electrical. Taking the stairs pinned you down if you encountered above or below any enemies and had no way to exit. The elevator shafts though provided cover and a way to go between floors. You needed to get inside one, pop the emergency hatch to get on the roof, and climb the access ladder to wherever you wanted to go.

Secure and safe if you didn't fall.

The pitch black was another story. He hoped the creepy crawlies scuttered away as his headlamp illuminated the way.

Getting inside unseen and unheard to pry open the elevator doors, with no idea if any were on ground level or not, was the unknown factor throwing shit into his plan. Silence was critical and speed crucial and having to repeat the process if he failed meant possibly drawing unwanted attention. It was a crapshoot for sure and the only way to get to anywhere inside. He wasn't thinking the passenger lifts.

That was crazy.

The freight elevators were the key. They'd likely be ground floor or basement level in order to move goods up and down between floors. A building that size he knew had two on opposite sides to expedite deliveries and office moves.

Getting to them?

He needed a way to do it.

The layout of the ground floors meant little since he had no clue where anything was, and taking the time to find what he needed was playing with fire. The option was finding the service entrance or side door that led to one of the elevators. He didn't like being a sitting duck and exposed while he searched.

Really, he had no choice.

Bypassing the front entry, he headed down a service road leading between the building and the sandwich shop next door. Passing the shop brought back memories of stuffing a large pastrami loaded with cheese and produce in his mouth and washing it down with a root beer.

The saliva began to pool in his mouth, and he had to swallow twice to get rid of it.

Getting right back to thinking about the present, he was careful to watch for any movement of Lurkers ready to pounce and end him. He moved swiftly along the building's exterior wall, rifle panning left and right in search of any target that needed expiration.

The small two-lane entry and exit turned right into a service entrance.

The rollup door was shut, and a tug with his right hand yelled it was locked tight. To the left was a nondescript door. He reached behind and pulled out his pry bar, and using his weight for leverage, jammed it open.

The stench nearly made him puke.

He applied some old Mentholatum inside his nostrils to drench it out. Putting the pry bar back in his ruck and trading his M4 rifle for the MP5 for the tighter surroundings he was sure to encounter in the building, he sniffed once, and moved inside. As he stepped in and to the right in front of the rollup door, he flipped his goggles down to let the night vision kick in.

The darkness crept up with the putrid smell, and once he got accustomed to it, he could understand why.

A horde of dead lay fifty feet in near a parked bus. From the looks of what used to be expensive suits and silk ties, a bunch of dead bankers. The smell should have dissipated long ago. It was cooler in here than expected.

Maybe the temperature took longer for the bodies to decompose.

Or, and this was an off chance, they were more recently dead and had been holed up in the building. It didn't really matter though. He had no time to figure it out and simply didn't care enough to know.

He scanned around for movement or sound, and hearing nothing, stepped forward with care. As he walked and watched, vigilant for any rapid attack, he found it. A cart sat in front of the elevator door, empty except for toilet paper and flats of soda. As he gently moved further inside, he heard a sound, far off, a scuff or kicked bottle, he wasn't quite sure.

Turning in the direction of the distraction, the movement caught his attention.

Five Lurkers, slightly hunched down, moving slowly towards him.

Fifty yards or so he thought.

They fanned out and kept coming, looking like some disturbing creepers from a horror movie, fingers articulating like undulating waves, mouths opened baring their teeth, eyes shining brilliantly in his goggles. He kept still, keeping them in his field of vision, not wanting a surprise attack from either side. A human raptor meal he wasn't excited to become anytime soon.

Thirty yards and closing.

Pffft, Pffft, Pffft.

Three Lurkers fell, the muffled shots from the suppressor catching them in mid step with head shots. As Ryan focused in on the other two, he let two more bullets fly with a squeeze of the trigger and then another. The perfect shots from the MP5 took them down.

He listened and waited.

Pretty sure they were it, he pulled the weapon's strap back tight across his chest and crossed the garage. Pulling the pry bar out from the side of his rucksack again, he went to work pushing it between the freight elevator doors. As the hydraulic doors caught pressure as he pulled them apart, he saw them.

The elevator must either have been summoned to the lower level or they took it down. It didn't matter as the cart never made its trip and neither did the maintenance workers. The skeletons sat against the back wall, peaceful. From the looks of it, the men causally sat down waiting to be rescued when the power failed.

That's what Ryan thought anyway.

The telephone hanging down from inside the comm system seemed to point to it. They could have crawled out the top.

Why do that if they assumed a rescue was imminent?

Minutes could have become hours, even days, and maybe the virus finally got to them. At least they had company to pass the time. Many died alone or had the unfortunate end come violently after episodes of intense, body lurching tremors that broke bones and crippled once sound minds.

No one deserved that kind of end.

Putting the dead men out of his thoughts, Ryan blocked the doors open with the cart and checked out the access shaft above the elevator. Pushing the corpses aside and stepping up on the handrail, he popped the top and peering around, found the ladder. It ascended into the darkness and looked in good shape. So, he hopped up from the handrail and climbed in, careful to replace the hatch to cover his tracks. He didn't need to be caught inside the shaft trying to fight in the pitch black while trying not to fall to a certain death.

That was suicide.

Climbing twenty-seven stories in a dark and dank freight elevator shaft sucked. The weight of his ruck and gear made it a bit slow going until he got in a groove. It had been a long time since he had done something similar during one of his deployments. He had forgotten how bad it was when he was much younger, compared to with some age under his belt.

Suck it up solider.

Ryan managed it, pushed the pain away, his thoughts focused on keeping David safe and finding his wife and daughter. Three years and unexpectedly his world turned upside down. For the better in knowing that they were all alive, yet adding uncertainty on where it went from here.

Success had many different outcomes.

Saving Julia and Emma, killing Mark, giving the world a chance to be reborn. Even if he died in the process and saved them and fulfilled his mission, that was still a success.

Failure was definitive.

That wasn't an option.

Ryan played it all over in his mind, going through his checklist, the mental prep, everything he was trained to do to ensure the operation worked as planned. The ease in falling back into the mindsight, the soldier who did the impossible, the death dealer who knew many ways to deliver the ending, felt a part of who he was that it scared Ryan a bit. He had lived that life and left it, created a successful business with purpose, found his love and married, become a father, and been a real member of society. If people knew his real past, his previous life, they would feel differently about him.

He was sure.

Julia didn't know about it. Even among his oldest and closest friends, a locked door sealed in concrete was a must. Too many skeletons and questions that had no answers. Family was left in the shadows too, only knowing he had served, told a tale of mundane work behind the scenes.

If they only knew the truth.

He didn't want it to paint such a wicked picture of the man she loved. That life was long before they met, and security work was all she knew about him. It was *the code*, the bond among those he served with and did the deeds. *Never talk about it*, at least not with anyone outside the sphere. They couldn't begin to comprehend the life or why someone did what they did.

Plus, there was Mark.

His mentor, his confidante, his friend. Someone he trusted with his life. Mark had reached out, asked for help, and Ryan, always ready to help an old friend, came to his aid. As the chaos erupted and spiraled into madness, the lies piling up along with the dead and the lines between who to trust and not blurred and unrecognizable, the real researchers, scientists, and doctors who worked the problem versus profited from it needed protection from the death threats and stalkers.

It wasn't even a question with all of the risks.

A sense of duty, supporting an old friend and doing something to help. He was going to be there and do what he could for the greater good. Who better to provide for them than Ryan?

If only he had seen it for what it was, things might be different.

The small things, the little deviations to Mark and his increasingly bizarre behavior that Ryan blew off, figuring it was the stress. The outbursts he had never seen, the cold eyes on occasion that stared someone down.

He should have recognized, been more in tune.

Mark was his friend and seeing what someone was or was *becoming* a difficult realization to grasp if such a divergent from what you knew or thought you knew.

The past was the past.

Today and getting to tomorrow, the only things that mattered.

CHAPTER SEVENTEEN

He got to the twenty-seventh floor after an hour of climbing.

He took a few breaks along the way, listened at a few floors for noises, and made mental notes for later. He planned on a recon of the floor to clear and secure it. Take some time to check out visibility from behind the glass and set up a few nests. The roof was his top priority. Having backup plans to backup plans the way of the special operations life.

You always had to have contingencies and drop back positions.

Ryan figured the top floor offered what he needed if the roof failed to produce. He didn't like the idea of putting any holes in the tempered glass almost three hundred feet up since that would create instability once wind made contact. The pressure produced could weaken the panes and prove catastrophic.

Left with no choice, he would though.

It would work better to simply remove the glass altogether and throw up a blind to hide himself. That would be suspicious if all of a sudden, a window was gone that had been observed there before. He'd take the time to scout everything out and see what he could actually do and when ready move forward. His plan was fluid until he had his intel to back it up. Take a breath and relax.

Things were getting real.

Getting ready to breech, Ryan listened and waited.

His headlamp off and his body secured to the ladder with a D-ring in absolute blackness, he kept his ears wide open for the smallest scuff, drag, or voice.

Nothing caught his attention.

With his lamp back on to see, he positioned himself in front of the doors in two footholds and connected another D-ring attached to his rope to a secured eye-nut bolt recessed into the wall. He grabbed the pry bar from his ruck and wedged it in between the doors. Throwing his shoulder into it, he heaved.

The doors didn't budge.

He pushed the opposite direction. Nothing.

Looking around the shaft he spied a cover to the side. Leaning closer to illuminate the faint wording, it said it was a manual door release. Lifting the cover and pulling down the lever, he heard a sound, likely the door catches, and pried. The door slowly inched apart and enough to let Ryan grab one side and pull it open. Quickly, he flipped off his light and let his eyes adjust to the darkness.

The hallway was dark.

Light from the right penetrated enough to see. From the looks of it, it led to an office beyond a set of double doors. He saw light in the distance and leaning in through the opening, saw enough of the cubicles to venture a guess it was an open floorplan by the way they were spaced out. Grabbing hold of the floor, he threw himself up and in and immediately took a knee, pulling the MP5 strap to loosen it and have at the ready. Releasing his safety line, Ryan crept forward, his weapon aimed true, and stopped inside the doorway.

Debris was strewn everywhere as if a tornado had rolled through the office.

Papers, folders, even the file cabinets were haphazardly strewn all around. It looked like the place had been ransacked. Monitors and chairs thrown about, cube walls pushed over. Even the fluorescent lights had been yanked down, the wiring exposed, the bulbs shattered below. He waited and watched, let his ears absorb, and the only sounds he heard were his breathing and the occasional squeak of a mouse.

Slowly, he stood up and walked in.

From the looks of the wrecked nameplate behind the receptionist's desk, the office was a former financial firm. Probably one of the high-end client types that invested and supervised assets. The art on the wall and framed mantras seemed to confirm it. He browsed, looking at old photos, scanning documents, opening drawers in search of any potential supplies. Coming up empty and the morning moving to afternoon, he needed time to scout and set up a perimeter to avoid any unpleasant company.

As Ryan secured the office, ensuring the exit doors to the stairwells were locked and barricaded and broken fluorescent bulb shards scattered around to warn of any intruders, he placed a few tripwires with flash bangs for added protection.

Satisfied with his work, he investigated the view.

The top floor office, with its three-hundred-and-sixty-degree panorama, provided an excellent base of operations. He could see for miles in all directions. From different vantage points throughout the floor, in two corner offices and around the open areas where they had placed couches and chairs for relaxation and conversations, he could see down the main streets of the city as they led out to the suburbs and industrial parks. For any mass movement along the normal transit routes, he had superb visibility.

Activity would happen soon, Ryan was positive.

Whether a full-scale assault on the old fort if they didn't know it had been abandoned or ripping the city apart piece by piece, it was only a matter of time. Brainers fixated on their targets, like bloodhounds. Call it something that misfired in what was left of their cerebellum or an attribute of the virus in predispositioned people. They would keep going until they either found what they wanted or were killed.

No in-between.

Mark and his soldiers would be a bit more vigilant and cautious, given what he witnessed of their precision movement and execution. Military tactics and responses. He had some idea of how they would operate and could predict to a certain degree. Their actions said they still thought like a soldier, though he wondered if this was a new category of virus intertwined with evil.

He knew he'd soon find out.

There was no radio traffic on the secure channels and that was a good thing. It meant the survivors were safe and secure. Mark and his team could have access to transmission monitoring gear and use it to pinpoint the group.

Unless there was an emergency, Ryan and John agreed to keep quiet.

There were plans they could put in place if they had to draw out their adversaries or misdirect them away from the garage. One meant having one of the lookouts stationed blocks away to transmit a signal and move the soldiers in the opposite direction. The second was one Ryan knew they'd use when the time was right.

He'd make a call and lead them to an ambush, manipulate the situation his way, and get the information necessary to advance the plan through the stages of action he outlined in his head. Unless there was imminent danger he saw coming, the radio was set to scan for signals to catch any wayward traffic that bled through the air waves.

The afternoon passed to evening and the eerie quiet of the twenty-seventh floor hung like a dark cloud over him. He noticed the storm clouds, eerie and foreboding.

The roof lookout took a backseat.

Maybe later if the doom subsided.

Normally, the office would have been buzzing with life and white noise people could drown out and continue working and going about their day. Absent life, every creak echoed and quickly dissipated, leaving another round of nothing in its wake until the next ghost in the cycle. Ryan had spent countless hours and days before in similar situations.

That was a long time and a world away.

Those days at least had some activity to watch to pass the dreariness. Here, he sat in a comfortable leather executive chair watching out the floor to ceiling windows and saw nothing roaming the streets except wildlife that had proliferated since the fall and begin to regain its numbers. Boring was an understatement.

He thought he'd fall asleep at the monotony.

Daylight meant being seen and nighttime offered the shadows. As the temperature rapidly dropped with the impending storm that was on its way, he could see the black clouds from earlier were nearing the city limits. With luck, fires for warmth might pop up. They might be specks, unseen at ground level miles away. Up here he could see them.

He could try and zoom in with his scope and gather intel.

It was the small insignificant details that the unaware or absent-minded let slip and those were the clues he would pounce on and use to his advantage. They could even be traps, meant to entice and cajole the survivors into an offensive attack.

He knew he'd do that if the table was turned.

It all depended on what Mark sought to put in place and the effort to get David. Knowing Mark, it was in the playbook along with some other cheats to try and win.

The Brainers on the other hand, subtlety was not a strong attribute of their makeup. They were more likely to reveal themselves. Ryan hoped to catch a glimpse, see their numbers.

They were the wild cards, the unpredictable factor in the equation.

There was no rhyme or reason in their actions, no way to know exactly what they would do beyond trying to ravage and kill. Soldiers acted in specific ways according to their training and if you knew the military branch and were familiar with the training, you knew the maneuvers.

He could work with that.

Brainers though, they were the ones that needed to be eliminated sooner than later or at a minimum, hampered enough to prevent any coordination and thin the field of opponents.

With no heat and the temperature outside continuing to drop, the office got cold quick. He began to see his breath billow out, the warm air from his lungs hitting the cold to create mist. Ryan had spent hours checking his observation posts with negative results. He managed to scarf down some food, an unappetizing MRE of chipped beef and stale bread known better as SOS, shit on a shingle. Some people really liked it.

He loathed it.

The spaghetti was better and tastier. Unfortunately, he'd grabbed and threw packets into his ruck without looking and got the crappy one tonight. The canned fruit was better, and he relished in the cherries last from the fruit cocktail mix. The caffeine from instant cold black coffee hit the spot, though he dreamed of a nice steaming cup with some real milk and sugar sitting at a table reading a book.

He missed those days.

Bundled up for warmth, the walking from post to post kept his body limber and he hoped maybe, a night free of tremors.

Of all nights, he needed to focus and watch the darkness to find his foes.

As the evening turned to night and the storm hit, the flecks of snow fell. Ryan watched them as they worked their way from the clouds to the ground, a gentle stream of flakes that reminded him of some old Renaissance painting.

From high up it was a beautiful sight, the glint of the moonlight catching just right, drawing lines in the air he would focus on and watch to the end. The production increased until a steady stream turned to a flurry and the once blackened streets turned white. Maybe a blessing he thought, as tracks in the snow would leave imprints for some time before being lost to the next layer of ice. If he found any, he could follow the line. With visibility narrowing at his altitude, he wasn't going to hold his breath for it.

Soon, old memories flooded in to replace the tranquilness of the falling snow.

Real war was a lifetime ago. Too many years to count reflecting his age. He was an idealist with no direction, a want to do the right thing and not in a place to do much about it. High school was a nightmare in the academic sense.

Not as a failure of a student.

He was bright, intelligent, someone who excelled in different areas of academics from a knowledge perspective.

The exams killed him.

There was something about the tests that didn't carry over from what he knew. He understood the content, knew the concepts and underlying reasons. Ask him for dates and it was failure. He never understood that, why a date was more important than the who, what, and why.

Why the facts tied together coherently failed because of a date in time.

He was smart, though it took time for the numbers to sink in. As he got older, it got better to the point he was a walking encyclopedia as his friends and family called him. In school it troubled him to the point that a four-year degree was out of the picture unless he went the junior college route. After graduation, with no idea of what the next year held or the next ten, a recruiter tried the sweet talk routine about the military and the GI Bill. A few years for Uncle Sam followed by free money for college.

Ryan wasn't interested.

Even though both grandfathers and his own father served, it was a different time. There wasn't a war his senior year and he felt little allegiance to join up. Persistent, the recruiter asked Ryan to at least test, see where he fell in line with military jobs.

Keep your options open, was the suggestion.

Wanting to end it, Ryan did. The results got him to today, the man he was, and the man he used to be a world removed.

Highly intelligent. A natural leader. Ability to make decisions and effect action. Focused, with clear direction.

He wasn't surprised by the results, but it sure did make for a conversation with the recruiter once all of it was revealed. His numbers placed Ryan in a category for the specially selected, those who functioned well as part of a small team of specialized members.

Call it special forces, elite operators, whatever you wanted, they were the ghosts of ghosts.

Not SEALS, not DELTA, not Marine MARCOM or RECON, not any designation anyone outside of top-secret clearance in the highest echelons of military leadership knew. Even the CIA SAD/SOG before it became the SAC/SOG was not as secretive or the top dog, and they took their numbers from the ranks of former special operators from the various branches best of the best.

Ryan bypassed them all and joined a group that went beyond politics and war.

For someone right out of high school with no previous military experience, he faced the typical backlash from those who had put in their time and were older. Hazing and outright cruelty attempted to break the young kid.

He put a rest to all of it right away.

Never one to back down and someone who despised the idea that hazing was acceptable or even tolerated before being a member of a team, he met it head on. First to complete runs and obstacle courses. First to capture the flag during exercises. Best marksman. He excelled beyond imagination, almost to the point of being obsessed and driving himself to exhaustion. He used it to his advantage, calling out his tormentors to throw them off their own game. He gave it right back without a pause.

They thought they were tough, he showed them he was even tougher.

He played the game. Didn't let them being assholes prevent him from being a team player, putting others ahead of himself if it meant succeeding on a mission assignment.

Even when they pushed him, and a few opted for the physical altercation, he came out on top with an extended hand.

When push came to shove, he showed he was the guy they wanted watching their backs, that no matter what, the team succeeding meant more than him. As time passed and his worth and decision-making in some tight spots saved lives, the young kid soon became the leader even the most hardened soldier would follow everywhere.

Mark was one of those who went from enemy to dear friend.

Years of service together, blood, sweat, and tears for fallen comrades, their bond was like big brother to little brother. Mess with one and you got the other. Mark left first, older and the time right, and went on his way to lucrative research. Used his science degree to save lives instead of take them. Years doing productive work and travel.

Towards the end Ryan thought it was the stress, the pressure to succeed and save people that got to Mark. A trained soldier should never have failed to recognize the changes like Ryan did, miss the mark on a friend who fell into the abyss.

Where it went wrong, he wished he knew.

CHAPTER EIGHTEEN

Old thoughts from Ryan's past floated in and out of his mind.

There was no way to prevent it. With time on his hands to think, inaction until presented with something beyond sitting, watching, observing, Ryan had a racetrack in his head going down straights and bends, each memory competing with others for who would make the finish line. So many competing ones his head hurt trying to reel them into an ordered and coherent list to tackle one by one.

Watching the warmth of his breath float out like a vapor trail provided a small distraction. Short puffs, pursed lips, dismal attempts at creating shapes to glide in the chilly air. He could make plenty of O shapes big and small. That was about the extent of his talent.

He'd love to trace a finger on the glass to draw shapes in the condensation. This high up with the weather he doubted anyone could see. Make a pirate ship pillaging a Spanish galleon. Cartoon characters jumping off a cliff. A self-portrait, though his drawing skills left a lot to imagination.

His luck someone with eagle eyes would focus in and his hidden lair would be exposed.

Pressing his luck was not a smart decision. Besides, getting up meant some effort and he was fine sitting in the comfortable leather executive chair, feet propped up. Comfort was hard to come by, so why miss out?

Around midnight he saw the first flames. A small one, partially hidden by the snow and trees, about a mile from his location.

Closer than he thought, but an indication of life.

One after another the rest followed, ten in all, spread out across the city. Only visible high up, there was no way anyone would know unless they were close enough to see the orange glow or smoke billowing up. Otherwise with the weather, they were lost in the haze. He couldn't see much, just the glow.

Focusing in meant little until the storm lifted.

Besides the hidden nature of the fires, trees, buildings, and all sorts of obstacles to line of sight prevented seeing who lit them. The city was decimated, ruins and rubble from one side to the other pockmarked intact and partially standing structures.

Visibility was his enemy.

Ryan guessed the dummies having fires were Brainers, since military personnel would have cold weather gear. Ten fires meant a good amount of the psychopaths around. He wished he knew how many in total. Missing information led to all kinds of trouble.

Around two o'clock in the morning, the storm still alive and the streets blanketed with snow, Ryan heard the first blast.

The windows shook violently from the vibrations.

He had been asleep, maybe an hour in, figuring the storm would keep his enemies hunkered down. The sounds jostled him back to reality. He cracked his neck, one eye glued shut from exhaustion, the other trying to adjust to the darkness while waking up, and sat upright.

The sounds came from the west side of town.

He grabbed his rifle and binoculars and bolted to the large windows along the side. Taking a knee, he scanned with his naked eyes and immediately saw it.

The flames illuminated the sky, vibrant orange fingers piercing through the haze of the falling snow.

He took his binoculars and scanned, searching for the target, when other blasts erupted to the east. He ran across the floor in a sprint, the brilliance lighting the way. As he slid to a stop, volumes of wild orange and red shot high into the night. The crosstown bridge was exploding into pieces and fires were raging along its path.

It hit him square in the gut.

The first explosions probably blew the main bridge over the river, the only way to the west out of the city on the freeway. The other bridges were local traffic, crisscrossing through town.

Containment, he thought. *They're locking everyone in and directing their potential escape along routes the bastards control.*

Running back to the west side of the building his suspicions were confirmed. The freeway bridge over the river was gone, its span resting halfway out of the water, the river footings that had stood tall nowhere to be seen. The other two bridges remained, one a small foot bridge and the other a commuter connector, still stood, though likely by morning or early the next day would be blocked and manned to prevent any escape.

As he sat in a chair taking it in, Ryan moved from plan A to plan D. Plan A was centered on a more defensive approach, gather intel and wait for opportunity. Prepare a counterattack when it presented the best chance at success.

Plan D was balls to the wall.

An offensive *fuck you* that would catch the Brainers and Mark off guard and throw them into chaos. It relied heavily on surprise and the right execution. If done the right way, it meant wresting control away and directing events the way he and the survivors needed to stay alive. The plan also propelled everything miles ahead of schedule and to a certain degree, he would have to wing it. Not exactly what he wanted nor what made him feel comfortable.

The situation aggressive and moving along like this, there was only a bit of wiggle room to respond and keep people safe. As a ghost, he had more flexibility to act, and as someone hell bent on getting his wife and daughter back, a lot to lose if it all went south.

Ryan flipped his goggles down and turned on his night vision.

The fires would blind his vision with bright light and the best thing to do was avoid focusing on them. He hoped to catch the heat signatures of people or vehicles and track those instead. As he scanned back and forth, he caught what he was looking for, though it took a second to register.

Faint at first, the temperatures stood out.

Heat from heads a few inches above the sides of the Zodiacs, fast inflatable boats used by the military and various special forces for rapid water assaults. He had spent a lot of time in them during his service. He watched as they vanished down the river and out of sight around a bend.

He had a good idea of where they were headed.

The port was not far away, and he ventured a guess it was being used as a staging point for a ship or submarine Mark was using as his base of operations.

This was great intel, though it did add a new dimension to the situation. With the main freeway bridge blown to shit, there were only two land routes across the water to get directly to the port. Sentries would be guarding them for sure. Trying to cross would be a bloodbath or he'd end up captured.

There were other options.

A much longer journey to the north to another river crossing and head south before circling back to the east. Ryan guessed it would be watched too.

Same issue to the south.

Miles of travel through unknown territory to a country bridge to cross. You'd be seen long before you got there if traveling by vehicle. A water crossing was possible, though swimming in cold water against currents was a precursor to a drowning. Even with diving gear, if he could get his hands on some tanks that still had air, it would be difficult and near impossible without the right equipment for pitch black water.

He sat watching the shooting flames as they died out and turned to glowing embers. His mind flashed a crazy idea.

Ryan laughed at the thought.

It was doable. Stupid and risky for sure and likely a one-way mission. It was an option if it worked. It meant having the right setup and finding it damn near impossible. He knew where to look. It depended on if he could get to it and whether he could get it to work.

"Why not?" Ryan shrugged, catching himself saying the internal question out loud. "What do I have to lose?"

CHAPTER NINETEEN

The municipal airport sat to the south of town.

Tucked between two old established and completely different neighborhoods contrasted by the divide between the have and have nots. Bordered on all four corners by small businesses servicing local clientele and homes well below the poverty level to mini mansions no average person could afford, it had been primarily a local pilot and corporate parking lot for aircraft.

Some distance from downtown, it wasn't a short journey if you were on foot. By car a twenty-minute drive if you went the direct route along the old highway turned boulevard and considerably longer if you circumvented and went through the neighborhoods and back roads.

Ryan was sure the airport was long left to decay and rotting away as he had not seen an airplane or anything remotely close since he took up roots and made this place his home away from home. He figured it was the best place to find what he needed, though it would take some time if he simply went hangar to hangar and rollup door to door. He needed to find the office and manifest of all planes and aircraft housed at the airport. That would lead him to what he needed, and he hoped was the answer to his plans.

He couldn't just drive on over and through the front gate.

Brainers and Mark's scouts were likely roaming free and getting caught in a vehicle, though it offered more protection, was much more visible and a target versus being on foot or taking alternate transportation. Besides the noise of the Humvee to draw attention, he didn't want to take everything with him. It was loaded with weapons, ammunition, and supplies, and if he had to bail out, it was a goldmine for the person who found it.

He went with the best he could find, an old black Electra beach cruiser from a bike shop that with a little bit of WD-40 to silence the squeaks from sitting for three years, would get him through the back streets and across parks in the dead of night. Portable air pump to juice the treads and ensure he could easily glide along, and for grins a cup holder to make it feel slightly normal.

A cold night ride was in store.

He hoped to avoid any of the Un-Dead on his journey and any Brainers using the back roads. He didn't want to be the center of attention for any death party.

The previous night's storm had blown through town and was finally gone. Warmer weather prevailed and the streets were left with puddles instead of blankets of white.

Bike tracks in fallen snow was a telltale sign that would lead straight to him.

If he had been forced to delay longer, it meant more chances for the enemy to strike and wreak havoc around town. He didn't really have the luxury of playing the wait game and simply sitting and biting his nails he might as well drag them across a chalkboard. He needed to do something, and with fortune shining down in a warm sun, he had to manage a smile.

With the dark of night returned to aid his anonymity and astride the comfortable cruiser, Ryan sailed quietly along the streets, passing businesses and homes that had once teemed with life and action. Long abandoned and overrun with weeds, the front yards of once nice homes sat derelict. Local mom and pop businesses once the mainstay of neighborhoods sat vacant and as he passed each, wondered if watchful eyes stared back.

Such focused quiet was the most troublesome. Eerie like a horror movie killer lying in wait.

The only sounds were the rubber tires on the pavement and his own breath. He heard the occasional cat screech or howl as roaming bands of dogs sought refuge and company with other animals that still felt like house pets.

It weighed heavy on his mind, and he wished he could save them all.

As a "fur dad" himself before losing his beloved ones to old age right before the end, finding Pete and taking him in gave Ryan a new sense of purpose and something to care for that had left a hole in his heart. Knowing all the ones who longed for a comfy lap or to curl up next to their human, he could imagine the loneliness they felt akin to his sadness before Pete.

One day maybe soon, the ones not fully turned wild, they could find someone to love them again.

Thinking of his old cats and dogs, and his new best buddy Pete, provided some distraction on the ride. Pedaling took three soul crushing hours to complete. Having some warmth of thought and memories helped bide the extended time. More due to taking precautions and staying off the beaten path, he finally arrived across from his intended destination, a bit tired, his skin exhilarated from the cold air.

The front gate was too out in the open, a long drive from the main road and a stop at the guard shack. He would have to take the service road out to the hangars and be visible from anywhere if anyone were around. He was set on the chain link fence closest to the hangars as it was a short distance from the public road to the first row of sheet metal boxes and offered some concealment between the rows.

The problem was getting to it.

The hangar complex sat right out in the open too, though only ten feet off the thoroughfare behind a long meandering ditch and another one hundred feet to the first hangar wall. Besides getting to the fence and over the chain link quickly, it was a sprint across four lanes of traffic and a concrete median from a starting point that left little room to hide.

If he decided to go, he had to commit and keep going.

The oleander bushes on his side of the street offered some protection to watch for any signs of life. Parking the bike and pushing some limbs around to hide it, he waited and scanned the property, searching out anything that yelled it was a trap.

The occasional raccoon and possum scurried the grounds.

From what he observed the place was dead, or as dead as dead was unless he encountered some psychotic weirdos lurking between the buildings. It was a little after midnight and he still had a lot of time to devote to this part of the plan.

He cracked his neck to the side, took a few deep breaths, and thought, *what the hell*, and went for it.

Keeping low and moving quickly, Ryan was across the street in no time.

As he hit the edge of the ditch he jumped, and catching his boot flat against the chain link, in one motion he kicked down and grabbed the top rail to flip over the bar. Landing square and bent at the knees to absorb the impact with all the weight he carried inside his ruck, he kept going forward until he reached the wall of the first hangar and going right and immediately left, went straight down the row.

The office was at the end of this building according to the sign and with twelve rows to cover and over one hundred hangars and storage doors, getting what he needed soon if he had issues was better than being caught during daylight. He kept pace and in less than a minute from the time he hit the fence to stopping, reached the office door. Standing still, he listened for sounds outside first and for any inside, and hearing nothing, took a chance and tried the door.

The knob turned and with a push, it creaked open.

Musty and dank from years of no air circulation and free to vacate, the odors passed him on their way out. Dabbing at his nose as it twitched from the smells, he proceeded forward cautiously, closing the door behind. Waiting a scant minute, Ryan let his eyes adjust to the low light of the moon coming through the old and battered blinds. He didn't dare use a flashlight for risk of being seen and saving the batteries for his night vision was more important. He could see well enough.

Time his enemy, he needed to quickly find the plane manifest.

The office was decent size for a small airport, probably nine hundred square feet with multiple desks and two closed door offices in the back. A row of tall cabinets lined one of the walls and mid-chest cabinets lined another.

Ryan had no idea where to even start.

He went straight for the offices and picked the door on the left. The stale air was ripe with the decay of withered plants that with no one to care for, dried up and their aroma caught within the confines of the four walls of the closed office. He walked in slowly, more for time to glance around and create a picture than of real caution. As he stepped forward into the dark room, its lack of light made it difficult to see. Reaching over to the interior window blinds, he opened them up, hoping to illuminate the office more.

No luck.

Tucked far back and with no exterior windows, illumination was hard-pressed to find its way here. He reluctantly turned on his flashlight and hoped the red glass of the lens diffused the beam enough from being seen in the far back of the building.

The wall map caught his attention at once.

It was a diagram of the hangars and placed on each was a pin with a card. Glancing at one, it listed the owner, rental date, and type of aircraft. He quickly scanned through each row searching for his target. He found it located in one of the last of hangars near the taxi road to the airstrip. He hoped it was there, if prayer meant anything at all since the planet had been abandoned by all higher powers.

Wishful thinking on his part. He could use it.

Getting inside the hangar was a different story. He searched for the master keys to the hangar doors. He rummaged through the desk drawers, opened all the file cabinets, and found nothing in the office. Repeat for the office next to it. He searched all the outside desks and cabinets and came up empty.

Time was ticking and wasting more precious seconds was a bad decision.

Ryan made a mental note of the hangar number and set out to locate it. He still had a few hours before daylight and wanted the darkness for cover. Twelve rows of hangars stood between him and his destination. Up to now, the night had been calm without distractions or noises that hinted at trouble.

He was smart enough to know silence was an enemy, especially with Lurkers.

Hangars could be used as hideouts and even for the Brainers, a place to congregate and watch for any intruders looking to make an escape by airplane if they could get one operational or scavengers seeking parts. Proceeding cautiously was paramount and being a phantom his asset. He had played the

part all too well for many years and countless missions.
Why screw it up?

CHAPTER TWENTY

The lights at the old airport had long stopped working, the only illumination coming from the glow of the moon.

Even with the small solar panels for the floodlights to save costs, they had stopped working as the batteries extended life ended. Ryan kept to the shadows along the perimeter walls facing the taxi road, stopping at each intersection to listen and peer down the asphalt between the hangars.

As he moved from row to row, he encountered nothing except the sound of his own breath.

His footsteps were light, the quick pace purposeful as he panned the nine-millimeter MP5 around corners in search of a target. The close quarter nature of the assault weapon and its silent and deadly suppressor were better suited for quick shots and ensured the element of surprise between each round before being recognized, and by then, it was too late.

Rows five, six, seven, and eight passed quickly.

He reached row nine and stopped cold. Even with voices low, they echoed off the sheet metal exteriors and traveled to his ears.

"This is a shit assignment," the voice whispered. "Why are we stuck out in this crap hole? Nothing is here and nothing works."

A deeper voice responded. "Because that's what we were told to do and that's what we do."

Ryan heard them clearly now and took a knee to absorb. *Take intel, assess the situation, eliminate the threat.*

He ran through it and waited.

The whispered voice raised its tone, the irritation at the answer evident. "Planes haven't flown out of here in years. No upkeep, no maintenance. The runways are overgrown. What does he expect, a bunch of civilians are going to come and fly out of here, to where?"

Ryan heard a loud thump and decided to peek.

The man with the deeper voice had a fist full of uniform shirt and his face a few inches from the other man. They were outside an open hangar door on the opposite side of rows from him. "I don't give a shit what you think. We do what we're told, that's the deal. We sit and watch. Better this than dealing with those crazy assholes," the man spat as his voice trailed off and he pushed forward to let the man go.

The whispering man grunted and raised his middle finger. "Whatever dickhead."

He turned and began to walk in Ryan's direction.

There was no more than a hundred feet between them, and the distance began to close. Ryan had no clue which way the soldier would go once he made it to the end of the row. Left towards him meant being discovered if he stayed put. Turn right and Ryan was behind him. Sneak up to eliminate the threat. It did mean distance to cover and possibly being seen by the soldier at the hangar.

The options weren't the best.

He backed up quickly, his MP5 trained ahead, and reaching the end of the row, stepped around the corner and watched. The soldier appeared, staring straight ahead. He looked around a few minutes as Ryan waited in the dark of shadows. Still as a statue and unflinching, the soldier's gaze seemed to focus on something out in the field between the taxi road and the runway.

Ryan scanned it and saw nothing.

Focusing, he heard rustling in the weeds and saw the quick flash. A jackrabbit scurrying around, probably in search of food. The soldier raised his own M4 rifle up, intent on target practice or outright killing of the innocent animal. He walked forward about twenty feet to the center of the taxi road, keeping aim at the hare. The soldier let his rifle come down for a moment, appearing to check something on it. He raised it back up and looked through the sight.

Reaching up to his throat, the solider pressed the receiver button and squawked in his microphone. "Found something to keep me occupied. Want a rabbit foot for good luck?" He must have received a reply. "OK, more for me. Don't be surprised when I blow the little dude apart."

A thought entered Ryan's mind. With his left thumb he flipped the switch on his MP5 from three shot burst to single fire. He had to do this just right. He could see the soldier grin, he was only forty feet away.

Ryan watched intently, waiting for the moment.

A rock kicked forward as the soldier's shot echoed through the silent night. Surprising the jackrabbit, it quickly bolted away. A split second later the soldier crumbled to his knees, leaning slightly forward.

A few seconds later footsteps pounded the asphalt and reverberated against the sheet metal as they grew closer. The deep voiced soldier ran out from the protection of the hangars straight to his comrade, oblivious to what had happened.

Coming up from behind he threw his helmet at the kneeling man. He raised his rifle and growled, "Asshat, it's not that big a deal to pray for a good shot killing a rabbit like you just sunk a winning three pointer. Get your ass up. You probably signaled to all the dead meat to come and rip us apart."

As he made contact, the soldier fell forward, face-planting the road.

Ryan used the opportunity to strike.

He moved with speed along the wall outside of the soldier's peripheral vision and came up behind him. Ka-Bar in hand he grabbed the man by the top of the hair and yanked him back, the sharp knife against his jugular. Startled, the soldier tried to move. The blade pressed more firm against his neck and the movement stopped.

"You know the drill. I won't bore either of us. Tell me what I need to know, and you can live. Lie and you die," Ryan whispered in the man's right ear.

The soldier sneered. "Screw you."

His blood began to trickle as Ryan's blade moved a hair.

"Not my type asshole. Your choice. You won't be my first and not my last. This isn't my first rodeo. So, what's the word Buttercup?"

Ryan gripped the man's hair and pulled. He caught some anguish in the soldier's response at the pain being inflicted.

"I tell you I'm dead. Go ahead and make it quick. You're wasting my time."

The blade thrust into the back of the left thigh and returned immediately to the throat. The soldier cried out in pain, grabbing his leg as the metal left the muscle and blood poured out.

"Never mentioned it would be quick," Ryan whispered. "This can be pleasant, or extremely unpleasant. Your call."

"Mother fu-" was all that came out before the blade found its next mark in the other thigh and returned straight back to his neck. The soldier fell to his knees, the pain excruciating, no longer able to stand.

Ryan sunk down with his adversary to keep leverage and the ability to strike if required again. "I've got time, do you?"

The soldier nodded his understanding of the situation. "What do you want to know?"

As the soldier answered each question, Ryan felt more anger rising inside of himself. The information gave a grimmer picture of what he was up against. The cracks in it provided some sense of possible success over certain death and failure. There was more to everything, beyond getting his wife and daughter back, but to humanity itself.

That weight felt like it was crushing his chest with each breath.

He wasn't a real soldier anymore and his family meant more than anything. If saving them meant a life expectancy short on time because worse was coming, the old dog of a soldier had to shake off the rust and play his own way.

"That's a lot of information. How do I know it's not a trap or a bunch of bullshit?" Ryan asked.

The soldier managed a short snort of laughter before answering. "You don't really. I lost everything when shit went down. Wife, kids, family, all of it. Being some madman's errand boy for world domination or whatever he's thinking is not what I had in mind. Staying alive versus becoming one of *them* wasn't a hard decision. Kill or be killed. I chose to be the one doing the killing."

Ryan understood it.

Either join or go against the grain. Stay alive or be in the crosshairs as a target for death. A stronger person would choose right. He knew he wasn't dealing with a lot of that. Sheep following the herd and the shepherd, though the wolf was really the one leading them astray.

As Ryan was about to speak, the soldier's radio came to life.

"Sit rep Thompson?"

The soldier chuckled. "You're screwed. I don't answer, they come."

The blade pressed back against the jugular.

"We both know that a first non-response won't do that. They'll try again in fifteen. If you don't answer, they might come," Ryan sneered in the man's ear.

Shifting his weight, the soldier quickly reached up attempting to dislodge the knife at his throat. Ryan pulled it away in one motion and came up from the back to press the tip at the base of the man's skull. Surprised at the swift and fluid action, the soldier went limp to the ground. He placed his hands behind his head and interlocked them.

"Who are you?" the solder asked as the butt of Ryan's MP5 came crashing down at the side of his head.

"I'm your worst nightmare," Ryan snarled.

He zip-tied Thompson's hands and feet before relieving him of all his gear. Grasping the soldier's uniform, Ryan dragged him to the hangar and locked him inside.

By the time he was done, Ryan had five minutes before another radio call. He couldn't afford to ignore it this time or reinforcements would come. With no idea where they might be or how long they would take to arrive, and as he still had work to do, he needed all the time he could manage to prepare.

Leaning against the metal wall, he patiently waited for the call.

The radio squawked again.

"Thompson? You better answer this time."

Pressing the mic button, Ryan answered in a low and slightly muffled voice. "All clear."

Noticing the muffled response, the voice asked, "What's the deal

Thompson? Your voice sounds weird."

Ryan pressed the mic. "Got a bunch of *them* wandering the airstrip and trying to keep them away."

"I'll send some men. They could use some target practice."

The mic chirped back. "Not necessary. They're milling about and Jackson chucked some cans in the ditch to get them to fall inside."

"Affirmative Thompson. Don't need to waste men if I don't have to. Too much other crap to do. I'll sit rep again at zero five hundred. Over and out."

Ryan had some time to get his ass in gear.

He knew things didn't always go smoothly and something always put a wrench in even a great plan. He had to act fast and get the hell out of there. A quick check of the airstrip with his goggles to check for any Un-Dead wandering around came back empty.

Satisfied, he hit the hangar for his prize.

The hangar door was locked from the inside. Moving cautiously, he went to the side door. It was too. Taking out his pry bar he wedged it between the lock and frame and gave it a swift push.

The door popped open with little effort.

He crept in and closed the door behind. It was blindingly black inside and he couldn't see his hand in front of his face. Flicking on the flashlight attached to the barrel of the MP5, he panned around to see what he could see.

Sitting in the middle of the hangar was something draped in a huge gray tarp. He couldn't tell what it was. Hoping for the gold, he walked over and grabbing a corner, pulled it off. Dust from years of sitting filled the air and made him cough. He wiped his face with the back of his glove and with the light gave it a once over.

Jackpot.

The ultralight stared at him, the once vibrant paint job covered in cobwebs and dust. He walked over, gazing at the aircraft and the simple design.

Fixed wing, open body, large rotor in the back for liftoff.

Takeoff and fly all over or get airborne and kill the engine to glide silently without detection. He had used one before on a few occasions, with a more sophisticated design and attributes for military use.

Flying wouldn't be a problem.

Light and agile with carbon fiber bodies, the military versions he longed for were silent and deadly depending on the armaments onboard. The civilian beasts could be loud and lumbering depending on the manufacturer and model. This one seemed expensive and probably well-constructed. He hoped it fit the bill.

Getting it running in his timeframe was the issue.

Plus, the color scheme stuck out like a sore thumb day or night. It needed some dark paint to blend into the dark of night and getting that might take some effort. A longshot he could even get it to work after sitting forever.

He felt it worth a chance to try.

Ryan checked his watch and had a few hours before sunrise. Working with only a flashlight complicated the process and his fingers ached. He knew he had to get it done and set out to get the beast in working order to at least move it to another location and finish the job. Dead battery, oxidized gas, flat tires, he had multiple fail points to overcome.

Wasting time meant at any moment soldiers could rain on his parade.

He hoped the gas cleaner and carb fuel he picked up from an auto parts store still had enough juice in them to spark the beast to life.

Sitting gas turned to almost turpentine.

He hoped it still had enough juice left in the tank to resurrect into some viable combustion. Pulling a metal waste bin over and throwing some added papers inside, he lit it up and hoped if he stoked it enough, he'd have sufficient light to work by and make quick repairs to get up and running.

The longer Mark had to search for and find David, the less chance his son and the others would be safe. Add to that Julia and Emma as captives and the information Thompson supplied, and the world was about to see a shit storm come to cement the end of humanity and welcome the rise of absolute madness.

The idea was crazy, insane in fact, though if he could do it and was successful, it was brilliant.

CHAPTER TWENTY-ONE

The ship sat docked at the first pier, a behemoth overshadowing the silos and warehouses of the old port.

It rose mightily above everything, a throwback to when naval superiority of the air was owned by America. The U.S.S. Yorktown, last of its name, had been officially decommissioned in late 1970. Eventually after many years and considerable refurbishment, it was turned into a floating museum, as the official account and story was told.

Behind the scenes, it had never left the Navy nor been relieved of its operational status.

The engines still fired, all electrical was left in working order, and armaments stored below deck at the ready if ever called back to service. When the public government failed and the world was lost, the shadow government of the United States, the real deep state, called the old workhorse back once more.

The Yorktown was one of many carriers like this, operating as museums in strategic locations around the country waiting for an opportunity to regain life and go active if ever the modern fleet was decimated or lost its ability to render aid. The virus swept across crews and ships the world over, leaving them literally dead in the water and unrecoverable. With bodies and madness aboard, the ghost fleet became the backup option and floating bases of government to continue forward.

The old ship was the only one to move to active status and utilization.

Some, through various predicaments and unforeseen screwups that prevented launching into duty, were left lifeless with no crew to support. Others were taken over in the early days by groups vying for safety which turned to bloodbaths as soldiers attempted coups.

The fires and explosions that followed essentially scuttled them to the bottoms of the oceans.

Sitting docked again made the Yorktown look like it had returned as a museum.

The activity and buzzing of soldiers aboard gave a different impression.

It had left port too early to be fully operational and the old planes on deck, long ago turned to tourist attractions as their engines and fuel were removed for safety, had been left on the flight deck or in the hangars below with plans for refurbishment instead of finding their way to the bottom of the ocean.

Collecting rust, the relics didn't matter much beyond places to take a break or hide from duty until air crews could help the birds rise from their deep slumber. Even three years later, the seamen worked tirelessly to repair and get the old carrier back to full use in the event she was needed longer than planned.

Food supplies were always an issue as no one had ever thought the Yorktown would be at sea and active for three years. Supplies dried up six months in.

Re-supply efforts at sea failed to materialize from any active ships.

Alone, the Yorktown wandered the seas cannibalizing other ships for goods. That only lasted for a short window as most vessels found their way to the bottom after incidents aboard or were too haphazard with what remained on board to risk Yorktown crew from attempting salvage efforts.

She sailed aimlessly for some time until a defined mission and plan was put in place, and then the old boat went about its business and ended up in the port to scavenge and re-supply itself with test subjects.

At least part of Thompson's intel was on target as Ryan watched from the opposite bank, hidden by the cattails growing high and cluttered together to offer him an unobstructed view.

It had been two days since the airport incident and avoiding detection as he maneuvered himself close enough to the Yorktown to see the activity onboard. It meant a slow creep through the vegetation. He was able to get the ultralight to fly and found a safe location in the countryside. Scrounged up some tools with the right supplies, and fixed it.

It had been a guess really.

He figured any farm or agri-business with machinery had their own shops and tools. He found one on the second pass before sunrise, and not too far away from the port in case he had to venture completely on foot.

An old family vineyard he knew by name.

It wasn't until he landed near the barns used to store the grape bins and passed the old fading sign that he put it together. It was the last wine he enjoyed with Julia and figured it was fate that brought him to the farm. Maybe find a bottle or two to pack away and hopefully enjoy if their reunion was successful was a thought that kept his spirits high.

Get drunk during the end of times with your wife.

Sounded like a great date night.

The property had long been abandoned. Though for him, not ransacked like many places given its country location. He rummaged around the sheds and found most of what he required in old black paint used for trailer frames and a surprise in a sealed fifty-five-gallon drum of gasoline. Taking a few ounces out and throwing a light to it, it burned nice and bright. Plenty of spark left to run the engine of the ultralight.

The tires had not quite gone flat from sitting in the hangar which made the takeoff and landing as bumpy as it could be without rattling everything apart. An old hand pump for tractors took time to prime and air the rubbers and with a lot of work he got the tires full.

Some extra bolts to hold a few necessities, a good wipe down of the electrical and gauges, and he was good to go.

With the ultralight fixed and crudely painted to blend in with the black of the night, he had flown in the day before using the dark to scout locations and glided to a remote dirt road to land.

Hid it deep in the tall vegetation that had overgrown the land.

From there he hiked through fields and crawled the rest of the way to his present spot before light and made himself at home.

He kept vigil listening to the transmissions from the pilfered radio to see if any alarm had been raised from his time at the airport. He couldn't leave a witness and take a radio without word getting back to Mark and the possibility of him putting it all together. With not many quick options for his time crunch, he did the only thing that came to mind.

He made things look like the soldiers got caught by some Bolts.

Sacrificing a life was an easy decision and given his final conversation with Thompson after he came to, it was evident the man had lost his humanity to the virus. Ryan thought he might be able to spare him his life, show some mercy. The callous nature and extreme final vitriol the soldier spewed forth showed any amount of decency left him long ago.

Killing someone like that made the deed acceptable, though far from the man he felt he was today. He chalked it up to what Thompson had said about kill or be killed. He made it quick with a blade to the back of the skull and disposed of the bodies as best he could to fake a Bolt attack.

Well-placed frags detonated and blew apart the remains.

Ryan smashed one radio to pieces along with a two-way he found in the office and mingled them together to look like they belonged to the soldiers. Some old towels dipped in blood and wiped along the hangar doors completed the faked scene. He hoped it worked, and given the radio play he heard later, it fooled Thompson's replacements.

Crisp air kept him awake. Sitting concealed watching the ship and foot traffic as the sun rose and life aboard awoke was boring work he considered a necessary task to gather intel on his enemy.

Clock the guard patrols, shift changes, who left and came aboard.

It was mundane for anyone else but an ex-special forces operative who knew what to look for and plan his attack. The patrols were pretty consistent with their routines, though they seemed lax in paying much attention.

Thirty minutes between passes on the hour and half hour.

Two guards together circled the deck and would stop fore and aft of the deck for a smoke break before moving on. Below deck was a bit different. The deck doors were open and the occasional person spotted gazing out over the fields before disappearing back inside. He saw people dressed in scrubs, soldiers, civilians, and even what looked to be patients in gowns with escorts.

The test subjects, their faces worn with fear and eyes vacant, tore at Ryan.

He could only imagine what they had gone through and continued to face. He thought of Julia and Emma, wondering what their life had been like for the last three years.

Julia was a strong woman, Emma, she was only a child.

What went through his daughter's mind every day? Did she feel abandoned by him because he couldn't save her, though not by choice? That thought killed him. He had always been her protector and had failed.

He had to right it, no matter what.

Still and hidden by the weeds, he watched for hours taking mental notes. Drew diagrams in his head of potential access points that could be breached with relative ease. Counted the soldiers who guarded the port. Scoured the aircraft carrier for any sign of Mark.

He came up empty.

He did see plenty of action around with soldiers gearing up and heading out in vehicles to only come back hours later seemingly empty-handed. As day to turned to night and his intel piled up, Ryan developed his plan to breach the Yorktown. It was supposed to be a recon mission only, a chance to learn and observe up close and get out.

Since the day he had left John and the survivors, things had gone a different path from their original conversation. The first plan had been to watch from the high rise and gain insight. Then the bridges blew, and he saw the soldiers retreat in watercraft towards the port. Flying in by the ultralight, even a few miles out, the Yorktown was visible.

The old ship put a completely different spin on the situation.

He had hoped to track back to Mark and some building or camp. Having the aircraft carrier in the mix and its ability to weigh anchor and leave, time turned critical and plans no longer concrete.

It was the way of the special operative to be fluid to current events and be able to adapt.

The rust kept flaking off, the old ways returning. It was a bit unnerving the way it all came back easily, so fluid and controlled.

Like it never left.

And to a degree, it never had. He knew deep down he had evolved, the way in which he let it still involved utilizing the methods and habits of his old life. He knew what needed to be done, and as events unfolded, he sensed he was beginning to enjoy being back in the saddle, reigns in hand, riding into the abyss guns blazing and his blood on fire.

Damn, Ryan thought, *I am what I am.*

It was clear he had to alert John and share the information. It left him faced with a dilemma. Leave and go back to tell John and risk exposure or the Yorktown leaving port.

He could radio a cryptic message.

Hope John understood it and without the signal being triangulated to Ryan's location as the source and if John responded, the survivors exposed. None provided the perfect response or answer and his options were limited. There was one solution available.

It was crazy, stupid, and downright idiotic to even think about it.

The risk was great. If it succeeded the outcome would buy them time. It also would be unexpected, and he ventured a wild guess, that a sense of superiority ran rampant. An old aircraft carrier and trained soldiers at your disposal might make some feel like they had overwhelming odds in their favor. The world was gone and the new order attempting to seed their future reign felt invincible as there were no real enemies in their way that they felt they couldn't overthrow.

Thompson had spilled as much.

If they felt anyone offered a legitimate threat, guards would be posted at strategic points and not on a thirty-minute patrol that offered up a window to launch an attack or diversion.

Patrols would be in the water to keep watch.

And from his observation, the port would be more heavily guarded than what he could see besides the few men walking around. Attacking the interior of the ship probably never crossed anyone's mind.

He thought it might work.

If he could get close enough to do it and high tail out of there, it was possible. Old navy ships like the Yorktown, were not nuclear-powered aircraft carriers.

They ran engines with boiler rooms.

It meant that exhaust had to be vented somewhere, and those vents, or funnels, traveled up through the decks and superstructure to release fumes and hot air. Well-protected by the design of the ship, any kind of bomb or targeted hit by a plane was by chance.

The original Yorktown had been disabled during World War II by a direct hit from a lucky bomb.

Its funnels ran up through the island, the command center of the ship that sat atop the flight deck and ran all ship operations. The stack wasn't straight up like most funnels and for this version of the Yorktown.

Not directly up through the middle of the island.

It angled to the rear at around a forty-five-degree angle to vent the exhaust away from the ship as it sailed. A better design, and a much better location isolated to the rear versus the old one that came up the middle and presented problems with all kinds of obstructions in the way.

The way the ship was positioned with the island closest to the dock was what meant it might work.

Ryan went over it in his mind. If he glided the ultralight towards the ship in the dead of night, between patrols and when activity was at its low point, he could approach from the water side and aim for the funnel. It would have to be quick and very precise.

He would be an object in motion and only have one shot.

Float to the funnel and heave a bag of grenades down the chute and hit the engine on the ultralight after he was well clear, as the first explosion rocked the ship. He would use the port's siloes as cover after he went on by and be gone before anyone knew what had happened.

It was insane and absolutely dangerous. He liked it.

If anyone saw him approach, even all blacked out in the ultralight, he was a sitting duck out in the open with little recourse to do much of anything. Timing had to be perfect and the flight path direct to keep altitude and be able to drop low enough to be close on the pass and drop the bag in the right spot.

There were a million factors that could go wrong.

One screw up sent the plan south and meant getting caught, failure, or death. The odds were well against him and given the scenario and circumstances if he could succeed and do it as a ghost, it bought plenty of time. Disabling the ship with no way to repair it quickly meant a chance at a rescue and possibly putting an end to the evilness lurking aboard.

He let the idea percolate and watched for a bit longer.

More to build up his resolve at the absurd feat he was contemplating to carry out than gather more information.

He wasn't scared.

He had done similar things in the past when called upon to do them and succeeded. Special operators were a functional bunch of lunatics, not in a bad sense or meant to be derogatory. They took on the impossible and made it work. Fear never entered their bloodstream. It made you weak and vulnerable to mistakes.

Caution? Sure.

Every man and woman who wore the uniform and was adorned with special patches gave testament to it. Women started serving in the shadows, though as a matter of public record or the growing whispers were never acknowledged. They were the ace card to call upon for those special times a softer touch was required. A lumbering man might muck everything up and screw the whole mission.

Women performed the rough jobs and did it right alongside the men.

As more recent additions to the arsenal of tools they had been earning their places and progressing into full-blown assets as time went on. He knew a few who he'd want at his side over some men. Times were changing, and a resource regardless of gender who could perform the task at hand was the best choice.

Then, the world decided to go dark.

Great soldiers worked the shadows and acted with cautious intent to protect themselves and their team members, always to ensure mission success. It meant intelligent thought over recklessness.

The drive to fight and live for another day.

Ryan had seen the gung-ho renegades who ran into the fray never to return. They were usually the young ones, eager to make their mark and show their worth.

Those imbeciles washed out in time.

The young ones like him when he started out, who questioned and reviewed, looked outside the box for solutions, were the ones who got the brunt of hazing and ridicule at first. Eventually they won out their counterparts to become true leaders when they showed that thinking it out over being a chicken with its head cut off and guns blazing away ended up tagged and bagged in the end.

There was a difference between being reckless and cautious, and doing the impossible or running right into the fire.

Some things seemed like the only logical choice when all else got checked off the box. You weighed options, debated, ran a scenario, and did it all over to ensure it was the right call. No mission was ever perfect, and some seemed at the outset a sure death sentence. It was the cracks in the impossible that allowed options, the weak links that presented opportunities.

Sometimes, you had to find the silver lining and take the risk and costs for a chance to win.

CHAPTER TWENTY-TWO

Ryan waited until it was dark enough to conceal his retreat.

Having to crawl through the fields and along ditches, it took some time to get back to the ultralight and begin preparations. He was midway through when the radio crackled.

"Base to scout teams. Acknowledge, over."

The sudden interruption startled him. Ryan stopped his work and immediately sat down to listen.

"Alpha Team. Go. Over."

"Bravo Team. Go. Over."

"Charlie Team. Go. Over."

Three scout teams on the prowl. It meant more ground to cover and a wider berth between teams. That meant in the event of discovery the survivors might have a window to escape.

The voice spoke. It lacked any emotion, the words almost monotone.

"Sit rep. I want information."

Ryan knew the person on the other end. Even with the lack of humanity in the words he knew Mark's voice. It had been a long time, since the push out of the helo, that he had heard him speak. The words always echoed in his mind, the vitriol Mark spoke as he pushed Ryan and he fell to the ocean.

He could never erase the voice from his head.

Alpha and Bravo reported in an hour later. Neither had come across anything extraordinary besides a group of Un-Dead wandering a corridor of town stuck between buildings. Most, because of the loss of brain function to key areas necessary for survival, had died out over time since a living body required nutrients and water. Ryan rarely came across them much anymore. A group was a bit significant, and Mark must have thought that too.

"Bring me three and eliminate the rest. Over."

Charlie Team didn't immediately respond. The lack of punctuality must have hit a nerve.

The anger in Mark's words spilled through. "Sit rep Charlie. Answer me you fuck. Over."

The radio cracked and a muffled sound could be heard and instantly disappeared.

A few seconds later, Charlie Team answered. "I'm not sure what it is. We found some fresh bodies. Not eaten. Looks like they were tortured and strung up. Over."

The silence lasted for a minute, maybe more.

When Mark spoke, the depths of his rage leaked out the earpiece into Ryan's head. "Bring me Rebel Fucker! Over."

"Roger base. Over and out."

Rebel Fucker?

Ryan couldn't help laughing at the nickname. His guess was the person using it gave it to himself and not something Mark pinned on some poor sucker.

A Brainer with a sense of humor?

Not likely. Probably a description or attribute of what the man had done or liked to do.

The revelation of bodies being found and at the hands of Brainers caused concern. Fresh kills could mean any number of things, and without more information there was little to go on. It didn't mean the hiding spot of the survivors had been found.

It also didn't mean it hadn't and David and the others weren't in serious trouble.

He needed to know more as it might change the plan, though diverging from it meant losing an opportunity to cripple the Yorktown. He was in a tough spot and no amount of weighing options over others was the right path.

His gut would need to proceed on this one.

It had never been wrong. Got him in and out of some tough spots. Saved hundreds of lives and earned him respect. That was years ago in the rearview mirror, and he had the now to worry about.

Not that he was worried.

He believed in himself with the rust attached. He just wanted to get it done and be over. That wasn't much to ask. Chip away at Mark and get the family band back together. Focus and get the job done. Nodding to himself, Ryan smiled and got to work.

He felt like a lone gunman.

The man on a mission, only he can rationalize the purpose. Manifesto in hand ready to reveal his words to the world. He knew he wasn't insane, at least didn't think he had boarded the bus.

Felt his resolve tightening and mind ticking off the boxes.

The inner dialog helped speed along his preparations and when he was ready, he knew there was no turning back. Switch on and a breeze to carry him, Ryan hit the gas and lifted off.

Taking in the view, the air was crisp, the cold of the night eating at his old bones.

Adrenaline provided a bit of comfort against it. Nothing except a warm bed and good night's sleep was going to erase the feeling in his muscles and once it was over, the tremors that would only add to the misery.

Ryan tilted to the left a bit.

The ultralight followed suit and maneuvered to the new path. The Yorktown in all of its glory was right in front of him and he'd be right on top of it in seconds.

Still undetected.

The patrol was on the opposite end of the flight deck and no one else ventured out in the cold night. As he approached, he knew he had one shot at it, as if he missed the chance making a turn around the ship's island might be seen by someone on watch or caught in full view through the large windows around the tower.

His path followed an obstructed view as no windows or doors offered detection.

Make the move and hit the target and a hard right turn between the siloes and he would be gone in moments. Miss and he had a split second to decide yes or no on making another pass. Hoped he didn't need to think.

Three seconds. Two seconds. One.

On three Ryan pulled one of the pins and shoved it into the bag with the other grenades he had recovered from the soldiers at the airport. On one he leaned out and over, arm extended, and dropped the package. Immediately banked hard right and aimed for the middle of the old siloes. As he looked down and around, he saw a vast sea of emptiness.

Literally, nothing. No soldiers. No vehicles. Nothing at all around the port's dock.

The desolation was troubling.

He figured there would be something to see and the lack of anything made him feel an uneasiness inside. As the ultralight made the turn and he took it back to center headed for the siloes, he caught it out of the corner of his eye. A sudden flash of light lit him up and he could see his shadow emblazoned on one of the siloes.

A larger-than-life image painted black against the soft gray cement of the silo wall.

It reminded him of a dragon, something some poor farmer or castle dweller would have seen after a fiery attack burned their village to the ground, the figment of their imagination running wild.

It was momentary and like a blip, he was past it.

The explosion came and deafened the quiet of the night and he took the opportunity to hit the ignition and fire up the engine. He pressed the button and waited.

Nothing.

He hit it again. Hoped it would start.

Silence.

His altitude began to fade, and the ground crept up beneath him. Even hundreds of feet in the air, his decent was rapidly dropping the ultralight. Within ten seconds he'd be hitting buildings and miss his window between the siloes. Reaching down, he pulled the primer for the carburetor. Never a praying man, he muttered one this time to the gods of machinery and pressed the button.

Dammit, come on! Ryan yelled in his head.

Finally, the blades roared to life, the sound hidden by the noises erupting from the ship. In an instant he was gone, a ghost that if anyone had seen him would second guess themselves amid the ensuing chaos aboard the old aircraft carrier.

He charted a path on the outskirts of town, away from the heart of the city and where he knew and believed was the focus of Mark's search. It took him far out on a course to land near the hidden garage where the Humvee was stored. With the ship disabled and the crew diverted to the hard work of ship repair and nowhere to go, his attention centered on checking in with John and seeing his son. The Brainer killings brought a new sense of urgency and especially the nature of the deaths.

If they were John's people, what happened?

If not, who were they and where did they come from?

Answers were needed immediately and how they moved ahead with the master plan of rescuing those on the ship and ending it once and for all had to move forward.

He couldn't see any other way.

Nearly out of gas, the ultralight floated to the ground and came to a stop. He had killed the engine and simply glided for a few miles to ensure he wasn't heard and conserve fuel in case he had to fire it up again. There weren't any hazards blocking his descent to the road and he came in rather hot and hit the brakes. Thankfully he didn't smash into the wall that was the dead end of the street. Rolling it to the side, the garage entrance at the old storage yard was still closed and the access door secured.

The toothpick he left to check for any incursions was wedged firmly in place.

He climbed the down spout up to the gutter and hoisted himself atop the wall. Listening, it was quiet. He hopped up, grabbed the plumbing vent pipe and pulled himself onto the roof. He gazed around from his vantage point.

Nothing moved.

Quietly, he worked his way to the skylight, checked that toothpick was still there, opened the top, and climbed down.

The interior of the shop was as he left it.

Ryan quickly raised the door and wheeled the ultralight into the safety of the garage and secured his makeshift interior lock. The Humvee sat in the corner and his gear all lined up, ready to resupply. He dropped off a few items he had picked up, the remaining grenades, extra ammo, vest plates, and put his own ruck, vest, and weapons down.

Settled into the recliner near the tool bench.

Spending days in uncomfortable positions and places didn't help an aging body. Being able to stretch and relax was a much-needed break to rest his weary bones and prepare for what was ahead.

A few winks of shut eye would do him some good, and the well-worn chair a relief to lay flat for a change.

Ryan closed his eyes briefly, enjoying the rest and comfort. He had listened to the radio on his escape from the port. By all accounts, no one thought they had been attacked. Seemed they believed there had been an internal ship issue to cause the explosion. The extent of the damage undetermined, at least it bought time. Deep in thinking about the Yorktown, he drifted until dreams overtook his thoughts.

He must have fallen asleep from pent up fatigue.

The tremors and muscles cramps came all at once, sending his body writhing in pain. These were the worst he had ever experienced. He tried to ride them out as the pain grew worse. His head started to get fuzzy and he felt woozy, things that had never happened. Maybe he was dehydrated from being gone and had not had enough water intake.

He wasn't sure.

He thought he had kept liquid consumption at the right level. It could be the virus and age catching up all at once. A tired body vulnerable to it.

He didn't know.

The torment went on forever or what seemed like it. Finally subsided and the waves of pain washed out to sea. He ached, hurt like hell. His head spun and his thoughts were convoluted.

It took a few minutes to get back to a sense of normal.

When he felt like he wouldn't keel over, Ryan got up and grabbed a water from the top of the tool bench and slugged it down in a few gulps. He chucked the empty into the big blue bin used for garbage and took another water, this time sipping it. His head began to feel better, and his brain hurt less. After five minutes his body felt back to its old self, minus the usual aches and pains from an episode.

What the hell was that? he thought.

The tremors and shakes had never been like that before. They were somewhat consistent in duration and pain level. This was a nuclear event.

His earpiece chirped to interrupt his internal monologue.

"Base. Charlie Team. Over."

Base answered. "What?"

"Rebel Fucker is M.I.A. Over."

He heard the dismay in the man's voice. It wasn't Mark. "What do you mean? Over."

"The group is gone. No one is here. Over."

Shit, Ryan thought. *The game is getting complicated. Brainers are a wild card and with them on the loose and bodies being left around something is going to happen and make a bigger mess of things.*

The man responded. This time, composed. "Affirmative. Your orders are to track and find. Bring him back ASAP. Over."

"Confirmed," the soldier of Charlie Team replied. "Over and out."

It was one thing to have to deal with Mark and his band of merry men. It was another to have psychos on the lam wreaking havoc on survivors. They were teamed up with some kind of agreement.

Did something change?

It seemed the Brainers were going AWOL and not keeping the pact and information flowing to Mark. Otherwise, the discovery of dead bodies wouldn't have been much of a surprise. Ryan assumed regular updates were a prerequisite for the unsteady relationship. And if it was failing and the Brainers were off doing their own thing, a chink in the armor maybe, he might be able to use it to his advantage.

Sunrise was fast approaching, and he needed sleep. Tired and foggy headed wasn't going to do anyone any good. A few hours of rest to recharge were in order and soon refreshed, hit the day hard.

Miraculously he fell right back to sleep.

When he finally opened his eyes, it was well past ten. Feeling refreshed for a change, he got up and grabbed a water. Thirsty, he drank another and another. His thirst finally quenched, a protein bar filled his belly and some old coffee to wash it down.

The day ahead was filled with unknowns and radio traffic had been silent since the last dispatch.

The Brainers must not have been found yet and he was sure soldiers were still canvassing the city. Moving around would be difficult though necessary, if he was to update John and find out what was going on with the dead bodies.

He changed out of his all-black special ops garb to his urban BDUs to help blend back in with the drabness of the city grays. Replacing his gear with the appropriate colored tac vest and rucksack from the Humvee, he brought along his sniper rifle and scope as an extra precaution. The M82A1 sniper rifle with ten round magazines was his first rifle in the service.

He knew it inside and out.

Converted for a lefty sharpshooter, it was like an old friend back after years of being estranged. Which way the round pulled depending on the wind, the maximum distance he could squeeze out of it and still make a kill, even gravity's attempt to alter its trajectory. He figured he was going to need it to send some messages and level the playing field.

Maybe, not as soon as he thought.

All geared up and ready to vacate, Ryan set out.

CHAPTER TWENTY-THREE

The morning was cold and brisk.

The bridge explosion fires continued to smolder, shrouding the sun in clouds and smoke. Throw in a few new ones from burning buildings in the distance and the city was cast in a blanket that wouldn't turn down.

A soft wind blew it all inward.

Between the buildings a gray haze limited visibility some, a good thing for him, bad for the lungs. He draped a bandana around his face to help quell the ashes from getting into his nose and made the trek to the garage to see John.

Like a fly on flypaper Ryan hugged the walls of the buildings, vigilant for any sound or movement.

Daylight with soldiers and Brainers around was a disaster waiting to happen and left him little choice. Waiting until dark lost precious hours and the possibility of David and the survivors being compromised. He knew the risks.

He wasn't some ordinary guy.

While the odds were greater, he'd been in worse situations. He was a trained ghost and killer, adept at being unseen and striking from the shadows to strike fear and chaos.

Mark's soldiers had nothing on him.

He had seen it, based on their retreat when confronted by the survivors. Their plan of attack was weak, their execution poor, and seeing their grim faces as they slunk away told him all he needed to know about them.

He knew a few were braver than the rest.

When push came to shove, he could isolate and engage them effectively and eliminate one by one to reduce their numbers. Separate the groups and cause confusion among the ranks and he'd gain the upper hand. It would take time to whittle them away, hitting at the right time and place.

That would start the downward spiral.

With the Brainers, there was always a wildcard to deal with that meant no plan of attack went right. In his experience you had to cut the head off the snake to create a mass effect. While they usually fought as individuals without much coordination, they did follow a leader.

Find and kill him and you had an opportunity to strike hard.

They worked on a hierarchy of rule. With the head gone some vied to step up and into the top dog spot. Sometimes it was obvious who would ascend, and the rest would eventually obey. Other times it created factions and infighting. Use that time of disorganization to drive a wedge and annihilate and they would turn tail and run with whatever remained.

He had seen their disorganization up close and from afar over the years.

As he made his way from city to city, hiding and staying an arm's length or two in the distance, he saw a few bands of them in his travels. Even witnessed them implode on themselves when vying for control. When he could sow chaos from a sniper scope away, he plucked them off, then scurried off to live another day.

He found a small amount of pleasure in the shootings. Not from a thrill killer mentality or the love of death. Simply in knowing one less asshole meant some innocent person might live to fight for life.

When their numbers got whacked, the Brainers, clueless to his accuracy with his long-range killing machine sending a large caliber head shot, they became paranoid and struck out on the closest member of their factions.

Always mistrusting, each assumed the next guy was going to kill them.

When death struck the only recourse was internal revenge, and what a show when an entire band decimated itself to oblivion. He hadn't had a chance in a long time to deliver the kind of anarchy the Brainers required to send them into a fighting frenzy and reset order.

The light needed an advantage over the dark, and hope was in short supply.

Brain on overdrive, the journey to John and the survivors proved slow and steady. The sounds of ripped banners still flying in front of businesses flapped with the wind. The occasional animal scurried across the street in search of food, though within the inner city any street faire was long gone. Ryan kept his pace and stayed as hidden as practical given the openness of this particular block. There were few entryways to recede into and no alleys to duck in for cover. A few broken windows could be crawled through.

What lurked inside was a guess.

He kept going, another thirty minutes of careful travel ahead. He could see his destination, he simply needed to maintain caution and ensure no one came upon him as he closed the distance.

It was less than a full city block when he saw them.

They looked like mannequins at first. As he neared it was evident, they were people. Ryan stopped and hunkered down to make himself less of a target and visible, backing into a doorway carefully and raising his M4 sight to his eye.

As he peered through it, he recognized two of the bodies.

One was one of the guards he passed on his trip into the old fort. The second was Roger, part of John's leadership team. The men were in the open and visible, having been obstructed from his view down the block by an empty shopping cart and old tube television set. They were posed on the ground as if runners who had fallen over and were still in step. It wasn't natural and the hair on Ryan's arms stood up.

Trap? he thought to himself.

Any sane person upon seeing them would run over to see what had happened. Offer aid and assistance.

They looked alive.

He knew better and could see the blood pooling around the heads through his scope. This part of the block had no windows opposite him and hugging the wall kept him hidden from above. If it was a trap, the killers were either above or down the block. If not and meant to send a message, he wouldn't know unless he walked on over.

He wasn't the stupid kind. He needed another way to know.

Ryan scanned ahead through his scope in search of tracks. He had noticed a bloody footprint and looked for any companions to it. A trail of blood wandered off to the right and disappeared. Beyond that, he heard no noises and saw nothing else to assist a decision. Taking a deep breath, he stepped further back into the doorway to completely hide his presence.

He turned and pushed gently on the door.

It was locked.

A good sign as unlocked could mean trouble, though locked from the inside presented the same dilemma. Reaching into one of his vest pockets he pulled out a small pouch. Setting his M4 against the wall, he pulled out two tools and began to pick the lock.

A lock pick set was a standard tool of the trade for ghosts since bashing down doors created too much noise and destruction.

He worked the keyhole, fidgeted around a bit, and catching the right part of the spindle was able to turn the lock and gently push it open. Returning the kit to its pocket he grabbed his rifle and carefully stepped inside.

The interior of the first floor had not seen life for years.

The dank smell of dust and stale air lingered in his nostrils. No decaying stench permeated his nose and it seemed free of any Un-Dead. As he glanced around and accustomed his eyes to the low light, he realized he was in a department store. From the outside it didn't appear that way, a single door leading in. As you got past the entryway and it opened up, the enormity hit home. It was deceiving if you had small expectations.

An oddity for sure.

He kept an eye out to listen for a few minutes and scanned the first floor. Quiet reigned supreme. Taking the hint, Ryan stood and moved to the escalator towards the back and walked up to the second floor. As he reached the top, bent down and stopped out of caution, he was met with silence.

Nothing moved or made a sound.

Moving swiftly around the corner, he proceeded to the third-floor escalator and went up. Nearing the top, he stopped and crouched low. He heard voices, low and muffled off to the left. Slowly, he crept up each step until he had nowhere else to go for cover.

"He'll be here," one of the voices offered.

"Can't miss them outside," the other answered.

Ryan leaned around the corner and back. Catching a glimpse, and seeing the two men facing the opposite direction, he quickly moved around the corner up behind them. Pressing the barrel of his M4 into the back of one of the men's heads, he tapped the other's leg with his foot.

"Don't move or you die," Ryan whispered.

He heard the piss flow and leak to the floor.

"Ah shit man, don't kill us please," the man on the left pleaded, his voice shaking with fear.

"What the fuck have we done to you assholes? You crazy ass mother-" the man on the right began when Ryan kicked the back of his locked knee, sending him crumbling to the ground.

Ryan lowered his rifle. "You can turn around."

The man still standing threw his hands in the air and turned. As he came full face with Ryan and recognized him, he lowered them. "You made me piss my pants."

The man on the floor looked up, the pain on his face from the knee blow still reeling. "What the hell man?"

Ryan stared at them both. "Backs to the escalator, really? Were you waiting to die or what?"

The men nodded, realizing the stupidity of their actions.

The man on the left, who Ryan knew as Peter from John's introduction before he left, motioned with his hand to keep their voices down. "I'm guessing you saw the welcome party outside, right?" he began. "When shit went down John left us hoping you'd find a way back here if you made it out alive."

"What happened?" Ryan asked.

The man on the ground finally got up. Ryan didn't know him. "Still an asshole," he mumbled.

Peter reached over and smacked his friend in the side of the head. "Shut it, Mike."

Ryan's impatience came out. "I'm waiting."

Peter nodded. "Sorry dude. You left on whatever it was you were doing. It's been days man. Well, those crazies started circling around getting close and then too close. John gave the order to bug out. Told us you would know where since if we got captured, we were done for anyway. The less we knew the better. Left some of us back if you came."

Mike nodded furiously in agreement.

Ryan saw something in the younger man's face. Noticed the tattoo on his upper arm and softened his demeanor. "Where'd you serve, Son?"

Mike looked confused at first, before it registered. "Kandahar. A few other places too. How'd you know?"

Ryan tapped his upper sleeve. "Marine tattoo. Unless you know someone who has that particular ink, you wouldn't have a clue. I know a few good men."

Mike laughed and nodded. "Only the few. Dirty work, Sir."

Ryan leaned over and patted Mike on the shoulder. He knew the dangers the young man had faced. He'd been there too. Mike's particular tattoo was for a specialized combat platoon that rooted insurgents out in the mountains. Risky work mountain climbing and staying alive against really bad odds.

"Sorry for the knee kick. You know not to turn your back, right?"

A sheepish grin and nod from Mike. "Yes, Sir. Complacency and comfort get you killed. Won't happen again." And, thinking for a minute, eyebrow raised, he asked, "What about you?"

Ryan shrugged his shoulders. "Me? I'm a ghost."

The words registered and the meaning was clear. He had heard the rumors, had caught wind of stories. Glimpses of people in and out of base. The interloper attached to his team that in the dead of night was gone in the morning. While he wanted to know, Mike knew some things were better left alone.

Getting up, Mike reached out, hand extended. "Thank you for not killing me, Sir."

Ryan accepted the handshake. "Call me Ryan. No rank in civilian life."

"Thank you, Ryan. I won't fail again." Mike sounded sincere.

Ryan smiled. "For the unofficial record, I wouldn't have killed you outright. I'd see if you had intel for me. Then, well…" His voice trailed off to make the point clear, more as a joke to lighten the mood.

Peter's face turned ashen white. "Shit. I'm glad you didn't."

Turning back to Mike, Ryan responded, "And, you are welcome."

Confused at first, Mike frowned, and realizing Ryan was responding to the not killing him part, nodded.

They took seats near the upper floor windows, keeping watch on the street below. Peter and Mike told Ryan what had happened, and the details left a pit in his stomach. The survivors had been secure and safe until a returning group of lookouts got caught and tortured.

They must have been the bodies Charlie Team found.

Before they were finally captured, after some time eluding and hiding in abandoned stores, they managed to send a coded message to John. He had no idea when or which way the assailants would come, and not even who they were since his people had not been close enough to see while hiding out and he gambled on the evacuation. Some went one way while the others went another.

A division of strength and numbers with more opportunity to have people live to fight another day.

The result was to secure predetermined safe locations with the other group not having knowledge of either's whereabouts. When the time was right and according to a preset time, they'd communicate and regroup.

One group went east toward the suburbs and hit a blockade of some type. Mike told him the radio calls seemed to indicate they might have made it through, though it had been silent from them for a while.

Ryan wondered if it was the crosstown bridge debris that affected their escape.

John's group headed north towards the more industrial part of town. Lots of places to hide and defend, but also potential exposure because of buildings being spread out. He knew where they were going and hoped they made it.

It was the best place to hide and be unseen among ruins and debris left piled high from destruction.

No word since from John and the uneasiness Ryan felt ate his insides. He had to trust the silence. If it was a massacre, John would have sent a warning over the radio.

The only people who knew the locations of where both groups headed were John and Ryan. It kept people safe to minimize information. The death of the lookouts proved that point. He wondered what to do as the plan seemed to be crumbling away. He needed to talk to John and confer, share what he had seen, see if the plan would still work.

The ship was an outlier, an unknown that became a player in the game.

The vacant dock offered some trepidation. While that might have been due to soldiers out searching for the survivors, he expected at least some men and vehicles there. Nothing around painted a very odd picture and one that didn't sit well. He had to think and decide what the immediate work ahead entailed and move forward with the knowns.

Taking a last bite of his energy bar after letting Peter and Mike's story sink in, Ryan looked at the young men. "What are you two going to do?"

Peter looked sideways at Mike. "My ass is staying put. We've seen too many of them crazies around. I am not getting tortured and left to die. I'll take my chances here."

Mike swallowed the last of his Twinkie, a rare delicacy and find given its shelf life. "I don't wish to get dead either. I'm also not a pussy. I did my time and can be an asset if you need me."

Ryan grinned. "No time for pussies. And I appreciate the offer of help. I need you to do something else for me. Ghosts are a solo mission."

Mike smiled. "Understood Sir, I mean, Ryan. I couldn't not offer and leave a fellow, what should I call it, another brother from a different mother twice removed hanging?"

Ryan laughed at the funny analogy and appreciated the attempt. "I'd probably say the illegitimate child of the third mistress sent off to a boarding school on an uninhabited island with no return ticket."

"I have no idea what you two are talking about," Peter shrugged.

"Probably best," Mike chimed in. Looking at Ryan, his face serious, he asked, "You've seen some stuff I'm sure, and I'm not asking for details. What are our chances? This is nothing like anything I've seen."

Ryan sighed, knowing the answer Mike sought. "I'll answer the second part first. Seeing something doesn't mean you can't overcome it. You trained for it and just never got to confront it. Fall back on what you know inside and use it. As for chances. I won't lie to either of you. It's crap. They have an old aircraft carrier docked at the port. It's disabled and it can't go anywhere. Men and supplies outnumber all of us, and throw in the crazy Brainers as I call them since they've lost what brain they had, and we're all outgunned and outmanned. Dismal at best. But," he winked, "they don't have a ghost to even the odds."

Peter's eyes grew huge after hearing Ryan speak.

Mike simply laughed and patted his friend. "We'll be fine Pete. We have our very own superhero on our side."

"What the hell is a Ghost, and no one ever mentioned anything about an aircraft carrier. And what do you mean it's disabled? We're screwed," Peter trembled, his voice shaking with each word.

"Think a ninja on steroids, Pete. No one sees him coming or going," Mike answered.

Thinking about it, Peter's eyes narrowed. "Ninja. That's badass. Only one?"

Mike shook his head. "How many movies have you seen? The good guy is always a lone black figure taking out a hundred bad guys."

Pete still didn't like it. "But one? We need an army of ninjas to take on these crazy people. They're all over the place. The living ones and the nuts hiding in the dark who grab you to eat. One guy isn't going to make a difference."

"Dude. Chill on the negative energy. I've told you a bit of my days hunting insurgents down, right?"

A nod.

"Okay. And the guy who came into camp by himself, kept to the side, went out with us, and then was gone?"

"I remember."

"Well, every time that happened, all kinds of shit went down. Made our work easier. That guy did things quiet and quick and the enemy never saw it coming. Gave us a chance to go and do our jobs."

Pete still wasn't convinced. "I'm just saying. One guy seems like the less-than-ideal number to get things done."

Ryan reached out and tapped Peter on the leg. Knowing it would help calm the young man and focus the two on what he needed from them, he filled them in.

CHAPTER TWENTY-FOUR

Ryan set out after dark.

Nighttime was his, the place for an old ghost to float among the shadows. He had spent some time before heading out simply talking to the young men, a chance to banter and have a semblance of normal conversation with two humans.

He missed conversation with people.

While Pete the adorable gray cat was a great listener, he wasn't the chatty type. Having a chance to converse with actual real live individuals, not knowing if he would ever be able to again, was important to his mental health.

Not that isolation had sent him down the road to insanity.

He did prefer the coziness of just him and his cat. If he were going to reunite with his family, he needed to dust off the rust and get back to being able to put some conversational words together more in tune with life than simply existence. Julia and the kids deserved better than hearing about survival tactics and how to spot the dens of the Un-Dead.

He left Peter and Mike with some frags and MREs to wait it out until further word from him or John giving an all clear and a specific destination and path to follow to get to the next safe place. While he could use the help and knew Mike could be useful, he needed the ease of travel and movement free of responsibility and worry over protecting another life.

Tight spaces, quick steps to cover, staying frozen for hours to watch and wait, it was not something you could teach in a few minutes.

Mike had some of the skills from his service time and was not your average grunt from his background. He was not experienced enough, forced to make life or death decisions on the edge of a razor. Being boots deep in blood and dirt and still alive spoke volumes.

Still wasn't the same.

The young man could follow orders. Act and think on his feet when faced with multiple threats? Stare death down and accept it if the odds were against him, and keep going until the end without curling into a ball?

Ryan couldn't ask him to commit to a potential one-way ticket to death's door.

He knew he might survive if luck fell his way. He couldn't guarantee the same for Mike. Tucked away in the top floor of the department store with exit strategies if it came to it, Peter and Mike had a better chance of survival staying safe than mixed up in the fray that Ryan knew was coming.

He circled back to the Humvee for supplies and to swap out some gear. The path forward required a few special things to bring and a weapons cache for a variety of situations. The haul added weight and being prepared for anything thrown his way was the only answer since he was a team of one.

He had no idea what might come his way.

Having a party favor to shoot or chuck at someone was the difference between life or death. Satisfied with his choices and packed ready to go, Ryan set out to find John.

From the old garage Ryan had a few paths he could choose to get to the industrial area of the city. The streets offered direct routes and were breeding grounds of the Un-Dead this time of night. He knew Lurkers haunted the old machine shops as he came across some in search of spare parts and tools he needed at the hospital. Bolts were somewhere around and after the incident a few days ago, their whereabouts were concerning as they added a threat to safely maneuvering the city. Brainers were holed up somewhere around town and Mark's merry bunch were in hot pursuit.

Any one or a combo of whack jobs impeded his movements.

While the old railroad tracks along the levee took him outside of a direct line, there was a cut across he could use to get back in line behind the industrial park and to where John and the others were hiding away. The tracks didn't offer much concealment. He hoped being away from search parties and inaccessible for vehicles, they would be a forgotten trail he could safely pass.

Ryan walked along the old rail line and kept to the dirt sides to avoid the crunch of rocks under his feet. When he needed to, he crossed to the other side quietly and kept going.

The view was wonderful.

He could see far down the streets that dead-ended into the levee and with the river to one side, the peaceful rush of water as it flowed by him. He had to stop and bend down a few times to wait out some of the Un-Dead wandering the streets a few blocks over.

He could hear them in the quiet of the night, their familiar moans and screeches carried easily with little competing sounds to filter out.

Much of the area beyond the tracks were large storage yards filled with trailers and big rigs. Even without streetlights the moon gave enough illumination to see beyond the yards. Not wanting to be caught in the periphery of some dead's eyes and risk them chasing his dark shadow, he simply waited them out and went on his way.

The trek left his mind to wander in thought about his family.

A week ago, he thought his family was all dead. A few days ago, he found his son and a bomb dropped that his wife and daughter were still alive.

It was hard to grasp and wrap his brain around without a pounding pain right in the front.

He felt like the worst father of the century or a dead-beat dad bailing on his kid. He had left David and went on this crazy mission. He knew it was right. That didn't mean it didn't eat at him or cause momentary bouts of second guessing.

Even for a grizzled warrior like himself.

Taking David with him to hide away at the hospital with little Pete meant what? Leaving his son alone to go and retrieve his mother and sister and possibly never to return? Get that bad dad award ready to put on the mantle.

Like that would have been a prudent decision.

A cat was not the best babysitter or protector, even if Pete was kickass at keeping mice and rats at bay. An eight-year-old boy left alone with no protection or how to keep alive was a disaster in the making for a made for television special. Staying with John meant more people to protect him and for Ryan, to keep his focus on what lie around the corner.

As Ryan came to a bend in the tracks that headed back towards town, he caught it.

The low rumble of trucks off to his right.

He couldn't see anything from his location. Risking it, he hiked down the levee and followed the street towards the intersection. Parked tractor trailers, long left abandoned and forgotten, gave him some protection from being seen. Like a rat, he scurried along and hid behind the massive tires of the last one.

The street vibrated and the familiar humming sound of diesel engines and tires mashing down on old asphalt pointed him a block away.

He peered over the top of a deflated tire, concealed between it and the bottom of the trailer deck. He hadn't been through this part of town before and only ventured around it on his walkabouts. The surprise appearance in front of him made his jaw drop.

Military trucks were going into a tunnel into the side of a levee. Guards stationed outside guarded the traffic.

You wouldn't have known it was there if not for the two open large steel doors recessed far back into the earth. The trucks went down and disappeared out of sight. It wasn't the train track levee along the river.

It had to be something else.

He watched five transport trucks go in and two leave with no idea how many in total he had missed before taking cover behind the trailer wheel. By the looks of them they were full of soldiers and not a stretch of a guess, the ones missing from the dock. John had mentioned tracking a transport and no idea where it was going.

This had to be the destination, but what the hell was this place?

With his right knee planted in asphalt and breathing regulated to hide the steam from the cold air, Ryan waited until the trucks were gone and the doors closed. From the outside, you wouldn't even know it was there as the camouflage made it appear as a parked trailer. The dead-end street was a great location to hide whatever lay behind.

How to get inside was the million-dollar question, and he was going to find out. Propped on elbows prone on the hard ground, Ryan took a long time with his binoculars focused on the trailer.

It looked normal enough.

He figured whatever was that important to conceal behind a fake trailer had to have a security system to keep it protected. He took his time to check every detail and got a clear picture of what he was up against. He only caught the hidden cameras in the top trailer lights because of the glint of a glass lens the third one in. The light cover was a much softer shade of yellow than the rest of the row and focusing in, he could see it.

Each third light along the top was a camera.

The cameras incorporated into the streetlights were a bit easier to recognize, though if you happened to glance and not focus on them you could barely tell the difference. Not too sophisticated security. The added dimensions were high tech and someone trying to hide something of significance in this lonely part of town.

A tin can blew across the street and into the chain link fence that ran perpendicular and ended against the levee. The sound was distinct against the dead of the night.

A quick flash of blue light coupled with a quick crackle, and nothing.

High voltage fence Ryan thought.

As he scanned the perimeter more popped out to his trained eyes.

Ground sensors imbedded in the levee to look like plants. Interesting. A single entrance through a tunnel and protected by trailers used as a bottleneck and only way inside by the looks of the construction. Slits painted gray trying to hide their presence in the sides of the trailers that were likely gun ports for crossfire if required. Can barely make them out. The small rectangular gaps between the siding and removable metal are there. Damn, this place means some business.

Ryan wondered how far the security efforts went. Some things appeared new, like the fence and the fake plants. The disturbed earth and too green foliage led him to believe that one. If they were newer the extent of measures might have some dead zones to breach. He'd need to know where and how to gain access. Not through the front door. He figured a fortress always has a back door.

He would need to find it.

Retracing his steps, he went back to the train tracks and flipped on his night vision. It gave him extra eyes to catch any abnormal glass or wires he might encounter as he sought to circle around behind the hidden entrance. Reflected light would be caught by his goggles sooner than later and hopefully capture any traps long before he walked into one.

He didn't need to get this far and wind up blown to pieces from a trip wire.

Walking the left side of the levee he scanned slowly ahead and around. The only reflected light came from some rocks that glinted momentarily and went away as he approached. Fifteen minutes of methodically observing the terrain he finally got to the spot where the train tracks intersected the other levee and kept going forward. Bent low to the ground already, he looked out over an empty field. There was a long ditch between the levee and the field and water flowed through it.

Twenty feet wide, unless you wanted to get to the other side you would stay away.

The field was overgrown with grass and had no buildings or any structures at all. The only items around were what looked like fifty-five-gallon drums scattered around. Their placement though fit a particular pattern, like a grid.

They shouted out fake.

Reaching up and clicking on the infrared for his goggles, he caught the steam coming out. His guess was air vents for a ventilation and heating system.

A potential weak point to breach.

No other cameras could be seen. He walked the length of the field, bent low to limit his presence, and around to the other side.

Nothing stood out.

The field was bordered by the ditch and levee wall, a huge rectangular indentation in the ground that likely would normally be partially submerged to add to its security and keep people at bay. He ventured that leap as he saw two water pipes submerged in the ditch that came out to empty in the field.

Probably run by electric pumps that no longer functioned.

Ryan's guess was some type of underground facility, what type and what they did, he had no clue. His team had not provided any protection details for it which meant it was off his radar.

Given the nature of the work he fathomed was going on below, there had to be patrols checking on the perimeter. He saw no one and with no cameras this side, the ones he caught must only be directed at the front entrance.

From the looks of it all, it was a quick and dirty set up.

It might give him an advantage, especially if he found the secret exit or access tunnel he knew was somewhere around. People would need an escape hatch or exit in the event of an emergency and this place was no different. The field could be boobytrapped or have pressure sensors. If water was supposed to cover it, he doubted there were sensors.

Mines or other explosives could have been planted recently, though it was hard to tell in the dark. The danger of that weighed on how thick the barrier was between a blast and the facility to prevent damage. If a Bouncing Betty was used, all to shoot the explosive above ground and then explode outward in all directions, it went for body parts and would have no effect on the ground.

Those types of explosives were supposed to have been banned long ago. Ryan knew otherwise.

He had no clue and really didn't want to find out the hard way. His suspicion was nothing was buried around the field to offer impending doom. He could wait it out and see if they might venture out topside, force the issue, or move along to find John. As always, new intel put forks in the road and clouded any decisions.

Much like the Yorktown, Ryan had no indication if the facility below was for long-term use or simply a temporary solution. He didn't even know if it was an actual facility. It could be a storage depot for all he knew.

Everything was conjecture on his part from past experiences.

Soldiers could be holed up inside for eternity or a few days. There was no real way to tell. All he knew was that something was going on and having information to assist in making well thought out decisions was the right and practical approach.

Or, he could wing it and see what fell in his lap.

What to do Carmichael? What to do you old ghost, Ryan thought to himself.

He had learned that the waiting game can suck and put you behind the eight ball as actions you could have taken passed on by. Recovering was worse than biting the bullet and going for it. Too many game pieces clouded the board with no sense of order or even rules.

It was chaos in his mind.

A soldier usually faced a single enemy and had a specific target to neutralize. Plans were solidified and actionable with results that could be quantified.

Here, none of that really existed.

There were multiple enemy combatants. Mark's goons had the numbers. The Brainers were wild cards. Add to that Lurkers and Bolts and you had a recipe for disaster. The targets kept adding up as new intel hit him in the face around each corner. The information were tidbits, little nuggets of gold that like puzzle pieces, began to fit together. For a one-thousand-piece set, the picture was a blur. He had to get something juicy to stop chasing a tail.

The thought hit him like a brick.

Rebel Fucker.

He seemed to be on the outs with Mark. And, what if the Brainer was the same piece of shit that had tried to get David? He looked like some backwoods reject that probably still thought the Confederate flag wasn't racist and about white superiority over others. Just a Southern heritage thing was what Rebel likely argued.

Ryan chewed on it for what seemed like an hour.

If he could get the Brainers to engage the soldiers and each thin the herd of the other, it might allow for some distractions. Open opportunities for him to throw some chaos into the fire and find information on Julia and Emma. Getting his family whole again was *his* end game. He still had to deal with the eradication of Mark and his efforts, or he'd never be able to rest.

It would be a constant life of looking over his shoulder.

Sometimes a crowded field allowed for missteps, and he hoped what he thought might work would get him in the door.

CHAPTER TWENTY-FIVE

Concealed by the shadows, Ryan scouted around and looked for the right place to do the deed.

He found it above a warehouse that overlooked the field. He had a few old incendiary grenades that should still work and cause a big enough blaze to get some attention. If the Brainers were on edge like he thought and keeping a vigilant watch, it would pique their curiosity and draw them in. The soldiers in seeing a cavalry of crazies at their doorstep, would have to respond.

Plant the seed to get them to the front door and start the melee.

He settled in for the day and waited for night to return. To say waiting was boring was an understatement. All you could do was wait and watch, be vigilant and still to stay invisible, keep focused and think at the same time.

He knew about the front door. Finding the back door?

The focus.

For all he knew the access point was in the warehouse. If not and he was stuck inside searching aimlessly, he might miss seeing it revealed if they all happened to spill out the real location. If for some reason it was inside and soldiers came bursting out suddenly, it made the game a bit easier to play.

Activity was non-existent and time simply shuffled its feet making an hour feel like a day. No movement out the front entrance and no one popped out of the ground from the field or levee. Ryan had managed some shut eye while it was still dark and rolled awake when sunlight hit his eyes. From then until evening, he sat and scanned with his scope and listened on the radio. A few transmissions here and there, though nothing that appeared out of the normal range of radio chit-chat.

As dusk fell and darkness enveloped the night, Ryan prepped for the coming events. Throwing the incendiary canisters was going to require some great aim and distance. He only needed to get them to the exposed dirt and let the hard ground bounce them further. He hoped it worked since nothing was for sure. If it did and some chaos reigned, it might drive a wedge or at the least foment distrust.

Any cracks were welcomed.

He lined up his cache meticulously, spaced apart within ease of grasp, and ran through it in his mind. Over and over, he envisioned it until like clockwork it repeated the same each time. Satisfied, he ate an energy bar and thought of his family, trying to keep positive at what would hopefully soon be a full reunion once he found Julia and Emma.

He waited a few more hours hoping to catch people sleeping. Figuring now was the time, Ryan began to launch the canisters one by one. Left, right, and as far down the center as he could they flew, hitting the ground and bouncing like playground kickballs further and further away. As they rolled and the hot material spewed out, small fires caught the dry grass and blossomed. The sparks from them started others, until a raging sea of orange lit up the sky.

It caught Ryan a bit by surprise at the suddenness of the blaze.

He had thought it would take some effort to get going and swiftly fade out to smoke. Time to get it all going and catch some attention. The fires taking hold and sending flames up sooner than later might miss the mark and as it grew brighter, he knew the Brainers wouldn't be able to ignore it.

He didn't have to wait too long for an answer.

Twenty minutes after the flames hit the sky, he saw the cars coming up the street towards the hidden entrance and lost count at how many piled out. The sudden appearance of armed men at the front door must have incited a panic.

From below, he heard one of the rollup doors being pulled open and footsteps moving out.

He peered over the edge and solider after soldier fanned out, some going left around the levee towards the front and others heading right along the railroad tracks. Heard the large metal door close below and a minute later someone exit the building's exterior door. Not wanting to waste a potential opportunity, he scaled down the pipe and proceeded cautiously to the door. Taking a deep breath, he flipped his goggles down and reached for the doorknob to turn it.

It was unlocked.

As the door slowly swung open, he moved inside, the MP5 sweeping from side to side in search of a target.

No one caught a bullet to the brain.

Precision steps guided his feet as Ryan moved swiftly into the interior, his eyes glancing around the large expanse of space. Even in the dark, with only moonlight peering in from the skylights high above, he could see well enough.

The place was completely empty.

He continued further in, checking the floor for any gaps in the cement. Maybe even some scuff marks to indicate where heavy items had been moved.

Not a trace.

Nearly the whole length of the building, he kept going. Fifteen feet ahead was the end, the wall staring back at him. Not even an office to check. Perplexed, he began to turn and face the opposite direction to begin a new search in case he missed something and as he did, he heard a noise from off to his left.

A soft sound of a lock mechanism disengaging its bolt.

Quickly stepping back to put himself flush against the wall, he saw two soldiers come out of it and head for the exit on the other side. Letting them get far enough ahead he ran to the opening before it closed and slipped silently inside.

Ryan found himself in a stairwell with red overhead lights leading the descent. His MP5 aimed forward and tracing the steps as he moved below, he kept a fast pace step after step, hoping not to come face to face with anyone in the cramped space. A firefight in a stairwell with potential ricochets was a hole through your heart waiting to happen. Drop dead and game over.

Thirty steps and he met a sharp right turn.

Leaning against the wall he listened and hearing no sounds, shot his body around it and looked at where he needed to place himself safely from view. He found himself in a large tunnel that intersected another to his right and then disappeared. With no cover and totally exposed, he kept moving and turned left to follow the tunnel. He hated being visible with nowhere to hide and time an enemy.

He had to find some answers quick and get the hell out.

A long corridor appeared in front with glass walls the length of the passageway as far as he could see. Hospital beds lined the walls, machines and tubing hooked into the people laying in them.

Bed after bed he passed, the patients either sleeping or eyes glazed, staring at the ceiling.

Momentum kept Ryan on a course moving forward and he could only imagine what was being done. His stomach soured and anger began to well inside, his desire to simply kill every person he could find and liberate each soul growing increasingly as an option to carry out immediately without regard.

He knew to tame the rage, it was a natural response.

Level-headed actions were the answer. He was causing problems aboveground and gathering intel now urgent. He'd still make some waves here, it just needed to wait.

He could justify that.

Ryan worked his way along the tunnel and came to an intersection. He must have been deep inside the underground facility. He hadn't seen a single soldier or medical staff. He thought it odd given the chaos he created outside.

Maybe it wasn't time for rounds and people were asleep.

Someone should be wandering at least. Looking left and right, he scurried left into a darkened hallway, smaller than the tunnel. Closed doors and numbers lined it.

Sleeping quarters? he thought.

Only one way to find out.

Ryan reached for the door handle to one of the rooms and quietly turned it.

MP5 ready, he pushed open the barrier and peered inside. A bed sat against the far wall and the soft illumination of a night light cast a faint glow in the tiny room. The figure in the bed was small and turned to the side facing him, sound asleep. Pictures lined the walls, drawings of animals, shapes, and what stuck out and hit home were the ones of a family. What must be a dad, mom, boy, and girl, and the beloved family pets. As he looked, a tear formed at his left eye and started to roll down his cheek.

Dammit Carmichael. Keep your shit together.

He forced his brain to grab onto the thought and with his gloved hand wiped away the tears welling up.

Slowly, Ryan moved inside and shut the door behind. A young girl around eight lay sound asleep, snoring softly through her open mouth.

She was beautiful.

Light auburn colored hair, pert little nose. Almond shaped eyes. Her pale skin made her look like a vampire. The purple pajama top had what looked like a unicorn on the front. The atrocities she faced were unimaginable and he pushed them deep down inside. Even in the faint glow of the nightlight, he knew.

There was no mistaking his precious little girl.

He lowered his MP5 and stood still. The last thing he wanted to do was startle her and she screamed.

That might bring trouble.

His mind clouded and his thoughts scattered.

What the hell am I supposed to do?

Ryan took a deep breath and held it for a moment. Letting the knots inside subside, he exhaled softly and regained his inner calm, the deadly soldier that nothing ruffled coming back to life.

Whether it was a sound escaping or her sensing a presence, Emma opened her eyes. For a brief second, he saw fear wash over her. As wide as saucers, her eyes stared at him.

She didn't move a muscle, just lay as still as a statue.

He could only imagine what was going through her head. Was she dreaming? Was she dead and seeing him? Was her dad a ghost visiting her? Attempting to quell her fear and ease her mind, Ryan walked slowly over and bent down. Taking his left glove off, he touched her cheek and then put his finger to his lips. Emma recognizing the signal, did the same.

Using his best sign language, he asked if she knew if there were any listening devices inside. She responded no. Taking a chance, he whispered, "Hi, Princess. I have missed you so much."

Emma's cheeks turned red, color erasing the paleness of her skin. A warm smile washed over her. "Hi, Daddy. I've missed you too."

Keeping his cool Ryan asked, "Where is your Mommy?"

Emma's smile faded. "I don't know."

Reaching out and stroking her arm, Ryan asked, "Where is your Bub?" He was curious to know what she knew.

Tears started to fall down Emma's cheeks. "Gone."

Not wanting Emma to break into full blown tears, Ryan smiled and touched his daughter's cheek. "Stink Boy is safe. Daddy found him Princess."

Emma sniffled and nodded. He wasn't sure what all she knew and he needed intel and time was ticking away. The radio traffic in his ear had been buzzing fiercely as the soldiers dealt with the Brainers and from the sounds of it, chaos reigned. He had some hard and fast decisions to make, and quick.

Ryan kissed Emma's forehead before kneeling to look deep into her eyes. "Sweetheart. I wish I could give you a big hug and read you a story. I need to ask you some things and if you can answer that would help Daddy. Do you understand?"

Emma nodded.

"Good," Ryan began. "When was the last time you saw Mommy?"

"Before Bub was gone."

Ryan nodded. "OK. When did you get here?"

Her brow frowned. Hesitantly, she answered, "A few days ago?"

Ryan stroked her arm again to offer reassurance. "It's OK. Whatever you remember is all right. Have they hurt you?"

The tears formed again, and her mouth quivered. She nodded yes.

"When was the last time?"

Emma thought hard. "I can't remember Daddy."

The answer, though hard to swallow, made Ryan really think hard. Mark was using test subjects and disposing of those who were dead weight. John had told him. Where Emma fell if they weren't testing on her anymore, it made him wonder why she was here.

"Hey Sweetie. A few more questions. Daddy promises."

"Okay," Emma smiled, the familiar twangy voice warming his heart.

Staring intently at her to gauge the answer, he asked, "Has Uncle Mark been nice to you?"

She smiled and nodded yes.

It was something he might be able to use. What was about to happen made his stomach want to throw up and take his Ka-Bar out of its sheath and drive the sharp blade straight through his heart.

"Listen Princess. There are bad men outside who want to hurt Daddy. Do you understand?"

"Yes."

Ryan smiled. "OK good. Daddy wants to take you with him and keep you all safe. But those bad men might try to hurt you too. You know Daddy would never let someone hurt you right, if he could prevent it?"

Emma frowned. "I know you couldn't Daddy."

Not quite understanding, Ryan began to speak and Emma shushed him, holding her finger to her lips.

"Uncle Mark pushed you and you fell. If you were here, you would have hurt the bad men."

It was that moment he knew how strong his daughter was inside and she still loved him, even after all this time. It didn't keep tears from flowing, and meant nothing would stop him from saving her.

Sniffing the snot back up is nose, Ryan nodded. "Yes, Princess. Daddy would have hurt them super bad. T-Rex style," he winked.

Emma reached out and touched his arm. "Roar. Hehe."

His earpiece threw fire to the flames as he caught the last transmission. He knew getting out was going to be tricky and probably pretty bad, and bad had left the building and damn near impossible was entering the door.

Relishing in the moment, Ryan cradled her in his arms. "I need you to be strong and my tough girl, OK? Daddy has to go before the bad men come and find me and they try to hurt you. I need you to not tell anyone Daddy was here. Can you promise me that?"

Emma started to cry, and he held her tight. She kept it soft, and nodded.

Kissing the top of her head, Ryan looked back at her. "I will be back to get you and Mommy. I promise. Bub needs his partner in crime, right?"

Emma chuckled at the thought of her brother. "He does Daddy."

Ryan began to stand up straight when the sound of the doorknob engaging behind him sent a shiver down his spine. Letting instinct take over, he stepped back behind the door and pulled his Ka-Bar from its sheath on his tac vest.

Quiet and quick was the intended scenario.

Motioning to Emma to close her eyes, she rolled over and pretended to be asleep.

He watched in the dim light as a woman walked in and over to Emma. Dark hair pulled back into a bun and wearing hospital scrubs, she stood staring at his little girl. Seizing the moment, Ryan stepped forward and grabbing the bun, pulled the woman's head back to expose her neck, the deadly blade at the ready to slice her jugular. The woman immediately threw her arms up in protest in an attempt to grab the knife.

"Get the fuck away from my daughter," Ryan sneered in the woman's ear.

The woman froze, her arms falling to her sides and her body beginning to go limp.

Feeling it was a ploy to get him to release his grip, Ryan hissed quietly through clenched teeth, "Don't even think about it."

The woman nodded. As his grip tightened on her hair, she tried to speak. Her voice was dry and crackled, the words unintelligible. She let out a slight cough and tried again.

This time, barely a murmur, she managed a single word. "Ryan?"

His grip remained firm.

Anyone could know his name after talking to his kids, wife, or even Mark. Prey on his emotions and get him to loosen his grip. He'd been there before with enemy soldiers, trying to make a connection, thought they didn't know his name. They played the human card in an attempt to buy some time.

Reaching her left hand out in front of her, high enough for him to see, he saw it. Two rings adorned her finger.

Still not convinced as he pressed the sharp steel edge against her skin, he sneered, "That doesn't mean anything to me."

He felt her body tense this time as she seemed to gather her senses.

Barely audible, she managed to get out, "Oatmeal stout and Shepherd's pie. Our first date. My first Samuel Smith."

Only one person knew that.

Slowly, the blade retreated, and he let go of her hair. The woman turned around and stared at the man in front of her. Decked out in black fatigues and armed to the hilt, his face camouflaged in black grease paint, the features weren't hard to miss with his beard shaved off. She touched his face, her soft brown eyes staring intently at him, taking in his green eyes as she outlined his lips with her fingers. Flecks of gray washed through her brown hair. Tears formed and began to flood down her face.

"You're dead. I must be losing my mind."

Ryan managed a smile. "I'm not that easy to kill."

Julia laughed, and catching herself, tried to contain it. "I saw you fall. How could you have survived?"

He simply shrugged. "Not the first time leaving a helicopter over the ocean."

Confused at his response, Julia started to speak, and Ryan pressed a finger to her lips. It wasn't the time or place to get into it. The radio traffic was picking up and his time was limited.

He looked deep into her eyes. "A million questions. I can share it all later. Right now, I need some." His face tightened and his previously at ease demeanor changed. "Emma told me she had no idea where you were. Why?"

Understanding what he was thinking, her head nodded.

"After David-" she began and soon started to cry.

Ryan pressed her close, his eyes wide. Taking the cue to suck it up, Julia wiped her tears with her sleeve.

Sniffing the snot back, she nodded in agreement. "After Mark lost David, he sent Emma and the other kids here. Punishment for me and being pissed off he failed at getting him back. I finally was able to come today. Emma's medications and knowing the right doses." Her eyes started to well up again. "I don't even know if he's alive Ryan."

A crossroads lay in front of him. He could spill all he knew and risk it, not knowing exactly where Julia's loyalties were after three years. He hated even having the thought in his head.

It was a legitimate one to at least weigh until something told him otherwise.

He had hoped to come and go, use the advantage of being a ghost and take the knowledge of this place back. He saw Emma and it all fell apart as soon as Julia came through the door. Their life had been one of trust, and as much as he didn't want to, he couldn't discount anything until proved beyond a doubt.

"Why are you able to just walk around?"

The question stung.

She looked up at him, the pain at it evident. "There's nowhere to go. This wing is locked down. The soldiers are all near the entrance to this place, wherever that is."

"What about Mark?"

Her spite at the question even being asked reflected back at him.

Her brow furled and he could see her jaw clench. "He's tormented us for three years. Experimented on our babies. He's evil Ryan, pure evil. You have no idea what all he's done." Julia knew deep down he had every reason to question her, and after three years believing him dead, it was hard to think the conversation they were having was not what she had hoped.

Ryan took a deep breath, the sigh escaping his lungs. "I'm sorry I wasn't there to protect all of you."

Julia managed to smile. "You're here now."

His stomach soured, vomit wanting to escape. He grimaced at the thought of what he had to do, and his eyes must have betrayed him.

"You're not taking us with you, are you?"

Ryan touched his wife's cheek and caressed it. "Finding you here was a big surprise I didn't come prepared for. In a few minutes, the soldiers are going to come back in the way I got in here. I don't know if I'll even make it out, let alone be able to keep the both of you safe. Bullets might start to fly and if you got caught in the crossfire-", he stopped as his voice trailed off, trying not to think about what would happen. "I need to bring reinforcements to take this place down."

Tears dripped down her cheeks. "You can't leave us here Ryan. I've already lost you once and David. Emma needs to be safe away from here."

His voice hard and firm, Ryan responded, "You and Emma are safer here than with me. Outside of this place," he pointed over his shoulder, "is a death trap. Soldiers, crazies killing anyone, and virus infected who eat people. Safety is far away. The three of us stand little chance skipping through all of that. Me solo, I can get help and rescue you and everyone here."

"How can you just nonchalantly do this? Like flipping a switch?"

Shaking his head, Ryan grabbed Julia by the shoulder. "Listen, you think I want this? Would you prefer Emma," now lowering his voice to a mere whisper, "get torn apart right in front of you? The outside is not the place for her, and I'm going to have a hard enough time keeping myself alive. You both are better off here, even if it means I die trying to get help."

Julia's eyes welled. "That's almost heartless Ryan."

He knew she was right. The radio chatter was getting dire and his window closing. Taking a chance, he decided to share. "He needs a haircut."

"What?"

"David. His hair is too long. And I gave him a friend to keep him company."

Shocked at the revelation, all Julia could mutter was, "How?"

Ryan shook his head. "Later Jules. He's safe with some new friends. If I don't leave here immediately, I can't guarantee that. I'm the best shot at ending all of this. Emma told me they're not hurting her anymore, so you have to trust me. As bad as it sounds, you're safest right here."

Not quite sure what to say at being left, Julia hesitantly asked, "You've seen him?"

Ryan nodded. "And, gave Stinky Little Man a big hug and kiss."

Another transmission. Above ground was becoming a nightmare and enemies preparing to come back inside. Time to leave.

She smiled at the thought. Looking over at Emma, who was now laying watching and listening, Julia pointed at their daughter and turned back to face him.

"Promise me you'll be back."

Ryan pursed his lips. "When have I ever let you guys down? Except the time I got chucked out the door of a helicopter…" he shrugged and gave a wink.

Emma and Julia both laughed, and realizing it was a bit loud, shushed each other.

"I will be back for my girls, and I will make Mark pay for what he's done."

Julia leaned in and kissed him. "I feel like there's something about you I don't know Mr. Carmichael, but I'll take it. Please, don't be too long."

"I promise."

"You better Ryan."

Ryan kissed her forehead and handed her a radio set to a secure channel. "In extreme case of an emergency before I am back. Keep this hidden at all costs. Listen at 4:00 am for two beeps. If you hear it, it means get ready to leave that night. I'll be back with the calvary. See you girls soon."

He listened first and hearing nothing, blew air kisses to Emma and Julia, and then vanished out the door.

CHAPTER TWENTY-SIX

He was the shittiest father and husband.

The absolute bottom of the barrel. He didn't deserve their love or affection for what he had done. Dad of the year? Yeah, right. Best hubby in the world? Not a chance in hell.

Ryan might as well put his pistol to the side of his head and pull the trigger.

He had abandoned his wife and daughter just like that, without any deliberation, when they were right in his grasp. Even as he worked his way down the hallways and corridors towards his exit point, he couldn't help think it. The decision had been easy, too easy to make. It didn't even take more than a few seconds to go from initial thought to final answer.

And that was the problem.

Really Carmichael? You just found your precious daughter, the little love of your life, and you bail on her? Your wife materializes, you put a blade to her throat, and you up and leave them both? What kind of sick and twisted asshole are you?

He couldn't jettison the inner monologue no matter how hard he tried.

It kept coming back, word after word, spinning inside his head like a Ferris Wheel. Even as he shuffled along, the clear windows exposing all of Mark's victims, he didn't feel any guilt about leaving them behind. Maybe being a special operator and having eliminated a ton of people in his time killed his ability to feel regret. Could have been all the times he had to make dire life and death decisions in a split second. There was no wrong or right answer to placate it.

He did what he had to do, and always would without a second thought.

Regret was a failing, and that notion they engrained out of his being from the harsh training and mental preparedness required to be the best of the best.

Never look back, move forward.

You simply weighed options, evaluated the scenario, and ran solutions. The most effective shot to the top and if it meant success, you rolled with the punches. This situation was no different than any other op he had been a part of or run.

Evaluate the intel and broker the plan.

The only difference this time around was it wasn't some unknown asset or HVT with intricate value. The kind of high value target that reaped rewards.

Those types meant nothing to him.

This was personal. His wife. His daughter. Two extremely valuable people in his life that he put into an equation and measured results. The math didn't add up, so he changed the variables and recalculated. Such a soldier to the core. Parent and spouse?

Worst of the bunch.

Snapping out of the woe is me beatdown, Ryan moved with precision. As he silently moved down the corridor, he couldn't help take it all in. Young, old, men and women. Wheelchairs of the infirm.

Even the familiar faces like Emma's laying in hospital beds.

Mark was pure evil, subjecting innocent people to experiments and trials, their value as human beings an end to a means. If they didn't produce, discarded as trash to him and his glorious cause of self-righteousness. How anyone could follow the man was beyond comprehension to someone who still had his faculties. Decency and what was right still mattered, or at least, did to Ryan. It seemed to the others, those aspects of right versus wrong and black and white had vanished into oblivion.

How else could you justify treating children as test subjects, mere guinea pigs, to be used and discarded?

The disabled and elderly, beings who brought joy to the lives of their families and friends, left to wither hooked to tubes and strapped to beds as their essence was extracted into vials?

What kind of lowlife thought any of that was justified?

Ryan didn't have a clue beyond the virus had screwed up the brains of what was left that nothing could bring them back. He hoped it wasn't the case, and deep down inside, he knew. Once the road was travelled, there was no turning around. The crazy train kept going, and nothing was going to stop it.

They didn't figure on Ryan Carmichael blowing the tracks.

Pushing the thoughts from his mind and refocused with cruel intent, Ryan kept moving past the glass windows, soft lights and machinery glowing to expose faces. Row after row of beds and technology, a crowded existence and less than optimal for life. The innocent locked away as convicts with no chance for parole.

No one paid him any attention.

Until he neared the last pane and from the corner of his eye, he caught a glimpse that made him stop cold. An older man, his temples graying and his face slightly mottled, stared right at Ryan. Even in his pallid condition, his eyes still sparkled bright, a blue like Emma's. He laid motionless, as if Ryan was a dream or spirit. Ryan turned to face the man, and sensing that the vision must be real, the gentleman raised his arm.

And then waved.

The air left his lungs, and Ryan felt intense anger and sadness conflicted within. He knew in his heart what the man must feel. Scared, afraid, and not knowing the truth of what was happening to him.

Like everyone else behind the glass partition.

Raising his hand, Ryan waved back. Hoping to add some levity more for himself, with the intent to let the man feel some security, Ryan smiled and signed *Friend*. Not sure what to do, the man wiggled his fingers.

Emma did the same sometimes.

Ryan touched the glass with his left hand. Taking a deep breath, he blew on the window and a large swath of steam clouded the surface. Taking his finger, he used it to write his name. The man looked and with the biggest smile, signed *James*. Nodding his head, Ryan stood up straight. Knowing every second was precious, he finished with the best he could muster from his own rusty sign language.

Be strong and I will come back and help you.

James, the fear vanished, grinned, and waved goodbye.

Walking away, tears crept down Ryan's cheek. Fear and confusion, hell, anyone in the situation James found himself in, would feel the same. He had seen it the day he walked into the old fort when he saw hundreds of eyes watching him. Threat, enemy, friend?

First glance no one could say.

Ryan was a stranger, some mysterious man in black who appeared out of the shadows and told him he was a friend and James took him at his word. Trust, something most people were hard to give, the man allowed in an instant. Emma was much like James, able to read people to a tee and know their inner being. Who was good and who were complete a'holes.

Intuition, Ryan always thought. *A gift of being able to see beyond the façade and see into someone's soul.*

Ryan felt it deep inside, that the shortcomings of most people and their walls simply could not keep a special soul from seeing someone's true nature.

Taking the last turn before ascending the stairwell to safety, the radio barked in his ear.

It stopped him cold.

Frantically, he glanced around, trying to find a place to hide before the soldiers came down from above. Metal fifty-five-gallon drums were stacked in a recess in the wall. Seeing a small gap, Ryan wedged himself through it and hid, waiting.

He barely fit within the confines of the space.

Ten seconds later, he heard the thud of boots on concrete and flashes of bodies going past. One group and another flew by, until the noise of activity echoed all around.

Trapped, he weighed his options.

Listening to the radio he waited until he found the crack he could exploit. More soldiers were on the way. From the chatter, he had five minutes before the place would be crawling with troops. Taking his cue to get the hell out, Ryan sucked it in and slid out. Turning into a full run, he hit the corner and went up the stairs two at a time until he reached the top and hit the door release. MP5 ready to put a head shot into anyone in his way, he sprinted for the exit and as he ran full speed, he couldn't help smile.

I am fucking glad I let the professional soldier overrule the family man, or we'd all be dead.

CHAPTER TWENTY-SEVEN

Helter skelter.

The phrase came to mind when Ryan exited the warehouse. It was complete chaos outside. The fires he started were subsiding after burning bright orange in the sky and had been contained to only the empty field. Soldiers ran amok with the last of whatever water sources they could find to douse the blaze.

Sporadic gunfire could be heard in the distance, intermixed with elevated voices that drowned out competing sounds.

From the radio transmissions buzzing in his ear while deep inside the facility talking to Julia, the Brainers had come full force. A lieutenant from the facility attempted to make contact and found himself an instant casualty. Not from a Brainer bullet, but from a trip wire explosive Ryan had planted earlier as part of sowing the seed of confusion. That episode sent panic spewing on both sides and add in the raging fires, the groups hunkered down prepared to fight their unseen enemy.

As time wore on it became apparent something was amiss and cooler heads, at least on the professional solider side, began to prevail. They started work putting out the fires while the Brainers acted as protection. Without that right part of the brain left to reason, the Brainers shot at everything that moved.

Trees, paper, cans sent floating and rolling along in the wind, even each other.

Eventually something sunk into their diminished capacity and with a more controlled approach, they moved forward. Less anarchy and more deliberate responses, though no enemy was hiding in the shadows.

Except a ghost named Ryan.

Taking advantage of the situation, Ryan crept through the darkened night along the side streets, using the shadows and bushes as cover until he came around to where the Brainers leadership, a loose description at best, were sidelined in discussions with some of the officers from the facility.

From a safe distance away, Ryan watched through his scope at the animated talk.

The conversation was heated, ready to explode if a match struck. He saw the guy who must be Rebel Fucker, the same skinny dipshit with the dirty-blond mullet who was commanding David's beat down. He was energetic, his hands rapidly moving in an attempt to convey something of importance.

The homemade duct tape tag with the nickname scribbled in big black ink was laughable.

From what Ryan could lipread, the Brainer was attempting to explain that his people weren't responsible for the fire or the explosions. They had come when they saw the initial fire and smoke and had hoped it was the survivors they had been tracking for days. The officers were asking why Rebel hadn't let anyone on Mark's team know about coming across the survivor group, the victims left behind that Charlie Team had found. As far as Ryan could tell, Rebel's response was it stemmed from being surprised at catching survivors, extracting information that sent him on a wild goose chase, and having lost a whole team of men in pursuit of David, when the Bolts attacked.

The conversation between the groups continued on and finally ended when Rebel spat and attempted to turn and leave. One of the officers grabbed his arm and it sent the Brainers into a frenzy.

They surrounded Rebel and trained their guns, ready to shoot and kill every solider.

Seeing they were currently outmanned, the lead solider put his hands up in front of him, seemingly to show there was no threat, nodded, and took a step back. Rebel mumbled something Ryan couldn't make out as he was partially blocked from sight, and the Brainer leader retreated with his security intact.

Time to sow discontent.

Having swapped out weapons and staring down the barrel, Ryan focused the scope of his M82A1 sniper rifle, turned the sight dials to pinpoint his target, let his breath exhale to steady the shot, and took aim. He depressed the trigger with his left index finger and the firing pin hit its mark on the cartridge. Passing through the barrel and the end of the sound suppressor, the bullet left.

P*ssst.*

As the first piece of deadly lead flew on its way to its mark and the brass ejected from the chamber, he lined the next target up and pulled.

P*ssst.*

Within a split-second, both kill shots hit dead center.

The first projectile blew apart the head of the Brainer leading Rebel away. The second tore through the middle of the back of one of the soldiers turned watching the simmering fires. The shot propelled him backward after spinning him around, making it look like he was shot from the front. Immediately after seeing his own man fall and the leader of the soldiers seeing his, Rebel yelled out, the soldier barked a command, and a barrage of gunfire erupted. With the two sides shooting at each other and focused, Ryan took his cue to leave. His enemies would be engaged for some time. So, he took advantage to leave the area and get back to John and David.

Ryan was about to stand up and hustle off when he heard it. The cries and hollers of death stampeding like bulls on the run.

He knew the sounds too well.

Glancing around for a safer place to hide, he ran between two old Victorians. A wrought iron staircase led to the second floor of one and he took it. Reaching the top, he grabbed the doorknob and turned.

It was locked.

Taking the butt of his sniper rifle, he smashed it against the lower pane, sending glass crashing inside. Hearing the sound of his beating heart filling his ear drums and not much else, he stuck his hand through, found the lock, disengaged it, and went in. As he shut the door and secured the latch, he felt the crash against the door and looking out, saw him.

It, was probably the better description.

The eyes were the first thing that caught his attention. Pupils huge and black. In the light cast by the moon, above the white part of the eye, the sclera was laced with red, the blood vessels engorged and pulsing. As he stared into them, there was nothing there. No humanity, no reasoning, no compassion, absolutely nothing.

Two vacant holes to hell.

The man, or what was left of the twenty-something Emo based on his ripped skinny black jeans, tattered green plaid shirt, and holey retro Vans, was as retched as any horror movie make-up artist could visualize.

Curly ginger hair was a rat's nest of kinks and leaves.

It looked like a really bad wig, more from years of neglect without a proper brushing and sleeping in the dank recesses of some Bolt enclave.

Ryan swore he saw worms slithering around in it.

As he caught the mouth, the lips curled back to reveal pointed teeth that had been purposefully shaved down, the man bit at the air trying to get to Ryan from behind the glass. Ryan couldn't miss the blood-stained cheeks, and it sent shivers down his spine.

He did not want to be the next meal.

The young man hissed and slammed himself against the door. It was only a matter of time before the glass would break or the barrier would fail. Bracing the door with his right foot, Ryan placed his rifle against the wall and reaching to his left thigh, pulled out his Sig and shot through the broken glass. Three quick pulls of the trigger tore through the stomach of the Bolt.

It didn't even flinch from the blasts.

Ryan pumped two more shots into the Bolt, this time aimed upward. The action made the Bolt madder. Tossing its head back, it let out a blood curdling scream that pierced his ears from the high-pitched noise and made Ryan grimace from being ear-splittingly loud. The head dropped level and the young man simply stared at Ryan and smiled.

It momentarily caught Ryan by surprise, the response reeking of sarcasm laced with psychotic intent.

It wasn't a warm and fuzzy smile. It projected a level of hate and rage, a statement of what it planned to do next. The eyes widened and the brows arched, and it reared back and slammed the door once more. Ryan sidestepped it as the Bolt came crashing through the entryway. Grabbing a large swath of dirty curls, Ryan pulled back with his right hand, pumped two shots into the back of the head, and then let go. The body fell to the ground, twitching and writhing as a pool of blackened blood formed on the wooden floor. A few seconds later it stopped moving and Ryan could feel the adrenaline levels in his body begin to ease.

It was barely a minute of respite before Ryan heard the pounding footsteps coming up the stairs. Grabbing his rifle from the wall he ran, not knowing where to go in a place he had never visited.

A wrong turn or decision meant being trapped with no way out and surefire death.

Down a hallway and past a bathroom he kept going, the footsteps echoing inside the upper floor apartment. Straight ahead was a door partially open so he went for it.

Closing it behind, he heard them coming.

Quickly looking around the room and seeing a dresser to the right, he moved to the other side and pushed as hard as he could to get it to block the door. It must have been laden with tons of clothes as one, two, three pushes before it began to slide and caught just as the Bolts in the hallway slammed into the bedroom door. The dresser rocked forward a sliver, and thankfully held tight. Again, they crashed forward, and it rocked a bit more.

A few more hits and the room would be breached.

Not wanting to wait and find out how long it held, Ryan crossed the room to hanging curtains and where he figured would be a window. Pulling the curtain aside he was met with French doors and as he looked out, a small patio balcony.

Grabbing the knob and opening one side, he went out.

The next building over also had a balcony and about eight feet between the two structures. Looking down he had nothing to really break his fall except bushes and hidden in them could be pipes to impale his body or anything that might break a leg and leave him vulnerable. He could hang over the side and drop down. Same problem.

He was pretty much screwed.

The door creaked louder as the Bolts ravaged it to get to him. The dresser moved an inch, and then another. With each attempt it kept moving further. Ryan had to decide quickly what he'd do before the dresser crashed to the ground.

"What the hell," Ryan sighed as he closed the French door behind. "Let's fly like an eagle."

He pushed a chair to the front of the balcony and stepped up on the rail. Draping his rifle across his back between his neck and top of his rucksack, he counted to three and jumped. As he launched himself up and out the only thought in his mind was making it and not killing himself on whatever lay on the other side.

Three feet, six feet, foot out to catch the railing on the other side and hopefully not slip and fall to his death.

His boot caught the barrier and with momentum carrying him forward, he went with it and stepped off and immediately went down.

Lying motionless on the ground, he heard the Bolts rampaging the room across the way. Objects bounced off the interior walls, screams echoed, and Ryan could hear wood breaking apart.

Taking his cue, he crawled behind a small chaise lounge to hide.

The sounds grew louder until the French doors across the way were thrust open and the screams pained his ears. Taking a guess, it seemed they were either spreading the word to find him, or really pissed off. With nowhere to go, all he could do was lay still and hope to stay hidden from view.

A figure appeared at the door, its head lifted, nose turned up, searching for a scent. Panning side to side, it hunted for Ryan hoping to catch his odor. Five minutes it stood, another young man, this one more from an upscale men's clothing store than the other Ryan put down. Dirty khakis, soiled pink polo shirt, loafers that had seen better days.

Same void in the eyes of lost humanity. All that was left, vitriol hate.

He could have been some rich kid in his former life. The class pretty boy in school. Every girl's dream date. The list went on. All Ryan saw was the rage, the desire to kill.

With the other Bolt dead, this kid must have moved up the food chain and into being in charge, as much as Bolts had a hierarchy or leadership. He occasionally turned, grunted what must be orders, the whole time continuing to stand and stare out from the balcony. All Ryan could do was lay still, keep his breathing regulated, try not to sneeze or cough.

That would get him killed.

He waited, listening, thinking over and over, until the Bolts gave up and left.

If I had let my emotions decide instead of my training and experience, Emma and Julia would likely be dead. I made the right choice and I hope they can understand and forgive me. Dragging a kid and wife through the streets and trying to elude killers and monsters would have ended in disaster. I'm not even sure I am going to make it another hour. I have to though for them, or this is all for nothing.

He knew it to his core. It gave him the strength and perseverance to keep going and fighting.

A Carmichael always keeps their promises.

CHAPTER TWENTY-EIGHT

It had been hours since the Bolts ransacked the apartment and not finding him or any traces inside or out, retreated into the night.

Ryan knew once they got something in their heads, just like the Brainers, they were killers on a mission. They would keep going like rabid dogs until something else caught their attention.

He hoped that the chaos at the facility might have attracted them to it. Given the small horde that showed up to support their fallen brother, he ventured to believe this group was a subset of a larger one drawn to the area. Sunrise fast approached and he didn't want to get caught in daylight. He had a tough choice, to stay and wait until night, or set out and risk being seen to get information back to John.

With lives at stake, he made a choice and hoped it was the right one.

He hoofed it as fast as he could away from the facility and blocks in the opposite direction. It was an attempt to elude any danger. The soldiers and Brainers would be tired, and he hoped either going to catch some shut eye or dealing with the Bolts.

The horde looking for him had gone towards the chaos.

He felt he had some distance he could make up and give him more time to get far away. He ran most of the way and only stopped when he caught the sun peaking its head over the horizon. About two miles away from the facility and needing to cut across town, Ryan found a parking garage and worked his way to the top to get a bit of rest.

The parking structure, five levels up, gave Ryan a great vantage point to scour the city. He could see the smoldering black smoke from the field fire fading out and hear the occasional gunshot. Beyond the smoke, the city was eerily quiet, which was expected, given real life had left a long time ago. It still sent shivers through his spine knowing that evil hid in the shadows, actual people who preyed on others.

Still physically human and alive. Dead inside and out.

As he sat on the hood of an old faded blue BMW and looked out, he wondered about his old friend Mark. Ryan couldn't put his finger on it. There was too much deliberation, too many intricate decisions, to peg Mark as a Brainer. They were reactive types and prone to disharmony. They worked together haphazardly without coordination.

Mark and his group were too refined, too decisive, in how they reacted and responded.

Ryan knew the virus had varying effects on people. The sloth-like Un-Dead wandering around with the life sucked out of them, but harmless. Lurkers and Bolts hunted bent on killing, their primal instincts intact and everything else vacant. Brainers who had a semblance of society by how they interacted, relished in torture and a good kill. Mark and his band of cold and intelligent psychopaths who somehow still had a semblance of order to their chaos.

There were the minority of survivors like Ryan who had been infected and were still as normal as they come. Ryan knew the virus had morphed and mutated, he had seen the research papers. Maybe Mark and his disciples were the next generation of evil the virus spewed into the world. No matter what Mark was, he had to be stopped.

And Ryan was going to make sure it was final.

He watched the sun rise and enjoyed the cold morning air. A small window of solitude with rest for weary bones. Feeling refreshed and ready to head out, Ryan heard the diesel engines approaching from the west.

He slid off the BMW's hood and knelt behind the concrete wall of the parking garage, peering through the slit between sections.

Three black Humvees came to a stop below and a dozen soldiers exited. He checked the radio volume and channel and heard nothing. Hitting the scan feature the radio spun through silence until it came to a transmission.

"Charlie Team. Fan out and search the perimeter. Bravo Team, secure the lower level. Alpha Team, move in. Over and out."

Ryan scanned the area and only saw the three vehicles. He paused, thinking, and out of the corner of his eye, he saw movement and focused. Twelve black clad figures hustled from an alleyway towards the parking garage. Looking right, he caught another group move slowly from the shadows.

Shit, Ryan thought, his adrenaline beginning to build up. *How the hell did they find me?*

A transmission interrupted.

"Two mikes out. Over."

Sweat began to bead across Ryan's forehead. He had been extremely careful in his movements and covered his tracks, doubling back here and there to throw off any scent or potential debris he disturbed.

"Lower level secure. Over."

One minute to go.

"Perimeter secure. Over."

He heard the diesel of another Humvee turn the corner and come to a stop. It sat idling, a fifty-caliber mount moving back and forth as a soldier kept watch for any intruders. He then saw Alpha Team hurry to the Humvee and take up a security perimeter around it. No one exited and no one moved.

"Package secure. Over and out."

Package? What the hell is going on?

Five minutes of nothing. The silence was overpowering, the only distraction the occasional morning chirp of a bird waking from the comfort of their nest.

And then, they came.

A caravan of black SUVs approached from the distance. Ryan looked around, trying to grasp how he ended up on top of whatever was going on.

It hit him hard.

Far enough away from the facility with multiple tall buildings to provide some cover. Streets that ran the length of town to provide escape points along any route if required for an escape. An open-air parking garage with plenty of concrete to suppress an attack from gunfire or grenades. For a quick impromptu meeting, it was a decent place to gather.

The SUVs rolled past the soldiers and into the garage. He heard the tire rubber squeak on the concrete as they came to a stop. Watching the reflection in the windows from the office building across the street, Ryan saw the passenger door of the black Humvee open, and a man emerge.

Ryan's skin crawled, rage beginning to brew. Hate seething deep within. Mark.

He knew the radio would be silent now and he needed to be a fly on the wall for whatever was about to happen. Getting bold, he took the far stairs and descended quietly to the third level. Seeing no one around, he crept to the center of the garage and took the exit ramp to the second level. Taking up a position where he could hear down to the first level, Ryan listened in.

The words echoed off the cold concrete.

"I need a status report. You've had ample time to finish this and I need answers."

The voice was full of anger and sounded familiar to Ryan, though he couldn't quite place it.

Ryan recognized the second voice.

"Don't ever speak to me like that. I don't work for you," Mark answered, his words calm and cool. "If you choose to it may be the last time."

"The last time for what?" the man growled.

"Mr. Vice President," Mark began, and Ryan could tell he must be smiling by the tone of his voice. "The last time you take a breath."

The deafening silence was broken by what could only be a bunch of semi-automatic weapons, likely the Vice President's men, being pulled to attention and the safeties disengaged. Laughter erupted and filled the void as it became louder and from what Ryan could tell, purposefully meant to exert Mark's perceived dominance.

"Tsk tsk James. Do you really think you have any power here? You are nothing, a cling-on from the old days. I raise my hand and you and all of your men are dead, and I go about my day and life like you never existed. So," Mark sneered, "you will grovel and give me the praise and respect my efforts have afforded your boss."

The Vice President began to speak, "You son of a bi-" and stopped when Mark raised his right index finger.

The fifty-caliber hummed to life and from the sound of it, decimated one of the SUVs. Ryan managed to peer through the slat of the retaining wall and saw the black SUV parked behind the others, ripped apart and smoking from the carnage. The sound of the deafening blasts bounced off the concrete structure and continued to reverberate until finally fading out.

Ryan saw the satisfied look on Mark's face and couldn't help wanting to shoot him right there. The smugness needed to be ripped off his lips. Ryan knew if he sent a round from his current location it would be obvious it wasn't retaliation or a hit by the Vice President.

But, what if? He thought.

He moved further back up the ramp and back towards the retaining wall. There was a sliver of a line of sight. He quietly took his sniper rifle and propped the lethal barrel on the wall and peered through the scope.

"Enough!" The Vice President yelled. "We're all on the same team here. He wants a report and after you lost the boy, wants to know how you plan on completing your work."

Ryan saw Mark shrug. "Don't know."

The Vice President's jaw dropped. "What do you mean, you don't know?"

Ryan sensed the bullshit, and simply waited for it.

"I'll get the boy back. It's a matter of hours. I still have the girl and if I need to, I can use her."

His stomach churned and Ryan nearly puked. He knew who Mark meant, even without him saying her name.

The Vice President waved his hands frantically at Mark. "The boy is the *key* you preach. The girl because of her condition, a reject. How do you plan on getting it from her?"

The tone struck a nerve with Ryan. He knew what the asshole meant and hoped he didn't go there.

Mark walked over slowly and stopped. "For the stupid like you I'll simplify it. We tweak her DNA to remove her *condition* as you say, and let magic do the rest."

Ryan could see the anger in the Vice President's face. He spat his words out, and they stung. "She's a retar-" was all the Vice President managed to say before Mark struck him in the nose, causing the blood to explode.

The Vice President's men quickly moved forward to surround the VP. They were met with a barrage of red dots and the sound of disengaged safeties.

Holding up his hand, Mark waved his hand back and forth. "No need for violence, so stand down men." The red dots from the soldiers' rifles clicked off. Turning his attention to the Vice President, he motioned for the Secret Service detail to part. They didn't budge. Shaking his head and looking at the senior member of the detail he shrugged, "Easy or hard way. You can choose."

"You son of a bitch!" the Vice President yelled, wiping the blood from his nose with a handkerchief. "How dare you!"

Mark made a parting of the waves motion with his hands. "Step aside gentlemen. We need to finish our talk. I will not ask you again."

Realizing his team was outmanned and outgunned, the VP spoke up. "Give him room Richard."

The Secret Service men parted, though kept their weapons ready to respond.

Mark stepped forward, hands behind his back. As calm as anyone could convey the words he hissed, "Do not ever say that word to me. Especially about her."

The Vice President glared. Not one to take being reprimanded, he spit the blood from his mouth onto the concrete and stepped forward, jabbing his finger into Mark's chest.

"I will say whatever I damn well please about anyone. She is a re-" he spat before Mark slammed his fist into the Vice President's nose again. Reeling backward and grabbing his face as he fell to a knee, the blood really gushing out, the VP yelled, "You broke my nose!"

Mark casually walked forward and bent down, looking deep into the Vice President's face. "The next time you attempt to say that word it will be the last. Aren't you supposed to be a godly man? Love everyone and all of that crap? That little girl is better than all of us. She might be different, but she is as close to an angel as you will ever see," he finished as he reached out and pushed the Vice President to the ground.

The Vice President fell back and sticking out a hand, caught himself. Looking up he spat, "You have experimented, poked and prodded that kid and her brother. You lost the prize and have the bottom of the barrel. She's some end to a means."

Mark chuckled. "It's people like you that don't deserve to have survived any of this. I may have utilized her and her brother to get what I need. That doesn't mean that child is worth less than the piece of shit you work for and she certainly is worth more than you. You're crap on the bottom of my shoe. I have known her since she was born. Watched her grow up and brighten the world that once was and enlighten the one we face today. I may be insane as they say, but she is the only one who genuinely has compassion, love, and the intelligence you lack to move beyond our current circumstance and help rebuild the future. Down Syndrome is not a deficiency. In many ways, it's a gift."

Ryan listened to it all, confused at the exchange he witnessed. There was a lot there, yet not nearly enough to piece together. He could draw a lot of conclusions based on what he heard. Whether he was right was another matter. The Vice President's boss?

He could surmise who that was, though it seemed out of the question.

In the last days of the world the White House had been overrun, those left behind from the Administration who chose to keep going despite everything had been strung up, their heads piked atop the residence's fence for all to see.

The President had long before been sequestered in a secret bunker to protect him and what remained of his family.

When some in the military and his own Secret Service finally came to terms with his intentions, they supposedly staged a coup and by reported accounts the President met an untimely fate. Unfortunately, it was too little too late and the ending chaos ensued, gripping the country and world in a divisive death roll that sent everything and everyone into a tailspin.

It was the end of the world as everyone knew it.

At least, that was the story he remembered. Seems the President didn't meet his maker.

As he thought about what was unfolding below about his little girl, Ryan's blood raged like a volcano. Emma was perfect in his eyes. She brightened everyone's world. Hearing the Vice President denigrate her, dismiss her life and value as if she was garbage, the dad in him clicked on. A really bad combination of trained killer and dad blended together.

Never make the loving and protective dad beast mad.

"When you are done with her, she is to be disposed of, understand? He doesn't want anyone to produce the serum and ruin his control over it." The smirk on the Vice President's face pissed Ryan off to the core.

Mark backed away. "No."

The Vice President stood up and brushed himself off. Staring at Mark he barked, "It's not a request. You either do it or I'll have it done. You can be gentle or ruthless. Let her go to forever sleep or torture her to your heart's delight. Get it done."

Mark's head titled to the right. As he began to speak the spatter of blood and brain matter shot forward and drenched his face as the Vice President's head exploded like a watermelon.

Instantaneously, the Secret Service opened fire in all directions.

Mark retreated as his men leveled a barrage of bullets that left nothing except dead bodies. With no one left standing of the Secret Service detail and the area now quiet, Mark yelled for the unit's commander.

"Who the hell shot him?" Mark barked as he grabbed the uniform of the commanding officer.

The commander stood fast. "It wasn't us, Sir."

Confused, Mark shook the uniform shirt. "What do you mean? He didn't shoot himself and his men wouldn't have done it. Unless-" his voice trailed off. "Secure the area, now!"

Realizing the seriousness of the command, the officer hit the mic on his radio. "Secure the area. Find me the shooter."

CHAPTER TWENTY-NINE

Ryan was in a full run to the top of the parking structure.

As he leapt up the stairs to get to the top level, his disappointment in himself boiled over.

What the hell have you done Carmichael?

He made a stupid move and there was no taking it back.

Listening to the exchange and the Vice President's order he knew he had to act or risk losing Emma. He had crept as far back as possible while still having a line of sight, which in reality was a tiny sliver between a concrete wall and Mark's head.

He was sure Mark felt the breeze of the seven hundred and fifty grain projectile whizz by his ear.

As soon as it left the barrel, he knew it was straight and true.

Wanting to get ahead of what was sure to come next, he slung the sniper rifle across his back and ran like hell.

As he made the top floor, Ryan ran for the opposite corner. He had scoped out the area during his downtime to find a potential exit point if required, and with an entire city street to clear his options were limited. He couldn't jump to another rooftop or wait it out as he knew the soldiers would go floor to floor to clear it. There was a single, risky route which probably would get him killed, and as the VP sought his daughter's death, it flashed before him.

What the fuck, he had thought, before pulling the trigger and racing to escape.

Not even bothering to slow down, Ryan kicked off the ground with his left leg, landed on top of the retaining wall with his right, and in a single stride, jumped. As his body thrust forward with all its momentum and propelled itself up and out, he reached up and grabbed the wire. Firmly in his grasp he held tight and as his body weight pulled, the wire ripped from its support. It was a matter of gravity and whether it stayed secure to the tower on the other side. As he swung across, he hoped it carried him to safety.

Five stories up to fall was a splat waiting to happen.

Twenty feet to go crossing the city street, Ryan thought he was clear, until he felt the wire slacken. With nothing else to grab and keep him going, he simply road it out. Body weight and forward motion got him to the rooftop on the other side, though the landing was rough as he hit hard and rolled to a stop against a vent pipe.

He immediately pulled the wire as fast as he could to prevent it being detected and left it next to the tower. Back on his feet and feeling the aches beginning to course his body from the hard hit of the roof, he got up and ran. Putting as much distance between him and Mark was critical if any plan were to succeed. He had no idea where to go or which way offered the best path.

All he knew was to keep going and let luck guide him.

He ran the length of the roof, a full city block, and reaching the other side, came to an abrupt stop. It must have been an old apartment building, because as he looked over the side, he smiled. A fire escape was a short hop below and a quick jaunt down the ladders to reach the alley. From there, to what he hoped was safety and rest before he had to move on.

As Ryan fled, he couldn't help think about killing the Vice President.

The image stuck vividly in his head. He knew it was an emotional action on his part, something he might not have done years before. He also knew it served a greater purpose to sow discord. The Secret Service detail had been obliterated and the Vice President dead.

That would not go unnoticed by the President.

Mark would need to explain the incident and make some appeasement. However, Ryan knew his old friend could massage it to his favor. Which for Mark, was a likely scenario.

Ryan had thought about all the possibilities, and each one still gave Mark an advantage.

The survivors catching Mark and the Vice President by surprise and taking advantage of the meeting. The Brainers seeking to make a statement and get themselves back some leverage. Even Mark himself eliminating the Vice President as a threat.

As long as Ryan wasn't part of the story, he had the upper hand.

He hadn't planned on shooting anyone. Simply listen to the conversation and grab as much intel to guide his next movements. Like a bad headache the words spoken about Emma, her being disregarded callously like garbage, fed his mind.

Her whole life was a fight against assholes who thought she was less than others.

The proud father acted to protect her, and though it was wrong, he felt the soldier inside pat his back. Talking about Emma always evoked the dad bear when anyone strayed into shit talking or messing with his baby girl.

He had even set a few straight when making comments about her right before the end of the world.

Like the time they were all out meeting for pizza at their local hangout when Emma was four and being a typical little kid. A group of good ol' boys sitting and drinking a bit too much thought it would be funny to trip and push her to the ground as she tottered by with her brother. Having recently started walking since hypotonia of her muscles made it difficult to stay on her feet, she had progressed well. Even the slightest bump offset her balance and sent her to the ground.

The man sticking his foot out didn't help her stability to move around it.

She had been a bit loud, happy and jubilant at being out with her family, though nothing that warranted the assault on a little kid. Ryan had just arrived from work and caught it through the large front window as he went inside the door. Proud seeing as David helped her up and over to Julia who tried to console her.

He walked over to the offending table and commented about the little girl. "Loud little kid."

"Someone needs to get them in their place. They should stay home and not bother the rest of us."

Ryan smiled. "I know, right? A four-year-old that is having fun. No place for it."

The good ol' boy didn't quite catch the sarcasm. "I remember when you never had to see people like her around. Messing up a good time tonight. Little tard."

"I'd hate for her dad to be here. He's probably some suit that would get in your face and wag his finger at you," Ryan mimicked as he mockingly shook his finger back and forth.

The table erupted in laughter.

The good ol' boy snickered, "Probably some little piss ant. I'd like to see him try that."

As Ryan laughed, he bent down and whispered in the man's ear. "No, not a piss ant. A papa bear who hates bullies."

With the last word Ryan grabbed the back of the man's head and smashed his face down on top of the table, holding it there with such force the man couldn't move. Staring on in shock the others at the table simply sat still, until one man, a big burly guy with a brown beard and American flag t-shirt, started to get up from the opposite side.

"I'd think twice before stepping into this," Ryan cautioned as he held the good ol' boy's face buried into his pizza slices.

The burly man stood and slammed his chair back. "You're a dead man," he threatened as he moved around the others towards Ryan.

Ryan shrugged. "I warned you."

As the man approached, Ryan pulled the good ol' boy's head back and slammed in back down before letting go. As the burly man got close, all three hundred pounds of him rushing forward, Ryan pivoted and struck the man in the side of the jaw, sending him falling forward and into a wall. He got up and ran forward to tackle Ryan, who juked to the right, turned, and pushed the man into the table, sending his friend falling to the ground. The others had stood up and looked at one another, trying to see what the other planned.

Ryan glared and shook his head. "If you're smart, sit your asses back down. If not, pay the price."

The men stared at one another, nodded, and retreated to the bar area and watched. The good ol' boy and his friend picked themselves up and stood, wiping the blood from their faces.

Pissed and enraged, they both jolted at Ryan.

Taking a lineman stance for a shotgun play, Ryan set back on his haunches and ducked his shoulder into the closest one and shot straight ahead. The motion clipped one man, sending him into the table while Ryan drove the other straight into the wall. Grabbing the back of his head, Ryan kneed him repeatedly in the gut and with one last thrust, threw him to the ground.

"Sucks getting your asses kicked by a little girl's dad, huh?"

The burly man yelled out and ran toward Ryan. This time, Ryan took him head on. He threw a left punch to the face, a right to his sternum, causing the man to lose his breath, and another left to the right side of his face to send him crashing to the floor.

The good ol' boy spit blood and got up. "I'm gonna end you."

Ryan laughed. "Really? You're a bully. My daughter is tougher than you."

The man ran at Ryan again and this time Ryan sidestepped to the left, hooked the man's arm, and pulled it behind him. With leverage to use, he pushed him to the ground and going with it, pushed the arm up towards the head. He could hear the shoulder squeak and the bone begin to break.

The man cried out in pain.

"Tell you what. You have a choice. You all apologize to my daughter with great remorse, or I break your fucking arm." Ryan made his point by pushing the arm higher.

"Fuck you, asshole."

Twisting, Ryan pushed harder. "One more push and it snaps. Can't use it to bully kids for a long time." As the man screamed in pain, Ryan tapped his head to make him focus. "I'd suggest you apologize or after this one I'll break the other. Won't be able to pick on little girls or jerk off for a really long time."

The good ol' boy laughed. "Screw you."

Ryan pushed and the arm popped out of the socket. The man shouted out in pain, tears welling up in his eyes.

"Shall I continue, or are you all going to be gentlemen?"

The burly man got up from the ground and rubbed his stomach. Breathless, he stood trying to catch his wind. "Come on Clem. Let's get him."

Ryan stared at the man. His face showed his intentions. "Are you serious? You two couldn't fight your way out of a pillow fight. And, you have been embarrassed in front of a whole room of people. Hear all the laughter? That's aimed at your stupidity. Give it a rest."

The man ran toward Ryan. and letting go of the pinned arm, Ryan punched the burly man in the groin. Grabbing his manhood, he doubled over and fell to the floor.

Focusing back to the man on the ground and grabbing the arm again, Ryan asked, "Had enough yet? Nod for yes or stay quiet."

The good ol' boy shook his head. "We'll apologize."

"Great," Ryan smiled and with a twist, popped the man's arm back into the socket. Leaning down and speaking into the man's ear, he whispered, "This is your one and only chance. If you don't and act up, I will put a hurt on like you have never seen. Understand?"

"Yes."

"Yes what?"

The good ol' boy paused a moment. "Yes, Sir." He motioned to his friends with his good arm as Ryan stepped back and looked on.

Gathering themselves up, the group huddled together and knelt. Ryan motioned for Emma to come over and with a smile she toddled on over.

"Hi," she announced with the warmest and sweetest voice. "Emma," she motioned, pointing at herself.

The men looked at Ryan and then at Emma.

"Hi there, Emma. Look, I'm sorry for what I did," the good ol' boy began. Ryan glared, so the man continued. "I didn't mean to be mean to you and push you like that. I'm sorry."

The burly man grumbled something under his breath, and Ryan coughed to catch his attention. Seeing the look in Ryan's eyes, he frowned and finally spoke. "Sorry little girl. I didn't mean to laugh at you."

Emma smiled and waved.

The other two men made apologies as Emma and the whole pizza joint looked on. When they finished, Emma went up and hugged each man. "Thank you," she smiled and then walked over to David and Julia. The onlookers clapped and hooted.

Stepping in front of the group of kneeling men, Ryan put his hands out, palms facing up. "See? That wasn't terribly bad, was it?"

Four embarrassed faces looked at the floor.

Smiling from ear to ear he stepped closer and knelt, being sure to keep enough distance in case they decided to be stupid again. "She's like you and me. Has feelings and emotions and makes any room brighter that she enters.

Take that to heart because if there is ever a next time that any of you pull crap like you did here and I catch wind of it, it will be the last. We understand each other?"

The men nodded. Ryan nodded and smiled back, and then stood up and joined his family.

As he thought about that long ago incident, Ryan wondered if violence was ingrained deep within. He had killed many times before, all for justified reasons, and now thought about his actions and how his past boiled over to his civilian life.

He was protective of his children and Emma for sure.

She didn't need to experience the cruelty of the world at such a young age, especially with no legitimate purpose beyond people simply being asshats. He had asked himself many times if he took the pizza place incident too far and each time the dad inside told him no, and the forever soldier smacked his face and protested he didn't go far enough.

He never knew if the responses were right, or meant to appease the man.

What he had done earlier to the Vice President was no different in his mind from a military action taking out an enemy. It happened that this time the enemy was targeting his precious Emma.

Being a parent and father to a child with special needs meant a certain degree of thick skin.

It didn't mean that you took it either. Besides, in the long run, sowing uncertainty for Mark was a game Ryan wanted to play. Who to trust, who Mark thought was after him, and keeping him guessing were all pieces on the gameboard. Ryan needed to keep his daughter and Julia alive, especially after what Mark said about Emma. It all played to Ryan's favor.

He could use the uncertainty and clouded reality to exploit it.

CHAPTER THIRTY

What remained of his lemon water quenched his thirst and the graham crackers as stale as they were, were the most delectable things to relax Ryan in this moment.

He took each sip and sloshed it around, the lemony taste erasing the salty spit that had built up as he was on the run. The graham crackers were old, the memories of sitting and having a few with David and Emma easing his mind.

His body needed rest after the last few days of chaotic activities.

He was nursing bruises along with aches and pains that an aging body, though still fitter than most active-duty special operatives, needed time to heal.

As he lay on the ground of the second-floor office, back propped up against a desk and looking out of the floor to ceiling window, he kept watch for any movement. He knew his actions caused dominos to fall and actions to begin.

There was a method to his madness and consequences to them.

Even taking out the Vice President was not a spur of the moment decision. It was in fact calculated with intense thought, though done in seconds from years of training and drills for these situations.

The master plan was to cement confusion and discord, force Mark to second guess everything.

That would create cracks in his resolve and provide Ryan an opportunity to strike. Being fluid to the current environment and acting on situations that could not be passed up happened. Sometimes, a precious moment appeared unexpectedly, and you simply had to take it.

Killing the Vice President was like taking the golden goose.

At least that's how his brain rationalized what occurred. A different time, a different day, he might have done something else. In this moment, tucked deep in a world gone to hell when so much appeared to be at stake, you did what you did to survive.

Step in his way, you get burned.

As the day wore on, Ryan longed for it to end. Nighttime would be his window to move, though he knew the soldiers would be out looking for a trail that wasn't there. A goose chase he hoped led them astray. Night vision would hamper his movements, but it was better to move around in the dark than daylight.

Shadows helped conceal and offered places to hide.

He was adept at traveling the night train and being a passenger seeking to avoid being seen. Countless times before he had been in similar circumstances having to traverse enemy territory or watchful eyes. Training came into play, and feeling the blackness a gift. You had to know where to go, how to step, how to be a real ghost.

Catlike and transparent.

He was the best of them and took pride in it. As he ventured more and more back into his element and the old solider dusted off the rust and threw some WD-40 on it, Ryan sunk back into the mental zone, if you could even call it that, of the war machine process. If Mark only knew he was alive he would be scared shitless.

The man knew Ryan and his deadly work.

Ryan also knew if Mark found he was alive, Emma and Julia would pay a steep price regardless of how Mark felt about Emma. Ryan was confident in that.

As dusk fell across the city and the black enveloped it, Ryan felt energized, rested, and prepared to head out. His body ached less with each muscle movement and adrenaline pumping through his veins. The tremors hit him early which was a blessing and a curse. He figured with all the activity his body chemistry had thrown the virus off and it decided to attack him sooner than later. Riding it out and getting it over with, he hoped it didn't come again while engaged in his journey.

That as they say, would really suck balls.

It took most of the night to find his way back across town and to the new hiding place of the survivors. It was only three miles from his original destination. Mark had sent extra patrols out in search of anyone or anything moving, or even a body found dead.

Ryan dogged and weaved from building to building, a step ahead until he ran out of ground to go further.

From there, the last leg of his travel was underground in the old subway tunnels which proved eventful. A pod of Bolts and Lurkers, which never congregated together as far as he knew or had ever encountered before, slept atop one of the platforms.

This was a startling new development, and an alarming one if these groups were experiencing some sort of community.

Language was long gone and most cognitive brain functions. He thought, what precipitated all of this? Ryan had wondered about mutations in the virus and some of the research he had read after the fall, though aligned a bit differently, you could extrapolate a bit. It suggested common denominators moving more and more to the center and shared.

Enemies going through a metamorphosis of consciousness and combined objectives was a dangerous partnership.

He had seen changes in each, more organization, though not structured, and a semblance of thinking and simple decision-making beyond the animalistic nature that drove the hordes. Maybe it was outliers in the groups who changed, and their brethren simply followed. He had no real evidence or clues and encountering this sent a chill down his spine. He hoped it was a long progression and not a sudden awakening that would throw gasoline on the fire.

New realities meant another threat to overcome and an all-out war for humanity that he wasn't sure could be won.

Ryan crept quietly, hypersensitive to his surroundings. One false move, a misstep on something that made a noise, even his own breath, could awaken one of the horde, and his ass was a goner.

He lost count of the numbers after making mental notes past a hundred.

He had expected some sentries, if you could even peg them at that, or a few awake to watch over the groups. His guess was they felt secure enough in their numbers and any threat non-existent.

They were killers after all. Why would they need protection?

He kept against the tunnel wall and walked the maintenance path, hugging the concrete and moving as swift as he could without sound. Even as the enemy got further behind him, he still felt his spine tingly with trepidation at eventually coming across another group and being pinned between the two.

That was a recipe for disaster.

When he reached the false wall in the tunnel, Ryan pushed the electrical box to the right. The wall slowly popped out enough for him to squeeze through and grabbing the handle, close it behind. The passage was pitch black.

With his night vision goggles, he found his way to the steel door.

He figured he'd press the intercom button, see if anyone was home before going inside. No one was supposed to be here, the industrial park the intended destination to meet up. This was a waypoint to rest and he needed to clean up.

A small opening retracted, and steely eyes peered at him. Surprised, he gave his passcode and waited. The reinforced locks disengaged and pulling the handle, Ryan walked inside.

His visible exhaustion betrayed Ryan's previous warm demeanor.

Matted hair from a buildup of sweat beneath his head cover. Clothes dirty and even though they were black, the large unmistakable circles of blood spatters popped out for all to see. His usually vibrant green eyes reflected back a haze of sleeplessness and internal pain from behind the grease paint masking his appearance.

The wear and tear of the last few days evident to John.

Shaking hands, John knew what Ryan required after days in the field, mission focused and his disheveled look speaking volumes. He needed a shower, even an ice cold one. Directing Ryan to the locker room, the weary solider stowed his gear and weapons before finding the showers and took a long, and very cold, relaxation under the spray. Refreshed and revitalized, he asked around and found David playing with an old set of cars as Pete lay asleep on the concrete floor beside him. Seeing his dad, David sprang up and ran, jumping into Ryan's arms for a huge hug.

"Dad! You're safe. I missed you," David cried as tears welled up.

Ryan held his son close, wrapping him in a warm and loving hug. He smelled his hair, his skin, as he rubbed the young boy's back and caressed it. His own tears dripped down his cheeks. The salty liquid catching the corner of his mouth. Happy to see David again, and fearful about the future, he couldn't help the wave of emotions washing over him.

Ryan kissed David's forehead. "I told you I would be back Son. Just a bit longer than expected. How are you doing Stinky Man?"

David pulled back and stared. "You're the Stinky Man, Dad," he laughed before trying to put on a serious face.

The father couldn't help laugh with his son. "I was really stinky but made sure I took a shower before I saw you."

"I'm glad you did Dad, or I would have to throw up. Bleck!" David pretended to lose his lunch in Ryan's lap.

Ryan nodded. "I agree Son," he began with a smile before taking on a serious tone. "Hey, I wanted to talk to you. It's been a crazy time and I have some things to tell you."

Sensing it was one of *those* discussions, David shrugged and taking Ryan's hand, walked him to a quiet place with chairs so they could sit and talk. Pete, excited at seeing Ryan again, ran over and hopped into his lap to find comfort and a warm place to fall back to sleep.

Three years of no contact, no hugs or stories, and being dropped from the sky made togetherness somewhat awkward. Falling back into old rhythms and habits soon dispersed that.

Seeing Ryan again made David feel like his dad had only been gone a short time.

Though he looked different, grayer hair replacing the once auburn brown strands he remembered and more lines around the eyes, even the fresher wicked scars, David relished in staring and a few times had to reach over and hold his dad's face. He hoped it wasn't a dream meant to torment him, like the ones he had every night since he saw Mark push his father out of a helicopter and watched him fall into the dark sea below. Tactile touch brought reality forward, and a whisp of a finger against the skin gave the boy comfort.

It had been far too long missing his hero.

When he was done talking to David and sure his son wasn't scared anymore and in a good place with what Ryan had planned, Ryan excused himself, kissed his boy, and went to find John.

Telling his son that he had found his mom and sister and left them was one of the hardest things he ever had to do.

Explaining to his son he used to be a secret soldier was even harder, though for a young boy who loved superheroes, David immediately thought his dad had super powers and could do even more things beyond what he already considered "super" for his dad.

Some details stayed sketchy to preserve as much innocence for David as practical. Ryan painted enough of a picture and with explanations that were age appropriate for David to know there was a plan and reasons for what had happened.

Confused at first, David didn't understand.

As his dad told the story and explained David began to get it, which for an eight-year-old, was damn amazing. Promising he would be back soon, Ryan left Pete and David sitting on a couch until he returned.

Ryan had to give the grim and gritty picture to John with all the gore, and that was the easiest tale to share.

After he finished his story and Ryan sat back in the chair, John simply stared at him, his right hand pulling at his chin. The events seemed utter bullshit if he didn't know Mark and what they were all up against. An action movie if there ever was one. Finally, John sat back himself and propped his feet up on the desk.

"I'm glad you knew of this place Ryan. Given what happened to our people we needed a place to regroup for a bit. An old government shelter off the books below ground. Got to love the preparations made during the Cold War," John sighed.

Ryan smiled. "One of the few I found out about during my travels. Outdated for sure. I knew the security officer who maintained it for the *just in case* and thankfully the knowledge died with him."

John leaned forward, elbows on the desk. "If I have not been living this, I wouldn't believe any of what you told me. They have the Yorktown and some underground base of operations? This puts a whole different spin on it. And if you believe the President is still alive and behind everything, I'm not sure how long we can last. We've heard rumors and rumblings over the years. Come across people that told some pretty far-fetched tales. It seems that the stories were grounded in a bit of truth. Damn. This really mucks it all for us. That's a lot of resources at his disposal if even remotely still available."

Ryan knew it.

The odds were astronomical. A bunch of civilian survivors helped along by some old retired soldiers. Outgunned and outmanned, death was knocking on the front door.

"Mark has his own small army and depending on where things are at with the Brainers after I pissed on things, we have cracks in their armor to go after. We have the advantage," Ryan answered matter-of-fact.

John shook his head. "How the hell can you be optimistic? You killed the Vice President. That right there, if anyone gets their stories straight, might add fuel to an already blazing inferno."

Ryan looked at John, his green eyes wide, which conveyed to the older man something he couldn't quite place. "One less asshole to deal with," Ryan shrugged. "Besides, after what he planned for my daughter, blowing the asshole's brains all over the place was inevitable."

The words lightened the mood. "True Ryan. If it were me, I would have done the same. Though I would have missed. I was never a real on the ground combat soldier like you. You guys were my heroes. Made my life a whole hell of a lot easier."

The compliment made Ryan uncomfortable.

He spent an earlier life doing what had to be done, things any good soldier would do, regardless of how they served. Given the chance, a cook or desk clerk was just as honorable and duty bound to step up and do what was right.

"Thanks. I do have to say, and it makes me feel bad, it felt good. What they've done to my kids, my family, death is too easy."

John nodded. "No criticism from me. You know whatever we can do to end all of this we will. After what you have shared, we have an uphill fight." Staring intently at him, John asked Ryan, "What *is* going through your mind?"

Ryan laughed, a nervous response more than finding humor in the situation. "The Yorktown isn't going anywhere. I think it's less of a focus. As a supply line for munitions, it needs to go. However, if we can keep anything coming from or to it, we can bottleneck supply lines. The underground lab seems to be the local base of operations from what I saw. And more pressing, is getting my daughter and wife out of there. If Emma is being used for whatever Mark is planning, she's a prized asset. Without her, they are left with little."

The furrowed brow and look screamed the confidence wasn't there. "We don't have the manpower, or firepower even. We can offer some temporary problems, though nothing I can see to solve it."

Ryan leaned forward and tapped the desk. "It's all about being strategic. The more we can distress their operations, the more we gain an advantage, if even temporary and only for a few days."

The old man sat back. "I'm listening."

"We know two locations where they have resources. They stupidly blew the bridge over the river near the port and the crosstown throughway. They only have a handful of ways to transport or move anything going forward. The silos at the port could block their access points, even if for a short period of time. Bring down the structures and block them in. At that point, any offloads of supplies would have to be on the water, and we could choke those routes. The underground facility has the backdoor. I left a radio with Julia and what to listen for to be ready. We could be in and out with a distraction. The President and the Brainers are the wild cards. His resources and whether Mark soothes things over with each of them, given we have no idea where their bases are, present a few problems."

John sighed. "Do you really think we can pull any of this off?"

Ryan nodded. "I know we can. We have a ghost and a desire to live, not under some dictatorship and constantly on the run. There's something else going on with this serum. If it's a cure or staves off the side effects, people will do anything for it. And, those who don't fall in line, will suffer. I can guess what happens. You want the cure? Round up the President's enemies. Make examples of them. Sound familiar?"

The thought of what could happen made John shudder.

History had evil dictators, and he knew what this President had tried before the pandemic took its toll. If he got his hands on the cure and controlled it, he would look to cement his authority and force people to bow to him. He felt above the law and Constitution, and with the end of the world and nothing and no one to reign him in, he could practically do whatever he wanted, and no one stood in the way.

"If he is alive and directing from the background, the President needs to be found and stopped too. That's adding a whole lot of crap on top of the cow pies already laying at our feet. We stop Mark, what does that accomplish? Is there someone else waiting in the wings to step up and lead this sadistic experimentation on people, on your daughter? I bet this is how the colonists felt about the king and his long arms and reach, though they had much better odds and support from friendly nations. We have a rag-tag band of survivors barely hanging on in an apocalypse. The odds of us winning went astronomical when you found out about the dipshit in chief," John exhaled as he felt all the energy get sucked out.

Ryan laughed.

He couldn't help it. He never liked odds, felt statistics could be manipulated any which way, and always rooted for the underdog. "John, sorry for laughing. It wasn't meant as any disrespect. I actually see a silver lining in this. And, I think I know how we are going to win."

John's brow furrowed. He leaned back in his chair, eyes closed, and didn't say a word. Seconds turned to minutes. Ryan lost count how long they sat in silence. Anyone walking into the room would think John was asleep by the looks of him.

Ryan couldn't take it anymore. "Are you going to say something?"

The old sailor finally opened his eyes. "Tell me."

CHAPTER THIRTY-ONE

Ryan walked John through his thinking.

It took some time to lay it all out. Breaks to add Scotch to their mugs a requirement to wash down the words and focus. A bit of banter back and forth to warm up for what was going to be as John knew, an important talk that meant the difference between life and death.

Ryan sipped, told a few stories about life and the near-death experiences over the last years. More to get John comfortable with the conversation and planning he was going to drop on him. The old man wasn't a retired operator. Never been special forces. Had met many during his service and travels, but not the kind of mission briefs that Ryan was going to roll out and draw for the old seaman.

First drink finished, Ryan dove right into it.

Step by step he articulated a plan, a rather lofty one, though it was grounded in a lot of details that John found not only intriguing, but plausible. The execution was the critical element as components had to be done simultaneously for it to work and others to follow. Ryan had mentioned the port and the need to choke off supplies and support.

An attack there would draw the attention of the Brainers and likely any local Lurkers and Bolts.

If some of John's group could lead them there to ensure there were enough for the party, Ryan believed it would draw out soldiers from the underground facility and leave it vulnerable.

Use that opportunity to rescue Emma, Julia, and any other survivors present and with vengeance, cripple the place.

Some well-placed explosives to cover his tracks if necessary and he and the rescued civilians would be gone. The idea was to divide and distract, install chaos and misdirection. Risky yes, although if successful it meant a whole new game to play.

John sat back in his chair and Ryan could see he was thinking hard.

The older man closed his eyes, sighed, and nodded. John knew the risks and as an old military man in charge of thousands of people and critical missions, there was a window of opportunity. Even with the band he had here, a few dedicated and well-trained men and women with service backgrounds, they'd risk it all if it meant a future for their families and friends. While not the well-oiled machine at Mark's disposal and whatever the President had hidden, he knew Ryan's plan could work.

It *had* to work.

"I am beyond impressed with the size of your balls there Ryan. I don't know much about you, but you sure have confidence and a mind like a genius. Mad scientist maybe. There are multiple fail points that affect this. How can you be sure it will work?" John stared at Ryan, waiting for his answer.

Ryan grinned. "The size of my balls is decent. It's the other part that is enormous," he emphasized with spread arms. A short laugh before returning to a more serious tone. "For any one part, if we simply attacked it, it would draw too much attention and leave what remained on high alert. By going after the port first and making it a spectacle, it creates a window. I'd say an hour, for the facility to send support and leave it vulnerable. While they deal with the explosions and the extra attention I think we can produce, the backdoor to the facility becomes our way in. Blow it and the research sky high and we create discord. Mark will fume and not thinking straight, look to seek some vengeance. The President will be pissed on losing his serum and I'm pretty sure want Mark face to face. That scenario is our chance to put an end to everything."

John scanned Ryan's face for any indication that the man had any misgivings as to his grand plan. He saw none. "Any one part could fail."

Ryan held up his hand. "Potentially yes. However, the execution is the key. Even if we simply affected the port a little bit, it is a thorn in their side. The facility would have to respond in some way. From what I have seen with their makeshift security out front, we could even send a car right past and they'd jump at it."

"The back entrance you managed to get into. How would you breach it again without them leaving it open for you?" John asked.

Ryan had thought of that. It was easier before when he causally walked on in. "That is the one spot that adds complexity. From what I saw, it's not a super secured door. Single lock mechanism. The hidden nature is what drives it. It may have been an afterthought of design or purposeful. The warehouse is empty, and my guess is that if fully operational it would be full of stuff and the door blending into the surroundings. All I know is it can be breached."

John's head moved slowly from side to side as he contemplated Ryan's words. "OK. If, and this is a big *if*, if this works, when do you plan on it?"

Ryan pursed his lips. "It has to be tonight. Me killing the Vice President and Mark likely scrambling for answers means we have a short time to act. Otherwise, we might lose it. And, if Emma is the solution to his problems, time is ticking."

"I'm not sure we can be ready," John answered back.

Ryan nodded, understanding what the man meant. "It's a lot to ask and a short time to prepare. I must get my daughter and wife tonight no matter what. Emma can't stay there."

John felt for him. As a father himself, though his children grown adults and no idea of where they were or even alive, he knew what Ryan was going through and would do the same if the roles were reversed. "I don't think we have the supplies to pull this off Ryan. We need some serious explosives to take those silos down."

Ryan smiled. "I don't think we need a huge explosion. I mean just bring them down. They're probably still full of rice that was waiting to be loaded. A tinder box waiting to burn with all of that dried out material inside. Add some fuel and some small and timed explosions to help it along and my guess is the heat will weaken the structures and help them along."

The concerned look on John's face began to fade. "All right. That might work. Except, how do we pull it off? We have to get there to do it. *And*, likely get past a bunch of guards or lookouts. Time is not on our side."

"By water."

Confused, John asked, "Water?"

Ryan nodded. "Yes. The quickest way is by the river. I'm not talking by boat the entire way. A surface boat would be seen. Something that resembles a seal or even a porpoise in the water might draw some attention, fade away if they crossed and submerged. Give someone a chance to sneak out of the water and cross over to the silos and light them suckers up. Use the same for the getaway."

John laughed. "Are you serious? We don't have anything close to a seal or porpoise we can use. This is crazy. I thought you had this thing thought out."

Ryan pounded the desk hard, catching John's attention. "Focus! I brought up surface boat and looks like. Take a canoe or kayak, paint it black or gray, flip it and add some mannequin head. Use it to float across while gripping the sides to see and beneath the dock to secure it. Get to the silos, plant the explosives, throw some diesel through the vent pipe, and get the hell out. We don't need perfect here. Just something that can be faked. Get it?"

John stared. "I get it. The problem I see is that we are not equipped to do this by any stretch of the imagination and to me, this needs to be perfect or a storm is going to send a tornado our way."

"No tornado. Not even a hurricane. And to your point, we are as equipped as anyone can be since we have luck on our side."

"Where do we get the stuff we need to do it?"

Ryan feigned shock like it was the stupidest question and threw up his hands. "Camping World!"

CHAPTER THIRTY-TWO

Time was an enemy.

Ryan knew it. He was asking a lot of people not designed for this type of work, or even warfare. He was built for it. Had lost track of the number of missions where he had to improvise to succeed when something got twisted and he or the team had to rework a solution on the fly. He remembered every mission in vivid detail and the times they went sideways.

This was no different.

He could plan for every little detail, address each possible speed bump that would alter or affect it. In the end, there was no way to be one hundred percent.

It wasn't possible.

What you could do was build a fluid framework with contingencies to use if a scenario or situation presented itself. Follow the plan to the letter until you couldn't execute it. Then, you checked your list of what-ifs and went for it.

He probably should have led with the fact that Camping World sat above them and was a treasure trove of goodies he planned on using for their excursions.

Where was the fun in that?

When he explained that the building had previously been a government headquarters for some agency and the shelter the go-to for the executive staff if nuclear holocaust arose, John eased up and opened his ears.

As the wall fell and the Iron Curtain threat eroded, the building no longer had a use and years later was bought and rented out. The shelter remained, though only a few knew or had access as time eroded and its protectors died out.

Ryan's friend, an old salt of a guy who was the last remaining caretaker before shit went south, had given Ryan the scoop. He knew where the access elevator to the basement was and knew there were enough supplies here to use for the show he planned to premiere tonight. Since electrical required juice to work, there was an old access door and ramp that went topside which was the secondary access point if the generators failed.

After getting all the details and seeing it develop, John relaxed. There were still some areas he worried about that gave him a lot of concern. As they talked and Ryan weaved an intricate plan together like a seamstress making a million-dollar designer dress, it all came together. The sticky part was getting the canoes and gear to the water. That, for lack of a better term, was the cock blocker.

"I get it. You could have been a bit more upfront and not given me a heart attack. The transport though, how do we do that part?"

Ryan walked over to a cabinet and rummaged through it. Pulling out a rolled-up sheet of paper, he walked to the desk and spread it out. "See this here? This is us. The tunnel goes all the way along this route," he pointed and showed John where the tunnel ran under the river to a station close to the port. "The station was closed years ago when they opened the new tunnel. The old escape and get out of Dodge line. The tracks were left intact from here and we should be able to use it. There aren't any access points from here to there, so I don't think we have any Un-Dead to worry about."

"We have a rail line with a train, and no way to use it?"

Ryan pointed to the map. "No, I think we can. In the event of a catastrophe, there probably wouldn't be any electrical to run the line. The old train is diesel powered. We just need to get it cranked up."

John sighed and spread his arms wide. "I stand corrected. I swear your dangles are *this* big."

Ryan laughed and snot shot out his nose. "Oh crap. Sorry, but that was funny."

"No seriously, you have a huge pair to even think this stuff up. And, to such detail and degree that it makes perfect sense it will succeed. I wish you had been my first XO back in my day to assist in some heavy decision-making that came my way. At least, you're on our side."

Ryan shrugged. "It's ingrained in me to prepare for everything. A plan is only as good as its framework and execution to get results. Make back-ups to back-ups and work it all out. Even under stress, we were trained to be able to make tough choices and carry a mission out. Even if it meant a one-way trip to the grave, if you were able to succeed it meant saving lives."

John put his hand on Ryan's shoulder. "That's a morbid thing to say and I'm sorry that's what we expected of you. Leadership too often means letting others sacrifice themselves for your own gain. From talking to you over these last few days I get a sense that I owe you my life. Not sure for what. I guess that in some shit hole around the globe you did some stuff that prevented a whole lot of really bad stuff. Thank you solider."

"You are welcome, Sir."

Patting Ryan again, the concern in John's voice was apparent. "What about you? I think we have the port all covered. You sure you want to go to the facility alone? I have a few good people, not as adept as you, good nonetheless. They were part of a Marine detachment for my ship. I'm sure they could offer whatever you need."

Ryan had thought about it.

Going alone was risky and really a stupid decision. Getting Emma and Julia out were priorities. He also knew that anyone else inside he couldn't leave there if he was going to incinerate the place.

Help would be a blessing.

Ryan knew he needed assistance once he managed to get people out and get them whisked away to safety. While he knew the Marines were well-trained and capable, they weren't operators or ghosts and he couldn't afford any screw ups.

"Thank you, John. The help I need is for getting survivors free and clear. I can handle inside. Once I get them topside, they need to be gone and gone quick."

John leaned back in his chair. "Understood. Lone wolf in action?"

Ryan shook his head. "No. Precision of execution. I can't afford to deviate from the mission. If these were teammates I had trained with, no question. People who aren't exactly in step and the same mindset are liabilities. I don't want anyone at risk and I know the layout and what to do and where to go. We don't have the liberty of working the problem and running it through a training session."

"I feel for you Ryan. I can't imagine what you've seen or done. I get the sense you are the best at what you do. I see it in your eyes. Best of luck. We need some of it."

Ryan smiled. "Thanks John. Please make sure if anything goes sideways at the port with the silos, I know right away. I'll be a sitting duck if the facility doesn't clear out enough and I have a whole lot of soldiers to engage."

John stood up and offered his hand. "Yes Sir. Go do what you do and see you real soon."

Ryan's mind wandered a bit, the whole day feeling like a cluster as they prepared for their assaults. Getting everything thrown together in such a short period of time and ready to execute was an undertaking of monstrous effort. Camping World provided many of the necessary pieces of the puzzle and surprisingly offered up a few bonuses that Ryan had not even thought about. That wasn't to say that it went spectacularly well.

It hadn't.

The canoes and kayaks required paint and since none was available for a quick turnaround to dry, they used black grease paint from the sporting goods aisle. It thankfully repelled water and wouldn't come off without a serious scrubbing. The crews doing the work ran out and had nothing left for the group that was doing the incursion to the port. It was supposed to be face paint to keep any glint from shining, so an alternative and less ideal means like mascara, prevailed.

The mannequin heads had to be duct taped on to stay in place and Ryan hoped they lasted the journey. Bolting on would have been the better choice. That required electricity and tools. It took a long time and effort to make them resemble some type of sea creature to pass for in the dark and if you focused long enough someone would wise up and realize they weren't animals at all.

The team did their best and hoped they passed fleeting looks.

The kid kayaks acted as the seals as anything bigger was out of place. The problem was they didn't offer much concealment or the ability to haul much beneath without a lot of drag. The canoes were great for fake porpoises, and with the air space inside could hold enough people to float across the river. That meant one had to act as the transport canoe and have everything hanging from it as it floated across upside down.

Two people could hopefully manage to maneuver it.

With a ton of weight and drag against currents, Ryan decided a second was required which meant more work to do. They had to haul all the supplies to land and to the silos undetected while keeping some of it dry, like the grill lighters and fire starters. All the dry storage bags were gone, and creative thinking meant some weird solutions using more duct tape, water repellant jackets, and pure ingenuity.

The bonuses happened with the propane tanks and a few other perks.

Diesel was the better fuel choice, though it weighed down any cans they would have to haul below the canoe. They would need full ones with no air pockets inside to ensure they had enough fuel to complete the task.

Propane tanks floated.

They added extra buoyancy and would help the teams float the supplies and themselves across. Untie and set them up with a connector and hose with a fitting, turn the knob, light the gas, and it would act as a propellant and fire source to stoke a blaze in the silos. Diesel could fizzle out. Not the propane.

The cluster was all the gear necessary to pull off a water assault.

The river was frigid cold and had current. Doing a free swim was out of the question and drowning not an option. The wet suits would provide protection from the cold water as much as possible, though they weren't the best cold weather kind and more aligned with summer dives. Layers were going to be required and the dry fit undergarments and insulation the team needed a mix and match of too small and too big, but the best they could do under the circumstances.

An issue were the air tanks.

Some of the air tanks still worked after three years which was phenomenal, though with the lapse of time didn't provide much in the way of extended air.

Fifteen, twenty minutes tops for most of them.

It was enough for what was necessary, though at the critical low end. The life vests that remained were small, more for children, and had to be stitched together with fishing lines to make a makeshift jacket for each team member to use before taking off and submerging below water to remain unseen.

It was cringeworthy how haphazard and dangerous the gear was for a night excursion in frigid and dark waters. The team of volunteers was adamant they could do the job. Getting the supplies for the fires and explosions proved daunting to feel they could remain secured and float to their destination.

The only saving grace were that propane tanks could float.

The ropes stringing everything together for transport would at least get the minimum across the river if something went wrong. It took the crew working on the project down to the wire to complete their tasks and get everything prepared and ready for the trek through the tunnels and to the launching point. With hope and some great luck, Ryan felt they had a chance to succeed.

Preparations for his own quest were the more worrisome and Ryan didn't want to put anyone's lives on the line.

He had to make the incursion into the facility alone to keep the element of surprise. Rescuing the survivors inside required an extraction and vehicles for transport.

That's where the others came into play.

He knew he could handle his side, and from talking to the men and women who were going to assist the mission, he felt slightly optimistic. Some had an extensive military background with combat experience, and from the small talk were beyond capable of handling themselves in any situation. A few were younger with less real-world experience, though their training and ship time with their detachment of Marines meant they could follow command.

He was even lucky to get two special operators from the Air Force and one from the Coast Guard.

At least if shit went south, he had some confidence Jack and Monique could step up and take lead if they must and Rich with his background in the Guard provide water support or rescue if it came to it.

While neither Jack nor Monique had his skillset, finding out he had them at his disposal forced Ryan to tweak his plan.

Let go a bit and let others step in and take an active role to lead.

Monique was one of the few women who turned heads and forced command to admit women into special operations. She proved her worth a few times over during her career and readily stepped up to show how special ops could be gender neutral. Rich was used to narco operations during his time at sea and in ports up and down the West Coast. He was a salt of a dog and his stories full of non-PC moments. Much like Monique, he listened, asked questions, and absorbed his role. Jack was the quiet one, his scowl a turnoff if you didn't know him.

It screamed leave me alone.

That perception was polar opposite of the man. He listened and followed directions to the letter and like the others, he was a needed asset. Any other time, Ryan would love to sit back and have some cold brews and tell some tales at length. He focused in on the primary details and what he needed of them, and quietly left to prep himself.

A half hour before he was set to go, David joined his dad as he sorted his gear and supplies.

Ryan felt strange sharing something personal and dangerous with his son. If it was the last time ever with David, he wanted his boy to know who his father was and clear up some of the secrets he had kept hidden away.

The boy sat quietly, watching and observing, before finally speaking up. "Uh, Dad, can I ask you a question?"

Intuition and knowing his little man, Ryan prepared for it. "Sure Son. What is it?"

A frown crept across David's face and his lips pursed before he spoke. Looking at Ryan, his brown eyes staring intently, the boy mouthed softly, "Dad, have you ever killed someone?"

Ryan sighed. He was ready for it, though had hoped he would be having the discussion many years in the future on his deathbed. He took David's hand in his own. "I have Son. Before I met your mom, I was a solider and met a lot of really bad people. My job meant sometimes the bad people died."

David nodded. "Um, have you killed anyone recently?"

Ryan paused a moment, didn't expect that one. "I have Son."

Fear welling up in his eyes, David shifted his body back a bit. "Are, are you going to kill anyone tonight?"

He hated seeing David fearful of his own father. Ryan knew he'd probably feel the same if his own dad had shown up out of the blue, armed to the teeth with all kinds of weapons and weird things, and proceeds to tell him he had killed people.

Bending down to get at David's level, Ryan touched David's cheek. "Big Man, I know all of this is strange and all of sudden you learn some things about me that are scary. You know I tell the truth, right?"

David nodded.

"Tonight, I am going to get your mom and Emma. There are some really bad people keeping them and as you know, have hurt your sister and you."

"Like Uncle Mark?"

Sighing, Ryan replied, "Yes, like Uncle Mark."

David's face softened and his shoulders became less tense.

"In order to save them and the others being kept, some of those really bad people are probably going to die. Well, that's kind of not true."

David didn't quite understand. "What do you mean, Dad?"

Peering intently at his boy and as serious as he could manage, Ryan had to do it. "I'm probably going to go all Hulk on them, though to be honest more like Darth Vader, and use my lightsaber and take every hand I can. Though some heads are probably going to roll too."

David couldn't keep the laugh inside and belted it out. He understood the reference and, as a kid who liked superheroes and knew his father's love of Star Wars, the picture of his dad all green and looking like Darth Vader at the same time popped into his head.

Taking a hold of Ryan's face with his hands, David peered deep into his dad's eyes. "Dad, are you a superhero?"

A laughed escaped Ryan and spit shot out his mouth. "No, Son. I am just a guy and your dad who helps protect people and the world. Superheroes are people like your sister, who every day works to make the world a better place by showing people that everyone is the same and that even if you have a disability, it doesn't mean a thing. She's my superhero, David."

David smiled. "She's mine too, Dad."

CHAPTER THIRTY-THREE

Every well thought out and executed plan finds itself confronted with a dilemma.

Sometimes it's a minor detail that changes the arc a tiny bit, allows for the completion of the task. Other times it's a major FUBAR that means completely changing course and winging it, though the final result remains ending in success. Tonight, in the dark and cold of the night, with odds against them and the spirit of surprise in their favor, the storm fell in his lap and all Ryan could do was let fate take over.

The mission to the port to blow the siloes worked, though barely, and the team returned to their safehouse to wait it all out.

The old marina road led to a storage yard and machine shop and being in the opposite direction and against the current, the team, once they made it safely back across the water, could let the fake seals and porpoises float down river and away from their intended destination.

A few days sequestered and moving at night to different locations, they would eventually meet up with their comrades. Waiting was the hard part as radio silence and being alone close to enemy territory was not ideal. Fortunately, they all made it out alive, though cold to the bone and beyond exhausted.

The silo explosion presented Ryan with his window of opportunity and his one-man rescue mission.

It had been nerve-racking sitting and waiting for the first glow of fire shooting into the sky. Ryan had been in place for some time, close to the warehouse and ready to act. When the first silo had gone up, he watched for his opportunity, about ten minutes after he saw the first trucks leave the front of the underground facility. By his count he saw six large troop transports barrel out and if full, he figured the ones left to guard were a skeleton crew.

With care he entered the warehouse, found the hidden door, and worked his magic to open it. That proved a bit more difficult in the darkness. Once he found the right spot where the lock engaged the frame, a well-placed charge of old C4 the size of a stick of gum to keep the explosion as quiet as practical, and soon he was able to breech the door and descend inside.

Ryan figured he had maybe fifteen or twenty minutes of solid time without much distraction, and it proved accurate.

After he found his way down the stairs and to the passageway, he encountered his first obstacle, a two-man team on patrol. He waited as they passed and seizing the element of surprise, eliminated them with quick knife thrusts through the backs of their skulls. Dragging them behind some storage barrels, he proceeded cautiously to Emma's room and hoped Julia had received his message to be ready.

As he moved, it was obvious the facility was in flux with all the disarray he passed.

Boxes of supplies being packed, crates of goods in prep for sealing and being transported. His guess, his exploits had hit a huge nerve or more likely, since he doubted anyone knew he had endangered the sanctity of the underground hideout, Mark was moving some or all of his prisoners elsewhere for some reason.

He needed to know where and why, if others had already been shipped out.

Quick steps and panning his MP5 to track any movements that might jump out, Ryan worked his way through the corridors. He didn't see any more guards and within a minute found himself at Emma's door. Testing the handle, he found it locked, knocked quietly, and waited.

A few seconds later a small voice asked, "Password?"

"Purple Princess," Ryan replied.

The door opened and to his surprise, Ryan saw a group of people huddled behind Emma, who was ready to go. Backpack on, shoes and jacket already, a warm beanie on her head. He smiled and she tried to wink at him, though her winks ended up being more of a two-eyed squint.

Julia stepped up and shrugged. "It got crazy around here. I gathered up everyone I could to wait."

Ryan nodded. "Great. Saves us some time."

She shook her head. "We have some problems though. The patient wing here has some who can't make it out. They're in vegetative states and we can't move them without wheeling them out the front door." The sad look on her face betrayed her because he knew she understood what had to happen.

Ryan sighed. "Are you absolutely sure?"

The tears crept down her cheeks. "I am."

Looking around the room, Ryan saw a mix and match of people, young and old, melting pot of ethnicities, and some with visible disabilities. Fear stared at him through transfixed eyes. He could tell they were scared, but saw the unwavering desire to get the hell out.

They nodded in agreement when he asked, "You all ready to bounce out?"

As he began to turn, Julia grabbed his arm. Leaning in, she whispered in his ear, "I know they have soldiers wandering around. How are we going to get out?"

Ryan reached and touched her cheek to wipe away the wetness. "Have some faith and trust Love. This is my kind of shit show," he winked with a sly grin.

A soft laugh, and then Julia wiped away the rest of the tears and put her hand on Emma's shoulder.

Motioning for everyone to stand up, Ryan pointed to the door. "If you want to live, do everything I say and when I say it. Single file line five paces behind me. No talking, no sounds. I am in the lead, and you follow. If I see anyone in front of me, I will take care of it and keep moving forward. Anyone have a problem with that?"

As he looked around for any responses, all Ryan got were affirmative nods.

"Good. Let's blow this place."

Peering out the door and seeing it clear, Ryan moved out and slowly down the hallway. Julia, holding Emma's hand, soon followed. The others left the room one by one until everyone was out. Reaching the end of the hallway, he heard the footsteps coming from the left and motioned for everyone to get against the wall. As the figure passed, Ryan, seeing the uniform, waited for the soldier to disappear down the hallway and then snuck up behind and quickly dispatched the man with his blade.

The body jerked momentarily and went limp.

He watched the frightened expressions as he dragged the body to Emma's room and pushed the body through the door and closed it. As he walked down the line of people, he saw them staring at Emma, who had put her tiny finger to her lips, motioning for them to be silent. Each one imitated her actions.

He knew from here on, the group would fall in line.

The rescue team had been blocks away to keep noise at a minimum in case the cars made a lot of sound. As soon as the second silo blew, they moved in. One team remained with the transports while another worked its way to the warehouse, wait to take out any soldiers that might be around, and then scurry the survivors to safety once Ryan emerged. Encountering no other soldiers and no resistance, Ryan led the group up the stairs and through the warehouse to the door. Glancing out the small window, he saw it was safe and opened the door.

One after another the people he had rescued passed him, with the occasional thank you or pat on the shoulder. It had been barely ten minutes inside and out. As Julia and Emma helped to usher the slower ones, he couldn't help smile.

Emma had turned into a little adult.

She held the hand of James, the older man with Down Syndrome who he could tell was scared and frightened. As she walked with him, she whispered encouragement and praise for him being brave. His gait became more confident and soon he smiled and waved. It made Ryan feel warm inside and that even in the face of such fear and a crap world, there was hope for a future beyond all the madness as kindness and humanity still reigned.

As Emma escorted James out the door, Julia, the last one, stopped in front of Ryan. "You're not coming with us, are you?"

Ryan reached out to touch her arm. "I can't. I have to tidy up or else this will keep on going."

Seeing the determination in his eyes, the stubbornness she called it, Julia knew there was no trying to convince her husband. Standing before her was a man she didn't really know and also knew inside and out.

He was complex, multi-dimensional.

She had thought about it since first seeing him after three long years, finally coming to terms he was dead and like a spirit he was standing in front of her, the little things that seemed odd or out of place popped out.

The locked cabinet in the far corner of the garage that was partially hidden and never opened. The talks with Mark that ended when she entered the room. The way he scanned his surroundings and took things in.

She thought it was all him being a security-minded guy.

He had run a successful company protecting all kinds of people from danger. It all started to add up. There had always been something about him she couldn't quite make out.

She hoped he could open up and tell her.

All she knew was her man was bad ass and had saved a bunch of strangers from almost certain death. At this point in time, he was more than her Ryan, someone bigger she couldn't understand. That was OK in this moment. He would have to spill later if she was to accept it.

Julia brushed the tears from her eyes. "I can't lose you again Ryan. I don't know what's all going on or how you are involved. You have to come back to me, to us."

Ryan smiled, pulled Julia close, holding her in his arms. "I love you and the kids more than life. I finally have you back, and I won't lose you again. You have to trust me. A Carmichael has to do-" he got out before she cut him off.

"What a Carmichael has to do." Looking up at him, staring deep into his green eyes, Julia asked, "Who are you, Ryan?"

He couldn't help laugh. "A ghost and as you probably have guessed, someone who has done this all before."

"And, the killing?"

Ryan sighed, the weight heavy on his chest. "What did Arnold say in that movie? But they were all bad, or something like that?"

Julia couldn't help laugh at him. If he could survive being pushed from a helicopter, manage to live three years alone, find his way inside a secret underground complex, kill enemies, and rescue people, she was sure he could take care of things and get back to her and the kids again.

"Go do your thing Mr. Hot Shot and get home safe."

"Have some chocolate chip cookies and cold milk waiting for me."

Emma had heard the discussion and walked over and gave him a hug. She was a smart girl and her ability to feel emotions a gift. "Be safe Daddy. Love love."

Bending down to kiss her forehead and give her a huge hug, Ryan relished in it before letting go. "I will Princess. Take care of Momma and Bub, OK? You're in charge until I get back."

"Yes Dad," Emma winked, before Julia ushered her away.

Ryan spoke to the rescue team leader for a minute and sure his family was safe and out of sight, headed back to the facility.

He had to plant the charges to destroy the research and all that was left and retreat quickly to ensure his own escape from the vicinity. A pang of guilt fell over him as he descended below for the last time.

There were still people inside, innocents, who deserved to be rescued.

In their current conditions, with no hospitals or doctors to keep them going and the possibility for a chance to recover, their odds of survival were next to nil.

He didn't want to kill anyone who didn't ask for it.

In the larger scheme of it all, he had to come to terms with the fact that locked in comas with little ability to regain their full facilities, going out this way was better than the alternative. Sometimes there was a greater good no matter how shitty or terrible it might be, and if it meant blowing the research sky high to leave Mark with nothing and back to square one, maybe life had a chance again to rise up.

Destroy the crap that enveloped the world.

He knew the asshole wouldn't stop his work, and Ryan wouldn't stop looking for him. Adding obstacles to prevent future tortures and foment chaos was a pleasure Ryan had to put in place.

With the last charge of C4 set and timed to go off, Ryan left.

On his way out he removed from circulation an additional eleven soldiers and ten research staff as he maneuvered the passages and placed each explosive near a highly combustible source to propel the blast. Oxygen lines ran overhead and gas pipes, used to fuel the Bunsen burners in the labs, had shut off valves outside the secured doors.

The soldiers were dispatched with ease, head shots straight and true as he encountered them.

They likely knew little and were simply following orders, no matter how complicit they were to kidnapping, torture, and death. Disposable assets, following the chain of command due to duty, even if the virus hampered their brains.

The research team though, he was sure they were aware of what they were doing.

They were actively experimenting on people, children, and even the disabled. He took some glee on erasing them from the face of the Earth and knowing they wouldn't be tormenting anyone ever again. The last one begged for his life, almost comical in his diatribe against his impending death sentence. Tried to sway Ryan that his work was brilliant and would revolutionize for a new world order.

Nazi doctors tried the same justifications.

It was too familiar, the words, the thoughts, the comparisons to past ideological scumbags who pushed their agendas and felt they were worthy of praise for their atrocities. Nazism, Fascism, even the President and his grip on his base of mindless drones who followed his every word as if they were gospel.

The ramblings of madmen who sought their place in history and couldn't fathom the evil depths of their deeds.

Ryan simply nodded in agreement before he raised his MP5 and splattered the man's brains across his workstation. There was no way he was letting any of these miscreants and soulless demons live another minute if he could help it.

Mission complete, he slipped out the same way he came, carefully placing one last brick of C4 to seal the stairs to the depths underground. He had enough time to retreat and be far enough away as the explosions would go off first at the front of the facility and one after another work their way towards the rear. Closing the hidden door behind him and heading to the exit, Ryan heard the words come through his earpiece. They caught him off guard and he froze in his tracks.

"Charlie Team to Command, over."

"This is Command, over."

"We've got vehicles leaving the vicinity of the facility. Engage? Over."

A moment of silence and then the familiar voice. "Eliminate the threat. Over and out."

Ryan had hoped the rescue team would be gone and to safety without being seen. While he knew it was a possibility, he had hoped they would zip out and be away without pursuers. Full of survivors, he knew the team would be hard-pressed to engage in a fire fight for fear of getting anyone killed. The soldiers had no idea anyone from the facility were riding inside and taking the vehicles out using any means a likely scenario. The only way to safeguard their journey was to act and act fast.

He ran for the exit and burst into the night, not knowing which way to run or go, except as far from his current location and in the opposite direction of the rescue team as he could. The next few minutes were critical to ensure he got away to a safe distance and draw the team's pursuers towards him.

As he ran, he pulled grenades from his vest and pulling pins, hurled them in one by one.

Sometimes he made sure to chuck two well intentioned grenades for the added kick necessary to create mayhem. With his M4 as his primary weapon for the ensuing firefight he was sure was forthcoming, he let off a few rounds to add to drawing the attention of Charlie Team.

The first explosion tossed through the broken window of a car blew out the windshield and vibrated along the street as it erupted in flames.

The second from a one-two combo next to a fire hydrant saw the water line blow with a loudness and scream a cannon of water high into the air. The next three along an old above-ground gas line that serviced the industrial area sent a huge plume of fire into the air.

If these didn't draw immediate attention, he wasn't sure what would.

Behind him, he heard the first facility blast and in the reflection of windows saw the plume of bright orange flames shoot high into the sky. A few seconds later, the next followed and the ground rumbled. Within five minutes the fire raged infernal, and from the sounds of it, his grenades had caused a lot of uncertainty as to who to follow.

"Charlie Team report, over."

A minute passed before a response. "The facility just blew, over."

Rage boiled over through the earpiece. "You incompetent fuck. What do you mean the facility blew up?"

The leader of Charlie Team replied, trepidation in the words as he sought the right ones to use. "We were in pursuit of the vehicles when we heard explosions and gunfire and broke off to investigate. When we got there the research facility was up in flames. We've lost the vehicles, over."

Two minutes passed before Mark spoke. "Do you have anything to report that will save your life? Over."

"We've got a line on the gunfire and are right behind it. Will update when we apprehend. Over and out."

Ryan smiled. At least the rescue team was on its way to safety. If Charlie Team was really on his ass, he needed to make sure they stayed on it. He crossed over streets and veered more into the city.

Taking a chance to sow even more discord, Ryan pressed the mic button. "Der hund ist los." His German accent was horrible, though super hilarious.

"Who is this?"

Ryan chuckled. He could hear the anger in Mark's voice.

In his best English accent, Ryan mocked him. "Bollocks. You're a wanker!"

Behind him he heard the squeal of tires and the fast approach of what had to be Charlie Team. Taking his cue, Ryan cut left and straight up the front stairs of an office building. Checking the front entry doors, they were locked.

A promising sign, he smashed the front glass.

Breaking the remaining shards, he went inside, managed to grin from ear to ear, and soon disappeared into the recess of darkness to prepare for what was to come.

CHAPTER THIRTY-FOUR

The front of the office building provided line of sight.

No retaining walls, bushes, trees, or any potential hiding spots existed. To get to the front doors you had to come through the open across the street or down the sidewalk, walk up the cement stairs until reaching the landing where the doors stood, and breach the entryway.

It was a perfect setup for some lone gunman

Sit against the interior wall and lean over to the side, rifle peeking out the broken glass, and pop off rounds as the police tried to storm and take the shooter down. In the dead of night with no lights and the interior pitch black, except for what managed to leech inside, anyone outside faced the wrong kind of odds.

Ryan wasn't a lone gunman.

This wasn't his first time being pursued and having to shoot his way out of a situation that left a lot of possibilities on things going really bad. While the front door offered a great spot for an amateur, it presented a one and done if someone managed to draw your fire and someone else happened to chuck a concussion grenade or worse yet, an actual grenade that would send metal shards tearing through your body. The off chance at severing an artery and you were toast.

No.

The smart move was retreating to higher ground, if in fact you insisted on a shootout. Above the fray with plenty of cover to lean over the top and shoot away.

That wasn't his plan.

A gun battle would pin him down, even if he managed to dodge and evade, taking his shots methodically to pick off his adversaries one by one. A firefight of one against many left too many scenarios that got you surrounded and your exit points diminishing until you were left with no way out. Ryan had been here before and he knew what to do, even if it meant encroaching on his time to get away. The important objective was engaging his enemy for long enough to give Julia and the others more time to escape.

Ryan moved carefully, silently maneuvering through the blackened building. The stairs leading to the second floor of the old building ascended up either side of the large foyer.

He went right and straight to the second-floor landing.

Took up a defensive position around the corner and against the wall. Tossing an old flare to the ground below, its red glow growing more intense as it burned, he waited.

Diesel engines and tires squelched outside.

He heard boots pounding the cement. If Charlie Team was any good, they wouldn't rush on through the doors after seeing the flare. If they were even half decently trained, they would approach with caution and maneuver through the entry with precision and purpose.

The flare was a ruse, a visual to distract.

He knew it would draw attention like moths to a flame. Just a matter of time for it to do its job. Anticipation ate away, watching and listening for them to come.

Ryan didn't have to wait long, which for a former professional was a bit of a disappointment. His expectations were maybe too high. The first line came through the broken door while the other entered from the right, coming down a hallway perpendicular to the foyer. As the teams met in the middle, he caught the chatter.

"Right side all clear to this point."

"All right," the team leader ordered. "Fan out and check the first floor."

As Charlie Team moved into position to secure the area, Ryan let it fly. The bottle splattered the tile right in front of Charlie Team's leader and sent a plume of liquid up in the air. As some hit the flare it sparked brighter and illuminated the room even more. He waited for it and within seconds he heard the pounding of footsteps echoing the previously quiet peace inside.

"What the hell?" one of Charlie Team's members blurted out as the sound roared and grew close.

"Open fire!"

Bullets erupted and tracers lit up the interior of the foyer as the Bolts descended upon Charlie Team. The wails of the killers drowned out the yells of the soldiers as they shot wildly in an attempt to stop the onslaught. One after another the Bolts fell, real death taking them. The next in line managed to jockey through the flying metal projectiles and find their way to the closest soldier.

Their grasp firm and ratio of numbers 5 to 1, the soldiers were ripped apart one by one.

All Ryan could do was watch the massacre and thank fate that he had been around long enough to know the smell of a Bolt den. With the bloody mess still going on below, Ryan took his exit. Hustling down the corridor and keeping his ears and eyes focused on any sound or movement, he found his way to the stairwell to the third floor and climbed up the steps.

He heard the sound behind him, and by then it was too late.

CHAPTER THIRTY-FIVE

Ryan awoke, his head on fire, not sure how long he had been out.

Slumped in a metal chair with his hands tied behind his back. Slowly prying open first his left eye and gingerly the right, Ryan saw a familiar sight standing across from him. Thin, skinny build, dirty-blond mullet.

Rebel Fucker.

"What's shakin' bacon?" Rebel grinned, his Southern drawl front and center. "Finally decided your cat nap was over?"

Ryan popped his neck from side to side, causally looked over his shoulder. They were the only two in the room. Looking bored, he shrugged, "Been a long few days of killing. Needed the rest."

The statement sent Rebel into a frenzy.

He did a little jig and twirled in a circle before coming to a stop in front of Ryan. "Woo hoo. I knew it was you man! You have some serious balls! Did you do all of that by yourself?" He was like a little kid who had learned the secret identity of his favorite villain.

Ryan smiled. "One man death machine."

Rebel slapped his leg. "A real-life bad ass mother. You are something else. Damn, I'm gonna be sad to kill you all dead and shit."

Ryan laughed. The high school dropout vocabulary was a bit comical.

Rebel tensed up, standing straight as an arrow, and pointed at Ryan. "Something funny asshole? I wouldn't be all laughy taffy if I was you. I got all carter blanche to have some fun torturing you for information and gets to kill you any way I want. And, I'm gonna." The gleam in his eyes showed he couldn't wait.

Ryan nodded and leaned forward. "Hey, let me tell you something. Step a bit closer."

Rebel's eyes grew wide. "Nah, I'm good right here."

"I'm all tied up and you're in charge. I'm not going anywhere."

Eyebrow raised, thinking it over, Rebel's head bounced up and down. "Yeah, that's right." Stepping closer to Ryan, he leaned in a bit. "What's on your mind fella?"

Ryan motioned to his right hand and stuck his pinky finger out.

Rebel leaned to the side. "Uh, what I'm supposed to see?"

Ryan wiggled his pinky. "My finger. Take a look at it."

Rebel moved to his left and glanced at the protruding digit. "Oh, shit man! That's one messed up finger. What the hell?"

Ryan pulled his hand back behind him. "I was doing some work for Uncle Sam and-" he began before Rebel interrupted.

"Your uncle did that?"

Laughter. "No, no. Uncle Sam, you know? The government."

"Oh," Rebel nodded. "Right."

Ryan kept going. "I was doing some work and got captured. Killed some people that were kind of important to this really bad guy. Well, he figured he'd even it up and have some fun with me. Kind of like what you want to do. He took my Ka-Bar, you know what that is? Well, he took my knife and thought it would be funny to start cutting my fingers off one by one."

Rebel's eyes grew huge. "Oh damn! That's what I'm gonna do!"

Ryan pursed his lips, disdain in his eyes. "Kind of standard torture procedure. I thought you might be original. Well, anyway, he started with my right pinky finger and boy, that mother fucker hurt like a bitch!"

The story was working. Rebel stepped closer, listening intently to Ryan's story. "Yeah, go on."

Licking his lips, Ryan continued. "I'm in serious fucking pain after having my finger almost severed off. He ties me back up to *think about things* and then comes back to cut off another. He was really pissed I killed his son, nephew, and two of his top generals."

"You killed his kid? You some bad man. You don't do that to no kid." Rebel seemed serious.

Did Ryan hear Rebel had some moral compass still intact? "Oh really? You and that reject tub of lard hillbilly were torturing that poor kid. I saw you."

Rebel squinted, his face tensing up before it relaxed. "Oh, that was business. Some pisser that was worth a whole lot."

Ryan frowned. "Ah, got it. Well, this guy's son and his buddies were doing some pretty bad things to some little kids. So, I splattered their brains all over the place."

The shock lit up Rebel's face. "No shit? What happened?"

Ryan leaned forward and motioned with his head for Rebel to move closer. He knew he had the man's full attention, and Rebel obliged. "Well, he comes back and beats the crap out of me, and I don't say a word. He walks over to take another finger off. As he walks and stands in front of me, he thought it would be really funny to take a piss on me. What could I do?"

"Ha! He did the old pisser on ya. Now that's a good one." The thought firmly planted in his head, Rebel unzipped his fly and whipped it out.

Ryan looked at Rebel's manhood, firmly grasped in his hand and ready to flow. "Yup. That's about what happened. But you know what?" Ryan let the words hang in the air.

Rebel looked down and grinned. "He pissed on ya like I'm about to?"

The chuckle echoed around the walls of the room as Ryan leaned closer. "You can't piss straight out of a penis if you don't have one."

The confused look on Rebel's face soon turned to horror when it registered.

As it did, Ryan's now free hands, having used the small blade tucked in the back of his BDU belt to cut through the zip ties, came forward like lightening. Rebel in shock, let go of himself in a vain attempt to block the attack.

Dangling free, Ryan grasped Rebel in his right hand and cut off his limp shaft with the knife in his left.

As he began to fall backwards, Ryan shot up and sunk the blade straight in the man's stomach, turning the blade around to make sure the artery he hit was completely severed and he'd eventually bleed out.

As shock took over and the life began to drain, Ryan leaned in and whispered. "Never ever fuck with a man's kid or hurt one. You'll lose your dick if you do."

"You cut off my junk man," Rebel got out in barely a whisper. "Not cool."

"Beating my boy wasn't either. You and all your buddies who hurt him are going to pay. See you in hell asshole," Ryan spit as he slipped the blade through the right temple, twisted it around, and watched Rebel's eyes glaze over.

He had no idea where he was or how many enemies were around. All Ryan knew was he needed to leave. Checking Rebel's body for any intel and finding nothing, he grabbed the dead man's radio and went to the door and turned the knob.

Unlocked.

The door creaked opened, and he found himself in a larger room. Walking across past a counter, he listened before opening the door and taking a peek to the outside. He saw a hallway and not a soul, and opening it up all the way, Ryan stepped gingerly over a broken bottle.

The torture room had been drab and ordinary, with nothing inside that indicated where he was or the type of place.

The hallway gave him a bit of information, though it proved disheartening. As he worked his way to the left, which seemed to be the way to go, the old high school corridor made his skin crawl.

Not from seeing any foe, just being back inside teenage hell.

The trophy case full of figures and cups, cheer squad and team photos, and even the game winning balls from multiple sports. He saw the name and mascot, had no idea who or where it was located, which put a black cloud over his head.

As he crept, careful to remain vigilant and silent, the office seemed to be part of the administration wing near the front of the school. The doors with a hint of light cascading through at the end of the hallway to the right screamed exit, and Ryan knew he needed to find a different path out. Brainers or Mark's men could be sitting right outside, and he'd walk right back in to being a captive. He needed to find a side exit and get the hell away before someone found the eunuch formerly known as Rebel Fucker.

Halfway down the corridor he found his stuff tossed on top of a table. Taking time to quickly gear up, Ryan checked his weapons, and scurried deeper inside the maze of a complex. With no working lights, it was dark.

Not completely, as skylights offered some hint of illumination.

Meant to cut down on electricity and use natural light whenever practical, it must be overcast out or the dirt and grime build up on the glass keeping all the light from penetrating inside. He found himself creeping down the corridors searching for a way outside. Some were dead ends into interior courtyards and the lunch area. Finally, he found his way to the back of the building and the breezeway to the playing fields.

An *oh shit* moment hit him smack in the face.

Ryan looked out at the expanse of open area, and in what he found out was the oncoming dusk that had been responsible for the poor light inside the school, his heart sank. The Brainer base of operations, or what he deduced was it by the hundred plus creeps he saw, milled about a rag tag encampment.

Tents, fifth wheel trailers, small pull tents hooked to truck bumpers, and even cots littered the fields. Wood fires were scattered all over and people sat in lawn and camp chairs around them. From what he could guess from the loud raucous noise and steam coming from pots and pans, it must be dinner time.

Life sometimes gives you lemons and you make great tasting lemonade.

Other times the lemons get squeezed on open cuts and hurt like hell. The remainder of times the lemons are putrid.

You still have to drink the nasty juice, and hope that you don't die.

Looking out at a sea of deadly Brainers who would like nothing more than to torture and kill him for days, his options, or lack of them, hit him like a ton of bricks.

Go back the way he came and hope he didn't meet any resistance or get captured. Retreat and hope to find another exit that could lead to safety.

Those options came with risks, though likely in smaller numbers, and were the prudent and smart choices to consider. There was a ballsy approach, and a sure road to death's door. Never one to back down, he figured why hide and run. Do what he did best and have a bit of fun.

Taking a deep breath, he walked straight out and faced the gauntlet.

CHAPTER THIRTY-SIX

The Brainers ate dinner like everyone else.

He smelled BBQ. What it actually was, Ryan didn't want to venture a guess. Large pots steamed away, smells like chili and stews, even potatoes and vegetables. The meat dishes made his skin crawl. The vegetables cooking away made his mouth water wondering where they managed to pilfer the prized finds.

He even caught a whiff of what had to be fresh bread and some sort of pies. None of it made sense. The friendliness, laughter, the breadth of food choices. It seemed so coordinated and natural. A huge group of people in one spot having a potluck.

During the end of time, they treated it as one big camping party. People sat together, plates atop their laps or on portable trays. Conversations flowed, though their topics strayed from the usual points of dialog to the more absurd or in many cases, disturbing.

Who could throw an empty treasured beer can the farthest. How fast you could skin a man and still leave him alive. The snippets of talk floated freely, interspersed with laughing and what seemed like comradery, or at least a fraction of unity with each other. To Ryan it seemed like some sort of evolution of spirit from what he had first encountered years ago. Maybe this group was different. He sensed something amiss, a difference in the way they interacted.

He tried to put his finger on it, and the reason became crystal clear.

Keeping his eyes wide and aware as the distance between the school and camp shrunk, he saw the marked drums. Emblazoned with the word *Regenetics,* he recognized the pharmaceutical company and its logo. It was one of the outfits his company supplied security for the research scientists.

Toward the end when the world was on the brink of collapsing, Regenetics had lost their funding and support due to the failure of their trials and scrutiny from peer review as to the validity of their work. The side effects bordered on criminal negligence and the CEO's push for expedited FDA approval and the President's eldest son running a character assassination campaign against any detractors smelled of the first family having a financial stake.

The truth proved the corruption when a whistleblower braved to come forward.

By then, it was too late. Black market release of vials hit the streets and people desperate for a vaccine paid thousands for a single dose, and ultimately suffered dire consequences.

Brainer after Brainer got up and topped off their mugs or cups from the open Regenetics drums. It didn't take a Ph.D. to figure it out.

Whatever cocktail was inside likely was having some type of interface with the virus brewing within the psychopaths.

They appeared to have evolved beyond monotone demons like the ones he met right after the world ended and had morphed into slightly humorous and charismatic crazies.

At least, this batch of hooligans who were sucking down the toxic contents of Regenetics' failure.

His conversation with Rebel started to twist his thoughts and hearing this group added to the checklist of things that didn't add up right. Seeing the drums and knowing the side effects cemented his conclusion. The nut jobs were getting an overzealous funny bone to make killing a whole lot more enjoyable for them.

The thought made Ryan shudder.

So much could go wrong at any point. It was like he blended in with all the lunatics and he couldn't help feel he made the right call.

Deciding to go into the lion's den was not a go by the seat of your pants decision. Ryan would have preferred to have avoided doing it. There were arguments in favor of moving forward versus stepping back. First was spending any time back inside where he could get pinned down and the horde from out here got called in.

He wouldn't last outnumbered and outgunned.

Second, wasting time seeking another exit meant precious time and the chance of not finding it. Third, and this is what sold it, walking straight ahead meant having his enemy right in front of him. If Ryan played his cards right, he could potentially get away in one piece, or at least with minimal damage. He also had his choice of vehicles to steal and secure a getaway if he chose to commandeer a ride. Plus, seeing the drums solidified he made the right decision.

The intel was something he could use.

Taking a cue from his observations, Ryan muttered to himself, low enough to not draw undue attention, though clear enough to be heard if someone paid him any mind. He rambled on about how best to filet the dermis on a body above the nerves and the right blade to utilize to keep pain flowing over simply skinning it.

He made it a two-way dialog, asking and answering himself.

He figured anyone who caught a whiff of him walking and it drew their threat radar would tune him out once they heard his conversation. It was a gamble, and one he felt could work.

No one gave him a second look.

Ryan maneuvered through the camp, careful to steer clear of large groups huddled together. He instead kept to the outskirts as much as possible. He was focused on reaching his destination, which had caught his eye when he first looked out the door window and assisted in his decision to go for it. Actually carrying out the plan was fluid in making it there, as getting a ride and pedal to the metal out of the school grounds was a priority if it worked out. He scanned the interiors of the vehicles he passed, searching for the right one he could simply hop in and take. Unfortunately, they were all too close to their owners to steal without drawing someone's wrath.

Thirty yards, twenty yards, ten, the object of his desire within reach.

Ten feet and quickly five, as he walked by, he threw two grenades. He had ten seconds to put as much distance as he could. Quickening his step, he moved fast and waited until two seconds were left, and suddenly sprinted.

The explosion threw him forward through the air.

Smack into the side of a fifth wheel. Hitting the side hard, its flimsy wall absorbed the blow enough to catch his twisting body and let him slide down. Hitting the ground feet first, he turned and looked to see the gas tanker send plumes of red flames hundreds of feet into the darkening sky.

Chaos ensued as the Brainers ran for cover.

Taking his own cue, Ryan kept going in the opposite direction with those doing the same until they all reached a safe distance and turned to watch the inferno. Standing in the back he simply took steps backward one after another until he was lost in the confusion. Watched them cheer on the flames with a chorus of hoots and hollers you'd experience at a rodeo.

Sure they were occupied with the mayhem, he ran like hell.

Across the field he bolted to what looked like a neighborhood fence. Occasionally peered over his shoulder to see if anyone pursued, and came up empty. As he neared the fence between the school and the neighborhood houses, Ryan prepared. Full sprint and still three feet away he jumped up, his left foot out to plant on the chain link and extended his arms to catch the top rail and throw himself over.

Ryan hoped to miss any obstacles on the other side. To his horror, he wound up crashing his ribs into a backyard lounger and twisted his right ankle as he rolled over the top and tried to stop his momentum.

His body kept going until coming to a hard stop against a large planter with a dead tree.

Reeling in pain he nearly shouted out, until he realized the amount of noise he had made crunching the old chair. Ryan took some deep breaths, closed his eyes, and focused as much of the pain away he could muster. Sucking it up, he listened to see if it caught the Brainers attention, until figuring out he was far enough away to avoid detection.

The Bolts were another story.

CHAPTER THIRTY-SEVEN

Ryan heard the screams first.

Too close. He must have landed right in the middle of a group or small pack. Trying to catch his breath as his ribs ached and get bearings on his senses, Ryan's eyes caught one shadow and a second running straight for him. With little time to react, Ryan swung the suppressed MP5 up and let loose with three shots.

He caught the first ghoul in the chest with all three rounds causing the woman to fall to the ground. After a brief pause, she got up and kept coming. The second Bolt he had more time to aim as it was a few steps behind. Quick pull of the finger and the bullet caught it right in the forehead and blew out the back, sending the man crashing down into the pool. Refocused on the female, he took aim and shot.

She went down for the count.

From the right two more came, and his eyes now adjusted to the dark, he realized they were teenagers and wondered if this was a family, maybe even the residents of the house. It didn't matter much. They intended on eating him and Ryan was not going to die tonight.

At least not right now.

He was on autopilot and instinctively fired first at the boy and then the girl. Two shots, two dead Bolts falling immediately into the pool. He listened for more, and hearing screams in the distance, knew the howls of this *family* had summoned support, and decided it was time for him to find his way out. The rampaging gang sounded like they were a few blocks away to the right. Taking the unlocked back gate, he limped off to the left and down the block.

The pain radiated intensely as he shuffled along. Soon his adrenaline kicked in completely and the pain subsided.

He still couldn't run.

At least he could bear enough weight to keep moving away from his current location. He had zero idea of where he was at. No clue how close or far away from where he needed to be. He had to get somewhere where he could at least get his bearings and figure out what to do next.

Continuing to put distance between himself and the Bolts was a matter of priority and given his current less than peak condition, it was imperative to put as much mileage between the Bolts and Brainers. He had no idea when Rebel's body might be found, with search parties sent to reel him back to purgatory.

Limping along as fast as he could manage under the circumstances, Ryan first headed left and immediately took a right down the first street he encountered. The hope was to head straight and keep going as far as he could to find some landmark, street sign, or other visual to give him an idea of his location. It was soon pitch black, and with no streetlamps to illuminate the way, it was bittersweet.

Lurkers lived in the shadows, ready to pounce. If he kept to the sidewalks and streets, he was more secure from being grabbed and killed. Street signs were only as good as coming across a familiar name, and not being able to read them in the greater scheme of it all didn't matter much.

What he needed was something more concrete, a thoroughfare he recognized, business he knew, freeway, something to say *hey dead meat, you are here.*

At least with something recognizable, he might know how far and long it would take to get back to where he had to go, and if too far away, to find some safe place to ride out the night and rest his throbbing ankle.

The high school must have been deep inside some residential area because all he passed was house after house until reaching a street that he figured would take him beyond suburbia. It ran perpendicular and on the other side of it was a small strip mall.

Left or right, he asked himself, not knowing which the right path was to take. He had been limping along for what seemed like hours and was fully exposed.

You need to decide quick.

So, he did.

Straight and headed for the strip mall, hoping to find a name that resonated or at least a place to rest for a while. He was exhausted and the pain was starting to penetrate past his fading adrenaline.

Mini mart. Donut shop. Dry cleaner. Check cashing.

He found everything that advertised *not the rich part* of town. There was even a cannabis shop right in the middle of business row. He dragged himself across as fast as he could, hoping to get out of the open and into some safe shadows.

It was wishful thinking. Maybe luck was still on his side.

Any number of things could go wrong, walk right into some Lurkers,

Bolts, or even Brainers. Given he'd made it this far and was still breathing, he felt some confidence in living a bit longer.

Hitting the first store front proved uneventful and as he walked along looking for something familiar, nothing jumped out. He could literally be anywhere, as he had no idea how long he had even been unconscious. For all he knew, it was days, weeks possibly if they hopped him up on drugs. He didn't feel drugged, thought likely last night was when they got him. And if that was the case, Julia and Emma had made it to safety and David was still locked away.

The pain became excruciating in his ankle and ribs, every movement a concerted effort.

Checking every window and store for a name he knew, he struck out. The small businesses led to the big box stores on the other end, so Ryan kept going. He wound up at a chain electronics store, an old two-story place with the front windows smashed from the looting during the last days of civilization. Taking a gamble, he went inside hoping to find some information to assist in finding his locale. Stepping inside and off to the side out of any light that might find its way in, he stood and listened.

Not a sound.

Flipping his goggles down to see in the dark, Ryan made his way quietly to the back and through the employee-only door to the storeroom. He needed to sit and rest. Finding the break room his first target, he went to an oversized couch and plopped down.

Being off his feet felt good.

Within a few minutes sitting the adrenaline faded out and the pain took over, his head feeling groggy from the agony coursing through his body. He started to think, ponder about all the wrong things that had happened, and like bad sex, self-doubt crept into his brain.

He was fucked.

It was only a matter of time before his card got punched and that was it.

Ryan Carmichael only a memory lost somewhere in this crappy town for his body to rot away. He had lost and finally found his family.

Had no clue how long they would be safe.

He was supposed to be there to protect them, keep them safe forever. He should have met up with them, hugs all around and tears of joy flooding the room.

He had messed up. Got pegged in the head and caught.

Lost a step in old age Carmichael.

He had no clue where he was, how to get to his loved ones, and was in a world of hurt.

How am I supposed to get to them like this? I can barely move, and I need to get the hell out of here.

He was sure Bolts were sniffing on his trail, on the hunt to devour him to the bone. If that piece of crap Rebel had been found, Brainers would be hauling ass to find him. He could only imagine the torture they'd throw his way for slicing the prick off of that asshole.

Death wouldn't come soon enough.

Not far off, maybe the worst of it. When word got to Mark, he knew it would send him into a frenzy. If he was fixated on finding David and Emma, Rebel's gruesome death would send his evil brain into overdrive.

As Ryan sat and the pain worsened, his mind darkening more and more, he felt helpless and completely hopeless with no bright rainbow around the corner. One beat-up middle-aged man against multiple armies of mindless Un-Dead, psychos, and well-trained soldiers was not a recipe for success. Even with his expertise and cunning, he was still just a man.

The Vegas odds were calling for his demise and paying pretty well.

He felt at a loss, that maybe it was time to pack it up and end it. He had done his job, liberated his precious wife and kids from hell, and given them a new chance to move on. Maybe that was enough, maybe that was what he was destined to do.

You can't win every single time Bud, he shrugged. *There comes a time when the writing on the wall tells you to hang it all up. Go out on your terms.*

As the thought penetrated and began to take a foothold, he felt a presence and jolted upright. He heard the voice, and it scared him shitless.

"Really? Do you think you have the time to sit and do this?"

Ryan looked up, his eyes trying to pinpoint the source.

"Come on. Julia and the kids need you to buck up soldier and get your head back in the game."

Sighing, Ryan shook his head. "Seriously? After three fucking years of a world gone to shit and you decide to appear?" A few moments of silence deafened the room until he got a reply.

Ryan's father stepped from the dark and into Ryan's line of sight. "Better late than never."

Ryan stared, the anger welling up inside. "Three years? You've been gone three years and decide this is the time? You've had plenty of time to talk to me since and I have enough on my hands than to do this."

Reg Carmichael moved closer and took a seat on the far end of the couch. "Seems like the right time Son."

The pain seared within, his ankle on fire. The last thing Ryan needed was this hallucination. "Dad, you are dead. D-E-A-D. I lost you after all this shit went down. I have a lot on my plate and no time to sit here and have a father-son chat."

The image of his father nodded and threw up his right hand. "You do Son. You also need a bit of help, so here I am."

Ryan was done, so done. His body hurt so bad and his brain a jumble of thoughts. He hung his head, trying to will his father out of his mind. Looking over, Reg was still there.

"Fuck."

Reg laughed. "Language Son. Listen, I'll make this short since time is not your friend. What did I teach you?"

Ryan winced. "Never ride the clutch?"

A hearty chuckle. "Yes, and what else? The one thing that pertains to this moment in time."

"Always believe in yourself no matter what," Ryan sighed as he answered.

His hallucination reached over, and he swore he felt his dad place a reassuring hand on his thigh. A tear fell down Ryan's cheek as he remembered him. Late-stage cancer right in the middle of a pandemic was a shitty way to die. There was no way he could have survived needing chemo and doctor care as hospitals turned to ghost towns.

Ryan was sure he was dead.

They had been fortunate to visit a few times when he was at Stanford Hospital undergoing care. It was one of the best places to be with cutting edge research and physicians doing extraordinary things in medicine and with cancer.

Ryan and Julia couldn't visit near the end with all of the chaos and restrictions due to virus protocols.

Even with all of his pull, no visits, and the kids didn't understand why their grandfather was sick and they couldn't see him. With the world ended as Ryan knew it, he could only hope the last days of his father weren't excruciating and feeling all alone.

The vision of Reg smiled. "Son, you've survived a ton of combat tours, capture and torture, and the most vicious of what life has thrown with those two little monsters of yours," he winked. "This right here, is a cake walk. You have always been my hero. The best husband for Julia and father to David and especially Emma. You have protected and nurtured that special little girl from the moment she arrived. Whooped ass on anyone who treated her other than a normal little girl. And David, that boy idolizes you. You bend over backwards to make sure you are the best dad he could ever have. All of that, well, gives you something to think about. Stop moping and get on back to them."

Ryan knew the truth of it.

His mind was telling him to suck it up and get back to doing what he did best. He had survived worse and frankly all of this, even stuck by himself with no support and reeling from injuries, was nothing.

Half asleep and full of bullet holes he could still kick some serious ass.

Three long years had been lost and being reunited with his family was a blessing. No one, not blood-thirsty Bolts, insane Brainers, not that psycho in a suit Mark, and especially not some mysterious fuck pulling strings behind the scenes were going to mess up his happy ending.

Looking over at his dad, Ryan wiped the tears away and slowly nodded. "You're right Dad. I'm a Carmichael. We don't take shit and we never give up or back down. No matter what. I've got people counting on me and no one is going to screw that up again."

The ghost of his dad began to fade away. The delusion had served its purpose and Ryan knew what he had to do.

As the image began to whisp into oblivion, his dad spoke one last time. "That's the Ryan I know. Now, go get them Son and give those little monsters a kiss from their Papa when you see them. And remember, you will never beat me in Dominos," his voice trailed off, and then he was gone.

Ryan sat a moment longer to let what had happened sink in.

Never in his life had he hallucinated like this. Had never felt lost like he had a few minutes ago, at the end of his rope with no success in sight.

The pain had really done its number on him, and he felt it.

There was no way he was going to let a bit of uncomfortable agony take him down. He had survived worse, had his pinky finger nearly severed off, been beaten to right before death, and gone on to wreak havoc and finish his missions, sometimes with the outcome for survival dismal. He always came out on top, and this was not going to be any different.

He had an advantage over everyone.

Ryan still had all his faculties, and key among them logic, reasoning, and fear. He could use their mental deficiencies against them. Quick to rage, lack of reasoning, sense of individual versus working together.

They also had lost their fear factor and could be rash to act.

Fear made you think twice, and if he could tap into any or all of his enemy's shortcomings to the maximum degree, Ryan stood a chance of coming out a winner.

CHAPTER THIRTY-EIGHT

A special operations solider carries a med kit full of goodies that can be used in dire situations.

Major trauma kit, in-use med kit, or a survival med kit. Depending on the type of battlefield one would encounter, the make-up of the kit would comprise some form of supplies from any or all. Ryan's current kit, given the urban nature of his surroundings and post-apocalypse world and from what he could scrounge up, contained key items that he needed to keep moving forward.

First up was the elastic bandage dressing for his ankle to support and suppress the swelling building up. Unlacing his boots and pulling down his sock, he wrapped the bandage around his swollen ankle and secured it. The compression felt good. Replacing his sock and boot, he stood, jumped up and down, and tested his ankle to see how it felt.

Thumbs up.

Taking off his tac vest he probed his ribs for any fractures. He didn't feel any. The spot he landed on the chair was noticeably painful, especially when he breathed. His kit had morphine, pilfered from the hospital's pharmacy and stockpiled back in his room, though going that extreme for a non-life-threatening injury and getting him loopy was not conducive to clear headedness.

The next step down was fentanyl citrate lozenges in eight hundred micrograms which would assist with the pain and discomfort. He could pop another lozenge if it didn't quite take the edge off.

He'd wait to see.

Taking out the pack he opened and took one, sucked on it, and hoped it would take immediate effect. It took a few minutes and he began to feel better. As he moved and felt less discomfort, his resolve boiled over and the next plan began to formulate.

Suited back up, he took his leave and ventured out.

There was always a method to his crazy madness. No matter how insane his plans might sound on the surface, they were grounded in careful thought, deliberation, and with ultimate success in mind.

His life was thinking outside of the proverbial box.

Find answers and solutions that might appear odd or even wrong, but when digging down into the details, made the most sense for a given problem or environment. On more than one occasion if he had taken the path others placed inside the box, the typical or textbook response, his teams or he would all have been dead.

Call it the deep thinker, the rationalist, the nonconformist to traditional ideas or ideology.

He simply felt that what one might go with from their gut for an immediate reaction could inevitably be the one your enemy also thought you would do and prepare for it on their side.

It left you high and dry.

Being able to take a different tact for him was something of a back pat, more of a using his brain to find solutions others dismissed or couldn't bother to take the time to think up. Why hand roll meatballs one at a time, if you can roll up the meat quickly into a log and cut off the balls one by one? Saves time, is efficient, and produces the same results.

The big box sporting goods store next door had been ransacked, leaving little of value inside if you needed to survive. The beach cruisers?

He had his choice of rides.

Quickly grabbing a hand pump off the shelf and airing up the tires, Ryan headed away from the old high school in the opposite direction. He kept to the main street until he got his bearings and finally figured out where in hell he was in comparison to the city.

He was out in the burbs, east of town, so heading west to try and rendezvous with Julia and the kids was forefront in his mind. Once he knew where to go, he took side streets to keep off the grid and still being able to hear or see if anyone pursued. It proved an uneventful and lonely trek, and within a few hours he was back in the city. As he came down the boulevard, the nearest path across town to circumvent high traffic routes he knew the Brainers and Mark's team would take, he stopped cold.

A hundred yards ahead the fading glow of debris, the embers soft orange, offered a hint of the destruction he would encounter as he closed in on the location.

An old pickup truck and camper, one he recognized from the old fort, sat burning in the dark. Charred remains, left posed in what could only be described as protective embraces knowing death was imminent, littered the street. The school bus smoldered, and he had to turn his eyes to divert his gaze from the wreckage and bodies lined against the side.

Children had been on the bus as part of the evacuation.

He knew David was not among this group as they had splintered off separate from John's. It didn't prevent the rage inside from venting to the surface. Children shouldn't be casualties of the sick and twisted.

Nothing was sacred anymore.

He saw the group further down, sifting through piles in the street. Pushing the cruiser to the side behind a shrub, he secured his six. Enemy locked in his sights, Ryan swung his MP5 around and took aim, moving swiftly and methodically to decrease the distance and take out his targets. The suppressor made quick dispatch. He put brain holes in the men farthest away from the group, who were turned away from the rest.

Tap, tap, tap.

As he closed in, he took down four sorting through piles of clothes.

Tap, tap. Tap, tap.

Coming upon the last one oblivious to it all, he pulled his Ka-Bar from its sheath in his tac vest and thrust it into the right triceps.

The Brainer screamed out in pain, and as she did, Ryan lunged forward and punched her in the side of the head. "Shut the hell up or I'll leave you alive for the flesh eaters."

The woman, blond ponytail pulled nicely back who looked athletic and no older than thirty, fell forward and caught herself on her hands and knees. Staring back at him she looked cute, a woman who could be your next-door neighbor, co-worker, or even PTA mother and parent of your kid's friend.

On the superficial of looks, she appeared *normal.*

If he were younger and single, she might be someone he would date if she checked off the boxes for compatibility. It was the eyes void of emotion beyond hate that painted another story. Ryan could see her ugliness and it was to the bone.

"Fuck you," she sneered through clenched teeth. "You don't scare me."

Ryan punched her in the face.

He knelt down, his knife hand resting on his left knee. "First, definitely not my type. Don't mess with psychos and I wouldn't screw you with someone else's dick. Second, you should be pissing your pants. You *know* who I am."

The woman's eyes grew wide as she put the stories together in her head. She looked up and he could tell she was about to spit on him. He raised his knife and waved her off, so she spat the blood on the street. "What the hell do you want?"

Ryan smiled. "Information."

"Drop dead."

He shook his head. "Again, not going to happen. Listen, my time is really valuable, and I do not have time to mess around with you. We can play nice and do this the easy way, or we can go the way your people do things and well, you know what happens if we have fun with that."

Her brow frowned as she took a minute to try and think. "I don't believe you. So, go off and screw yourself."

The blade lunged forward through the same hole in her arm, ripping the flesh. She screamed out again and he punched her one more time.

"I'm getting tired of this," he sighed.

She looked up, and a hint of fear shone in her eyes. It caught Ryan off guard for a moment. He had begun to see a sort of transformation among Brainers. This was the first time he had ever seen one show any hint of feeling fear.

She turned to face him, pulled herself close in, her hand covering her wound. "Why are you doing this to me? What did I do to you?"

Ryan slapped her across the face and pointed. "What did those children do to you?"

Frowning and looking over at the smoldering bodies, she pointed, "Them? We were looking for some kid worth a lot of goods and supplies. They were worthless so we- "

He punched her again and blood gushed out of her broken nose. "Children? Really? Are you and your kind that far gone that nothing is left of your humanity? Are there no children at all among you?"

Wiping the blood with her shirt sleeve, the woman shrugged, "We do what we have to do to survive. Anyone gets in the way pays the price. Children do not contribute anything to us, so what good are they?"

The words had no emotion at all, and he knew right there that while there was some evolution going on within their brains and bodies, Brainers were still psychotic pieces of shit and always would be until eradicated.

Staring at her and still kneeling, Ryan waved his knife. "Wow. Just wow. You all are beyond any redemption. Well, for you it's decision time. Tell me what I want to know, and this ends nicely for you. Don't cooperate and you know those crazies that eat people alive, like the ones who tore through your friends a few days ago?"

He let the words sink in and seeing her put two and two together, continued. "If you lie or I don't get what I want, I will leave you for them to feast. Probably will go for the soft parts first," he smiled as he tapped the knife on her chest.

Nodding she understood the ramifications, she answered, "OK, I get it. What do you want to know?"

He smiled, the kind of smug grin you give when being in a superior position. "Great. First question. Has the boy been found?"

She shook her head.

"Use your words please."

"No."

Ryan stood up and moved back. Being close to the Brainer woman made him want to kill her outright. "Thank you. Has the girl been found?"

A perplexed look. "Who?"

Ryan guessed that David was the priority and Emma the backup plan. Focusing Brainer resources to find his son would keep the crazies on task. Mark likely was using his own men to find Julia and Emma. Keep that one quiet and more executed with precision than the cluster Brainers left in their wake.

Stepping back Ryan considered what to ask next. "The man who is giving you the orders to hunt for the boy, where is he?" He didn't expect the crazy laughter.

"My *leverage*," she cooed.

Ryan shook his head. The game was going to be a nightmare. If she thought she had anything to bargain with, she was sorely mistaken. He stuck the blade into her shoulder and turned it.

"Wrong answer."

Glaring up at Ryan she coughed, "You are going to die a really slow death. Can't wait to see it."

Tapping his lips, Ryan pointed at her. "Rebel tried that earlier. Let's say he's not the man he once was or will ever be again. His dangles ain't dancing no more."

Confused, she started to speak, and then went silent. The thought of what might have happened flashing in what was left of her brain.

"Getting the idea there, little lady?"

"I can't wait for them to skin you alive!"

Ryan began to laugh, which caught the woman by surprise. Opening his right palm, he showed her the device, the red dots blinking and moving on the small screen.

"You mean them?" he pointed before pressing a button. As the explosion blew, the sound of ripping flesh and screams resonated behind him.

Her rage boiled over and she lunged for him, missing the mark as he stepped back and planted his right boot to the left side of her head. Catching her in the temple, she was out cold immediately, which defeated the purpose of capturing her alive. He needed information and her conscious to extract what he needed, though he could finagle a positive from this if he thought about it.

David was still safe and not in the Brainers hands. The woman had no idea about Emma, which for two high value assets he was sure Mark was keeping her for himself. If he wasn't, every Brainer if not out searching for her would at least know about her.

He took that one with some consolation.

His kids were secure and hopefully on their way to a deep dark hole to hide and wait. It also appeared Rebel had not been found yet or he figured the radio would have been blowing up with Brainer traffic. He had picked up

Rebel's radio back at the high school and beyond a bunch of backwoods chit chat about hunting and fishing, it was relatively quiet. Ryan could send them all into a tizzy if he wished, except he was saving that for when he really needed it.

He had to find Mark and end him before time ran out.

CHAPTER THIRTY-NINE

A one-man army against the world was a recipe for your own death.

No matter the man or the skills, the end was an inevitable and a forgone conclusion. It was a matter of reality and not living in a fantasy. The unknowns were when it happened, the proverbial how it struck you dead. There was always a formula to it.

At least, in Hollywood movies that solitary hero had a ray of hope and in the end came out victorious.

The real world, the lone gunman bent on rectifying the wrongs perpetuated by society or some secret organization found himself on the wrong side of a blade or bullet in time. Life didn't pan out that way where evil didn't wind up winning it all and throwing victory in your face.

In Ryan's case, he never thought he wouldn't wind up on top.

No matter what, he persevered.

Even if he failed time after time, he kept at it. Julia called it the stubborn blood of his ancestors coursing through his body. He called it never giving up, never allowing someone to win who didn't deserve it.

Evil was an enemy to what was right.

The stain that tarnished the color of black and made it something bad, and for him, he wouldn't stop until his last breath wiped out the sinister and decrepit who felt nothing was strong enough to stop them.

Ryan Carmichael was the thorn in their side.

Dawn approached and the early morning light was ready to cast its rays to advertise another day. He had a hell of a time hauling the limp body of the Brainer woman with him. Finding an old shopping cart from a local store left in the parking lot to rust away and using rope to keep her secure, he managed to pull the still unconscious woman behind the cruiser as he went to the first known location the survivors would use as a safe spot before heading out.

Tucked far back in a non-descript light industrial neighborhood to the south, the old warehouse complex was large enough to hide the group sight unseen.

Reaching the front gate, he stopped and scanned his surroundings.

Seeing nothing amiss he pulled it ajar, rode inside, and pulled it closed again. His destination was the second rollup door to the left. Back on the bike he rode, dragging her behind.

Fresh bullet holes in the cement wall made Ryan stop in his tracks. He didn't see any bodies or vehicles, but he knew. Parking the beach cruiser against the wall, he pulled his M4 around and walked slowly to the side door. Reaching for the handle he checked.

It was unlocked.

Hesitantly, he turned the knob and carefully moved into the dim interior. The survivors, or what was left of the group, were inside.

The unlocked door screamed out they had given up hope and from what he saw as he looked from face to face, he understood why. Bodies lay beneath blankets, drying blood pooling nearby. Medics tended to the wounded and those who were capable ferried water around. Not a single gun aimed his way as he emerged into the light of the lanterns.

Ryan dropped his M4, the sling dangling precariously at his side, and walked around in a frantic search for David and Pete. He checked every vehicle, every tent, and finding nothing, asked for John. A firm hand gripped his shoulder and turning around, he saw the old man, face bloodied and right eye swollen.

The dejected look, the pain staring back from the man's good eye, made Ryan freeze.

"Come with me Ryan," John said softly as he led him towards the back of the warehouse and motioned to sit in one of the camp chairs set up around a radio station.

Ryan shook his head no. "I've got a prisoner outside and she needs to be-" he began before John held up his hand.

"She's been taken care of Ryan. Here, please sit."

He sighed, the weight of the world feeling like it sat right atop his chest. Looking behind, he finally sat. "Straight to the point please."

Pursing his lips, John bobbed his head and took his seat. "As you can see, they found us. Seems we had a spy in our camp. Led them straight here. We're dealing with him."

Heavy sigh.

John leaned back and grabbed a Scotch bottle off the table. Taking two beat up tins, he poured liquid amber into each, and handed one to Ryan. "Expensive as shit. Figured worth drinking while we still can enjoy it."

Ryan took a sip and the flavor hit. Damn, it was not just good, but exquisite.

Taking his own, John let it sit there for a minute on his tongue before swallowing. The older man looked beaten, his spirit seemingly lost. Even though he was a career military man who spent his life at sea commanding a ship and thousands of men and women through missions and combat theaters, he was never prepared for this.

Taking another sip, he let it slide down and finally spoke. "We were compromised Ryan. One of my closet allies sold us out for a bunch of bullshit. Didn't stand a chance. Outnumbered and far outgunned this time. They took David and a few others, left the rest of us alone. Guess he figured we didn't pose a threat."

The words bit hard to the bone. His head full of fog and hurting, the thought of his boy in the hands of the enemy again hard to swallow.

"Was it Mark?" was all Ryan could say.

John nodded. "It was, here. Led the party himself. Left me a message. Said he won and there was nothing we could do this time. And, the really bad news. He has them all. That crazy band of nut jobs he uses caught up to our other group and got your wife and daughter. I am sorry Ryan."

All Ryan could mutter was, "How?"

"His spy didn't know where they were holding up. That wasn't it. My guess is they tracked them somehow. Killed my entire group and took them. Got word about an hour ago."

All the air left his lungs and his body felt like curling up into a ball. "Sorry for all of this John. I need to get my family back."

John shook Ryan's leg. "Hey, we are all in this. Your family or not, we are all targets and fighting these assholes is all we have to try and survive. You have to focus and clear your head. He mumbled something I didn't quite understand. Rambled on a bit about taking them where we could never find them, where they'd have a place they'd love close to all the places they would call home. Any idea what he meant?"

The rage within Ryan began to brew.

First, it festered, and soon it simply exploded. He had made a life keeping it locked away pretty tight, deep inside the bowels of his being, without ever showing a hint. This time, he absolutely lost control.

Standing up he threw his empty tin against the wall.

Walking over to pick it up he crushed it in his left hand, bending it into a ball. He chucked it all the way across the warehouse before sitting back down, dejected.

John sat watching the entire episode, wanting to speak, yet keeping silent as he observed the show unravel. He didn't know Ryan well. Had spent enough time talking and hatching their plans that he could tell he was a man who rarely lost control, who could seethe with anger, and still keep his cool. This was probably uncharacteristic for this hardened soldier that even letting it out was against his own internal code of conduct.

Reaching for another tin, John poured a hefty dose of Scotch and handed it over.

Ryan reached up without really looking and took a long sip. "That goddamn piece of shit," he whispered almost to himself, his voice hollow.

John moved his chair closer and touched Ryan's knee, trying to offer some comfort, knowing there was little he could really do in the moment. Figuring what the hell, he asked, "Have any idea where they're headed?"

"San Francisco Bay Area."

John wasn't sure he heard it right. "Did you say he's going all the way across the country?"

Ryan looked up, eyes red, not from tears, but from volcanic fury. Cold and menacing, he answered. "California. The Bay is a freeway hub of the state where a bunch of them all converge together. You can get to anywhere along the routes and close to our favorite places. Disneyland down the road, get to camping along the coast up above Bodega Bay, enjoy Mendocino and Shasta. And, Santa Cruz and Carmel within striking distance."

John felt the wind leave his own sails. Three thousand miles away with no transport, no plan. Seemed Mark had the resources and capabilities to do it. "Do you believe him?"

Ryan sat back. "I do. He thinks I'm dead and little anyone can do to get them back. Anything he tells you he knows you don't have answers. He doesn't need to lie."

Sitting back in his own chair, feeling for the young man, knowing he had been reunited with his family only to lose them in the blink of an eye, John felt a tear. Wiping it away he could only say, "I really am sorry Ryan."

Ryan shoved the tin toward John, and the old man obliged. Taking a slow sip, he finally answered, "I said little, I didn't say impossible."

Not sure what Ryan meant and knowing that getting across the country was damn near impossible given every unknown and bands of psycho killers roaming freely from town to town.

John smacked his own knee to get Ryan's attention. "What are you talking about? It's over Ryan. He won. Even if you managed to find a way, you'd have to survive the trip. And how long will it take? I'm sorry, you need to hope and pray they stay well and move on."

Ryan glared at the older man, and the way he looked caused John to shrink back in his chair.

John wasn't used to having anyone showing disrespect. As a man used to exerting his authority and power, he oozed being number one. Seeing Ryan stare at him, the eyes cold and void of anything besides wrath for Mark, it was a bit hard to swallow. While he could empathize with Ryan's plight, as a former leader of men it was his job to control and bring them back to reality when situations called for it.

This was no exception.

"Take it down a few notches soldier. There's a time when the battle is lost and you accept defeat. This is no different."

Ryan watched the man for a minute, two, three, before saying a word.

His words were coarse and cut deep. "I've killed more men than you can count. Been in shit holes and dug my way out. Taken out bullets myself and dressed my own wounds. I am your worst nightmare that comes in the night and kills you and goes back home and sleeps like a baby. I don't lose and never have, and this is no different. Your experiences are cake compared to what I have seen and done in my life. Don't think you can out rank me here with some tepid talk about giving up and moving on. I'm a civilian and take orders from nobody. Driving cross country is not an option. I'm going to fly."

Shock at being dressed down and the absurd talk about flying caused John to reflexively cough. When he stopped, he thought about drilling into Ryan and really giving it to him. However, he decided to listen and see what he had in mind.

"Fly? Nothing has been in the air for years that I've seen, though we've heard rumors and rumblings from time to time. Missiles blew everything out of the air that tried to break the no-flight bans and everything else has been collecting dust. Any plane would need a serious overhaul. Unless things have been going on in places we don't know, there hasn't been a plane or any aircraft seen in the skies forever. How can you possibly fly across the country?"

Ryan smiled. "Who said anything about a plane?"

CHAPTER FORTY

John never ceased to be amazed by the crazy clown car driving Ryan's mind.

His plans were unconventional and bordered on insane. At least, when told by Ryan that's how they seemed when he wove his tale.

On the surface they lacked any sense of success.

Having been recently exposed to his thinking and rationale, John knew that even the most far out scheme, laid out like it had been drawn with crayon by a psych ward lifer, had been methodically dissected every which way and that failure was not an option. There were multiple paths to success. Once he accepted Ryan worked it for this one, John was open to listen.

Ryan told a tale that seemed like it was out of a sci-fi movie.

Given his old Navy rank and command status, John was privy to the military details of what Ryan spoke about, though less about the civilian and commercial aspect. To him it was all too futuristic and not anything that he felt capable or ready for prime time.

"So," John began, trying to find the right words, "you're telling me that a blimp is going to first, miraculously be available, two, somehow be able to get you across the country, and three, get you there in time to do anything? I can't buy that."

Ryan understood the inability to grasp the information. He'd think it was too if he had not seen it himself and been able to take a ride. Wanting to keep John open to the idea, he carefully laid it all out and hoped he could make it work.

"For the last twenty years, and really in the last ten, defense contractors have utilized that great concept of skunk works to bring back some of the more extreme and futuristic concepts of flight and aerospace. One of the big aerospace companies worked on the idea of how to supply remote troops or research stations in inhospitable locations. Planes can't fly everywhere. What if you can fly some type of craft effectively, carry the cargo, and land on a dime? You solve a multitude of issues and offer up a bunch of solutions. Where to start? Balloons and blimps have been used for centuries and with ever-evolving technologies and materials it progressed to a hybrid airship. Can land in the roughest of terrain and not pop its exterior, can stay afloat for a considerable length of time due to its electric engines and solar regeneration, and is quieter than a plane. Stealth, robust, and longevity of the skies. Plus, really cool looking and fun to ride in."

John sat quietly, taking in Ryan's story. He knew of the military blimp use. This expanded on it and took it to another level. "Okay. Interesting concept for sure. There's the where, how, and do you really think it will work? Three years there's been nothing maintained or flying. How can you even manage to think it will run and actually be air worthy?"

Ryan expected the skepticism. It was justified. And, John was right. There was no guarantee it was even where it was supposed to be and fit for flight. It was a chance he'd take if it could work.

"The where, or at least the last where before shit went south, was about twenty miles from here. Research facility for the last of some flight tests. I know about it because it was a potential last resort to transport scientists and researchers to a centralized location to keep their work going, and we know how that panned out. I took one of the last flights and got to know it pretty well from talking up the crew and ground support. You know, cover your bases and all contingencies gathering intel from the ones who really know. The how is a shot in the dark. Since it's electric, it runs off a recharging station to juice the engines and batteries for takeoff and the panels built into the skin on top recharge it. It should have been hooked up and if the panels in the field are intact, the ground batteries should have been cycling on and off this whole time. If it was left hooked to the connectors, it is a matter of airing it back up and hitting the ON switch. Super easy."

John held up three fingers. "What about number three. Will it work?"

Ryan was confident. "It can and it will. If the systems still work it's a thirty-hour ride to get to where I need to be."

John nodded. "I can spare some crew to help you out."

Ryan shook his head. "This is a one-way trip. If Mark has a plane that functions, it means a runway at some airport. I land the beast and fail, he simply hops another ride and is really gone for good. No, I need to find the airport and runway he's using and make sure he can't ever leave again."

John held up his hand, motioning for Ryan to stop talking. "Have you bothered to think that maybe Mark has some other means of transportation? A plane seems to be a grasp. What if he has a train? Some locomotive that he got up and running to get across the country? I might buy into that one. Take a route that circumvents areas you know are hostile or can't get through. Pretty much see the nation unencumbered going past fields and pastures."

Ryan let the statement sink in.

He was amped up, his mind racing, searching for the right answers. His usually coherent and in-charge planning was showing signs of cracks, and he didn't like it. A train was a possibility, except time seemed to be a pressing thing for Mark. It would take days, maybe a week or more, to cross the United States. Add any issues with tracks, derailments, and prohibited passage and a train seemed like a liability.

Too many negatives if you got stuck in the middle of nowhere.

His arms crossed, Ryan waved a finger. "I don't think a train is viable for him. It would need to be able to run the length of the track without encountering any debris or decimated lines. Unless he has had it mapped and cleared ahead of time, it seems less plausible. At any point he could find resistance or destroyed tracks that leaves him high and dry with nothing. A plane, more of a chance. And with a plane, he needs a place to land it. Eliminate that avenue and he loses his advantage. Blow it and the strip and he's lost."

"What's going through your head as I'm not liking what I think you are saying? How do you plan on getting away?"

Ryan was looking off deep in thought. He knew that was a huge problem, how to extract and be gone. Some things were left to chance or once on the ground to assess the situation. Hostile territory and many unknowns meant he couldn't plan for every contingency. He at least needed to have something brewing to go on.

"My plan is to load up the airship with explosives and crash it either into the runway if he's using a small airport or straight into the plane and blow it sky high. That prevents him from using it if I initially fail." The words said Ryan was serious.

John shook his head. "That is the dumbest thing I have ever heard you say. If you do that and succeed, how do you plan on getting out of there?"

Ryan knew John was right, to a certain degree.

He very well could rescue his family and what? He had no way of getting anywhere safe. He could load up a vehicle onboard with supplies and offload somewhere first. Aim the ship for the plane and parachute out. Hoof it to the location with his family and try to avert unfriendlies. Risk after risk with little kids in tow.

Across the country and with no support, it was a recipe for disaster.

His family was his problem, since he was the one that failed in the first place. Asking anyone else to help was being selfish in his mind. Success was the most important factor.

Julia and the kids, and stopping Mark, were all entwined.

Each was critical and dependent on the other, as simply saving them and getting away without killing Mark and destroying his research meant little. He would keep coming and never stop. A life on the run, constantly looking over their shoulders, was not a healthy childhood for Emma and David.

"Thanks for the reality check, John. Putting others in harm's way for me has always been selfish and not in my DNA."

John patted Ryan's shoulder. "Hey, even the best of the best sometimes needs a slap back to Earth. What's the real plan?"

Ryan figured it was all chess moves.

Attack here and sacrifice there. Use Mark's weaknesses against him. If he had a plane and an airport, it would be lit up in some fashion and visible from the air. Disabling the strip and plane was not a requirement.

If he could, it added to setting up for checkmate.

Supposing Ryan had a working airship, he'd be able to sneak in quietly, do the deed, and get the hell out. That all hinged on the airship not being found and blown from the sky as it waited for his evacuation signal. If he could remove Mark's plane from the equation, pursuit wasn't possible.

Where Julia and the kids were hidden was a different story.

There were hundreds of square miles, really thousands, where they could be tucked away. Finding that location and facility presented a huge problem. He figured it would need to be close enough for transport and quick comings and goings and he had a few potential choices in San Francisco International, Oakland, and San Jose airports.

There were a few municipal airstrips strewn around, which might be finding a needle in a haystack.

Plus, there was the old military airstrip that had turned into the best spot for television shows and wild experiments. It could take considerable time to locate the right plane, and daylight was the enemy.

"We will need to come in at night to remain as invisible as possible. Search for landing lights at one of the airports. That will give us a starting point. Depending on the setup, and this is all a fluid discussion, I either get remote charges set and blow right away as a distraction, or after retrieval and blow the plane as we're getting the hell out. If the situation is sketchy, we find a place for me to rappel out and down and the airship finds a place to scurry off and hide, probably just offshore or hovering low over the hills. The missing piece is where Mark has them. I doubt he will have a huge neon sign to tell me."

John puckered his lips. He looked like a guppy. Ryan couldn't help laugh.

"Something funny?" John asked.

Sorry," Ryan sheepishly replied. "That face kind of threw me off and I couldn't help it."

John smiled. "My wife used to do the same thing to my concentration face. Getting back to planning, I get the dark of night, hide the ship, and search for the family. What if he is so confident that he isn't hiding anything?"

Ryan thought about it, and it made some sense. Mark had ego, and it was bolstered by the virus' effect on him. If he thought he was in absolute control and had a place ready and secure, why hide it.

Who was going to come for him?

"He could be in any number of facilities around. There are pharmaceuticals, labs, hospitals, and there's Stanford and San Francisco universities with top notch resources between their hospitals and med school research capabilities. Any large campus would require some serious juice. My guess is there would be some indicators, lights, solar panels, buzzing activity, and guards to ward off whatever is lurking on the West Coast. Find the airport and reduce the distance to search. We find the commotion and take the backdoor in."

John smiled. "That's the tactician come back to life. There's probably a bunch more that needs planning. My guess is if the flight has time to develop it, you need to get on the road."

Ryan nodded. "We do. First is getting to the airship and seeing if it's even viable. Load it up and get airborne."

John started to pour another drink for them both. "I've got the right people for you and I'm not taking no for an answer."

CHAPTER FORTY-ONE

The trip to the airstrip took a circuitous route.

Avoid obvious roads out of the city and deter any potential engagements with Brainers or soldiers.

The back roads hadn't seen life in years, at least not of the normal living human kind. The trip was a sightseeing adventure of playing what not to hit with vehicles. Wildlife roamed freely and were hard pressed to move on more than one occasion without being prodded to scatter.

The Un-Dead, the mindless ones that were more nuisance than anything, occasionally appeared from the tree lines, though it seemed more to see what or who was disturbing the quiet of their existence.

The attentiveness was a new phenomenon, the eyes less distant and void of humanity, a semblance of *color* to them.

As a whole, they usually ignored everything and simply went about their scavenging and wandering ways, or at least, that was what they did in the past. Ryan found it unusual to see this *life* in them, similar to what he saw with the Brainers. He had seen them drinking some wild concoction that he figured between the chemicals and the potential for a morphing virus to change some of the traits that previously were gone, they were slowly emerging into a newer species of evil. Maybe the Un-Dead were experiencing the same sort of progression, the virus taking a new path.

He didn't know and didn't have the time to stay and figure it out.

Moving along, the twenty-mile trip took about two hours. Time seemed to ooze forward at a snail's pace. It wasn't the obstacles they passed or had to remove from the road that made the time drag.

It really felt like time was at a standstill and barely moving in a linear direction.

By the time they reached their destination, the caravan of four vehicles, Ryan's fully supplied Humvee ladened down with firepower and John's ragtag team of volunteers and conscripts to the cause, everyone held their breath on what unknown would sprout from the ground and wreak havoc.

Nothing interrupted them.

They arrived at the facility, a non-descript blip along a back country road. The chain link fence surrounded an overgrown field and airstrip.

The only visible mention of its presence a lopsided and broken signpost near the guard gate.

The arm was down and the gate beyond closed so Ryan parked the Humvee. Stan, one of the volunteers and from the lengthy car discussion a former Airborne Ranger, hopped from the passenger seat to investigate.

Approaching cautiously, his pistol poised to shoot, if necessary, he walked to the guard shack, checked the door, and after opening it, immediately stepped back. He held up two fingers which Ryan knew meant the guards never made it out. Walking to the arm he unlocked it, pushed it out of the way, and waved the team through.

The facility gate was thirty yards from the guard shack. Closed with no electricity to open and close it, it required manual intervention. Without juice, there was no way to unlock it.

A cutting torch would make quick work of it.

Without one, they had to rely on more brutish measures. Ryan sifted through the back of the Humvee and produced a sledgehammer. Stan stared at him and chuckled. Ryan motioned to Vic, a former strongman competitor on the amateur circuit and mechanic by trade in the Air Force, and handed him the tool.

"Have at it," Ryan said.

"Really?" Vic feigned disdain at the task. "Because the rest of you are puny little people, I have to break a nail," he winked.

Ryan shrugged. "Better you than me if the electricity decides to kick on and you get electrocuted."

"Asshole." Vic laughed, and seizing the glee in being able to show off his skills, set to work.

The gate proved stronger than anyone could have imagined. With every heave, Vic brought the hammer down and the metal rattled. The lock failed to budge. Five minutes turned to twenty, and Vic was winded. He took a seat on the bumper of the Humvee and slugged down two waters to replenish his saliva. Looking down at the bumper, he got up and turned around. Slapping his forehead, he shook his head.

"That thing work?" Vic asked.

Ryan looked over. "Does what work?"

Vic pointed to the winch tucked under the bumper. "The winch. Does it work?"

Walking over to the vehicle, Ryan glanced. He hadn't realized it was there. Seeing the severed wires, he frowned, "No."

"Dammit," Vic sighed, dejected.

"Not so fast. I've got an idea." Ryan pushed the release, pulled out the cable, and secured the hook snugly to the gate. "Hop in and ram it in reverse."

Vic pushed down on the gas and the tires squelched. Smoke started to rise from the burning rubber catching hold and with a loud snapping sound the gate suddenly yanked off the hinges. Pulling it out of the way, he hopped out, gave a thumbs up, and one by one the team drove in. Ryan followed last after manually rolling the wire back into the housing and for added measure, set up a trip wire across the opening to blow a grenade to warn against any followers.

He headed to the far side of the facility, past the admin buildings and warehouses to reach the far hangars on the other side of the compound. They found the airship hangar door, still closed, and the solar panels next to it undamaged.

Ryan hoped the airship was still there and with some luck, they could get it airborne.

The large hangar door was locked from the inside. Walking to the small access door to the left, Ryan checked, and it too was locked. Yelling to Vic to open the back of the Humvee, Vic found the large pry bar and brough it over.

"Go ahead, Mr. Muscles," Ryan smiled.

Vic placed the end between the door lock and the frame, and with one hand, pushed forward. The door creaked on its hinges and with a loud cracking sound of the lock breaking, immediately swung outward. "My grandma could have done this," he grinned.

Stepping around Vic, Ryan pulled his flashlight out and walked through the door. A minute later he emerged and gave a thumbs up before walking back in. Soon, the large hangar door began to creep open and soon was open far enough for the team to drive in. Stepping to the entrance and waving them on, Ryan pointed where to park and went back to continue cranking until the door fully illuminated the interior of the massive hangar.

No one was prepared for it.

The team exited their vehicles and the enormity of the airship immediately hit. It was nothing like the blimps of old, the pictures everyone thought of seeing in the skies for football games or sporting events. This was a completely new image that boggled the mind, like cutting a blimp in half, putting a whole one in the middle, and gluing all three pieces together. It was enormous in size, far bigger than anyone could imagine. Sitting in the hangar and seeing it in person sent shivers down spines and made arm hairs stand.

The beast sitting in front of them was the latest model, built for larger cargo and extended flight. Its predecessor was a true hybrid, using fuel and electric to power motors and provide necessary function.

This new iteration was all electric.

Took the fly by wire approach to its infrastructure over cable and pulley systems. With reduced weight using fiber wire and eliminating heavy cabling and mechanics, it allowed for redundant electrical systems and increased maneuverability and distance.

All electric and light, its fuel economy was astronomical.

More space and lighter framework meant more hauling ability of cargo and goods. With flexible solar panels built into its skin, the craft could stay airborne for weeks without the need to ground for a recharge of its state-of-the-art batteries. It was truly an engineering marvel designed around hi-tech wizardry.

Ryan only hoped it could still fly.

He walked over and simply stood for a moment to gaze. A real sight to take in. As Ryan's brain dove into overdrive thinking about what needed to be done, Marcus, one of John's trusted advisors and his former executive officer, or XO for those aboard ship, came over and patted Ryan on the arm.

He reminded Ryan of John Thompson, the former head coach of Georgetown.

The voice, glasses, and a resemblance in his face that made him feel like you had known him for years from having grown up watching college basketball. He carried his authority with him, though the softer side always came through.

"Where do you want us to start?" Marcus asked.

Ryan turned, his checklist ready. "First thing is checking the re-charge cables. Hopefully they were left attached and cycling on and off. We need to get inside and see if we can turn it on and check out the gauges to see where we're at. If pressure is really low, we'll need to boot it up and give the pumps time to prime and begin the airing process. My guess is we need a bit since it's been sitting here. That's a start. From there, here's a list. I can walk you through it and you can assign to whoever you need."

Marcus smiled and took the written list from Ryan. "You are certainly something Ryan. I barely know you, but man, from what John tells me I'd follow you anywhere to get the job done. Well, almost anywhere and don't tell John. He's still my skipper."

Ryan managed to laugh. "Thanks Marcus. I know this seems like it's insane and a suicide mission. My wife and kids can't be a science experiment for a psychopath. If Mark wins, we all lose in the end."

Marcus nodded. "I hear you. I only knew Mark for a short time and it got worse towards the end. All of us here lost someone or watched them die or go off the rails. If we can help get life back, even if a tiny bit of what we used to have, we'll all die to help."

"Thanks," Ryan acknowledged knowing it was true. "Let's get to work."

It took an entire day to get the airship worthy and prepped for flight.

Sitting for three years saw natural leakage of the helium and getting it connected to the fill lines and the tanks working to fully blow it up took hours. The electrical systems started up without an issue and going through the paces took time, to ensure all of the automated checks came back successful and in knowing what was what. Loading supplies and securing the Humvee to keep it from moving and shifting during flight was a bit guesswork and some hope. No one had ever done it before. Even using your best guess was just that, a guess.

It wasn't like they were packed down for months.

They had a few weeks of food and water stores and the extras for the basics of sleeping and living arrangements. It all had to go somewhere and with most of the gear loose and not in containers or boxes, the best they could do were cargo nets and rope and hope nothing got away if it shifted.

Familiarizing himself again and their pilot with all of the flight controls was time-consuming. Once Ryan got into it, the knowledge transfer was fairly easy.

He had spent time talking up the airship pilot.

Watched him when he took his first flight before the world fell. Being nosy and inquisitive gave Ryan a pretty good grounding in all the displays and switches.

This flight's pilot, a woman named June with short red hair and intense blue eyes who was more at home flying a big C-17 to deliver troops and supplies, listened intently, asked questions, and was the type of professional anyone would want at their side. She also had a sense of humor, which helped to lighten the mood, and occasionally poked Ryan in the arm when he got too far down into details.

"It's not a big lug of a plane like I'm used to, but I think I can keep it afloat. No wheels so crash landing is the best I can do there," June joked.

"I'm glad you have confidence. I'm a foot on the ground type guy. Though I've spent my fair share of time jumping out of perfectly good aircraft. Hoping that I'm not going to have to do that on this trip."

June smiled. "This thing seems to hover pretty well based on the turbines I'm seeing out there. If we can find a spot with enough clearance, I can put us down and you can hop off. No room to do that safely and I'll personally push you out the door."

"Awesome," Ryan's sarcasm evident to everyone. "Another hot shot pilot who can't land. I hate crash landings."

"Me too. I'm an O-fer."

Not sure what she meant, Ryan asked, "O-fer?"

June grinned. "You know, zero for zero. Never had a successful landing in my life."

Marcus who had been sitting in the navigator's seat, couldn't help laugh out loud listening to the banter. Humor was a good tension release, and he knew they all needed it. "Ryan, I can vouch a tiny bit for June. I've been on a few of her flights, and while she isn't the most hospitable host there is, she can fly like the best of them."

Peering dead at Marcus, Ryan pointed his finger. "If not, you end up jumping with me."

The former XO violently shook his head. "Hell no. I'm a seaman, not one of those SEAL nuts or airborne weirdos. My feet stay inside the ride, not leaving a perfectly good one."

Ryan gave a thumbs up. "Guess it's only me."

With the airship prepped for flight and towed outside using its mooring lines, the team lifted off and headed West. While the team finished all the preparations, Ryan, June, and Marcus had time to chart a course towards California.

The direct route seemed obvious and was the most vulnerable in being caught.

Ryan thought taking a path through the southwest region offered less inclement weather. Marcus thought go as far direct as possible and depending on conditions come down from the north or up from the south.

June thought otherwise.

"Hear me out," June motioned with her hand. "If we're looking to stay invisible, if we go straight and veer off here, there could be spots along the way they have outposts or lookouts. Just saying. Go along the southern path and come up from Los Angeles and it's all flat land or the ocean once we hit the farmlands. We go along a northern direction and then head south, we at least have the mountains and terrain to hide us. Plus, if you think they're in the Bay Area, we come down and we have plenty of places to hide. Could even come in low over the water and under the Bay Bridge if we had to or in from Vallejo and high and along the ridge behind Berkeley, Oakland, and Hayward. Park it and watch to see what is lit up. Maybe find some time to stop in Napa and snag some really expensive wine while we all wait for you?"

June made sense. She *was* the experienced pilot in the group. Weather was a factor. Being seen could be a death sentence. Remaining hidden provided their advantage, and if they managed to sneak in undetected and could get Ryan close enough and hide themselves somewhere safe until called, it might work.

It had to come together and succeed. The whole mission a shot in the dark, searching for needles that could really be anywhere or nowhere. There was little lying presented for Mark in the way of gaining anything of value. If he felt he was on top and controlled life, ego would leech out his pores like a bad odor to rub it in. He had zero to lose in his mind.

A whole coast away and no way for John to rescue the children.

Ryan was the tactician. The one with experience pulling off missions that were fated to fail, but by the grace of chance or some otherworldly alien being that seemed to like his ass for some crazy reason, he managed to pull off the impossible. To Mark he was fish food, long dead and not a threat. The crazed old friend also had all of the resources it seemed and the backing of a cabal of lunatics following the whims and desires of the President. If Mark really felt no one could or would stop him, his guard wasn't up.

Ryan knew the man. He could exploit the weakness.

"No real argument from me. Options of what we can do and flexibility to change plans on a dime if we must. Stay invisible and out of sight. Not like we're a gunship with cannons on this ride to protect us in the sky."

"Yup," June agreed. "But I'm really serious. If we can stop in Napa and pick up some really expensive wine, it will make the trip worth it."

"Ok," Ryan joked. "You drive, I'll buy."

CHAPTER FORTY-TWO

It was a long flight and time to rest and prepare for the fight ahead.

Ryan had no clue what all lay ahead. Knew it was going to be rough and possibly his last mission. Being confident in his skills and abilities was one thing. Knowing he could accomplish anything he set his mind to was one of his biggest assets. He also knew when the odds were totally against him and the likelihood of success minimal at best.

He was a realist.

Ryan was only one man, even with the support of this ragtag group of former soldiers and civilians. A ghost can only hide so long before the hunters find you in the house and look to send you packing. This trip sought to drop him right in the middle of a shark feeding frenzy without the benefit of a steel cage.

He would be exposed, working off his wits, and trying to find a needle in a very large haystack.

Even if he had his crack team again, there was so much at stake and so many unknowns going in basically blind. If there was luck or mojo that had kept him alive this long, he needed to tap into it and really milk it for all it was worth.

The team had their list to complete while he grabbed some shut eye and Ryan had faith they would carry out their assigned tasks. While he didn't know any of them personally, in fact some he had only met when they showed up to leave, he had been able to chat with most a bit here and there. They were fathers, mothers, brothers, sisters, and all had lost most everything when the world died.

The one thing they all had in common was a sense of hope and a belief that Ryan would succeed.

Even if they perished in the process, they felt their contribution to his effort and the mission worth the risks if it meant stopping the madness and finding a way to get the world to start over.

That pressure weighed heavily on Ryan's shoulders.

In a sense, it lifted him up from his self-doubts and gave him energy. His body was tired, his mind numb, and knowing the team were working hard to support his crazy exploit allowed him to drift off and find a rest he had not felt in years. For the first time, the effects of the virus remained at bay.

Not a single tremor or convulsion coursed through his body, and he slept like a baby.

He got lost in a dream, his family on vacation on one of their famous "Carmichael" road trips. Ryan at the wheel focused on the road and listening to the satellite radio as Julia talked about something he tuned out. The kids in back, Emma pretending to read her books and singing to herself while David played with his dinosaurs. They were little and fragile, his most prized loved ones in the world. Glancing at Julia as she asked a question to a topic he wasn't paying any attention to and being annoyed at him. Good times for all, moments being together.

He longed for their next trip, being together in one space.

A firm hand gripped his shoulder and jostled him to consciousness. He stirred, opened one eye to see who it was, and slowly came back to reality.

"Are we there yet Mom?" Ryan whined.

June frowned. "Really? We've only been gone ten minutes and already a whiny boy," she winked. Letting go and her tone suddenly serious, "We're getting close. Hit some rough weather patches you probably felt that cost us some time. Now we're getting some smoother flows. It's getting dark and I thought I'd wake you up to watch as we approach."

Ryan nodded. "Thanks. I'm interested to see what this side of the world looks like."

June looked at Ryan, her bright eyes dim. "It hasn't been pretty."

Even at their high altitude and with the sun setting, he could tell the picturesque landscape he knew as a boy was gone as he watched from the front window of the airship. Flying home in the past usually took him this way and he enjoyed the scenery from Utah on down as the plane crossed each state and showcased its rugged terrain. Now, they were nearing Reno, its casinos easy to see against the Nevada skyline and the housing tracts going towards Lake Tahoe abundant in the cheaper to reside state.

Nothing of value lay below.

Houses were piles of rubble, a long-ago fire swept by winds and storms that raged unchecked leaving little behind as it burned everything to the ground. The once proud gambling towers sat looking forlorn, many with the top floors gone and what was left of the hotels open to the elements. The streets were littered with debris, and the occasional small fire, likely from some fledgling band of survivors or even Brainers. The former beacons of decadence stood limp, and as they passed overhead, Ryan could only guess what California looked like as they neared their destination.

"Has it all been like this?" Ryan asked, the sadness apparent in his voice.

June nodded. "Most everything. A few cities and towns with some things still standing. Seems the more rural places are the most void of any signs of existence. The larger cities have shown some wayward life, but nothing to really say one way or another."

Maybe being a gambling city caused people to bring the house down, to steal some gambling terminology. Get back at the filthy rich owners who stacked the deck against the regular Joe. The brain wired for death and destruction taking control and leveling the odds.

It might fly as an answer.

Ryan knew why the houses were gone. The blackened trees for miles from Tahoe heading north along the border told him that. Without fire management and resources to combat there was nothing that could be done. California was a fire magnet with all of the national forests, and he cringed at what he would see below as they kept moving south.

"All of this, for what? This country had it good, or at least thought we did. Look at us. Nothing left except a pile of crap mile after mile and divided all over again between the living and those who want us dead or imprisoned to rely on their graces. We got so far and have lost it all. Makes you wonder what the rest of the world looks like, doesn't it?" Ryan's voice betrayed the sadness in his heart.

June touched his hand softly, not with any kind of affection meant to go anywhere, more out of a sense of compassion. "All we can do is live day to day until we can change the world again. I think we're not the only ones in this boat. Maybe there are others like us, fighting the good fight. One day, we'll know. I have faith in it."

Ryan hoped she was right.

He decided he would sit and watch as they cruised further into California. They had to decide if they would head across and come down from Santa Rosa in the north or wind along between Sacramento and Stockton and towards the hills they'd use as cover.

There were pros and cons to each choice, as coming from Santa Rosa covered less populated cities and lots of land to potentially hide them and a straight shot between the capital city and Stockton would place them right behind cover to sit and scout.

To Ryan, aiming for Mt. Diablo and coming right up behind the hills seemed like a better choice to scope out what lay ahead and allow for strategic concealment for a surprise incursion. June and Marcus concurred.

Ryan put up his feet, drank some cold coffee, and waited.

More of the same materialized as the airship passed city after city. Careful to stay high enough in the darkness and along the outskirts to minimize detection, they could still see clearly and far in the distance to absorb the destruction of civilization. Ruined buildings, decimated housing tracts, freeways littered with abandoned cars and big rigs. The lone fire peeked out from below, and beyond the isolated camp, only darkness resonated. Ryan had hoped they would see some kinds of real life, encampments, houses with their backyards lit up, a picture of life staring up at them.

The dismay was crushing, though not totally unexpected.

Ryan's heart sank. He had hoped more than anything some tangible evidence would scream out people were in fact massed into rudimentary communities trying to survive and hang on. Mile after mile the bleak answers stared up, cried in desperation, speaking volumes without uttering a single syllable.

As he passed close to his hometown the stark reality hit that life as it had been known was forever gone.

His old elementary school was nothing. A shell of its former self, the cafeteria building a pile of bricks. The wooden playground structure, once a home to tag and hide and seek games, was burned to the ground. His junior high school, once a bastion of academic excellence, no longer had a roof.

And to his complete horror, his former high school, the argonaut of sports for the region producing countless athletes and pro stars, wasn't even left standing. The entire campus was rubble, the football and baseball fields graveyards for two crashed cargo jets, their failed deliveries strewn everywhere, the wreckage having annihilated the home bleachers.

Damage done long ago, the effects everlasting to see.

The obliteration of what used to be his backyard to roam from this high up, over miles and miles of the city, was a crushing blow to his soul. To rebuild would take generations. Ryan wondered if even a sliver of the past could crawl back and be a brick of a new future. No communities to speak of, no cities or towns left unscathed. The remnants of death, decay, and destruction as far as the eye could see. Even if he found success and triumphed, did it even matter?

The question festered and itched, and like a bad headache, reality came back.

They reached Mt. Diablo and hovered in place, the Bay Area from north to south unraveled in front of them. They could see to San Jose and beyond and all the way to the Golden Gate Bridge. A blanket of pitch black stared through the window, with dots of light here and there, sporadic at best and so small that anyone or anything warming themselves on the cold night were insignificant.

Using the high-powered lens of the airship's front camera system, the entire Bay was visible in high definition on the large monitors. The Hubble telescope has nothing on the micro details the high-tech system had in producing clear and full color images up to fifty miles away. It had to work effectively for harsh conditions in the Artic and deserts with the lowest light possible to ensure the safe operation of the craft.

San Francisco International Airport lay dormant, not a single runway light lit. Same with Oakland. All the municipal and general aviation fields towered and non-towered were quiet. It was eerie beyond belief and looking to his left to check San Jose International, Ryan couldn't help see it.

Like a pimple in the middle of your forehead before prom night, Moffett Field showed signs of life.

You couldn't ignore it.

Building lights hinted at activity, and the runway lights yelled at the top of their lungs. Panning and focusing the camera in, Ryan observed dozens of people scurrying about. For an old military complex that Nasa took over and ran operations for various missions and flights, though Ryan knew from experience its covert activity never ceased, it seemed as if the virus simply skipped over and left the place intact.

"Jesus," June stumbled as she caught it in her sight. "Can't miss it, can you?"

Ryan adjusted the focus on the control panel and moving the joystick, scanned the complex. As far as he could gather, it was a working and fully functional airfield. He could see various aircraft scattered around and a few with their landing lights on.

As the shock subsided, they heard the roar of an engine off to the right and saw a huge cargo plane, from the looks of it a C-17, on its descent headed towards the near runway. Far enough away and shrouded in darkness with Mt. Diablo offering some cover, their visibility blended in, and Ryan was hopeful they stayed that way.

"So much for blowing a single plane and runway," Ryan shrugged as he eyed June. "This really complicates things."

"You think?" June shot back sarcastically. "Any great ideas rolling around up top?" she motioned with her finger, pointing at his head.

His head nodding up and down, his brain working the problem, Ryan closed his eyes, deep in thought. There was no way to disable a whole airfield without getting caught.

It didn't play out well for success.

He could wreck some upheaval and dole out some explosions and given the circumstances it seemed like a lost cause and a detractor from the mission. Once part of the plan, it made zero sense to dedicate time and energy to it.

Looking back at the monitor, Ryan focused past Moffett and squinted his eyes. He knew it had to be there somewhere, and taking a good hard look, he found something, though being miles away, he couldn't be totally certain.

"This is obviously a bust. I'll state that upfront and right away. We hoped finding a working airport would point us in the right direction. We did, but not as active as this. Something insane is happening around here, and we found the hornet's nest. I have a hunch, though it's weak this far out. Take a look," Ryan pointed her in the direction of the dim lights. "See, right there?"

June focused her eyes and saw what Ryan directed her to, beyond Moffett. "I *can* see something. What is it?"

Ryan sighed. "State of the art research and hospital facilities tops in the world."

June frowned, the drama he was creating unnerving. "*And,* that would be?"

Ryan grimaced. "Stanford."

She sat down in the captain's chair, the time to do it now more than ever. June knew the university and its medical facilities and reputation well. The picture was revealing itself little by little.

West Coast isolation within the Bay Area with the ability to cut off access in all directions. Mountains and hills offering protection. Freeways, roads, and bridges that could be blocked or access prevented. Only so many access points to guard and then it was tough back roads to try and travel.

A great place to hide and continue on without undue attention.

From a military perspective it made sense. Choke access and bunker down. Anyone wanting in had to work for it, and the paths were not easy or offered swift passage without facing some kind of death.

Looking at Ryan, June asked, "OK, so what *is* the plan?"

Ryan walked over to the navigation desk, clicked on his light. Looking it over, he ran his fingers from their current location to their next target. "We need to get here," he pointed, his finger on the expansive Stanford campus. "Problem is, we have what looks like an active airport dead ahead. We can't go straight on over without catching attention. We need to avoid any flight paths like the plague."

June peered down and let her eyes adjust to the red light of Ryan's flashlight. Studied the map and had an idea. "We have two options. Head north towards the Golden Gate, turn south, and follow the coast. Once we reach San Gregorio, we go east hugging the hills and drop down the other side of the 280 near the Pearson-Arastradero Preserve. Open land free of obstructions. A hike gets you under some cover. Second choice is longer going deep to the south near Morgan Hill and cutting west to ride the mountain range. Similar landing destination. Longer and more obstacles to circumvent, and it avoids a lot of potential eyes looking to bring us down."

"My guess is either takes considerable time or gets us close to daylight."

June nodded. "Yessir. Not much choice. Could find a place to call home for a bit. Get close enough and bed down with some cover. We will be a sore thumb sticking out if we don't find a good hiding spot."

Ryan looked at the map again, and walked back to the monitor. Looking closely, he scanned the area near Stanford. Three minutes of nothing passed, before he sighed and sat back down.

"What is it?" June asked.

"There's something else. Stanford is not the only place lit up. This keeps getting complicated and venturing outside of what I'd call needing to *wing it*. Not sure what, though it might offer up some intel. Worth investigating," Ryan offered.

The frown on June's face showed her dismay. She liked solid plans, not the kind that changed midstream and put people in danger. "I'm more the stick to it type. If we go off and check on every little thing it leaves all of us exposed to a crapload of unknowns and potential pitfalls. Stanford seems surefire. Why go off elsewhere?"

Ryan looked over, already deep in thought and working out a plan. June was right to a degree. Follow the plan and execute. In his world, sometimes shit hit the fan, got dropped in your lap, or you stepped right in it and had no choice to clean it off.

Stanford was lit up like a beacon screaming *come and get me*.

The rest of the Bay Area was a black hole.

No lights, few fires flickering and even those were tiny. Another building or complex might be where Julia and the kids were or offer him clues and information. He could ignore it, move in and out. What if it was a lab that could continue the research and taking his family meant saving them, but leaving Mark enough to complete his work? He couldn't ignore that.

Risk or not, he had to know what was there.

"Mark isn't the stupid kind. Even if he's crazy and completely gone. He'd have a backup plan or facility. Is this one or *if?* I don't know. It could be and I have to find out."

June turned in the captain's chair to face Ryan. She reached out and touched his knee. "I know this is hard for you. For all of us. Risking the team for a hunch, I can't get totally behind. Give me something to shake my doubts."

Ryan touched her back. "My gut is screaming at me. Get us close enough to recon from the air and I'll be able to tell you yes or no."

Head halfcocked to the side, June responded somewhat sarcastically, "I'm supposed to rely on your gut?"

He couldn't help laugh. "Not entirely. However, I was very good at what I used to do in my other life. Some might say too good. Diving back into my old shoes my spider senses are all tingly. Get me close to see. If it is something, I'll check it out. If it's not, we continue on. Deal?"

June slapped the top of his hand. "Mr. Carmichael, I wish we had met a long time ago. I'm betting you have some stories you could tell. From what I can put together, my guess is if you told me, you'd have to kill me."

Ryan smiled sheepishly. "You've kind of grown on me. I would, but I'd feel really bad doing it."

"I'm sure you would Sir."

Marcus came over and looked as if he'd seen a ghost. "Hey, you guys caught any of the activity at Moffett? It's like a flurry hit it. All kinds of movement going on. Can't see too well this far out on the small screen. It's buzzing like a hive."

Ryan walked over to the large monitor.

Marcus was right. Moffett looked like it was on alert with vehicles and lights weaving all over the place. As he watched, he heard the roar of the engines whining and saw the large cargo jet on its approach front and center outside the window, a mile out. For all the activity sending the place into a tizzy, the incoming aircraft must have serious value onboard. Sitting and waiting for it to land and taxi, he could only guess.

When it finally came to a stop and the rear cargo door dropped, he focused the airship's camera. Zoomed in close to observe and see what came out.

"Shit," was all Ryan could say.

June and Marcus looked at each other, confusion at the words. Neither spoke, and the silence growing in the cockpit left everyone feeling dislodged. After a few minutes, Ryan stared transfixed, not uttering a word.

Marcus saw too and spoke up. "Um, I thought he had a jump on us days ago?"

Ryan, still looking at the monitor, held up his hand for Marcus to be quiet. Eyes transfixed, watching the movements and following the activity. The occasional deep sigh. A few unintelligible mumbles under his breath.

If anyone dropped a pin, the sound would blow out their eardrums.

Five more minutes passed. Becoming a bit agitated, Marcus started to speak, and Ryan's hand shot up immediately. "Keep quiet."

Ten more minutes flashed by, and Ryan's head dropped. Sitting back in the chair, his eyes closed, June could tell something was seriously wrong.

"What is it, Ryan?" June finally asked.

His head shook. "I'm getting too old for this crap."

Confused, she took a step. "We're all too old for any of this. Something catch your eye we need to know about?"

Marcus raised his hand. "You saw something. Seems like it might be one of those things that turns a party into what do the young kids call it? A raver?"

June couldn't help laugh. "Rager Marcus. Though from what I hear, a rave is a pretty wild experience too."

"Ah, got it. Old guy here. Not up to speed on all the young people lingo."

Ryan had been oblivious to the banter. Tuned it all out. Moffett was forefront in his mind. Three thousand miles and smack in the middle of California. The soldier ached for it. The father cringed at what was dropping in his lap.

Marcus waved. "Earth the Ryan. You on the planet or off in space?"

"Yeah, looks like you ventured off into la la land with that blank stare out the window. Can we join you or is this a one man show?" June hoped they weren't losing him to something they couldn't see.

Sighing, Ryan opened his eyes and turned. "It was Mark. He has Julia and the kids. Stanford is secondary. He took them to the other place lit up like Christmas. You're dropping me off there."

CHAPTER FORTY-THREE

The airship was not like driving an inconspicuous old Mini Cooper around that could easily blend in or hide behind a garbage can.

It was huge, close to half a football field in length and extremely wide given its tri-hull design. Throw on a grayish exterior skin and subtlety was not its strongest attribute. Keeping out of sight kept the team safe and alive.

What Ryan asked was beyond insane.

"I know what you are asking. Are you serious?" June's voice cracked, the pitch higher than it should be. She was a hardened vet with multiple deployments under her belt. Had done a few things most pilots wouldn't try. Safety for her crew was always number one.

Ryan nodded. "Absolutely serious. There are only two ways as I see it, and you don't like my first option. This is about as good as it gets."

Marcus, usually a voice of reason if you knew him well enough, piped in. "I'm with him June. I don't really see another way to do it."

June slapped her forehead, knowing how unbelievable this was going to get. Shaking her head, all she could mutter was, "Your funeral."

Intel was in short supply, and given the pressing need to produce a rescue, eliminate the threat, and get out of town, sound, or reasonably sane options, could be counted on one hand. The element of surprise was theirs, if they managed to keep clear of obstacles and any soldiers on patrol.

Ryan had a plan.

If it was a spy movie the plot would fall in line nicely with it. For real life, even the best imagination probably would not have thought this insane feat up.

The risks were astronomical, the potential reward worth its weight.

He had thought about safer and somewhat saner approaches. Take the airship above ten thousand feet and parachute in. It would work, but if anything went sideways on the decent, catching a massive wind draft that

252

blew him out over the water, or a hard landing given all the gear he was planning on bringing, and he'd drown or break something and be chum or a feast served up on a platter.

Nothing was eating him alive.

There was coming in from the west like they had planned to hit the Stanford campus and then hike his way to the target.

Use the ocean and coastal hills as cover.

Distance and time were enemies, plus if he encountered anyone or anything on the way, a gun battle would seriously impede progress. Even if he managed to evade, the jig was up and security would be tightened like a vice grip squishing a grape. With residential and business ruins all around, and countless unknowns or watchful eyes, he couldn't get dropped off a block or two away. June needed clearance unless he roped down from above to the ground.

That meant being a sitting duck.

With a gleam in his eyes, Ryan had hatched up a new idea.

"Look, we need space and a way for you to high tail it out. It's open, close to the water, and means you can turn and run away. No one will be midnight golfing so it kinda works."

June stared at Ryan. "A golf course? I get the concept. But, really? There are other places that to me work better."

Ryan shook his head. "Maybe, although from a practical standpoint and hoofing to get there, it offers the most direct route and potential places to hide."

Nervous eyes, or was it concern? Hard to tell. "Are you absolutely sure about this?" June asked.

"Yes I am. The San Francisquito Creek puts me one street over. My guess would be besides dark and spooky, no one would be watching it. Take it from the golf course and keep low. Anything else puts this big gray bird too close for comfort. We can only see and venture a guess. This at least, we can see first and hope for the best. Get out if it smells rotten." Ryan's fake smile made him snicker, more to add some levity and ease June's concerns than he thought his idea was funny.

Marcus patted June on the shoulder. "I'd think he was nuts too if I didn't see the value of the creek and keeping the element of surprise. Plus, all we have to do is throw him out the back and run like hell."

Taking the joke in jest June laughed. "I'm with you on that. What's the whole plan? Hike in, see what's going on and attempt a rescue? If it works, how do you plan on escaping?"

Ryan smiled. "That's where the real fun comes into play. You get to see how well this big balloon can fly and do a touch and go."

After more conversation and pouring over the maps, Ryan laid out as much of a "plan" as he could muster. Given zero intel, no clue as to the enemy's numbers, and absolute lack of knowledge on what was left of the neighborhoods and businesses for structures, it was a masterpiece in potential failure.

All in a day's work for him.

The only constant was his family being taken to some secure location deep inside a neighborhood and sequestered inside some compound. Ryan vaguely knew the area and the homes from when his father was hospitalized and he and Julia, needing a food break or to clear his head, mindlessly drove around and dreamed about moving back West and finding a place to throw roots down alongside the mansions of millionaires and billionaires who turned regular lots into walled fortresses to keep people at bay.

The uber rich of Silicon Valley throwing their money around and driving up real estate beyond the reach of normal folk.

His guess was Mark had taken over some industry tycoon's house for its security set up and proximity to Stanford. A smart move. And if it was hard to reach by street or had barricades in place, the more isolated and out of reach from infiltration by potential enemies it presented itself, though he thought that was laughable given society was gone and organized bands of anyone beyond Brainers seemed like a fairy tale.

Ryan wondered about that one.

If Mark was confident he was in charge and no one could get in his way, there was the potential for lax preparations. Possible breaks and holes in his thinking processes. Maybe he simply had a place and took it because he liked it.

Station a few guards to ward off the Un-Dead or survivors.

From all he had heard over the last days, Mark thought he was God and nothing could stand in his way. If he really felt that way, locking down the place was overkill. The answer would be known soon enough, and maybe, just maybe, luck rolled the dice Ryan's way one last time.

Simply moving forward this late was out of the question, and as dawn would be coming, finding a place to hide a huge gray airship for the day was a must. Bald Ridge, below the summit of Mt. Diablo, offered concealment and a place for the crew and team to get out and stretch their legs. June landed the big bird and with a few hours of dark left, Ryan took up the first watch with a small group while everyone else got some shuteye.

He found a nice spot to lay and watch the stars.

Being out in real nature had been a long time ago, and while he didn't relish becoming prey for wildlife all by himself or a wandering band of Lurkers or Bolts, this high up away from any city he figured they were safe enough. All stretched out, rifle ready to engage any threats, Ryan took a bit of time to unwind. He knew sleep would come later and had to disengage and not go over and over the plan in his head.

Almost two weeks ago, Ryan was alone, except Pete for much needed company, surviving and barely eking out an existence.

Everything he thought written in stone began to crack and slowly chip away. Seeing David for the first time in years, though not knowing it at the time. A roving band of Brainers back in his town, who hadn't been seen in over a year.

Seeing the caravan of survivors at the old fort.

Mark and his soldiers attacking. He could have simply walked away at that point, self-preservation to remain alive.

He didn't, couldn't contemplate it, as the image of the boy stuck in his mind.

By the grace of luck, that gnaw in his belly turned out to be the right decision as he was reunited with his son.

Then, one by one his world began to devolve.

The information John shared. Mark having the Yorktown parked at the port. The underground facility. Finding Emma and Julia alive, which all turned the current reality upside down. No matter how hard Ryan focused on the positives, something felt *off*, the numbers not adding up. He couldn't quite place it, the weird feeling in his stomach.

Ryan knew something was *wrong*.

The last days had been a whirlwind, with hardly any time to do anything except absorb, react, and plan.

No ability to really reflect, dissect, or think in detail about everything that had been dumped in his lap. With a grandiose mission mere hours away and time to kill, he had a chance to pull all the bits and pieces forward and put the puzzle together.

The funny shapes didn't snap in place, and that sent a shiver up and down his spine.

Maybe it was all the rust dusting itself off his exterior. Could be the shock of recent revelations. Three years thinking your family was dead could do that.

Possible he didn't want to think it.

As he lay under the dark sky and all the information swirled around in his mind like a tornado, he kept coming back to what felt out of whack with all he knew.

And smack, it hit him.

Emma and her speech.

For a kid who required speech therapy and could not string together enough words for a sentence when he last saw her, even though her receptive skills were top notch and she understood everything, she was quite proficient using language. The stay at home and virus numbers kept schools totally remote with zero in-person therapies when everything went downhill. While Julia did a great job supplementing them, three years without the proper resources and a world gone to crap meant Emma's progress had to have been affected. Either Emma hit it out of the park and shined, or something didn't add up.

Julia in scrubs. The lack of total shock at him rising from the dead.

While the scrubs he could get, a replacement outfit, maybe? Her reasoning for her movements being a locked down wing and getting Emma her meds, Julia appeared a bit too together.

Him presumed dead and like a specter standing in front of her armed to the teeth and dressed to kill?

She only knew his security work. His military background was concealed from her and everyone else. She should have responded differently and acted more, *upset*.

Was that the word?

Ryan thought it was too tame. For not seeing her husband for three years he expected hysterical tears. It didn't sit right. Throw in the most recent revelations and you had a brew cooking.

The traitor in John's group.

It was true there was a spy. Too close to John and someone privy to some specifics. Not close enough to the inner circle to know about John and Ryan's conversations. While the defector could give details about David and their whereabouts, the group with Emma and Julia was kept locked tight. The rescue party was led by Ryan and their eventual final destination after getting the hostages and survivors not divulged until *after* they had left and been on their way. Julia knew he was alive and he had given her the radio.

By all accounts, the only one who knew enough was....

Julia.

Ryan felt all of the air leave his lungs. It felt like a baseball bat had been sent full swing for a home run right across his chest. He couldn't breathe, hyperventilating, his head getting light. The thought of his own wife betraying him, subjecting their children to torture, was a foreign concept he couldn't rationalize.

The tremors spewed a hate through his body like never before.

His arms contorted, the angles painful, the muscles pulsing a thousand times a minute. Back arching, head thrown back with chest protruding forward. Legs flailing wildly up and down, side to side, bending and extending, the tendons pulled tight and, in a minute, relaxed. Fingers pulled in and out of closed fists, punching the air. The pain excruciating, with no way to fend it off.

Ryan could do little except let nature take its course.

Fifteen minutes of extreme torturous spasms and his entire body posed in unnatural ways. When they finally subsided, the last wave washed away to return to sea, Ryan could not move. His body lay still, the neurons ceasing function.

Not even a twinge.

He stared at the night sky, tears sending water down his cheeks, no way to wipe them off.

For the first time in ages, Ryan cried.

When it was all over, he reached and wiped away the remnants. Not much left but salty residue. The crust was there and needed to go. Ryan sat up, his mind spinning, trying to grab at his thoughts as they sped on by. If Julia was his betrayer, and the one behind the death of John's people, she had turned against not only him, but her own flesh and blood. Allowing David and Emma to be guinea pigs, test subjects used for torture, was the highest betrayal of parenting and love for your own. He didn't want to stomach the thought, couldn't find a plausible explanation, had no reason to doubt the information smacking his face.

Prove me wrong, Ryan thought to himself.

Rolling it over and over from every angle, no other canvas showed bright colors. Only the black and white of deceit dripped down, like wax melting slowly down the side of a candle. Maybe he was jumping the gun, so to speak, to put a really bad analogy to it. It all kept coming back. Nothing added up and that made it even more troubling to the equation.

The anger began to rise.

It welled from the deepest and darkest corners of his mind, a foam that kept boiling to the top. Ryan felt the heat, his ears warming to the touch even in the cold of the night.

It wasn't the knit cap doing it, that he knew.

He felt the blood pulsing, swore he heard the beating as the fluid traveled in the miles of veins and vessels that traversed his body. He hadn't felt like this in forever, and as the anger took the turn and became rage, trying to keep it wrapped in a tight bow became nearly impossible.

Rolling to his side and pushing up with his left hand, Ryan hopped up on his feet. The steam from his breathe rose up with each exhalation, so he bent his head down and tried to think. Digging deep, he realized he needed to clear his head of everything and focus on the mission ahead, or death would come knocking and he'd answer the door this time. Closing his eyes and clearing his mind, he slowed his breathing and relaxed his muscles.

Let everything go.

One minute turned to two, five to ten. Fifteen minutes later his focus returned. The determination to kill stronger than ever.

Vengeance will be mine.

Ryan let it percolate.

He wasn't the type to let emotions take control. He was always cool under pressure and level-headed. While he knew days ago when David came back to him that the seed of revenge was planted, and the surprise of Emma and Julia that death for Mark was too easy a solution, he never before had felt an almost glee in going to kill someone.

Now, it was right there.

He sensed the smile, warmed up inside against the chill of the night as he played it out. He wanted to kill, to exact pain and suffering beyond imagination. With the thought of Julia being an enemy, he threw her into the mix.

Killing his wife didn't even phase him.

The pain struck and he fell to his knees. Blood trickled from his nose. He reached up, wiped it away, and in the moonlight stared at it. The color appeared to be black and oozy, not the expected red of normal human blood.

The sight sent a shiver down his spine and immediately he lurked forward and threw up.

With both hands planted in the dirt, he wretched, his dinner of cold canned beef stew vomiting a pile inches from his face. The entire meal came up and when it was done, he continued to dry heave until nothing remained.

Grabbing a water bottle from his pack Ryan took a swig and spit out the taste of puke. Mouth free of the sourness, he drank the bottle in a few gulps, not worried about slugging it down too fast. The liquid hit the spot, filled his stomach and eased the nausea to the point of feeling one hundred percent. That made him feel normal again, yet there was more to it.

He didn't feel right, felt amiss.

Something was going on and he had to know what and why. His mind was running laps, marathons of thoughts all huddled together with no rhyme or reason. Oozy blood had drizzled from his nostrils. He blew chunks. Maybe all of the stress of what was about to drop was the answer. The physical toll from the last week finally catching up.

It had been too many years to count since his last major operation and body count.

Maybe he was going insane, at least with the way his brain was gurgling up concocted scenarios based on what he knew, or thought he did. That was possible, though if he was questioning his sanity, he was sure it meant he was actually sound of mind, or close enough.

What the hell is happening to me?

Ryan stood up slow, letting the cold air slap his face. Eyes closed, deep breaths, he let his muscles relax. The spasms and tremors made his body ache like never before. He had played high school football and had been on the receiving end of a vicious hit that made the stars appear. The pain from this made that blow feel like a tiny finger brush against the skin.

He was the meticulous kind.

A man who planned and planned even more. He sought the truth, all of the facts and information he could gather, and made the most articulate and well-constructed decisions. He rarely acted out of character, at least, the soldier Ryan was composed and a stoic rock.

Even the husband and father had his act together.

Somewhere he felt he had lost that edge. Couldn't pinpoint it. It felt like he was a different person. Not all of a sudden, had diverged over time from the linear path and was on a tangent timeline.

Three years of being alone probably did not help his train of thinking and having a whole new reality dumped in his lap.

Add a week like the one he lived and any sane person might begin to contemplate if the asylum had a room available. Whatever was going on had to wait.

Suck it up soldier. The mission comes first. Your internal crap can take a backseat. We'll deal with it once this is all over.

His children required immediate focus and extraction from an evil using them for profit and gain. Not necessarily monetary since paper and coin were extinct.

No.

Profit and gain based on control and fear over who remained. If Mark could truly create a cure for the virus, or at least stave off its aftereffects, even if it was a maintenance dose on a schedule, people would flock and do anything for it.

Anything.

No one would care about the fate of Ryan's children. Given the self-absorbed and *me first* attitudes and selfishness that got the world in this mess in the first place, two kids were simply collateral damage. No matter what, he would get them and ensure they survived.

Even if it meant no cure.

The world would need to suck it up and deal with reality and move forward the best way possible.

Screw anyone and everyone that thought otherwise.

It must have been hours lost inside his skull because sunrise peeked over the horizon. Pissed at himself for losing track of time and not getting some shuteye, Ryan hurried back to the airship and checked in with Marcus. There hadn't been any radio traffic to note and lookouts using high powered specs didn't notice any unusual activity at the airbase or their intended target later that night.

The only thing that was reported back, and something that didn't register any warning flags, were the fires that speckled the area.

A dozen more sprouted from the time they landed to right before dawn. While they were in proximity southwest of where Ryan was planning on infiltrating the city, they were small enough to suggest a few people, not a large contingent.

Nothing in the immediate landing area.

The news was worrisome, yet not enough to alter his plan. Taking his cue, Ryan went to find a quiet and dark corner of the immense beast and find some slumber to rest and recharge. Tonight was going to be a grueling endeavor, and being solid of body and mind required.

An A game was required as anything less meant a potential loss. Get in the headspace, loosen the muscles, hydrate and be ready.

He hoped his aging flesh and troubled mind allowed it.

CHAPTER FORTY-FOUR

Ryan approached death and war in much the same ways.

Death was inevitable. One day your card was up and called in. The only thing you can do is keep moving forward and do your best, and then do more to ensure you completed your mission to success.

Once that happened, you could keel over.

It was a fatalistic approach. He knew it. The Reaper always knocking on your door asking for a cup of sugar. You could graciously fill it up and tell him you were busy and had things to do, so goodbye for now. Or, you could slam the door and piss him off.

Do that and face the wrath when he brought the sickle down and split you in two. Ryan preferred a friendly walk with Death and some nice chit chat before they had to leave the living and pass through the gates of Hell.

War never changed. For millennia people had fought. Killed each other over stupid things. It was a cycle, repeated over and over with no end in sight. You did what you had to do to survive.

The places and people changed. Not the outcome.

This was war, no matter how you spun it. His children were captives, taken for experiments and used for their bodies and what they possessed. It was a personal war, one that his enemy had no idea was coming and when, though he figured if Julia was in on it, Mark had some inkling Ryan would be coming.

Just not this soon.

Traveling across the country with little resources and roads and highways littered with death and destruction, Mark probably assumed a lot. Like if Ryan even managed to gather up enough supplies and could manage a cross country road trip, it would take weeks or longer to go from Point A to B.

If, and a huge one, *if* he was lucky to survive the trip.

Underestimating the resolve of a father who possessed the skills he had, was a ticket to definite death. Ryan would never stop, like the Bolts. He'd keep coming until he finished the job.

Mark knew it.

Mark had no idea how he'd actually succeed, and that was Ryan's ace in the hole. Let Mark think he had the time to prepare, and then cut his balls off from below.

Ryan snickered at the image. Creeping up from below and taking his Ka-Bar out of its sheath. Grinning from ear to ear as he reached up and slid the blade across the skin. Watching testicles pop out and fall to the ground.

That was all it was, a mental picture with limited details.

Not like he could come up from the bowels of the toilet like in Roman or Medieval days, attack, and sink back down to oblivion. It was a fanciful thought to humor and pass the time. Plus, crawling around in crap and urine wasn't exactly high up on the bucket list of creative ways to kill someone.

If, he could actually do it.

Shaking his head to jostle the insane words filling it up, Ryan came back to Earth and his focus. He was all prepped, magazines stocked full, clips all in line in his tac vest. Sniper rifle primed and ready, tucked peacefully in its protective soft case, though he didn't think he'd really need it.

Close and personal to keep quiet was the goal.

Any kills in close proximity to keep his presence secret and sounds to a whisper. His M4 with suppressor would suffice as he maneuvered from the airship to the creek and hidden below street level. Once he reached his destination, the MP5 and Sig with their silencers would eliminate any immediate threats.

Worse case, he'd use his Ka-Bar and slit some throats or severe a few spines.

The thought of really getting inside someone's personal space again and hearing the last breath of a dying asshole sent happy shivers up and down his spine.

He had one last operation meeting to go over all the specifics and check in on his target. With pitch black to cover their ascent, the airship came to life. Rising up to altitude to let the cameras work and focus in, Ryan checked the area and the landing point.

Moffett Field was awash in activity.

Vehicles sped from hangars to aircraft, loading and unloading crates and pallets. He had a pretty good sense of what they were based on the shapes and sizes. Armaments and munitions cans.

Hundreds of them.

Using the joysticks to turn the cameras and adjust the lenses, Ryan watched the monitors until the intended landing area came into view. Grass overgrown, the tree leaves offering shade and privacy, the golf course would screw up even the best handicap in its dilapidated state. It looked more like the surrounding nature area than a recreation spot. He panned left to right, covering the expanse of the fairways and to the clubhouse.

Nothing moved.

Scanning further, Ryan searched for lights. To the north of the course along the shore only shadows stared back. South, a few small campfires he assumed for warmth were far apart and inconsequential. Towards the west and his intended destination, sporadic lights glared, small and indicative of some type of activity. Fortunately, the creek, below the streets and what was left of the neighborhood, was shrouded in black and devoid of any illumination.

It was as thick as soup.

His target was lit up like a Christmas tree. Not the grounds of the mansion, the interior of the house. Ryan expected flood lights or some feature that lit up the street for any potential encroachment or breach since streetlights had long been silent.

Nothing peered back.

It seemed odd and out of place. If you were Mark and felt superior, being attacked or anyone having the gall to try and climb the compound's exterior walls was not on your radar. Smug in security protocols being able to deter and repel. Looking at the building, Ryan thought it probably had looked no different three years ago. People at home, lights aglow, enjoying their perfect life without a care in the world.

Completely oblivious to the rest of humanity who struggled to survive.

Thinking about the entitled rich assholes who used to live in the sprawling house sent Ryan's blood boiling. They were long dead, victims of the virus succumbing to it or turning into one of the hordes rampaging and eliminating survivors.

Their privilege lost, he couldn't help his distain.

Even though he was a former CEO of a successful company and made some good money, he also poured it back into the organization with great salaries and rewards for his employees. He lived modestly, and that was all right.

Not to say he didn't live comfortably.

They did.

Raising his kids to respect value and earning with integrity and hard work instead of on the backs of others was an important lesson he passed on. You can't take your money with you. He felt that to his core. Being a person who amassed tons of it seemed not only selfish, but counter to being a real human. Who needs billions of dollars, expensive cars and artwork, and donates small amounts to charity and pretends they're for real?

He loathed them all.

Taking a deep breath to curtail the rising anger inside, Ryan closed his eyes and thought of his children. Emma, her smile a heart melting sight that he couldn't wait to see. David and his funny faces. They were his world and getting them back the most important thing in his life after losing them to Mark and apparently, his wife.

Julia would get her own justice.

Mark was the one that made him feel on fire inside. Watch the life drain and fade out from Mark's corpse. Julia though, Ryan wouldn't take pleasure in her death. She was after all, the mother of his babies. Given what she had allowed to happen, there was no way she would escape punishment. It would be quick, as painless as practical.

Maybe.

"Everything good to go there, Mister Fancy Pants?" June snickered.

Ryan turned away from the monitors and glared. "My pants are not fancy. Off the rack."

Laughter erupted in the confined space. Marcus held a hand to his face to keep from being too loud. June, recognizing the sarcasm, shook her head. Ryan winked, and began to chuckle.

"More like taken off a dead body I'd say," Penny piped in.

A spitfire of a personality with a shaved head and more tattoos than a renegade biker, she was managing Ryan's drop inside enemy lines. Get him in quick and safe, that was her mission.

Ryan feigned hurt. "Seriously? A dead body would have that lingering smell. These are crisp and new. Or, *newer* I should say. No blood stains on these bad boys."

Marcus patted Ryan's back. "Not yet, right?"

June rolled her eyes. "What is it with men? Always have to go out and kill stuff to feel like a real man." The words were meant to be fun, with no ill intent. She could see in Ryan's eyes as he raised his brow, that something lurked beneath. She couldn't place it, and not wanting to go there, offered some light-hearted teasing to go along. "My guess is the body count will make the last days of civilization look like a birthday party compared to what's coming."

He couldn't not think about it. Ryan realized he must have either grinned or lost his poker face based on the look he caught from June. Wanting to keep focus and play along, he shrugged. "Only the bad guys."

Penny tapped the window to get everyone's attention. "OK people. Back to planning here. We got stuff to do."

Ryan nodded and motioned for the team to gather around. He went over each detail using the map and what his movements would be if left undetected. In the event his path was obstructed or he had to improvise, he showed them ten contingencies in order of priority. If he succeeded, he'd use the same location for pick up at the golf course. If events got hairy or desperate, he had alternatives.

The problem was that if he had to go with back-up locations, it meant breaking radio silence.

There was a pre-arranged time for the primary pick up. If that got scrubbed, he couldn't provide a timeline. Unknown terrain, potential enemies in pursuit.

There were too many factors that came into play. The team would have to be close enough and use the dark to get in and out quick.

It was the only way they'd all make it out alive.

CHAPTER FORTY-FIVE

Silence filled the cabin.

You could hear a pin drop.

As Ryan finished up, June couldn't help feel trepidation at the mission ahead. She was seasoned, too many combat flights to count, and never in a situation like this. Penny, the lone civilian of the group, great at details and managing others to get assigned tasks done from her days running logistics for a big parcel company, felt a pang of angst. She didn't know Ryan at all, yet felt for him knowing what he was up against.

He hadn't hid any details as he went through the plan and explaining why he was doing it.

Marcus felt a twinge of sadness and a sense of pride. Being an officer who had to make some of the tough calls alongside John, he had directed men and women for tough work. Ryan, being in a completely different category than any seaman yet with the same duty background and sense of getting the job done the right way, personified every person who ever served.

Do what is right and for the right reasons, Marcus felt.

The former XO had been around many special operators during his time as John's number two man. His ship the launching point for many missions over the years. Those soldiers personified a certain commonality to him, same demeanor, stature, the way they carried themselves 24/7, even the way they spoke most times.

Ryan was different.

Marcus could see the hardened operator's mind at work and also a softer side, almost hidden, that came out. Maybe it was the jokes and sarcasm, the raised brow or wide eyes on occasion. If he had met the man in the real world, the way things used to be long ago, he thought he'd have no idea what lurked below the surface unless Ryan told him.

In a different time, sitting and talking over a beer would have been a great way to know the old dog, make a new friend.

Marcus envied the soldier, a man who had been deep in it and suffered great loss, and still put one foot in front of the other and kept going. Being at sea was easy to support freedom. Putting your life on the line in the middle of the muck something only a few had the servitude to tackle head on.

"Are we all in agreement and good with the plan?" Marcus looked around for any objections and saw none.

"Great," June sighed. "I have my end. Never done a dump and run in a big airship before. Fingers crossed!" she animated as she threw up her hands.

Penny looked around. "Come on. Easy job people. We have our own superman taking on the evil villains. Seriously though Ryan," she complimented as she patted his back. "You are one hell of a guy and mad respect. We owe you our lives when this is all done."

Ryan, eyes closed and head down, pursed his lips and looked up. "Thank you all. I appreciate it. My family is my life, and my kids my world. I'd be lying if this was not all about them. It is. Everything else is kind of secondary. I promise you, this will end. One way or another."

Marcus nodded. "Family is everything. Holding onto them and making sure they're safe and with you, no one can blame you for putting them first. We've all lost. If we had the chance to get any of them, we'd do the same. Being able to help someone out to get cherished ones back, hell, no question there. We've got your back."

June and Penny smiled. Ryan felt some comfort in knowing he wasn't all alone, a twinge of guilt at risking others for his own selfish efforts. Family was pivotal and foremost. Mark a priority. Anything else he could do to cement discord and impede the evil, icing on the cake.

Stepping away, Ryan walked around and gave his personal thanks and headed below to gear up. As he walked, the smiles and nods from the team made him uneasy. He had the world on his shoulders and had to produce results.

It wasn't the first time he'd been in that position.

He'd been on missions before where freedom and chaos hung in the balance, failure on his part creating a new world order that swept democracy into the gutter. Those times never phased him.

This was different.

Democracy was gone. Freedom a lost ideal. A virus had toppled the world and left nothing. It could not really go much lower. He guessed everyone could end up as crazy psychos or dead.

Really dead.

That would absolutely kill any chance of putting the world back together. The difference with this was more on the line to end the craziness and give the world a chance at surviving and everyone he had encountered knew it. They all looked to him to succeed, and that was more pressure than anything he had ever felt before.

Fail and the end was inevitable.

Ryan did one last check of all his gear. It was all as expected and ready to go. He found a quiet spot in the cargo bay, just inside of the large exterior door used for supply drops. He sat and closed his eyes, beginning his routine to get in the head space he needed before stepping into the fray. Went over the map in his head, out the airship, hustle to the creek, along the banks, under the freeway, and to the neighborhood.

Hoped he didn't encounter anyone or anything that blocked his way.

He had no way of knowing since his intel was from miles away and couldn't dive into the details as if he had overhead satellites or a drone to provide information.

This was shooting from the hip in the starkest sense of the words.

Over and over, he envisioned what lay ahead. Potential kills, obstructed paths to circumvent, scaling the compound's walls. Moving expeditiously to breach an exterior door quietly and unseen. Finding his kids. Confronting Julia and dealing with her treachery.

Killing Mark.

He must have been fully absorbed in his head as he didn't even hear Marcus speak.

"Ryan? Hey Ryan? We're almost there." Marcus was knelt down and had to touch Ryan's knee to break him from the zone.

"Huh? Oh, right," Ryan nodded. "Sorry. Deep in mission thought. Thanks."

Marcus stood back up. He looked worried. "You, OK? Not really my place to step into a world I've never been a part of. You've seemed a bit, I don't know, edgier, than from before. Is it your kids?"

Ryan looked up.

He wasn't sure how to answer. He had felt something was not quite right. Could be the sudden jump back into soldier mode. Lack of sleep these past days. Finding out about his wife and kids. Everything in such a short period of time all at once. He couldn't put a finger on it, knew deep down there something gnawing at his soul.

"Just want my children back in one piece," Ryan managed to spit out before the airship shuttered and dropped altitude.

"What the hell?" Marcus had lost his footing and wound up in the seat opposite Ryan.

The intercom came to life. "Sorry everyone. Still trying to get used to this beast," June answered.

Taking his cue, Ryan stood up and winked at Marcus. "Be ready for me. I have a feeling I'll be inches ahead of a death squad trying to help me meet the Reaper once I get done."

Marcus laughed. "Roger that. Call and we'll be there for you."

Putting on his tac vest and utility belt, Ryan adjusted the leg strap for his Sig. Nice and snug, he threw on his rucksack, pulled the straps for a tight fit, and put on his helmet.

It had been years since he had been part of a mission drop.

Those were all with his team or at least a spotter if a two-man incursion. This being his first solo adventure, besides the ones he'd been conducting since seeing David and stepping back into creeper mode.

It felt liberating and surreal all at once.

He didn't have to rely on anyone else or worry about their life. Deviate from the plan and wing it if required. While having others with him might prove beneficial, take some fire and direct the focus away from him, he didn't trust any of the people he'd met enough to let them tag along.

Out of step and not in sync meant mistakes that got people killed.

A team or partner trained with you, knew your every move, was one in mind and body. A rag tag bunch of former soldiers who never worked together, let alone had never crawled through the pits of hell in combat or a clandestine op, were more a liability than an asset.

He couldn't put Emma or David at risk.

He slung the MP5 halter around his neck and tightened it against his side. Picking up his M4 he pulled the cocking handle to engage a round, set the safety, and set it to three shot bursts. His sniper rifle was tucked away in his ruck, more as a precaution over feeling he was going to need it. He was packed full he knew, probably bringing too much for the occasion. He figured take an overabundance and lessen the load on the trip versus have a deadly need and not have the goods available.

Never get caught light. You died if you did.

The red light starting to flicker, indicating they were close to landing. As soon as the green light lit, the door would lower and Ryan would jump. June would get the hell out and hunker back down until signaled for the pickup.

Sweat started to bead on his forehead, not from stress or worry. It was damn hot with all his gear on. The cold night air would feel nice, refreshing even, and as anticipation began to rise waiting to depart, deep from the bowels of his soul he began to feel a wickedness he had never experienced before in his life. He *wanted* to kill everything in his path, craved pulling his Ka-Bar and plunging it deep in the gut of some adversary, yearned to watch Mark, and Julia if it came to it, slowly slip into death.

Thinking about taking lives put a huge smile on his face.

He had never killed for fun. Saw it as a blemish on the soul. He valued honor and integrity. Followed the code to heart. Taking a life meant erasing someone forever and when he had done it, it was always for a just cause.

Get rid of the demons and false prophets who wreaked havoc on the world.

Even post-pandemic his thinning the herd of Brainers, Lurkers, and Bolts had a higher purpose. Their departure meant some survivor might keep on living.

In the here and now, the thought of ending anyone who got in his way, friend or foe, even family who had once been loved and adored, tingled a joy within. Never in all his years had an almost pleasure in dealing death coursed through his body.

He didn't know what was happening to him, but Ryan liked it.

CHAPTER FORTY-SIX

The drop went off without issue.

He barely got out the door before the airship made a sharp turn and immediately sped off, low over the water, before disappearing straight up into the clouds. They had been fortunate the weather had turned to crap, with low hanging clouds hiding the moon and all-natural light.

It was perfect for a night mission like this.

It did mean he was moving in near total blackness until his eyes could adjust enough. He didn't want to use his night vision if he didn't need to, more to keep them from being a distraction than draining the batteries.

Taking a breath, Ryan moved swiftly through the tall grass.

Tree cover was non-existent over large portions of his trek and getting to San Francisquito Creek imperative to keep from sight. As he hit the dirt boundary before the trail that worked along the creek for bicyclists and runners, he decided to sprint.

Something felt off, he couldn't place it, and getting below the trail low on the bank felt critical to stave off the thought.

It might have been the too quiet of the night with only the sounds of animals or being in the open and exposed. For some reason he felt eyes staring from the shadows. Friend or foe, he didn't really care. Anything or anyone causing any kind of delay was a distraction and potential flare lighting up the sky to his presence.

The smell stopped Ryan cold in his tracks.

He hadn't had that aroma sneak into his nostrils since his last tour. Used Mentholatum dabs on his upper lip to stave off the stench. Here, death and decay permeated the air. Looking down over the edge of the creek, his eyes fully adjusted, he saw them. Bodies in various stages of rot, skulls void of hair and skin, rib bones protruding from unidentifiable masses of flesh. There weren't a few.

Hundreds of former living souls littered the creek bed.

Stepping down the embankment, careful not to lose his footing, Ryan kept a vigilant eye. Scanning the corpses, a consistent feature screamed back. Hospital gowns, the former white linens no longer pristine, were muddled dark from decomposition and dirt. He had seen similar dumping grounds during his service, civilians killed and discarded like trash.

Men, women, and children who became prey for ideological psychopaths who valued obedience and servitude through bastardized religious zeal over compassion and acceptance of their own people.

As he maneuvered amongst the dead, working around to avoid protruding bones and trip into a puddle of fermenting organic matter, Ryan pictured their last minutes and what must have been the end. Failures to provide Mark with results and sent to their demise without a second thought, a needle sending a cold fluid coursing their veins until the dark took hold. That was if any amount of humanity existed with the medical staff.

He doubted it.

He knew a bullet was quicker to save valuable medicine. Bring them out here, turn around, and one pop to the back of the head. He could only imagine if that was the scenario. What went through someone's mind standing on the precipice above, staring below at what would be their fate, and have time to watch as the bullet left your forehead and you still had a few moments of consciousness to realize what happened before death took control.

Fear. Anxiety. Calm.

Any one of those circulating before the deed. Ryan hoped that the people didn't suffer more than they had under the guise of medicine. Guinea pigs used for profit and science and slaughtered for an insane dictator.

They needed justice like Emma and David.

Same with the rest from the last three years, really four, if you counted all the crap that led up to the extinction of society. Everyone deserved to have someone avenge them, persecute the unjust actions, and as he slowly absorbed the stench and rot, Ryan's blood began to boil again.

He tossed the anger aside and finding a clear pathway, walked through the debris of discarded humans along the banks of the creek. Ears open for sounds, he heard nothing out of the ordinary.

He had thought eyes were lurking, might have been he caught a whiff of the bodies and it triggered a guarded response.

As he marched forward, he didn't encounter anymore dead souls, just garbage and junk that seemed to have found its way post-apocalypse by the looks of it. Navigating the old televisions, toys, clothing, and other miscellaneous items, he found himself staring up at the 101, the dark tunnels for water flow under the freeway no more than fifty feet away.

There was no way to venture through.

A massive wall of mangled cars and semi-trucks and their trailers blocked the passage. The rusting carcass of a bus precipitously hung over the edge. Ryan wondered if the next strong wind would finally send it over to the pile of wrecks below. From the looks of it, an accident or possibly purposeful act provided the carnage impeding his path forward. He could attempt to scale the metal and find a hole to the other side, although the amount of time wasted didn't fit into his plan.

Every minute was precious to saving his kids.

Sighing, Ryan decided to circumvent the blockade and go around. It required going topside and across the freeway to the other side. The retaining walls on either side were too high to scale, so he turned around. He had passed some type of a road before the bend in the creek, back on his right as he retraced his route.

It had to have been some access point to the water.

Coming to it, he walked along the side to prevent muddy boot prints, until he came to a locked gate. Peering through, he saw a public storage facility on the other side, the familiar orange roll-up doors visible. Kicking the mud off his boots and wiping them clean, he hopped the gate and landed quietly on the pavement, staying still to listen intently for any sound.

His own heartbeat was all he heard.

Heading right, Ryan crept low, eyes panning back and forth, his ears perked to catch any noise. He found himself facing a frontage road that ran along the freeway. Concrete barriers topped by chain link ran each direction as far as he could see in the dark of the night. Feeling his odds were better going right, he jogged until he was over the top of the creek and seeing nothing, sidestepped the wrecked cars and walked through the broken barrier. Glancing around, he searched for the quickest way across the freeway around the mess of scattered cars.

Seeing a break between bumpers, he took it.

He had seen freeways similar in the three years since the world stopped. Cars left running, doors open. Trucks fishtailed, their trailers flipped on their sides. The East Coast didn't have the traffic congestion like he saw here. Not to say that it had never had traffic jams. When everything ceased many roadways became death zones, abandoned vehicles littering the freeways and highways the country over.

None of it compared to what he was seeing in front on him.

Car after car all lined up, wreck upon wreck one after another. Practically bumper to bumper to where jumping on hoods was his next step to try to bypass everything. It was surreal that at the end people were still driving to some destination in an attempt to outrun the inevitable.

No one could hide from fate.

Getting to the median he paused. Vigilance kept you alive. With no noises or movements, he stepped up and jumped over. Soft landing. He again looked for the quick route and took it. Reaching the shoulder and staring up at the huge sound wall, Ryan looked left and right to find a break in the barricade.

A few yards to the left he found it.

A small opening between the brick sound walls had a short fence to scale. Putting his foot against it he thrust himself to the other side. Another frontage road to cross. Headed right until he knew where the creek would be, went straight, and over the rail.

A short retaining wall ran along the top of the embankment.

Ryan walked between what was left of backyard fences and the creek until he found a place to climb over. He wanted to keep hidden as much as possible, and being on the other side of the wall offered more than the battered fences.

Concealment and a barrier against an attack kept him sane.

At least as far as trudging along in darkness and with adrenaline building up for the fight to come could keep anyone together. Every creak and rustle were potential enemies, ready to strike. Most sounds emanated from curious felines watching from the shadows, their want for human interaction toying with their desire to stay alive. Other distractions to his perked ears came from a light wind blowing through all the overgrown vegetation.

He liked the thick greenery as it hid his movements.

It also prevented seeing beyond them. Anything could lurk and he hoped they kept away. He was so focused he didn't remember how he got to the cross street. Standing there and knowing he had to go right, Ryan stepped over the small concrete wall and knelt.

Silence.

The road, littered with forgotten debris and wrecks of vehicles, stared back. Layers of dead leaves, plastic bottles and cans blown from who knows where, three years of ignored cleaning added up. He chose his steps carefully and deliberately like a dancer or ballerina performing a perfect routine.

Eyes could be anywhere, and ears hypervigilant for a meal, his worst enemies.

The lights were beacons, beckoning Ryan like a lighthouse guiding him safely to shore. Against the backdrop of darkness enveloping the entire neighborhood, the house stood out like a sore thumb. It looked like it should have three years prior, full of life and continuing on as if the virus had never destroyed humanity. Not that from his watchful post he could see much.

The high security fence prevented it.

The second-floor lights, hidden behind curtains and offering silhouettes of figures, were his only view into the fact people were inside. Needing a better vantage point to see the grounds and any security walking about, Ryan found a large tree with a foothold and plenty of foliage to hide his presence. Ruck off to lighten the load and M4 against the trunk, he climbed up, positioning his body in the crook of a limb that acted like a seat. Letting his eyes adjust he scanned, looking for soldiers or anyone out for a stroll. All he could see were solar lights on either side of a few pathways and the porchlights for the front.

No one appeared from the shadows.

Looking to the front gate and following the driveway to the house, he spied a few Humvees, the culprits that transported Julia and the kids, and a few others of various tastes of the rich and famous. One though caught his eye, and shaking his head, he grabbed his binoculars and focused in. Blinking rapidly, more to see if his eyes were playing tricks than to clear dirt away, Ryan frowned.

A pristine midnight blue vision of excellence taunted prying eyes.

Classic lines. Chrome sparkling as hints of light caught their surfaces. American muscle under the hood. It had been ages since such a beauty waved a vigorous flag back and forth to say, *Look at me*! There was no confusion as to what it was, a beast of beauty long loved and never forgotten.

It was the license plate that sealed it.

"No fucking way," Ryan whispered under his breath.

Maybe his mind was screwing with him. Could be he wanted to see it. As he took it in, the 1968 Mustang Fastback, a restored with great care project from the days when real metal and craftsmanship to detail made a car worthy of the road, sat parked alone.

As if on display, there was no way to ignore it.

He came across another gem like this one while scavenging for food, parked beneath a tarp in a garage and seemingly forgotten. He wanted to try and fire it up, knew the hum and rumble of a meaty V8 would draw too much attention. He settled for sitting in the driver's seat and wishing he could go for one last drive. Since that encounter, he hadn't come across another. Sighing, he shook his head as confusion rolled within his skull. The odds of this?

One in a billion.

Scavengers collected. At least, the ones looking to survive picked up odds and ends to make life better. He searched for items to make living more like being back in the past. It kept his sanity going. Most people took the small, worthless things of little value. A mirror. Record or CD to reminisce about a favorite band.

Even those little gnomes people collected to adorn their lawns. Ryan had seen a house with them long ago. Probably a hundred or more. He knew they were taken and not the original lawn relics. The house obliterated, debris a pile of hazards. Each gnome meticulously placed around the carnage post-destruction. Someone either found humor in it, or it connected them to their own life left in ruins.

Collecting a whole car meant something else entirely.

Ryan wondered if it was there as a trophy or more meaning was at play. Getting it had to have been difficult. Transport and get gassed up.

He knew that for a fact.

It wasn't like this relic was easy to find. Too few existed when the world was still alive and living without the pandemic and chaos. Post shit storm with clogged freeways and tracking it down meant a concerted effort and desire to have it. Rage began to build, and his thoughts worked overtime.

It was a challenge, a taunting, and a real message.

"No one takes my ride."

CHAPTER FORTY-SEVEN

The last time Ryan saw his baby was before the pandemic finally overtook life and he and Julia had been in the Bay Area to see his dying father.

The Mustang had been his pride and joy for decades.

A project car when he was a teen that required tough love and hard work to revive, it was a father and son bonding experience to restore life back to it. First to drivable and as the years progressed more and more to customize and define its character as a true one-off, the car was a second love. Peering at it over the security fence sent a shiver down his spine, a flashback to better times.

It was when he saw the plate, *RCBEAST*, that the anger brewed.

His car, his love, sitting in the driveway of a mansion and stolen by some asshole. Ryan's beast didn't belong there and how and why sparked questions. Only a handful knew the warehouse where it was stored and he was sure he had never told Mark. Julia knew and his dad did too, and as he was long dead, his wife's treachery grew larger than life.

Pushing down his contempt and hate, Ryan looked for a way in.

While he didn't see anyone lurking, simply going over the front gate wasn't an option. No cameras appeared to watch the property, at least as he could tell using his night vision goggles to scan for heat signatures and the internal red dots of security lenses his specialized gear could see. He needed a quiet and secluded entrance and seeing none from high up in the tree, he decided a closer look would give some results.

The mansions in the neighborhood were silent ghosts of their former selves. Many had been obliterated, imploded more like it, while a few still stood proud. The house to the right of his target was a mangled mess while to the left it looked like you could move right on in. Retracing his steps, Ryan crept back up the street to the house next door to his target. Climbing the gate, he landed softly and waited.

Quiet.

Kneeling, he flipped his goggles down and peered around the front of the house. Nothing unusual popped out. Keeping low he hustled off to the right and in-between the home and the fence. Finding a potted plant in a big half wine barrel he hopped up and looked over.

His goggles gave the all clear.

He needed a good spot to hop up and staring down the fence he found a small fruit tree with a V-shape. Going to it he planted his foot, pushed up to stand, and in one motion jumped over, hitting the grass with a soft thud. Goggles still looking for enemies, he came up empty again.

This is really odd, Ryan thought as he processed the scene. *Either I'm missing something or he feels safe behind these walls. What gives?*

Choices scrolled before his eyes.

Find an unlocked door on the ground floor, maybe even a window, and go in. Climb up and breach the second story. The activity seemed to be upstairs by his initial assessment earlier. Watching, his knee on the lawn for support, the lower level was dark, the only house lights by the front door and around the back.

Third option, knock and see what happened.

Ryan snickered at that thought, the absurdity of it and the balls it took to do it. He had them, but he wasn't stupid. He had no inside intel and exposing himself that easily was not his style.

The lower level won.

Ryan had made it this far and had come fully loaded with everything he felt would come in handy. He could lighten up and take only his essential gear. He found a place to store his ruck behind a large pine tree, grabbed a few perks he thought he might find useful, and let himself go into offensive mode.

Low and with a quick pace, Ryan approached the mansion.

It was a modern style, one of those designs that had taken the original house, bulldozed it, and built a completely new structure with straight lines and energy efficient by the looks of the windows and multi-layers he saw on close inspection. Breaking one would make too much noise over a single pane window. Cutting the rubber weatherstripping to pop each glass out, a better approach.

Not getting caught by someone seeing or feeling a draft, ideal.

Meticulously, Ryan used his Special Ops knife, choosing the smaller blade over his Ka-Bar, to work between the double windows and pop the catch.

This option didn't damage the window and scream intruder.

He figured an alarm system was moot during the apocalypse when electrical ran on generators. He had heard the low hum of them somewhere behind the house.

Being that security minded with billions of people dead was total overkill.

Run the lights and priority appliances. With his gloved left hand, he slid the window open and waited. No resistance or alarms waking the Un-Dead, and taking a step back, put a foot up and jumped inside. Closing the window silently, he listened.

Eerily quiet.

Enough ambient light lit up the interior. Flipping his goggles up to let his eyes adjust, Ryan scanned his surroundings. An office, desk facing sliding doors opposite the room. Bookshelves lining the entire wall to his left. Massive big screen and electronics to the right. A couch and chairs facing it. Stepping forward, he gave the desk a once over, searching for information on who lived or had lived here. Sifting through a stack of papers, tech manuals mostly, he found an invoice.

Bringing it close, he sighed.

"You have got to be kidding me." He had to reign his volume in, the revelation hitting a nerve.

More invoices, added intrigue, and neurons on fire. The amount of money was astronomical. The products the toys of the uber-rich.

Putting the papers down, Ryan crossed the room, careful to avoid creaks on the hardwood. Stopping short of the double doors, he nodded, more to gather his thoughts than to answer the inner dialog shouting inside his brain about what was about to spring out as soon as he pulled one aside.

Pulling the strap on the MP5 loose, he set it to single fire.

The right-side door slid silent, offering cover as it retracted back into the wall. His eyes focused immediately, panning left to right and back in search of movement. His ears listened, catching not a sound. Leaning around the corner of the wall to see along the right side, Ryan stepped forward and into a large entryway. Front door some thirty feet to the right. Staircase ten feet to the left. Some closed doors on the opposite side of his location.

Taking a few more steps inside, the marble floor glistened from some light source. Looking around, opulent was an understatement. The paintings on the walls, if what he saw were true, bordered on a hundred million dollars at least. The artwork, sculptures, and vases spread around were in the same ballpark for value.

Ryan simply sighed. All the money in the world and the beauty of artisans and painters throughout history kept out of the public eye. Museums needed to be the venues to share them with the world. Though with no world left, maybe everything got pilfered and wound up in places like this.

Standing there he wasn't shocked, only yearning for life to return.

Once all this is over, I should start collecting everything back for when life and society resets and we start anew. Museums would be a nice outing for the kids.

A scuff of shoes, and he heard a door open and the sound of feet.

Turning quickly to protect his six, he nearly fired until the figure came into view. The shadow stopped, aware of Ryan's presence. Seeing a darkened figure lathered with grease paint and a red dot pointed at the intruder's head kept the mystery person still.

It took a step into the light, the hidden face revealed.

Staring in disbelief, emotions all over the place, Ryan kept the MP5 locked on the forehead of the man. Eyes locked and seconds, even minutes, passed until he managed to clear his throat and speak.

"Hi, Dad."

CHAPTER FORTY-EIGHT

"I didn't expect to ever see you again."

Reg Carmichael's words lacked emotion and any former love he had for his son. His gray hair, which had been long, was back to a short trim. The Unabomber beard was still present, though the current look manicured and presentable. He had gained back weight and looked healthy, the cancer having decimated his physique the last time Ryan saw him.

He looked like the Reg of old with a glow that made Ryan cringe.

Ryan, locked in place as if concrete trapped his feet, his teeth clenched and anger brewing, almost pulled the trigger. A split second of conscious thought retracted his finger. Keeping his aim true and his feet finally able to move, he stepped forward a few feet.

"Nice to see you too, Dad."

Reg shrugged. "What? Am I supposed to be thrilled to see you?"

Ryan nodded, lips tightly pursed, his emotions needing to be kept in tight check. "No. Not at all. The fact you're here says a whole lot."

"Like what?" Reg spit out.

Ryan didn't know where to start. Things were getting complicated with the story he had believed for the last three years. Facts were disintegrating in front of his eyes.

He could dive into all the shit or cut the crap.

His dad was supposed to be dead from cancer, yet here he stood. The fact he was in this house was a door he wasn't sure he wanted to open. He could waste time to find out or get to the point.

"My kids. I want them."

Laughter.

"Your kids, huh? You come back from the dead and think you can walk in here and leave with them? No. I don't think so."

The bullet grazed Reg's right ear and went into the wall behind him.

"You motherfu-" Reg started before the next bullet swiped his left ear.

His eyes dark and cold, Ryan spit in the direction of his father. "Next one is dead center."

Reg held up a hand. Taking his shirt sleeve, he wiped away the trickling blood from each ear. "Wow! My *son* has a pair of brass balls. I see the rage in your eyes behind all that clown face makeup. Since when does some fake security wannabe think he is so tough? Some pissant motor pool mechanic in the service. Prancing around like some kind of ninja assassin? *You* are nothing."

Ryan couldn't help laugh. The only person who knew his real background was Mark. Seems Mark had something left inside that honored the Special Ops code.

"My kill count of assholes like you has an acknowledged record. Then, there's the ones Uncle Sam kept quiet for national security concerns. You have no idea who I am." The coldness of Ryan's eyes radiated his hatred.

The words hit a nerve in Reg. He closed his eyes, thinking, and managed a short chuckle. Two and two from his boy's past started to add up.

"Mark never bothered to tell me anything about you. Just him. Makes some sense all these years later. Snippets of stories you told that had details that didn't quite add up. Interesting," Reg nodded.

"At least he managed to keep some secrets." Ryan could feel his anger, the rage coursing his veins. He had to keep his cool. He had to get David and Emma. He also needed to know the truth.

Reg sighed. "Seems to be the case."

Never a man to procrastinate, Ryan got to it. "What's your involvement in this? I know Mark's investment. What about you?"

The older man stepped a foot forward, and immediately stopped when he noticed Ryan move his finger. "Woe Son. Settle down. No need to shoot me."

Ryan shrugged. "No guarantee. And no promises."

"Tough crowd."

"You have no idea Dad," Ryan mumbled under his breath.

Taking a moment, Reg waved his hand. "All right. I guess you deserve to know the truth. Why don't you come and meet everyone? You won't be leaving alive. Might as well."

The old man's confidence was comical.

"Sure Dad. Whatever you say."

Motioning to Ryan, Reg walked to the right of the staircase and down a hallway. To the left, he opened a door and descended below. Ryan followed, not sure if it was the right decision or not. His dad went down into what must have been a basement and into a large room.

The space was enormous and some light source offered enough visibility to see four men sitting at a table, deep in conversation. As soon as he saw them his world, the one he had trusted and believed in, completely crashed at his feet.

Seeing the invoice, it pinged a warning inside, and now the alarm bells roared.

CHAPTER FORTY-NINE

The four men looked over, confused and hesitant.

A dark figure descended the stairs pointing a gun at them. With Reg in front of the stranger, they assumed the worst and started to rise before two well-placed rounds hit the table dead center and they sat back down.

"No need to worry gentlemen. Meet my son, Ryan."

Ryan looked around the table. Disgust didn't describe what he felt.

The wealth sitting around it would have totaled almost a trillion dollars, if money still existed. Philanthropy, technology, global business, media, and significant funding backers for the virus research and distribution. When he saw the invoice and name and knowing a bit about the neighborhood, he knew he shouldn't be shocked at the people he saw in the room. The shroud was unravelling, all the lies and deceit. These were supposed to be the good guys.

The real truth was hard to swallow.

Mike Goldberg, the founder of the largest social media platform in the world. Billions of users and his data collection that bordered on criminal, he possessed avenues to infiltrate and influence daily life.

John Beezer, logistics extraordinaire who created an empire for goods and services that expanded beyond books and packages into every nook and cranny you could imagine. Throw in his ownership of a respected newspaper and media company, and he wielded significant power.

Elliot Mann, automotive founder for electric vehicles who expanded into space technology with plans for Mars. His threats to move his company and manufacturing out of California despite the tax breaks and lucrative incentives held cities and counties hostage.

The last one left Ryan in shock.

Bob Gains, the creator of modern technology platforms and one of the largest investors in medicine and healthcare to assist third world countries join modern times. He was the godfather of them all. Bundled software, proprietary code, his products made companies dependent and ran the world.

Bob Gains was the first to speak. "You told us he was dead Reg. How is he *here*?"

Reg walked over to the table and took a seat, facing Ryan. "As far as I knew, he was. Why don't you ask him?"

Bob glared at Reg and turned to Ryan. Leaning back in his chair, he waved a hand for Ryan to talk, expecting him to obey. After a minute of silence, Bob raised his hands up. He was used to giving orders and people doing what they were told.

"You going to talk or what?" Elliott Mann began before Ryan glared and the man cowered back into silence.

Ryan cleared his throat. "I look around and see what was supposed to be people who valued and wanted to help save the world. The fact I find you all together mixed up with Mark and my own father paints a very different picture. Let me be clear. I ask the questions and you answer."

John Beezer's eyes grew wide with disdain. "You are in no position to dictate shit to us."

The bullet sprayed John's brains around the table. The remaining men, shock at the brutal and instantaneous reaction, looked at each other and realized if they wanted to live, they better play right.

Wiping away the brain matter and blood, they stared, emotionless.

"My Son, the killer. Didn't know you had the spunk in you. Seeing your eyes, I know you feel it. Deep down inside. A burn like never before. Don't you wonder about it?"

Ryan ignored Reg, but the words resonated a bit.

He felt a burn, a desire to kill that was never there before. Not like this. Maybe it was seeing his dad wrapped up in something that involved his children, or the fact he was still alive. He needed to keep his focus and push any resentment or daddy issues out of the way.

Mike Goldberg turned white as a ghost.

Ryan thought he probably crapped his pants. The youngest billionaire there, he was the worst of the bunch in Ryan's eyes. Let his technology platform spread lies and disinformation without consequence. All to make money. If he had stepped up and put an end to all the deceit at the beginning, the world might have survived.

He looked each man in the eyes and Ryan's stare screamed cooperate. "He was the first. Talk and you might live. Turn asshole and you get the idea."

Furtive glances all around. Nods to acknowledge they understood.

"Great. Glad you all agree for a change. Who's running this shit show?" Ryan watched for signs, a tremble, a twitch, to see if any man would lie.

Bob was the first to talk. "Your old man pulls the strings. Figured you already knew that by showing up tonight."

The gut punch nearly made Ryan double over.

Reg was supposed to be dead and as far as Ryan knew had no connection to any of these men. He wasn't some rich billionaire. An average guy, who on the face of it, was way out of place. The connection, what was it? The statement could be a diversion and the details needed specifics to know truth versus lies.

"The President is running the show and not dead like we were led to believe. I heard the Vice President." A bit of a lie, since the VP had not actually put a name to the culprit.

Reg frowned. "You did that?"

Bob glanced at Reg, looking for an answer. "He did what?"

Ryan's father shook his head, and laughed. "You are quite the man Son. The only way you could say something like that is if you were either psychic, or there. Given the VP is dead and you are standing here armed to the teeth, my money is you did it."

Elliot pushed his dark hair back. "He's the one who killed him? Mark said some survivor group was behind it, the ship, and the research facility. Your boy is part of the resistance?"

Reg shrugged. "Ask him."

Time was ticking and the Q&A getting sidetracked. Ryan had to direct the conversation and keep it focused. "The President. Why are they saying you are the one?" He looked at his father for an answer.

"Ah. Ever the one to avoid answering for himself. Well, if you must know, the President is dead. Coffin chum. Maggot food. Lost his head right before this wonderful world sprang from the ashes."

The rumors had floated.

Many from the Administration had ended up with their heads posted around the fence of the White House. That was true. Should have happened with the first insurrection over the election. The President? Ryan figured a lie to keep his ass from being hunted down.

"That asshole caused all of this to happen. Might have died, but he put the wheels in motion. Led the crazies down the righteous path." Ryan's words caused laughter to erupt around the table.

"You think that incompetent fool could have done anything without being told what to do?" Bob sighed, and leaned back in his chair.

"Enlighten me."

Elliott leaned forward on his elbows. "We needed someone who would play along in office. A puppet to dance. A little bit of leaks, sow discontent, fan the flames, and there you go. Beezer and his media reach at its best. Couldn't let that devil woman win, so we and some of our compatriots got the red menace elected."

The words seemed genuine, if void of emotion.

"Why?"

Mike chuckled, more to himself than to the others. "Money of course. Democrats like to tax and have corporations pay their fair share. We decide where we want to spend our money, not them."

Ryan pursed his lips. "Say I believe that. You get douchebag in office, then what?"

Bob looked hard, his gaze a bit troublesome. "He miraculously wins the first election because we can make it happen. He owes us because of all of the dirt we have on him. Also, because he can profit from the win as long as we decide he can."

Ryan thought about it. Puppet masters pulling the strings. The Deep State at work. "Where does the virus and everything else that happened play into it?"

Reg decided to take this one. "You see the boys here? Well, what's a great way to make even more money? Pandemic! Shut the world down and make people rely on you. Beezer made a killing on all the crap people bought online and had shipped to them. Mike there, well he was head deep in advertising all the conspiracy crap. Let the crazies speak and shop their insane ideas and products. Let them do whatever and he pretends to hide behind the First Amendment. Elliot pushed clean energy while people were forced to be at home. Bob killed on all the tech stuff required to do all the remote work and distance learning. Well, how do you get even more control? They're all philanthropists who give away tons of money. Create a virus, control the distribution, and get people locked into a vaccine. Brilliant actually."

Ryan stood, his stomach churning in knots.

If half of what he was hearing was real, truth and lies became a mess to sort out. Looking around at each face, Ryan wondered what skin they had in the game. They were all rich beyond imagination and philanthropists trying to help the world.

Their public personas didn't fit.

Bob and his wife founded a non-profit foundation and funded billions into it to help people across the world. Vaccines, medical care, you name it. Same with Mike. Founded with his wife, funded astronomically, aimed at helping people. Elliott was on a mission to curb waste and change fossil fuels to electrical consumption. Put settlers on Mars to help with over-population. Beezer's media company was one of the largest thorns in the President's side.

Nothing made sense.

"If that's true, and I don't trust anything mentioned in here, what makes you leader of the assholes?"

Reg put his hand to chest, the feigned hurt an Oscar performance. "Really, Son? Such contempt for dear old Dad?"

The anger rose. "Answer the fucking question!"

"OK, Ryan. Calm down there, Son, before you pop a vein."

Mike nervously shuffled from side to side in his seat. Ryan could see he might be the weak link if pressed. His testimony before Congress and subsequent statements around his company's failure to contain the lies and spread of disinformation to the public showed his inability to keep it together when on the spot. It was something to keep in mind for later.

Ryan aimed the MP5. "Answer me."

Reg threw up his arms. "All right already. Keep your panties cool. The virus was manmade right here in the good old United States. Been in the works for years. You know all that hubbub about bath salts a few years back? The naked guy in Florida on the bridge who tried to eat the face off someone? The college kid who attacked his neighbor in the garage and obliterated him? All of the wackos who did mass killings during golden boy's last term before the redheaded step-child took office? Dry runs to see how the virus worked. Move on to make a vaccine that controls it."

Shaking his head, Ryan sighed. "Our own people? Didn't learn from the Tuskegee experiments, did you?"

"Fuck ups happen. My cancer? Seems something lurked in my DNA, RNA, mRNA, or whatever they call it. Fragments. A Stanford researcher on our team caught it when my blood hit the hospital network. Mine wasn't enough of the puzzle to work. My grandkids had a lot of it. You can begin to see the bigger picture."

Things began to click.

Ryan stepped forward. "Why you?"

"Why not?" Reg grinned. He enjoyed toying with his son. It had been a long time.

The bullet shattered the wood between Reg's open legs. A few inches more and he'd be a soprano.

"Tick tock, Dad."

Reg decided to cut the sarcasm, if only for a bit. "You know all that business about Deep State? Who controls the strings from behind the curtain? Can't be the obvious, can it? The President wanting to root out and eliminate the players? Who do you think put him in office? This was calculated from the start."

Ryan stood listening and for a moment, believed it. It was a line of bullshit a mile deep. He'd play along, if only to root the truth from the lies.

"The world has devolved. Overpopulated by religious followers who think they need to keep having babies because God commanded it. Poor thugs and trailer trash who can't keep their panties on and dicks in their pants and have kid after kid on welfare. Third world civilizations that can't stop killing each other over ridiculous ideology and tribal disputes. Deep State? Try Global State. This is the U.S. faction. We're *everywhere*."

Ryan wiped his forehead of sweat. "Getting really deep in here with all the shit. I'm supposed to believe any of this?"

Reg laughed. "How do you reign chaos back in unless you start over? The Black Plague was a great model. Construct a little virus to whittle things back to manageable and start over again. Let it pop up here and there, spread like wildfire. Simple."

The anger boiled over. "Cut the shit, Dad. I've seen the research. It wasn't manmade. It was a natural evolution of a coronavirus. Virulent and deadly. Nothing more."

"You would like to believe that, wouldn't you?" Mike chimed in. "Control the platform and dispersion of information and you can make people believe whatever you want. Plus, make a crap of money in the process."

"Be the ones with the money to help everyone and the channels to distribute a cure. When you have a foundation of trust, people will believe anything." Bob was looking right at Ryan, his glasses perched a bit low on his nose. The smirk on his face said he wasn't lying.

Elliot was the last. "Act like you are helping humanity while ensuring they have no choice to follow."

Reg pointed at each man. "Beezer would have said something similar, but you had to go and kill him."

"One less asshole playing God."

"Tsk tsk, Ryan my boy. No one is playing God. Quite the contrary. God did all of this. We're cleaning up his mess."

"Still doesn't explain you."

Reg sighed. "True. Well, as I mentioned, things have been in play for a really long time. You can't go and let a virus run amok and not have a way to contain it. Deep State, remember? I got recruited back in college when I went to pharmacy school. My military time during Vietnam got me in touch with a lot of believers. Zealots all over the place supporting the cause. Well, that researcher I mentioned? My blood? They needed to get a purer source and David and Emma, *surprise*, were matches. You'd never have agreed to anything, so they came to me. Of course, I said yes if they could keep me alive. Got my cancer in remission. The plan went into motion and Mark was gracious enough to help out."

"You drove trucks for a living, Dad. I went on road trips with you when I was young."

Reg waved his finger. "Yes. I was. What better cover and way to distribute for our network than driving it all around."

Ryan was growing agitated trying to contain the rage. "None of this adds up. You're all lying."

Was it a sliver of compassion Ryan saw? Reg leaned forward. "Son. No lies. The truth. The virus got out of hand before we had a real cure. It was all supposed to be aligned and ready, but someone jumped the gun. The vaccines? You know they didn't work out the way they were supposed to. Rushed to try and show something was being done. Marketing to quell the noise. All those side effects turning people in crazies? Emma and David can stop all of that, or I should say keep the *turn* at bay. Once you're gone, your gone. I know you have seen them. Everyone else like us can keep on chugging and rebuild society. Though, under more strict guidance and control."

Ryan's ears burned. "Let me get this straight. You knew what would happen and you still did it?"

The dark evil in Reg's smile made Ryan want to kill him. "You can't gain control if you don't thin the herd and make them dependent on *you*." Reg emphasized the last word and it made Ryan's skin crawl.

It was all frighteningly unbelievable.

CHAPTER FIFTY

Ryan felt like his entire life had been an intricate web of deception.

He had no clue what was real or the actual truth anymore. The lies he had forcefully believed false if true would be the foundation madmen were using to reinvent the world. He felt the wind get knocked out, his knees wobbly. Sweat poured down his forehead and he felt lightheaded.

Elliot suddenly sprang from the table.

Ryan must have lost himself for a minute and looked vulnerable and the billionaire decided to feel like a hero. The blade came out and went straight through the throat and out the back. The body fell, convulsing on the concrete as the blood began to pool.

"Anyone else?" Ryan asked.

Rob and Mike shook their heads.

Reg glared at Ryan, hate reflected in his eyes. "What makes you high and mighty?"

Wiping the blood on his pant leg, Ryan pointed the blade at his father. "Shut the hell up." Replacing the blade in its sheath, he grabbed the MP5 from its sling.

The older man stood up, defiant. "Don't ever speak to me like that. I am your father!"

Play the game, or control the outcome. Ryan had choices. Too many. Things were going down a rabbit hole and the air thick with contempt all around. He could end it all and walk out. Dig deeper for information. Try to extract truth from all the lies. Argue with his dad and air out the family crap.

Sighing and taking a deep breath, Ryan walked over and punched the old man in the face.

"Shut the fuck up," Ryan spat.

Blood poured from Reg's nostrils. Shock shone in his eyes. He didn't think his oldest son had it in him. It was a bit exhilarating to think Ryan had the balls.

As the thought faded, the anger brewed. "You think you are better than me?"

Ryan laughed. "Yup."

The answer made Reg's growing hate boil.

Putting his finger to his lips in anticipation of Reg speaking, Ryan let it out. "You kidnapped your grandkids and allowed them to be experimented on. You are not only the worst grandparent ever, but a royal piece of shit stuck on the bottom of my boot. You have one shot at living, and only one. Keep lying to me and your death will give me immense joy as I slice you up slowly and let you bleed out. Goes for each of you. We understand each other?"

Reg sat back in his chair, smug. "Go fuck yourself, Son."

White as a ghost again, Mike shouted, "I'll talk. Please don't kill me."

"Great," Ryan smiled. "Where are my kids?"

Bob reached over and threw a laptop at Mike. It him in the forehead causing a huge gash.

"I really don't have time for this," Ryan sighed. Pulling the trigger, Bob's brains splattered all over the table and his body settled in a hump to the side of his chair.

"Upstairs!" Mike howled.

Ryan waved his hand. "Thank you."

Mike fell backward out of his chair as the bullet penetrated his heart and the force propelled him to the ground. He was dead instantly, a gracious gesture on Ryan's part. He believed the former billionaire had been so scared he would sell out his own mother. You could read it on his face as he blurted out. It was the least Ryan could do.

He was going to kill them all anyway.

"You are one cold blooded killer, Ryan." Reg sat, his eyes focused on his son, awash in hatred for what his boy had done and pride for him being such a ruthless mother.

"I just take out the trash."

Reg pursed his lips. "What now, Son?"

Ryan pointed towards the stairs. "Take me to my kids."

The walk upstairs felt like a death march. Silence, except the soft patter of boots on the hardwood. Ryan had just killed four men without even a flinch. His Dad, leading the way to where David and Emma were supposedly kept, was going to meet a similar fate. Though his death was going to be painful and gruesome.

Ryan couldn't help take some satisfaction in the thought.

Never had he been this cold. He had killed before, in circumstances that warranted it. Tonight, he could have tied the billionaires up, left them to chance of Bolts having a feast.

It never crossed his mind.

The rage and anger were deep and present, felt like he wasn't even the Ryan of old anymore. The calm, cool, collected hardened solider who had been in war and situations that would make most people puke and crap from fear, was nowhere to be found. The skills were there, yet the bubble wrap around emotions to keep himself in check was gone.

Reg turned to talk, some chit chat Ryan figured. A hardened stare made Reg think twice and he kept walking up to the landing, made a right, and proceeded until coming to a door on the left. Looking at Ryan again, he motioned, "They're in there."

"Open it."

Reg turned the knob and pushed the door. Light peered out, and he quietly stepped inside. Ryan kept close behind, vigilant, eyes darting left and right. Passing the threshold and fully in the room, the old man took a step to the left and stood. Two small beds, pushed against the far wall, had two small figures resting.

Ryan could hear Emma's soft snoring.

David's curly hair hung over his eyes. Seeing his beautiful children, a small tear formed and fell down his cheek. Looking around the room, another figure came into view.

Julia.

The rage seethed within. His wife, the mother of his children, the one who sold them out to the devil. She was asleep in the corner.

"Family reunion," Reg whispered.

A hard smack in the back of the old man's head. "Shut the hell up."

A boot squeak must have caught young ears. Emma yawned and turned to face the door. David pulled the covers down from his face and stared.

"Dad?" Emma and David asked, not sure if he was real or not.

"Hi, Princess. Hi, Stinky Man."

The voices woke Julia. She rolled over and slowly pulled the covers down. Coming to a sitting position on the bed, Ryan saw the handcuffs and the bruises around her eyes. Tears started to well, and in a moment she cried.

Confused, Ryan stood still.

Another trick, he wondered? If they thought he was coming because Julia had spilled he was alive, it was the perfect way to lower his defenses.

Reg watched it unfold. Saw the murderous intent in his son's eyes when he saw Julia. The confusion washed away by doubt. He began to snicker, until he laughed out loud. "This is wonderful."

Ryan glanced over. "What are you blabbering about?"

Reg slapped his leg. "You are oblivious! You're on your way to *turn*."

Julia's eyes widened. She pushed the covers all the way off and walked over to Emma's bed. Motioning for David to come, she held them tight, protectively, her eyes never leaving Ryan.

Ryan spit. "What are you talking about, Dad?"

"You, Son. Used to be in control of yourself, actions and emotions? A few times acting out, doing things that were out of character? Like the pizza place when Emma was little, right before the world ended? What about since you were last with the family here? Been able to keep it together or have you let your rage take over? You did kill everyone downstairs without any kind of justice, you know?"

The words were heavy in the air.

He had felt different, more reactive and violent, control a fingertip out of reach. Ryan chalked it up to the stress and circumstances. Lack of sleep and having his world turned upside down. Two weeks ago, he was alone with Pete, as happy as he could be in his world. Things were fine.

It all changed when he saw David and stepped into the fray.

In that moment he felt himself unraveling, and pushed it away. Events required him to act. Kill or be killed. He justified the feelings that had percolated deep within and like a volcano eruption had begun to spew out.

The nature of the shit storm, Ryan thought to himself. *The world is gone. Life obliterated. We survive or die.*

"Let me guess? Every time your adrenaline begins to pump, you are a bit impulsive? The Vice President? Blowing up all those poor people in the facility? Yes, I figure it was you. Since you got your vaccine shot and until this very day, a slow fall into the abyss of being able to keep it all together?"

He could see the fear in Julia as she looked at him. Never had he seen her like that. The eyes, reddened with horror, brown jewels shining brilliantly back at him scared to death.

"I've done what I've needed to do. No qualms."

"I saw how you looked at Julia when you walked in here. You wanted to kill her. Not once downstairs did you say anything about wanting your family back. Just the kids." Reg smiled. "I bet you thought she was a huge part of this, didn't you?"

Ryan ignored him.

"Answer him, Ryan." Julia kept her eyes focused.

He didn't know how to respond.

"Say *something,* Son. Your time is getting short before you, the Ryan we know and the man I can't wait to die, leaves the building and becomes one of *them.*"

"You're lying, Dad. Stop."

Julia shook her head, and in that instance, Ryan felt his old self crawl back. It felt good.

Julia's voice was calm. "It's true, Ryan. The side effects of the vaccine. Some are fine, have minor issues. The maintenance shot they are developing will keep the side effects at bay as long as you keep getting it. The ones like your dad, turn into psychotic assholes with no one left inside. Others turn into those *things*. I've seen it."

As soon as Julia finished, Ryan felt all the air leave and the good vibes vacate. "How do you know?"

"About what?"

"The side effects that make people turn? What are they?"

Julia looked at him, scared as she searched his eyes. Asking meant he had them. "The body tremors. They're worse when adrenaline has been racing through your blood. Progressively worse over time. Really bad when things are calm after a really stressful day. The violent streaks. Same thing. As adrenaline and stress become more prevalent, they get bad. Rational thinking, keeping a level head. All of that seem to dissipate until you go off the handle at any little trigger event."

Reg must have caught the glance. "Oh, damn, Son. You have it!"

Julia glared at her father-in-law. Tried to get his attention. "Reg, please."

Reg feigned ignorance. "What?"

"You know what."

The old man laughed. "Like I care about any of you. An end to a means."

Emma pulled her head from under the protective arm of her mom. "Papa? You don't love us?"

Bending down to eye level, Reg smiled. "Nope."

Hearing the word, Ryan slammed the butt of the MP5 into the back of his father's head, knocking him out cold.

"Nice, Dad!" David yelled. "Papa deserved it."

"David, stop," Julia ordered.

The boy winked at Ryan so she couldn't see.

Shaking his head, Ryan let out a deep breath. This was not part of the plan at all. His father tied up in it and hearing a bunch of talk that warped truth and lies into a spider web of doubts.

What was real, he didn't know.

He knew the lies that had been told over and over, couldn't pinpoint any valid information to prove or disprove. His head hurt bad from thinking that and all he wanted was to curl up and sleep it off.

"Ryan? You there?"

Snapping out of it, Ryan walked over to his family. "I'm here."

Julia frowned. "You really thought I was part of this? Could do this to our own children?"

All he could do was shrug. "My mind hasn't been my own it seems."

Reaching out, Emma grabbed Ryan's hand. "Thank you, Daddy."

Confused, Ryan asked, "For what, Princess?"

Smiling, Emma replied, "Keeping your promise and coming to get us."

Julia snapped her handcuffed fingers. "Look at me Ryan. How long have you had the effects?"

Ryan thought. Gradual at first. Worse over time after he lost them.

Agonizing since he found out they were still alive. "I guess after the first vaccine I started to feel a bit off. Nothing serious. The last three years a slow progression. Really bad when my adrenaline gets pumping. Calm days it's OK. Been bad since I saw David the first time and ever since."

He saw the fear in her eyes. Not for what was happening to his body, but afraid of *him*. Never in their time together had he seen that look. No reason for her to feel that way.

He saw terror and for the first time, Ryan was scared.

"Listen to me Ryan. I've spent enough time around Mark and his lunatics to hear and know what is happening to you. A small percentage have extreme side effects. They take time to develop. Most, it hit them within a few weeks or months, and then you get people like Mark who are raging psychotics. I've even seen it in those wandering killers. The ones it takes years, those are the severe cases. The cure keeps it at bay, or at least that's what Mark says. He kills them all off after studying them since once they turn there is no being human again. You need the shot, but it's not even close to being ready."

The precipice stared at Ryan.

A razor's edge to fall either way. If Julia wasn't lying, and he wanted to believe her, he was on his way to being one of the ravaging death dealers on a scale he had never encountered. Run and risk becoming one and putting his family at risk.

Surrender and let his family be pawns, test subjects, used over and over for the whims of a madmen.

He couldn't let his children live a life as prisoners, and losing the love and respect of his wife for allowing them to be subjugated to a world where they had no freedom, he couldn't allow it.

Even if he had to die to rescue them and get his precious loved ones safely hidden away, never to be found.

Julia saw it. She knew the look. When Ryan made up his mind there was no changing it. "No, Ryan. You *will* die."

He walked over, pulled out a master key, and unlocked the restraints. Bending down to his children, who had listened to their parents and had begun to cry, Ryan touched their legs. "Hey, hey, guys. Who is you Darth Daddy?"

David sniffed the snot back. "You are, Dad."

Emma wiped her face. "You, Daddy."

Pointing a finger at Ryan, David couldn't help it. "You know Dad, he did end up *dying*."

Ryan laughed to ease the tension. "No, he didn't. Remember, he found his true self and turned his energy over to his son to help the Force. Plus, you know me. I'm Super Dad. Nothing can get me."

"Super Dad," David grinned.

Looking at his wife, Ryan had to ask. "Why didn't you mention anything about my dad?"

Julia shook her head. "I thought he was dead, too. Saw him for the first time tonight."

"What about Mark? Where is he?"

Wide eyes. "He went to the university and is supposed to come back."

"We need to bail this popsicle stand. Grab whatever you need and get some shoes on. We're going for a ride."

CHAPTER FIFTY-ONE

Digging through Reg's pockets, Ryan found the keys to his Mustang.

Motioning for them to follow behind, he opened the bedroom door and peered out. No sound, no soldiers waiting to strike. Stepping out, Ryan raised his MP5 and panned left and right, moving swiftly with Julia and the kids right behind.

Reaching the stairs, he stopped, listened, and proceeded down the steps.

When they were all on the first floor in the entryway he pointed to the front door. It wasn't ideal, but the quickest route. Julia understood and holding Emma and David by the hands, kept a few paces behind as Ryan moved to the door.

He took a deep breath and turned the handle, opening the solid oak door quietly on its hinges. Staring outside into the cold of the night, no one shot. Taking that as a good sign, Ryan ushered everyone out and in the direction of his pride and joy.

"Really, Ryan?"

Ryan smiled. "Hey, one last ride. We'll never see him again." Handing the keys to Julia he motioned to the car. "I need to grab my stuff and take care of something."

"Hurry please."

Running off, Ryan ran back into the house and to the basement. Time was critical with the need to escape looming overhead like a nuclear bomb. The men had laptops, working on something that he had no idea whether it meant anything or could prove valuable. Scooping them up and taking them to be dissected for information might provide something to use in the future.

Same with the server racks lined up against the far wall.

He had noticed them, the blips and beeps of lights, the sound of cooling fans running, shadows in the faint glow from the lamps in the room. Ryan knew if these men took the time to run a small datacenter in the bowels of

Mike Goldberg's house, the disks had to contain a trove of data.

Maybe, and he hoped it was true, they had enough intel on them to bring the whole Deep State down for good.

Grabbing a backpack that was next to the cold body of Bob Gains, Ryan dumped out the contents and collected the laptops. Stuffed inside, he hurried to the server racks and opened the doors. Clicking each hard drive release and pulling it out, he stuffed them into the backpack and zipped it up.

About to turn and leave, he saw a cabinet tucked far in the back. Thinking what the hell, Ryan ran over and open it.

If this was the bonanza, he hoped he struck gold.

The words *Confidential* and *Top Secret* were stamped on the outside of manila envelopes. There had to be a hundred or more, thin and stacked neatly in stacks of three. The backpack didn't have the space, so he searched and found another, and stuffed the envelopes inside.

Checking his watch, he had been there for three minutes.

Time to take his leave, he ascended the stairs and stopped, once last look at the dead men around the table. Where things went wrong and why, Ryan wondered. Superficially, some of the most population friendly and supportive individuals in the world. Their non-profit work assisting the planet to become a better place and raise up third world countries and people. What they had become spit in the face of their generosity. So much said before he killed them, but so little that made any amount of sense.

Hopefully the haul here would shed some light.

Two steps at a time, full run across the foyer, and out the door. Diversion to retrieve his gear and then Ryan ran back to the house. Satchel in hand, he opened it and threw the bag inside. Hustling to the Mustang, he helped settle the kids in the backseat and threw his ruck, weapons, and the goods from the basement inside on the floorboard. Leaning in he ordered, "Do not touch anything. Understand?"

Affirmative nods.

Pulling his extra pistol from the side holster of his ruck and grabbing some magazines, he handed them to Julia. "You still got it?"

Smiling, she winked. "Almost as good a shot as you Babe."

Ryan ran to the gate and pulled it open.

No trucks or obstacles waiting to take them. Sprinting back to the muscle car, he put the key in the ignition, hit the switch, and the old beast roared to life. The low rumble and hum of the dual exhaust spitting out for the 428 cubic inch V8 engine that produced more than 400 horsepower soothed his soul.

He had missed the sound.

While not the most practical choice for a getaway, he knew the car inside and out and what it could do in a street drag. If anyone decided to give chase, the custom rod would outrun and maneuver anything short of a high-end racer.

The Humvees or trucks Mark were using couldn't keep up.

Rolling slowly out the gate, Ryan made a left turn and headed west to the first block. Making a right, he proceeded cautiously around three years of debris littering the residential street. Radio in hand, he clicked the mic.

"Big Momma, Awesome Daddy in route. Packages in hand. Extract at Charlie location. Repeat. Extract at Charlie. Over."

The speaker came to life. "Affirmative Awesome Daddy. Safe travels. Out."

Turning the radio off, he hoped the momentary break in radio silence didn't get pinged. Turning to the right, he knew what she was thinking and answered. "What? You thought I'd come all this way alone?"

Julia sighed and shook her head. "When we get out of this, we need to have a really, really, long talk Mr. Carmichael. I have no idea who you are, not a clue."

David leaned forward, whispering, "Super Dad, Mom."

They had to get the hell out and had some time to kill. There was a lot to say, but Ryan had to focus. He was edgy, his optics acutely aware of every movement and sound. He could still multitask, so driving, talking, and avoiding anything that came their way, he knew he could handle it.

"Do you know what the hell is going on?"

She turned away, not sure what to say. Staring out the window at the destruction staring her in the face, Julia finally spoke. "It's hard to place what is real and what is a lie. The truth is twisted, the lies grounded in facts. Saying there is a wide berth of gray area is an understatement."

He wasn't sure how to respond. "I heard a lot of things in the basement. Do you know anything about that?"

Julia shook her head. "Depends. What was said?"

Feeling he needed to cut to the chase, Ryan shrugged. "Tell me what you do know."

Julia started, and what she shared seemed surreal. Mark was quite the loquacious man given he felt the world was gone and he had nothing to hide. Shadow governments, puppet masters pulling strings, a global consortium that decided enough was enough and the world needed a reboot. So many players in the game it would make your head spin knowing the who's who of zealots and followers of the cause. He asked questions, and she answered affirmative or from what she had heard, what were lies.

Nothing made sense.

Ryan tried to wrap his head around it. He had believed in facts and perceived truths that turned out to be false. Throw in the lies that were perpetrated as misinformation and in reality, were factual, and you had a maze that a sane person couldn't manage to escape. Even the virus, the root of the pandemic and trigger for the apocalypse, was not the main ingredient. It was all a chessboard with moves and counter moves to checkmate civilization into total obedience.

"My head hurts," was all Ryan could spit out.

"Tell me about it. It's a horror movie times two."

They reached the main road, with the 101 straight in front. Sitting at the stop sign, the explosion sounded behind them, the flames illuminating the rearview mirror. The smile must have been too obvious as Julia elbowed Ryan in the ribs. Turning to the side he frowned and reached over and gave her hand a reassuring squeeze.

"Let me have this," Ryan whispered. "My Dad helped do this to you and the kids, and I let it happen."

Julia squeezed back. "Get back to being *my* Ryan, please."

Weighing options, he wasn't getting on the freeway. The side streets provided less obstacles to drive around and cover than the open highway. Going left meant heading towards University Avenue where it hooked up with the 109 and if he took that route, a straight shot to the wetlands and open terrain for the airship to land.

Quick getaway and be gone while darkness prevailed.

It was risky, taking a main thoroughfare. Ryan wasn't familiar with the area and getting lost in a neighborhood or stuck with no idea how to escape was not a great rescue plan.

Wind up in a dead end, cul-de-sac, or diverted from going where he needed to because of blocked or littered streets that wouldn't let him pass. A main road he could get off one street over if he had to and then get back on it. Going deep into a neighborhood with a lot of unknowns was a recipe for disaster.

He wasn't that bad a cook.

Stepping on the gas petal, Ryan drove with the lights off. Blowing the house was bad. Drawing attention with the V8 was asking for trouble.

Screaming *here I am* with headlights blazing was worse.

The other vehicles might have been less conspicuous. Could have been the better choices. Take one of the Humvees and use its ramming power if required to move obstacles. Big, bulky, and slow didn't bode well for a quick retreat. The Mustang had power and handling. He built it and knew it inside out. Plus, it was a much cooler car to use for the escape.

Ryan's luck, the other vehicles had working GPS devices that would let pursuers track them.

The lack of illumination made travelling difficult as they crept along at a steady pace following the 101 until reaching University. Hard right over the freeway and towards the 109 with a descent into East Palo Alto.

Gas station on the left. Taco shop and auto parts to the right. Mostly residential with pockets of low-income shopping spots. The poor side of town where real people lived. Not the rich and elite homes that made up Palo

Alto proper.

Though with the inflated home prices of the Bay Area, buying a home in this side of town would still have set you back half a million or more for even the most rundown and in need of a complete renovation home. He'd heard of bidding wars that went to a million dollars because nothing could be afforded anywhere else.

A sad commentary on America he thought.

High tech had ruined home prices. Widened the divide between classes of people. The haves and the I have nothings. Driven values to the stratosphere. And he had just left the home of one of the assholes who had been at the root of the problem.

No more.

Focused and eyes watching all around, Ryan kept driving, the desire to be gone from this place burning inside. All he wanted was his family safe.

He hoped the path was clear enough to reach their destination in time.

CHAPTER FIFTY-TWO

The first tracer exploded to the left.

The next round hit the corner of a building and sent bits of stucco and sheetrock flying. Looking in the rearview mirror Ryan saw the Humvee appear out of nowhere. Smashing down on the gas pedal, the Mustang roared to life, hitting sixty in no time flat.

More rounds whizzed past, the sound of shearing metal and houses being shredded filling the night.

Left, right, Ryan weaved back and forth to keep from being the next casualty of a high-powered round. The old car handled well and Ryan was glad he had updated the handling and suspension as it fluidly went around car after car with ease.

The lumbering Humvee was less fortunate.

The wide frame was meant for the open road. The chassis hit an old Volvo wagon and careened into a parked delivery van. The sound of crunching metal echoed inside the Mustang and made Ryan feel a bit better about their predicament. Closer to the extraction point, he had to break radio silence.

The airship was a sitting duck if the fifty-caliber mount atop the Humvee wasn't disabled.

"Big Momma, Awesome Daddy. Coming in super-hot. Prepare for a grab and go. Secondary pick-up per arrangement. Over."

"Affirmative Awesome Daddy. Packages will get priority. Stay safe until Delta. Out."

The confused look on Julia's face was momentary. She then understood the conversation. "You're not coming with us, are you?"

She deserved the truth. "The kids are the target. You all need to get away from here. I have to make sure that happens."

"Ryan, you can't do this again."

He saw David and Emma in the mirror, tears welling up. "I will be coming

303

with you. Just not this time. That cannon behind us if it catches up will obliterate your getaway to pieces. That happens, game over and done. My job is to slow them down, get you to safety. I disappear, and you guys pick me up later. It's the only way."

Julia touched his cheek. "Are you sure?"

"I am."

"You better, Ryan. Or, I'll kill you myself."

"Mom!" The kids screamed in the back.

"Kidding my minions. Mommy loves Daddy a whole bunch."

The neighborhood houses offering cover would soon end and the road across the preserve an open stretch. It ran into Highway 84 and go right to the bridge and over the bay. Left and through the remnants of Mike Goldberg's former campus.

Ryan saw a faint outline in the darkness ahead. Flashing his lights to show he was a friendly, Ryan slowed down and came to stop. Hoping out and grabbing his ruck and gear from the back, he leaned in and kissed Emma and David.

"Listen to your mom. David, big man in charge. Emma, keep your Bub out of trouble. You two know what to do."

David nodded. "Protect Emma and Mom. Got it, Dad."

Emma smiled. "Keep them out of trouble."

Motioning for Julia to hop over into the driver's seat he kissed her on the lips. "Turn the lights on and speed towards the airship. It will draw attention and give me a chance to take care of business. Get on and get out of here. They know where to find me when I'm all done."

She couldn't help crying. "Ryan, please come back to us. I can't lose you. We can't lose you."

Touching her cheek, he smiled. "I found you once to love and marry, and tonight to bring us all back together. Third times a charm. They'll be close behind and I have to get to work."

Julia nodded.

Stepping back and still low, Ryan motioned to the back. "There's two backpacks on the floor. Make sure to give them to Marcus. He'll know what to do. Now, go."

Ryan could hear the Humvee smashing its way down the street and approaching the end of the line, so he closed the door and hit the roof for her to leave. The Mustang roared as she floored the gas pedal and the rubber caught, shooting the car down the road.

He hoped he would give them enough time to make it.

Stepping off the road, Ryan hustled over the sidewalk and behind the curve of a fence. Quickly pulled the M82A1 sniper rifle from its protective bag. Grabbing the scope and snapping it into place, he took up a prone position, set the night vision, engaged a round, and peeked around to the right and towards the desolate darkness confronting him.

And waited.

A minute maybe, and the Humvee came barreling towards his location. Peering through the scope, he flipped the safety off and focused in on his target. The high-powered lens sent back an image to his mind he had waited a long time to see. A smile crept up the corner of his mouth, and with a controlled breath in and slow exhale, Ryan pulled the trigger.

His first bullet hit its mark.

The second connected soon after. The gunner slammed back from the impact, blowing a hole in his chest and soon slumped out of sight through the turret opening. The thick front windshield, designed to resist the impact of high-caliber weapons and projectiles, was no match for the heavy grain powder used for custom fifty-caliber sniper rounds. Add in a depleted uranium metal slug that melted through the glass layers and it blew apart the head of the driver. A sudden wobble back and forth and the Humvee kept coming towards him, finally rolling to a stop fifty feet away.

Mark sat in the front seat, frozen in place.

He *knew*.

Had seen it before, a lifetime and a world away. There was only one person who could make one deadly shot like that, let alone two in quick succession. The reckoning was here and he could either piss his pants or meet death head on.

Fear long gone, he reached over and opened the door.

Confidence fueled Mark as he walked down the middle of the road. At a disadvantage in the black of night, he could only hope to draw his adversary out in the open. He might stand a chance and the odds were abysmal at best.

He still had a good hand to play.

"Hey Ghost. Figured you were dead, my old friend." The words were hollow, no emotion in them.

The chirp of grasshoppers the only sound.

"How have you been? Me, have had a grand old time with your wife and kids. Been a blast. Sad you let all this happen to them. Poor excuse for a husband and father." Mark hoped the personal attack hit a raw nerve. He kept moving, waiting for a reply.

Nothing.

The raw silence unnerved his anger and it fumed. "I know it's you dammit! Fucking answer me!"

A black silhouette stepped into the open, drew near.

Step by step it came until it was no more than twenty feet away. Even in the dark and hidden behind a painted face, Mark recognized him. Ghost in the flesh. Seeing his former friend had cheated death made the encounter intriguing, a new spin on what could play out next.

The momentary clarity descended back into madness.

A sense of superiority rose to a level beyond normal comprehension and feeling it, Mark spit in Ryan's direction. "Your family is mine! You'll die and Julia I'll give to the crazies as a sex toy. Emma and David will grow up knowing you couldn't do a damn thing to save them from my hell."

Laughter hit Mark like a brick. It lasted ten seconds though felt like an eternity.

"Say something dammit!"

Ryan held up his hand. "Always think *you* are in control. How is that working for you? The Yorktown and the port? VP's head blown up like a watermelon? Your lab? Charlie Team? David, Emma, and Julia? Seems to me, you couldn't manage a hot dog cart in Central Park that was full of foodies."

The words sunk in. Mark closed his eyes, head bowed.

He should have *seen* it, should have *known*.

Ryan was the best of the best. That much carnage and destruction? The danger and potential for failure high? He was the only person alive who could remotely pull it off.

"You."

A smile from beneath the war paint. "Yup."

It hit, and it hit hard. Mark's head cocked to the side. Even in his diminished state lacking human emotion, the synapses fired to put two and two together and allow sarcasm to flood the room.

"How's the sleep Ryan? Able to get a real restful night without the old body bouncing off the walls?"

For the first time, Ryan wasn't sure what to say. "Me? Peaceful as a baby."

The lie didn't wash.

"Don't think so friend. See, I've known you since you were, what, eighteen, nineteen?"

"Nineteen by the time I hooked up with the unit." Ryan could see the grin on Mark's face.

"That's right. Been some decades I've had the displeasure of watching you work. Get a good insight into the inner workings of that shriveled up brain of yours."

The conversation was getting boring and Ryan wanted to end it. "Got a point?"

"Impatient! That's what I'm getting at, you pathetic fool. The Ryan I knew would never in a million years try to pull off the stuff you did. He was methodical, careful. Not the type to go rogue and attempt the impossible all by himself. You're losing your control, the ability to think rationally and not act on impulse. I'm betting the VP shot was unexpected, right? I've seen you make that shot before. Not much of a guess you did it."

Pursed lips as he thought. Mark was right. He only decided to shoot when the VP denigrated his baby girl.

Sighing, Ryan shrugged his shoulders. "No one talks about Emma that way."

Mark slapped his thigh. "No. The Ryan I knew would have followed for intel. Not assassinate a high value target."

"Whatever."

The air began to stink of confidence and power as Mark continued. "You blew up all my research. No one knew it existed! Now, I have to start all over. So, you need me. Need me to finish my work. Means you're on the fast-track to no return. You don't get the vaccine shot and soon, you turn into one of *them*. A new breed of death like never before. That the father you want for Emma and David?"

Ryan wasn't buying any of it.

Mark could see it in his adversary's eyes. "See, the kids possess this great enzyme that combats the virus. Doesn't outright kill it. But, and this is the great part, if you keep getting the shot it prevents turning into one of those bottom dwelling maggots. Don't get it in time, and kiss loving daddy goodbye!"

Even if it all were true, using his children wasn't in the cards. "Sorry. Am I supposed to care?"

The statement sent Mark over the edge. "Listen you stupid fuck! No shot, no one left on this miserable planet. Sacrificing your rug rats to keep humanity going is a small price to pay."

Calmly, as he felt the anger building and a pressing desire to contain it, Ryan pointed. "See, that's where you're wrong. There's a time and place where evolution decides enough is enough. Survival of the fittest. Whatever analogy you want. Emma and David *are* the start of something new. They just aren't the slaves to fuel your crazy shit."

Mark ran forward and immediately stopped when he saw the blade in Ryan's hand. "Big man now?"

Twirling the handle around, Ryan realized the action seemed deliberate and put it back in its sheath on his tac vest. "Don't need anything except my thumb to kill your sorry ass."

Mark knew Ryan was right.

He'd seen some firsthand and knew he wasn't facing his old friend who had a moral compass, but was in the crosshairs of a stone-cold killer. When it was all over, dissecting and seeing what the virus had done would be such a treat.

Trying to buy more time, Mark took a different tact. "You never thought any of this would happen, did you?"

"That my father and his asshats would send the world into a pandemic and screw humanity into near oblivion? No, thought never crossed my mind."

"Your dad? What about him?"

Deep sigh. "I met up with him and the boys club at the house. They told me everything about him running the show and their absurd make-believe world. Killed them all without a second thought."

Mark nearly doubled over. "Reg running the show? Seriously? Pawn in the game. An end to a means to get your kids. Nothing more."

Clouds started to form.

Ryan's thoughts jumbled with scraps of information with no connections. Truth and lies still occupied opposite camps. He was dealing with manipulators and liars at every turn. Finding out fact versus fiction was a blistering road to follow.

"Tell me. What's the real story?"

Mark shook his head. "No, you don't deserve to know. You can have your last precious moments spent wondering what you missed when you should have been paying attention to the details. Training should have taught you that."

Ryan shrugged his shoulders. "My training put your ass in a sling. You had no idea I was alive, let alone one guy able to throw a monkey wrench into your entire operation. All by himself. Kind of sucks being you right now knowing you lost. Doesn't it?"

"You are the one who lost. Can't save them this time."

The total conversation was no more than five minutes long.

Ryan knew it was an eternity and enough time for reinforcements to arrive and put an end to it. He hoped Mark would divulge some intel to connect dots and remove the gray over truth and deceit. Information sat convoluted and fractured, bits and pieces of this and that with nothing strung together coherently to make any sense. If anything about his own mental and physical state were true, and he had his own doubts, then his mind was losing its edge. The abyss to insanity a step off the ledge.

He knew deep down, he felt it.

Had known for some time and didn't want to confront the reality. Maybe it was disbelief or his own stubbornness that ignored the truth. The writing was there when he looked back. The pizza parlor brawl. Missing Mark's dive into cruel insanity. Hunting Brainers and Bolts over the last three years to "cleanse" his environment.

The events over the last two weeks.

If he had been in his right mind half of what transpired never would have gone forward. Choices had to be made and soon. Which path and journey to Valhalla were the questions he had to answer.

Ryan stepped closer. "Do you know why I was better than you as a soldier and even if I'm going to turn into one of them, a better human being?"

The question hit the right nerve. "You learned everything you knew from me!" The hate in Mark spewed a venom Ryan had never seen.

Smiling, Ryan nodded. "I did. That's true. I also never walked into a shitty situation without a backup plan."

Mark stood still, Ryan's words filtering through what little was left of rational thought. He smiled, wicked and evil, and in that moment the old friend was no more.

The realization registered, and when it did, the bullet hit home.

CHAPTER FIFTY-THREE

Julia, David, and Emma sat in the jump seats as the airship headed away to safety.

Immediately whisked inside as soon as Ryan's beloved Mustang got them to the pickup location, someone ushered them through the drop door before the air beast lurched right and low until it reached the water. A few minutes to get to full speed, and water spray from the turbines splashed the windows from the low altitude.

Julia knew no one. Ryan hadn't even given her a name of a contact. She sat with the kids until a man, late fifties and a warm smile, took a seat and introduced himself.

"So, you two are the ones causing all of this trouble," Marcus winked at David and Emma. "Your dad says I need to keep my eyes on you."

David nodded. "Both eyes."

"And your glasses too," Emma chimed in.

"Well, nice to meet you. My name is Marcus. I will be your escort until later."

Julia managed a half-hearted smile in return. "Hi Marcus. Julia, Emma, and David."

Marcus reached over and shook their hands. "Pleasure to have you all onboard."

"Thank you. We appreciate the ride. Wish Ryan had made it too."

He could see the fear in their eyes, the trepidation at being there without Ryan. They had been rescued by her husband and their father only to have the man stay behind. Marcus knew he'd feel the same if he was in their shoes. All he could do was try and make the flight as pleasant as possible.

Marcus kept them company, filling Julia in as best as he could on the past three years. A lot to cover, and he hoped it made her feel less of a victim and more a survivor from depravity and warped minds.

She wanted to know about Ryan.

Marcus tried to divert the conversation, more for the sake of the children than keeping her in the dark. She wouldn't have it, so he told her. If Ryan failed, it meant a one-way ticket and punching the clock of everyone within a hundred-foot radius. It was the only way to cover the airship's exit and assure its escape.

Barely a mile away the blast lit up the night.

Realizing what it meant, Julia began to cry. She didn't want to believe Ryan was dead. Couldn't take having to explain to Emma and David he wasn't coming back. It might have been better if they had never seen him again than to have a brief reunion. She wrapped her arms around her babies, tried to control the sobbing, yet there was no holding back.

The pain and sorrow were profound.

Someone motioned to Marcus, and he excused himself. There were hushed words, frowns and bowed heads, and hesitantly he returned. His face betrayed the words he didn't speak. Julia's head fell into her hands, more tears and sensing the sorrow in their mom, Emma and David began to cry too.

The loss of Ryan created a void, one that was bigger than it had been before they even knew he was alive. He had saved them from evil and sacrificed his own life to ensure they had a new one, free of pain and torture.

A new chance at a life.

The airship was making its way to Skywalker Ranch, meticulously over the darkened inland hills close to the coast and dropping in to hide. It was a temporary plan, stay the night and out of sight. Pretend to be some motion picture prop next to the sound studio.

An avid Star Wars geek, Ryan thought of it.

Off the beaten path and secluded, multiple buildings and trees to offer concealment. He and Julia had been fortunate to tour the facility before the kids came, an invitation from a close friend. Remembering the layout and the plan moving forward, he figured it was a place they could use until moving on.

Soon, more activity broke the silence.

Marcus looked over and seeing confused looks, excused himself. Standing near a speaker, static echoed. Three short beeps. Turning up the volume, he listened. A minute passed. Another set of three beeps. Sensing something what going on, Julia got up and walked over. Two minutes later a voice broke the silence.

"Big Momma, my packages secured?"

The tears welled and began to cascade down Julia's face. The familiar voice, the tone haunted and low. A hesitant smile slowly emerged at the corners of her mouth.

Marcus grabbed the receiver and pushed the button. "Awesome Daddy, packages confirmed."

"*All* my packages?"

"Affirmative. How you doing, Ghost?"

A cough and what had to be spit answered back. "Can't kill a ghost. Seems you can lay it on death's doorstep though."

Julia frowned. She heard the pain in his voice.

"Anything we can do to help get you home?"

Five minutes of static.

"Negative, Big Momma. This cowboy is riding solo. Posse looking to find a tree and make me swing."

"Affirmative. Plan C or Z?"

Silence.

Then, a hushed response. "Z. See you on the flip side. Awesome Daddy out."

Marcus put the receiver back in its holder and could see Julia's pain. Thinking her husband dead more than once, and mysteriously from the ashes he emerged, if only for a short time. Marcus stepped over to her and tried to offer comfort, if any outward gesture could begin to ease her suffering that moment.

"He's alive, Julia. *Alive*," Marcus let the last word hang. "He has nine lives and his card isn't up yet."

She stared back, shook her head. "I don't know, Marcus. Seems he might be getting close. I have no idea how many times he's been here before. What if this is his last? What do I tell my kids?"

Marcus looked over at Emma and David, huddled close with her head on his shoulder. They were fast asleep now, the conversations inside the cockpit of the airship white background noise. Touching Julia's arm, he smiled. "For some reason I think that man is indestructible. Like a cockroach, but in a good way."

She couldn't help laugh. "I don't know about that. He does get under my skin."

A snicker. "I can see that being true. Listen, let's take what we can get, right? He has contingencies to back up the contingencies and more plans than I can imagine. OCD to the highest power. We have to have trust and faith he knows what he's doing. He's batting a thousand."

Eyes closed, Julia leaned in. "It might not last. He's got symptoms, growing worse each time. The turn is coming and he might not make it back."

Concern shone in Marcus' eyes. "What do you mean?"

"Over the last three years Mark collected data. A lot of it. Experiments and people piled dead along the way. You've seen some of the results. The different ways side effects of the vaccines affected people. There's another result too. Grew over time and the world going to complete crap. The ones who seemed fine and then the symptoms came. Slowly, growing over time. Headaches, full body spasms, and irrational decisions rooted in the rational.

Split-second decisions a normal person might not make that are cold and calculated, but someone who is like my husband I guess, a highly trained soldier, can make and carry out on a dime. Succeed and move on. Stress and adrenaline seem to be the catalyst. I'm betting you've seen it in him."

His pursed lips gave the answer. "I have. Thought it was the super soldier. That special breed that keeps the world safe at night and we never know."

"I never knew. But the worst part is those that have fought off the effects for a long time who succumb. They either turn into the worst kind of monsters, or end up dead. How he's survived coherent this long is a miracle. He needs the shot."

Marcus didn't know what to say. "Hey. He's managed a whole hell of a lot of success even if he's not firing on all cylinders. I can only imagine what he could do if he was the whole super soldier. Heard some, and this is worse to a degree."

Julia had to ask. She didn't know if she'd ever see Ryan alive again. "His past is a deep dark secret. Who is my husband?"

Marcus patted Julia's hand. "I'll let him give you all the details because he *is* going to tell you. I can say this from what I do know and have heard. You have someone who loves you and those kids more than anything in the world. And keeping you safe is his priority. He is one of the fraction of a few who can walk into hell and face death and come out with Satan's head on a spike and no one ever saw it coming. They don't call him Ghost for nothing."

She didn't know whether to be proud or scared. The man she thought she knew was a shell hiding a life seeped in darkness. Julia hoped he didn't keep falling into the blackness, never to return. She'd heard the stories of soldiers who whether it was PTSD or some other mental breakdown, got lost completely. This was a million times worse she knew. Throw in a virus on top of whatever might be lingering inside his head, and Ryan's future might be short.

"Ghost, huh? I hope mine comes home. I'd like to know why he got that name."

Marcus excused himself again and went to talk to someone. After he left, Julia nudged the kids awake. Sitting on the edge and facing the door to make sure no one was listening, Julia hunched over. "OK, guys. It's us like always. Stick together no matter what. Use your big kid ears to listen and follow directions. Never leave my sight. Got it?"

Nods.

"Good. Your dad is going to come and get us. I'm not sure when. So, we need to make the best of it. In the meantime, we stay aware. You see or hear something funny, you tell me right away. OK?"

"Yes, Mom."

Pulling out the pistol Ryan had given her, Julia checked it to make sure the safety was engaged and tucked it back into her waistband. Patted her waist to make sure there wasn't a noticeable bulge.

She didn't want to have to shoot anyone. If it meant protecting Emma and David and not being separated, even if to keep them all safe, there was no hesitation.

She didn't care who got caught in the line of fire.

CHAPTER FIFTY-FOUR

The bullet hole ached.

He had been shot before, knew the drill. This time, and maybe because of the circumstances surrounding it, the intrusion into his old and battered body was the worst.

It was one thing to be shot by a stranger or in war.

Off in some shithole or third-world country, the guy on the other end some zealot thinking he was getting some virgins when in reality he was going to hell. The pleasure of women gone and instead demons making you their sex toy for eternity. The person pulling the trigger having no connection to you.

Being shot by your own father?

No way to ever forget the pain of betrayal.

It would have been better if Mark was the one. At least, Ryan could rationalize that. Mark had no blood connection, no familial bond that should have meant something of value.

Even a tiny shred of it.

Ryan's dad seemed to have none of it left. The comment to Emma. The way he had no qualms putting his grandkids in harm's way for his own selfish needs. How else to justify what the man had become?

The loving father and grandparent were gone.

Ryan saw it in his eyes in the bedroom.

The man he once loved and worshipped, longed to be like, was now a figment of Ryan's imagination. All that remained was a hateful and demented soulless void that deserved the kind of death that only Ryan could deliver. If he was a praying man he would get on his knees and ask that his enemies were dead. Blown to kingdom come, their bodies shredded into tiny pieces of flesh.

Absent that, Ryan was going to hunt every single man or woman down who had touched his kids in any way and bring deaths like no one could imagine in their worst nightmares. The Reaper was an altar boy compared to the man Ryan knew he was today.

And that was fine.

He sensed they were still alive, that he had miscalculated the blast radius and while they were injured for sure, the lights were still on.

He knew he'd rectify it soon enough.

Ryan drove, his mind wandering with no destination. He had to get far enough away and hope he could make the rendezvous. The target on his back was painted in neon and distance the only thing that might give him a fighting chance. Lick his wounds and stitch it up to get ready for the fight ahead. Having Marcus offload his Humvee was the right call since the Mustang, as much as Ryan wanted to keep his ride, was not suited for distance travel.

Plan three steps ahead and two more was what he did.

Besides, the weight of the military vehicle laden with all of his weapons and supplies prevented the airship from top speed. It would need every advantage to evade detection and he needed the tools of his trade to stay alive.

If only for a bit longer.

The showdown with Mark and the unexpected appearance of his dad made the future a mess. He had hoped to simply put an end to Mark and be done with it.

Kill the brain trust and move on.

When Reg shot him, Ryan knew it was really over and there was no coming back from it. Not the mission since his father was a poor shot, but any ounce of his real dad being left inside the shell of the man he had known. The mission was still going to go forward.

There was no question about it.

He wondered when the evil in his father took root. If what Reg said was true, it was a long time in the making and nothing would have changed it. Ryan thought maybe it was all bullshit, the virus having eaten away the man and his words meant as spite.

Distract and deceive.

That didn't explain what had happened to David and Emma. Could have been a last-minute plan to kidnap them. The virus' effects sending things into overdrive. If he was wrong, the virus wasn't the cause. Reg was just pure evil.

Ryan sighed, the thought hanging in his mind. A lifetime living with someone and not seeing any signs or signals. A trained soldier who was taught what to look for absolutely missing and failing to catch anything that pointed to a man who by all accounts was the devil.

Putting his wife and children in harm's way.

Seems he had lost a step if he couldn't see what was going on right in front of his face. Not that looking back he recognized any sign or telltale lie that jumped out. Everything he could remember, even as hazy as his memories were with the virus and misinformation playing tricks, he came up empty.

Maybe one day it would be clear.

As he lay on the ground, blood oozing from his shoulder, all Ryan could do was go to his backup plan. He rolled to his feet, slipped the backpack with explosives off, and ran. Catching them flat footed in the radius was his ace, though if Mark really knew Ryan like he thought he did, he'd know Ryan never backed down from a fight.

Running was not in his DNA.

Looking over his shoulder Ryan saw Mark step forward and motion to Reg to retreat. The Humvee was still operational and with Ryan on foot and the fifty-cal able to light him up, it was the better choice than a foot chase.

Clicking the remote trigger, the explosion threw chunks of asphalt and concrete crashing down on it, the front axle collapsing under the weight. With the Humvee disabled and a huge crater in the street between them and him, Ryan had the upper hand.

Though for how long he didn't know.

He needed to level Mark's Stanford research labs. Take out the new location and staff. From hearing Mark's desperate tone, Ryan knew he was back to square one. Two blasts in one night would send security into a frenzy and if good old dad and his former best friend had survived, there was no way Ryan would be able to step foot across Camino Real and walk on campus.

He didn't have that kind of luck.

Ryan needed help, real help, to stop Mark and Reg. To stop whatever scheme and Deep State shit was in the works. The main objective got Julia and the kids safe. Though he still had some lingering suspicions about her.

It was hard not to given the answers she provided didn't all add up nicely with a cute bow on top.

Maybe it was the virus, could be the old soldier dog radar going off. Throw in a tangled web of lies filled with deceit and the truth buried deep. He wasn't sure what to believe, but it needed to be sorted out one way or another.

There was little that Mark could do without them under his control.

He knew Marcus and the survivors would die to keep Ryan's family safe knowing what was at stake. Before leaving the airship, he had a frank conversation with Marcus about Julia.

Be wary and watch her every movement.

She was an enemy until otherwise confirmed she wasn't a traitor in their midst. The kids were priority one and their enemies would hunt them down, unless Ryan managed a Hail Mary win with no time on the clock.

He was one man against what he knew was an army.

Even with John's people, they were outmanned and outgunned. He needed real answers and only one person could help.

That depended on whether he was still alive.

It meant looking for a needle in a haystack in a city likely leveled to the ground and actually finding him. If anyone had a finger or pulse on the madness that kept a black fog over the world, Ryan knew one of his oldest friends was the one who did.

He needed to find Honcho. Fast.

Thinking of his old friend as the thought washed past, the lightheadedness made focusing difficult. The sun was coming up and daylight travel problematic. Ryan needed rest, to staunch the blood before he bled out. He had popped a couple of Yunnan Baiyao pills to help with the blood clotting for his wound. A Chinese herbal medicine with a hell of a lot of uses.

He'd used them many times before and was one of those weird and miraculous remedies that did the trick.

Seeing a grove of trees to the left atop a bluff, he pulled onto a dirt road and followed. Finding a break between the massive trucks, he parked within and concealed on all sides, hoped he could fix his wound and wait it out. Clean gauze, alcohol to clean, fishing line and needle, he wasn't sure he had the strength right now.

A few minutes was all he needed. Rest a bit and fix and repair the old body like all the other times.

He was a real patriot, a man who loved his country and had done everything he could to protect it. Given his blood, sweat, and tears for democracy and those who wouldn't hesitate to spit on him. Truth meant more to him than anything, and Ryan felt deep inside that most of it had been a lie.

He had been a puppet, called to dance for the whims of demented masters who had motives beyond justice and protecting the world.

What their real intentions were, he couldn't guess or begin to fathom the absurdity of their words on the world stage. Lies were rooted in truth and truths were deceptions meant to cast shadows. Seems even the drones following the President were nothing more than pawns.

Regular people just caught up in the mix.

Innocents that paid the price for their undying loyalty to his cause. How many might have lived if they knew the truth, whatever that was since the pieces were strewn about the board and making heads or tails of it lost in his mind.

Right side up and upside down meant little if you didn't have the cypher key to unlock the puzzle.

If Ryan had more time, more energy to fight, maybe there was a light at the end of the tunnel. Without something to guide him and the tunnel closing in around him fast, time was fading away. Power and corrupt intentions ruled the world.

Topple one dictator or madman and the next was right there to take his place.

Or, take her place since if the conspiracy was as vast as they were making it out to be, insanity was not solely the realm of men. Anyone could fall into the void and cheer the death of billions on.

He knew it deep down.

Friend or foe was a thin line where anyone was your enemy. Truth was subjective. Lies shades of gray. Ryan had heard it all and even now, sitting trying to stay alive and reunite with his loved ones, he had no idea what was real.

So many divergent roads to truth and knowing absolutes. Take one and journey far into darkness. Take another and never return. The choices endless, and for a man who had built his life on facts and trust, those bridges were burned to the ground.

The only person he could absolutely trust was himself.

And that was iffy if he was on the downslide of transforming into a true cold-blooded killer. Once he lost himself, he knew it was over.

He hoped the tech found in the mansion proved fruitful and could either lead everyone back from the brink or at least give them a fighting chance to overcome the demons in the shadows.

It was wishful thinking he knew.

If the computers and hard drives provided any amount of information, it might take months or even years to analyze, let alone decipher if encrypted.

Could the world wait that long? At the present rate things were heading, he thought the odds pretty slim.

His kind of betting to place the lucky chip and roll the dice.

The fog grew dense in Ryan's head, the peace of memories and dreams blending together. Julia, Emma, and David, their smiles once more to warm his heart. Julia's last kiss still fresh on his lips. The tears felt salty on his parched lips.

He wished he could simply jump into his mind and stay there forever. Live in the past and relish in the happy times. Never venture out again into the land of harsh realities.

If only that could happen.

Maybe when the turn came and he was no longer himself, those visions would in some way keep a sliver of humanity inside to reference as he was out living the life of a killing machine. Taking out anyone in his way.

He felt deep down that was his true self. The façade of Ryan the family man a mirage. A suit he put on each day when really, he had always been evil. Just never embraced the man and went along for the ride.

As he thought long and hard, Ryan was truly a killer. The best and worst kind. Once humanity left the building, he knew he would be unstoppable.

That idea brought a sly grin.

Kill them and kill them all.

A cough, and shortly another. Blood spewed on his hands, a mist in the air.

His skin felt cold to the touch and he knew.

One breath in, the lungs exhaling as the final calm awaited. His family was safe, and he had done his job, completed the mission and could relax to watch a beautiful sunrise to end the day.

One last time.

ABOUT THE AUTHOR

Jason McDonald is an American author who writes suspense and psychological thrillers steeped in twists and turns that keep you guessing and make you think. Stepping outside the typical writer's box, he bases his books in current events, historical references and personal experience, and then turns them all into a fictionalized world for your entertainment. With multiple novels waiting in the wings, he is now devoting his time to publishing his library of works for his readers and followers to thoroughly enjoy an escape with new stories.

Away from writing, Jason loves to spend quality time with his family, enjoying the outdoors, travel, and watching his imaginative twins grow. They inspire, support, and provide the drive to pay it forward.

For more information visit: jason-mcdonald.com
Follow on Twitter: @JasonMcD_Writer

Made in the USA
Middletown, DE
10 January 2022